MADEMOISELLE FIFI
AND OTHER STORIES

GUY DE MAUPASSANT was born near Dieppe in 1850 of cultured, middle-class parents. To school he preferred the holidays which he spent swimming and fishing at Étretat, one of the newly fashionable Channel resorts. He enrolled as a law student in 1869, but the Franco-Prussian War of 1870 ruined the family finances and he was reduced to earning his living as a minor civil servant in Paris. To relieve the boredom and to work off his excess energies, he rowed and swam at Argenteuil and Bezons (favourite haunts too of Impressionist painters), where he enjoyed masculine pursuits and feminine company, sometimes to excess. Flaubert, a childhood friend of his mother, encouraged his literary ambitions and helped shape not only the exactness of his style but also his pessimistic view of life. It was Flaubert who introduced him to Parisian literary life then dominated by the new 'Naturalist' movement led by Zola. The publication in 1880 of *Boule de Suif* in *Les Soirés de Médan*, a collection of stories about the War of 1870, made Maupassant famous. Lionized by fashionable society and courted by newspaper editors, he wrote prolifically and was soon France's best-selling author after Zola. In the decade which followed, he wrote nearly 300 stories, 200 newspaper articles, 6 novels, and 3 travel books. He earned vast sums of money and spent it all—on yachts and houses which symbolized his success, on travel, on his mother, and on his brother Hervé, who died insane in 1889. By this time his own health was beginning to break down. On New Year's Day 1892 he attempted suicide and was removed to a clinic, suffering from the syphilitic paresis which had driven him mad. He died on 6 July 1893 at the age of 42.

DAVID COWARD is Professor of French at the University of Leeds. He has published numerous articles and books on the culture and literature of France and is a regular contributor to the *Times Literary Supplement*. For World's Classics, he has translated *La Dame aux Camélias* by Dumas *fils*, Sade's *The Misfortunes of Virtue*, and a previous selection of stories by Maupassant *A Day in the Country and Other Stories*. He has also edited three of Alexandre Dumas's most famous romances: *The Count of Monte Cristo*, *The Three Musketeers*, and *The Man in the Iron Mask*.

D0608442

THE WORLD'S CLASSICS

GUY DE MAUPASSANT

Mademoiselle Fifi

and Other Stories

Translated with an Introduction by
DAVID COWARD

Oxford   New York
OXFORD UNIVERSITY PRESS

Oxford University Press, Walton Street, Oxford OX2 6DP

Oxford New York Toronto
Delhi Bombay Calcutta Madras Karachi
Kuala Lumpur Singapore Hong Kong Tokyo
Nairobi Dar es Salaam Cape Town
Melbourne Auckland Madrid

and associated companies in
Berlin Ibadan

Oxford is a trade mark of Oxford University Press

Translation and editorial material © David Coward 1993

First published as a World's Classics paperback 1993

British Library Cataloguing in Publication Data
Data available

Library of Congress Cataloging in Publication Data
Maupassant, Guy de, 1850–1893.
[Short stories. English. Selections]
Mademoiselle Fifi and other stories/Guy de Maupassant;
translated with an introduction by David Coward.
p. cm.—(The World's classics)
Includes bibliographical references.
1. Maupassant, Guy de, 1850–1893— Translations into English.
I. Coward, David. II. Title. III. Series.
PQ2349.A4E5 1993 843'.8—dc20 92-10105
ISBN 0-19-282923-8

3 5 7 9 10 8 6 4 2

Printed in Great Britain by
BPC Paperbacks Ltd
Aylesbury, Bucks

CONTENTS

CONTENTS

INTRODUCTION

GUY DE MAUPASSANT was born on 5 August 1850 in the Normandy which he loved and used as the setting of so many of his stories. His father Gustave, dandy, womanizer, and amateur water-colourist, lived comfortably on his private income. His mother, Laure Le Poittevin, and her brother Alfred had been childhood friends of Gustave Flaubert, the future author of *Madame Bovary*. Flaubert had hero-worshipped Alfred and was grief-stricken when he died aged 30 in 1846. He remained in touch with Laure and it was through her prodding and her ambition for her son to make a mark in literature that Maupassant was later to come under the wing of 'The Master'. Laure was cultured and took a personal hand in the education of Guy and of his brother Hervé, who was born in 1856. But she was highly strung and emotional and suffered symptoms consistent with a malfunction of the goitre. She was restless, suffered migraines, and was at times unable to stand bright light, and it seems likely that the nervous disorders suffered by her sons were to some extent inherited. Maupassant always remained close to both his parents, though he tended to blame his father for the breakdown in their relationship. Divorce, which was not legalized until 1884, was not an option in 1863, when husband and wife finally separated.

Until he was 9, Maupassant lived with his mother in Normandy. In 1859, he was sent to his father in Paris and spent a year at the Lycée Impérial Napoléon, before being returned to Laure, who was by then living on the Channel coast at Étretat, which was turning into a fashionable resort for writers and artists. There Maupassant learned to love boats and the sea, and there too he mixed with fishermen and country people, picking up a store of characters, anecdotes, and speech-patterns on which he would later draw copiously. His education was continued by Laure and the local priest until 1863, when he entered a Catholic boarding-school at Yvetot, where, in spite of the tall tales he later told of his pranks, he was a conscientious pupil. Even so, the discovery of a poem, judged by the authorities to be sacrilegious, led to his expulsion and return to his mother at Étretat in June 1868. There he helped rescue the English poet Swinburne, who had got into difficulties while swimming. For his trouble, Maupassant was twice invited to lunch, and observed for himself a collection of engravings and gruesome objects—including a withered hand, supposedly of an executed murderer—which Swinburne, an admirer of the Marquis de Sade, had assembled. It is likely that the experience (and the hand, which he later acquired and used as a paperweight) fuelled Maupassant's interest in horror—a theme of many of his stories.

In the autumn of 1868, Maupassant became a boarder at the lycée in Rouen. By now his literary vocation was becoming clearer and, through Flaubert, he met the city's librarian, the poet Louis Bouilhet, who read his verses, shaped his taste, and disciplined his style. Bouilhet died suddenly only days before Maupassant sat his *baccalauréat* examinations, which he passed modestly. Had Bouilhet lived, Laure believed, her son might well have become a poet.

In the autumn of 1869, he went to live with his father in Paris and enrolled for a law degree. But in July 1870 his formal education was brought to an abrupt end by the outbreak of war between France and Germany. He was mobilized and posted to Normandy, where he served in the stores. When the Prussians advanced on Rouen in December, he retreated with his regiment to Paris and, though he never heard a shot fired in anger, was almost captured when he lost touch with his unit: he walked thirty miles in the snow, he wrote to Laure, and spent the night in an icy cellar. When the armistice was signed in January 1871, he was back at Étretat, where he had ample opportunity to observe the arrogance of the Prussian conquerors and the spineless collaboration of local bourgeois notables. Although he was not demobilized until November, he saw no more of the horrors of the Paris Commune in May 1871 than he had of the late war.

During the hostilities, the family fortunes had suffered. His father was reduced to finding work as a broker's agent, while Guy, instead of resuming his legal studies, was taken on as a junior clerk at the French Admiralty in 1873. He was to remain a minor civil servant until the early 1880s, when he felt confident he could earn his living with his pen. He hated the drudgery, and a good number of his stories describe in sympathetic terms the life of genteel poverty, quiet desperation, and fear led by underpaid, harassed ministry clerks. But there were compensations. Holidays, all too short, were spent at Étretat, while weekends were set aside for rowing expeditions with friends on the Seine around Argenteuil, Bezons, and Chatou. Maupassant was a fine athlete and revelled in physical activity. He boated, fished, and became a crack shot with a pistol. He also chased girls, and it is likely that it was from a chance encounter in 1873 or 1874 that he caught the syphilis which was eventually to kill him. But he derived more substantial consolation from literature. Each day he remained in his office until six and spent the evening writing. In 1874, through Laure, he renewed his acquaintance with Flaubert, whose friendship and example he was to value above all others. 'For seven years', he confessed in 1888, 'I wrote poetry, I wrote short stories, I wrote long short stories: I even wrote a play which was ghastly. None of it has survived. The Master read it all and then on the following Sunday, over lunch, he would criticize what I had written and gradually drummed into me two or three principles which are the distilled essence of his long and patient teaching.' These principles included the punctilious search for the exact word which conveys what is unique and original in a character or a setting; and objectivity, or the self-effacement of the author who tells a tale but does not make his own views or personality unduly obtrusive. He shared Flaubert's pessimistic view that life is redeemed only by the greatness of art. He was also confirmed in his taste for cheerful obscenity, which Flaubert both practised and encouraged.

Increasingly frequent visits to Flaubert's flat in the rue Murillo brought him into contact with writers and publishers. In 1875 his first tale appeared in a magazine, a horror story based on the Swinburne hand. Two other macabre stories followed in 1876, together with a few poems and book reviews. By 1877, he was a member of the new 'Naturalist' circle which had formed around Zola, who had expanded Flaubert's practice of realism by linking it to a scientific analysis of society: human drives and motives are to be understood as consequences of physiology and circumstances. Or, as the philosopher and historian, Hippolyte Taine, put it, as expressions of 'heredity, environment, and the moment'. Maupassant admired Zola and yet, for all his own temperamental fatalism, he never fully accepted his determinist view of life or his ideas about art. Though he was to ride to fame on Zola's coat-tails, he remained emotionally attached to Flaubert, who had treated him as a son.

Although he began a novel, published a few tales and poems, and even staged a play, he made little headway. His breakthrough came when Zola's young men decided to collaborate on a collection of stories on the theme of the Franco-Prussian War. The volume was published in the spring of 1880, and Maupassant's contribution, 'Boule de suif', was widely admired. *Des Vers*, a collection of poems, appeared almost simultaneously, but it was his tale of the prostitute who acts with honour which caught the eye of the critics. Flaubert, who had read it in manuscript, had been lavish in his praise and Maupassant was hailed as his natural heir. He was besieged with offers from the editors of newspapers and magazines, who were eager to recruit his brilliant new talent. But Flaubert did not live to see his protégé's success. He died suddenly on 8 May 1880 and Maupassant sincerely mourned his passing: 'It is as though a great emptiness has settled all around me,' he wrote. For the rest of his professional life, he remained true to what he regarded as the spirit of Flaubert and celebrated his memory and art in newspaper articles and, notably, in the essay on fiction with which he prefaced his novel *Pierre et Jean* (1888).

But success was not to be denied, and in the summer of 1880 he began turning himself into what he later described, somewhat wryly, as a 'literary wholesaler'. In the dozen years which followed, his 'industrial output' ran to over 300 tales, 6 novels, 3 travel books, and 2 plays. He also wrote about 200 substantial newspaper-articles which express, in less dramatic but more direct form, the rather conservative, even snobbish attitudes which lie behind his tales.

He was a determined élitist in most of his social views. He

lamented the passing of the old urbane governing class, which
had been replaced by elected deputies who lacked style, talked
of little else but industry, progress, and democracy, and had
led France to a foolish dream of empire in Indochina; on the
contrary, he said, the French would be better advised to
withdraw from all their colonies. The middle classes spoke of
money, set up as gentlemen on country estates, and lived lives
of spectacular vulgarity, of which Monsieur Eiffel's tower was
the fittingly awful symbol. The prevailing enthusiasm for
universal suffrage was entirely misplaced. Equality does not
exist in nature and should not do so in society. The thought of
uncultured masses waiting in the wings to rise up and destroy
the flower of French culture was simply too appalling to con-
template. The notion that education would improve matters was
an absurdity, since schools, 'odious' in his experience, merely
brought stupidity and prejudice within the reach of all and
enabled larger numbers of people to declaim inane ideas which
hitherto they had been too inarticulate to express. For the
common herd Maupassant felt the same cool disdain which he
turned on women. The proposition that women should vote or
enter parliament or study medicine was quite preposterous,
since 'the experience of centuries past has shown that women,
without exception, are incapable of truly artistic or scientific
endeavour'. Their role is to ensnare men into marriage, and
Maupassant subscribed gladly to the misogyny of Herbert
Spencer and Schopenhauer.

Broadly convinced by the scientific positivism of his century,
he believed that life is a by-product of laws of physics over
which we have no control. There is no God. Human thought is
a chemical or electrical reaction to external stimuli, and its
purpose is to enable us to survive and reproduce. Man is a
helpless victim of mechanistic forces, an animal whose instinct
draws him unerringly to the lowest denominator: satisfaction of
the appetite for pleasure and power. To disguise the sordid
realities, we have invented comfortable abstractions. Religion
disguises the utter pointlessness of existence, while the idea of
Progress masks our inability to change. Love poeticizes the
horrible carnality of the procreative process, and Patriotism
applies a veneer of respectability to human cruelty, greed, and

aggression. These abstractions, which we raise to the status of moral and human truths, are illusions. If there are consolations in life—literature, music, painting, scientific discovery—they are victories over Nature, which is the enemy of the spirit. And they are won by an intellectual aristocracy of artists and thinkers who must be free to pursue truth wherever it leads. Sentimentality in art merely succours the common illusions, and the aim of the writer should be to show 'humanity bleeding' in ways that are neither forced nor fantastic but plain and ordinary. More observer than moralist or preacher, the artist strips life bare and reveals the human condition for what it is: a ghastly cosmic farce.

Maupassant's journalism is strong on impact and heavy-handed irony and probably overstates his case. But even in the twenty tales in this selection his cynicism, which deepened with time, is plain to see. Lawyers are crafty, mayors are pompous, and, like most of the representatives of the middle class, they pay lip-service to morality while ruthlessly pursuing their own self-interest. In time of war, they utter patriotic platitudes and leave the fighting to others. In peacetime, they pursue their compulsions—money and position—with single-minded complacency. To them Maupassant was inclined to prefer the grimmer obsessions of the uneducated, which, in comparison, were at least honest and refreshing. Indeed, Monsieur Chicot shows far more ingenuity in getting his hands on Madame Magloire's farm in 'The Little Keg' than is displayed by Monsieur Serbois's sordid compromise over the bequest or by the more routine confidence-trick of Lawyer Lebrument, who makes off with his wife's dowry. And if he commends the bravery of prostitutes and peasants like Mother Savage in the face of Prussian brutality, it is in part to emphasize the cowardice and inertia of their betters. For as a group, Maupassant's peasants are cunning, grasping, and violent and merely exhibit in a plainer form the cruelty and selfishness which he defined as the essence of the human soul.

Maupassant does not suggest that there is much to be said for marriage, a breeding-ground for unhappiness. Wives and husbands betray each other, and children are innocent casualties—but only until they grow up and, in turn, spread misery to new generations. The blame usually falls on woman, the crouching beast who is fair without and foul within. Madame Parent and Jean Summer's mistress in 'The Model' reach for marriage as a means of acquiring respectability, and they exploit sexuality, manipulate guilt, and use any weapon to achieve their end—which is to devour the unsuspecting husband who walks into their web. The only unions which work are the result of accident. If Hautot inherits a mistress and, in 'This Business of Latin', old Piquedent abandons Latin and acquires an unexpectedly agreeable helpmeet, it is through no merit of their own. For there is no logic in this world and precious little consolation either. The curé of 'Shepherd's Leap', impelled by a murderous puritanism to stamp a whelping bitch to death, is undone by the religious zeal which he pits against the baseness of his own nature. The Abbé Vilbois, when tested in 'The Grove of Olives', knows that 'there is no help from God or man' and he is left to face his destiny alone. Miss Harriet's faith is no buckler but an illusion, for the only immortality granted her is to be food for worms and for the plants which will flourish over her grave.

Maupassant's clinical pessimism shows humanity finishing a poor second to the forces of nature, the spoiling power of existence, and the yawning gap which separates desire from its realization. Disappointment and disillusion are endemic in these tales, which can at times feel like a laboratory in which the same experiment is rerun endlessly and nearly always with the same result. The innocent are at the eternal mercy of the cunning, and what is bred in the bone will come out in the flesh: Walter Schnaffs is a temperamental poltroon and it was written that Madame Husson's May King should turn out to be an unredeemable failure. A mixture of scientific determinism and old-fashioned fate overwhelms human dreams and human effort. Nemesis lies in wait for Miss Harriet, Monsieur Parent, and the Abbé Vilbois: a pure heart, idealism, and sincere repentance will not deflect the inevitable.

Yet occasionally, there seems to be a gleam of hope, and several stories actually come close to a happy ending. Monsieur Piquedent settles contentedly into his new life and young Hautot finds domestic peace. Of course, Nature, which is malevolent, is also blind and may well nod now and then. But it is hard to escape the conclusion that odds are beaten only with the complicity of Maupassant, who breaks out of his role as objective narrator and allows personal feelings to redress the balance. If Mademoiselle Fifi's victim eventually finds a good man, and Monsieur Dubois, much to his surprise, emerges victorious in 'The Duel', the reader may well suspect that an old personal score is being settled with the arrogant Prussian conqueror. But the contradictions are not limited to intermittent rushes of the armchair jingoism which Maupassant ridiculed in others. His contempt, rock-solid when he dealt with groups, readily evaporates when he gets to grips with individual cases. He may have hated all Prussians, but Walter Schnaffs, a victim of war like his 'Two Friends', clearly has his sympathies. He despised all women, yet he treats Miss Harriet (who is English to boot) with aching tenderness. He considered religion to be an illusion, but respects Abbé Vilbois's brawny Christianity. Maupassant drew many unsympathetic portraits of peasants and sailors, yet the widow Severini of 'A Vendetta' and Mother Savage are not among them. We are all Nature's fools, but holy fools are clearly a protected species: the help-less victims who cannot bear the strain, refuse to compromise, and resist with honour. It is Maupassant's vulnerability to the spectacle of 'humanity bleeding' which breathes, if not hope, then at least a sense of solidarity with suffering into these grim chronicles. The greedy, the cheap deceivers, and the selfish do not merit a second glance: they dig holes for themselves, and Maupassant is happy to push them over the edge. But the wronged, the fighters, and those, like Miss Harriet, who are 'singled out by the eternal injustice and implacability of nature', are a different breed and he does what he can for them.

Maupassant would be unbearable to read without this instinctive sense of complicity with suffering humanity, which was at root a reaction against cosmic injustice. His stories would also be bleaker without his lyrical feel for nature. The rocks and gales of Corsica may make a suitable setting for 'A Vendetta', but a truer expression of his feelings is given in his highly charged descriptions of the Normandy countryside.

Maupassant himself had a full measure of the sense of place which he extols at the start of 'Mother Savage', and while he could not believe with Miss Harriet that the beauty of nature was the handiwork of God, he fully shared her love of rolling landscapes which lift the spirit and quicken the senses. Of course, Nature will always win and the good green earth waits patiently to receive our bodies. However uplifting, the glory of a tree, of a sunset, of a running brook is no more than a stay of execution, an illusion like Love, which merely suspends for a moment the relentless advance of change, decay, and decomposition. In middle age, Monsieur Parent surveys the countryside, which does not beckon to him now but turns into a bleak vision of life which has passed him by. The moment is not philosophical, for he does not generalize. Nor is it cathartic, for he does not learn from it to go forth in newness of life. He does not rationalize his situation: he simply feels it. Maupassant does not suggest that he has a soul, or even much of a brain, but insists, as he always does, that his feelings lie on the surface of his skin. Crises are not a prompt to reflection but a spur to action. He never allows his characters to speculate about their predicament (they do not curse God or revile Man) and indeed are not, properly speaking, rational creatures at all. Their lives are lived on the level of the senses—fear, hope, greed, love, despair—over which they have no power. The joys of life, like the beauties of Nature, are short-lived. But knowing that this is so gives an opportunistic pagan like Maupassant the edge: consciously living life to the full subverts Nature's hidden agenda by enabling us to regain control of our drifting fate. Maupassant's moral strength lies in his determination to resist and his refusal to collaborate.

Maupassant approached his own life with the same defiant pessimism, and after he made his name he exploited his success to the full. He worked hard and quickly and ensured that he was well rewarded for his labours. Soon he was France's best-selling author after the immensely popular Zola, and he commanded astronomical magazine-fees for his stories, which were quickly republished in volume form. In the autumn of 1880 he had joined his mother in Corsica. It was the first of many journeys, duly recorded in articles and travelogues,

which he made mainly in North Africa and Italy. He acquired a
series of yachts and named them after his books. He bought
homes in Paris, Normandy, and the south of France. He was
lionized by fashionable society. He embarked on numerous
love affairs, which he wrapped in the tightest security. He
enjoyed parties and was fond of playing practical jokes on
friends (rather as he does on the reader in certain of his tales).
Rich, fêted, independent, Maupassant enjoyed the public
image of a successful and fulfilled man. This was how one
American caller, Blanche Roosevelt, described him to readers
of *The Woman's World* in 1889:

In personal appearance, Guy de Maupassant is of medium height,
solid, well-built, and has the bearing of a soldier; he has a fine
characteristic Norman head, with the straight line from neck to crane,
in the medallions of the old Conquest Warriors; his forehead is low
and rather too heavily lined; and his hair, brown and wavy, is now
combed straight back in the fashion of modern Roman youth. In short,
M. de Maupassant has such a look of cheeriness that he reminds
one of a clear autumn day—an agreeable harmony in russet colours
and russet tints; dark brown laughing eyes, a shapely mouth half-
concealed by a heavy brown moustache, an olive skin mantled with
red and a general ruddiness give this character and warmth to his
physiognomy.

But behind the confident façade of the successful man of
letters, there were strains. Although outwardly fit and healthy,
he was increasingly plagued by a series of symptoms none of
which responded to treatment. He suffered from migraines,
indigestion, and palpitations. His hair fell out and he could not
sleep. He experienced memory lapses and severe eye-troubles.
The many doctors he consulted diagnosed nicotine poisoning,
stress, and—that catch-all—neurasthenia. They recommended
travel and warned against overwork. He took pain-killing
drugs but also used ether, which had the added advantage
of stimulating his imagination. But he had other worries.
His mother's health was poor and he accepted financial
responsibility for her well-being. More disturbing, his brother
Hervé, who had proved unemployable, began to act irrationally.
Maupassant set him up in a horticultural business in the
south of France but Hervé grew violent and was eventually

institutionalized: he died 'quite mad' in November 1889 at the age of 33. Thus to the intimations he had received of his own mortality were added gruesome family duties and the heavy bills which went with them. Maupassant turned himself increasingly into a money-making machine.

As the 1880s advanced, he wrote fewer tales and began to explore the possibilities of the psychological novel. But though *Pierre et Jean* (1888) was adjudged to be 'faultless' by Henry James, Maupassant is best remembered for his mastery of the short story. He wrote at different lengths and in different inks, in part at least to meet the requirements of the magazines which published him. For *Le Gaulois*, a serious quality daily, he supplied serious, quality stories. He offered lighter, racier, bawdier work to *Gil Blas*, which had a reputation for being witty and scurrilous. He dealt with most levels of society save the urban proletariat, of which his knowledge was limited. But whatever his subject and mood, his natural bent was for the strongly plotted tale constructed on a firm narrative base. He liked dramatic reversals and situations which do not turn out as we expect, though he did not abuse the 'surprise ending' as O. Henry, an admirer, was to do a decade or so later. Indeed, he frequently withholds the final revelation (as in 'Monsieur Parent' or 'The Grove of Olives') and leaves the reader to share an enigma. So sure is his touch that our shock or outrage are directed not at the author but at life itself. Chekhov made stories out of less, and Zola was a more systematic realist. But Maupassant is more disturbing than either, for he turns the coolest of eyes on the illusions by which we live. Situations are peeled back with surgical precision, and his line, as Seán O'Faoláin remarked, is 'as hard and clear as a diamond on glass'. Maupassant does not preach; he simply reveals. His laconic manner and lucid irony make him chilling and uncomfortable reading. There is danger in his tales.

This is most literally apparent, of course, in his stories of the fantastic. Not for Maupassant the ghosts, magic, and diabolism of tradition, which he despised as puerile. On the other hand, he much admired Turgenev's ability to make the skin creep: 'in his books, the supernatural remains so elusive and hidden that the reader is never quite clear that the author actually intended

it to be there. It is rather that he conveys what he has felt
exactly as he felt it. He implies his uneasiness of mind, his
bewilderment at what he has not understood and the heart-
stopping sensation of inexplicable fear which comes to him like
a mysterious breath from another world.' These words apply
equally well to Maupassant's own tales of the supernatural.
There is horror in 'At Sea', but it is physical and unmysterious
and provokes no more than physical revulsion. But other tales
take us inside minds and have a more alarming resonance.
'Call it Madness?' and 'Who Can Tell?' activate 'sensations'
which are all the more alarming for being non-specific. The
first is a pathological study of sexual jealousy described from
the inside. The second involves strange visions and a wizard,
but the focus is squarely on the narrator's fear of a world which
has suddenly stopped making sense. Here, the inexplicable
does not have a separate reality but is the product of a dis-
ordered brain. The terror does not come from outside but
grows like some poisonous mushroom in the mind. Maupassant,
who knew such terror, turns our own fear of madness against
us.

At one level, he may be said to reflect the current fascination
with the new interest in the subconscious. He attended lectures
given by Charcot (as did Freud) and became interested in
hypnotism and early forms of psychoanalysis. In this way he
came to a better understanding of the cruelty and the sadistic
impulses which feature in so many of his stories. But his
interest was not merely academic or professional. He consulted
experts about the condition of his mother and, more urgently,
of his brother. But he himself had long since been haunted by
visions of his double, who he claimed to have seen sitting at
his desk or staring back at him from his mirror. His memory
lapses upset him and he grew tetchy. He reacted angrily to any
attempt to intrude upon his privacy. He took noisy neighbours
to law. He threatened his publisher, who had omitted to obtain
permission to add his portrait to a new edition of *Les Soirées de
Médan*. The strain of meeting deadlines and the ghastly death
of Hervé took their toll. To some, in the autumn of 1889—
Blanche Roosevelt, for example—he seemed 'lean', 'fit',
'cheerful', and 'talkative'. To others, who noted anxiously the

habit of 'perpetual locomotion' with which he tried to ward off 'cerebral fatigue', he spoke increasingly of death, his failing sight, and the memory lapses which prevented him from working.

Although he continued to write and publish, his behaviour became increasingly erratic and unpredictable. In December 1891, while he was wintering at Cannes, his condition deteriorated dramatically. He saw his own ghost. He believed a fishbone had entered his lungs and was rotting there. On the last day of the year he wrote to his doctor: 'I am utterly lost. I am dying. I have a softening of the brain brought on by the salt water with which I have been washing out my nasal passages. This has made the salt ferment in my brain which drips out of my nose and mouth at night in a sticky slime. It means that Death is near and I am Mad. I am wandering in my head. Goodbye, my friend, you will never see me again.' Five hours later, he tried unsuccessfully to cut his throat with a razor.

He was taken to Paris, to the clinic of Doctor Blanche, suffering from paresis, or 'general paralysis', which was syphilitic in origin. There were periods of lucidity but over the following eighteen months the delusions deepened. Friends visited him and came away appalled. R. H. Sherard, who had known him in his prime, was one such caller:

Poor de Maupassant's madness ran its usual course. He imagined himself the possessor of boundless wealth. His talk was all of millions and billions and trillions. He wanted to dig holes in which to bury his immense accumulations of gold. He shouted into an imaginary telephone orders to his stockbroker to buy the French Rentes *en bloc*. At times, flying into mad passions, he would dash round and round the room in pursuit of some phantom thief. The only mercy that was shown to him was that he died in one of these terrible paroxysms. He died while he still had the semblance and bearing of a man. His friends were spared the spectacle of that awful degradation into a condition lower than anything in animal life, to which general paralysis, where it runs its sacrilegious course, brings its victims. There was no very great change in his appearance when he died. Somebody who saw him after his death said to me, 'He looks like a soldier who has died on the field of battle.' (*Twenty Years in Paris*, London, 1905, p. 65.)

Guy de Maupassant, one of the world's greatest story-tellers, died on 6 July 1893, one month before his forty-third birthday.

Nature, exacting a terrible revenge, had won. But then, Maupassant had always known it could not be otherwise.

SELECT BIBLIOGRAPHY

OF the various complete collections of Maupassant's tales, the most comprehensive and the most fully annotated is Louis Forestier's edition of the *Contes et nouvelles* (Bibliothèque de la Pléiade, Gallimard, 1974–9, 2 vols.).

Of works by French critics, Pierre Cogny's *Maupassant: L'homme sans dieu* (Brussels, 1968) is probably still the most balanced and accessible general introduction to his ideas and manner.

Critical biographies in English by Francis Steegmuller (*Maupassant: A Lion in the Path*, New York, 1949; repr. London, Collins, 1950, and Macmillan, 1972), Paul Ignotus (*The Paradox of Maupassant*, University of London Press, 1967), and Michael Lerner (*Maupassant*, London, Allen & Unwin, 1975) are all helpful.

The most useful critical studies of the stories are Edward Sullivan's *Maupassant: The Short Stories* (London, Arnold, 1972, Studies in French Literature, 7) and *Maupassant* (New York, Twayne, 1974) by Albert H. Wallace. On Maupassant's style, George Hainsworth's 'Pattern and Symbol Style in the Work of Maupassant' (in *French Studies*, 1951, pp. 1–17) is invaluable. On the vexed issue of Maupassant's patriotism and attitude to war, see Rachel Killick's excellent 'Mock Heroics? Narrative Strategy in a Maupassant War Story' (in *Modern Language Review*, Apr. 1987, pp. 313–26). Mary Donaldson-Evans's *A Woman's Revenge* (Lexington, K., French Forum, 1986) deals interestingly with Maupassant's 'progressive gynophobia'.

For Maupassant's place in the history of the short story, the following may be consulted with profit: Seán O'Faoláin, *The Short Story* (London, Collins, 1948); Ian Reid, *The Short Story* (London, Methuen, 1977, The Critical Idiom, 37); Valerie Shaw, *The Short Story: A Critical Introduction* (Harlow, Longman, 1983).

A CHRONOLOGY OF
GUY DE MAUPASSANT

1850   5 August: Birth of Guy de Maupassant, probably at
        Fécamp. His mother, Laure de Poittevin, a childhood
        friend of Flaubert, was cultured but highly-strung. His
        father's family, vaguely ennobled in the eighteenth century,
        hailed from Lorraine. Gustave de Maupassant was worldly
        and lazy, and Guy later held him largely responsible for the
        failure of his parents' marriage.

1856   Birth of Hervé de Maupassant.

1859–60 Maupassant lives with his father in Paris where he attends
        the Lycée Impérial Napoléon.

1863   Separation of Gustave and Laure formalized. Guy and
        Hervé live at Étrelat with Laure.

1863–7 Maupassant attends a Catholic boarding-school at Yvetot.
        His teachers consider him able and industrious but finally
        expel him for indiscipline and for writing 'obscene' verses.

1867   Laure moves to Rouen and sends both her sons to the
        Institution Leroy-Petit.

1868   Summer: The English poet Swinburne gets into difficulties
        while swimming at Étretat. Maupassant rescues him and is
        twice invited to lunch at the 'Chateau Dolmancé', where he
        is lastingly impressed by the macabre and 'perverse'
        preoccupations of the Sadean Swinburne.
        Autumn: Becomes a boarder at the Lycée Corneille at
        Rouen. Meets Louis Bouilhet (b. 1821), the city's librarian
        and friend of Flaubert, who encourages his literary
        ambitions.

1869   18 July: Death of Bouilhet.
        27 July: Maupassant passes his *baccalauréat* examinations
        ('*mention passable*').
        October: Enrols as a law student in Paris, where he lives
        with his father.

1870   15 July: France declares war on Germany. Maupassant is
        mobilized and sent to Le Havre where he serves as a
        quartermasters' clerk.

1870   1 September: Fall of Sedan.
            27 October: Surrender at Metz.
            December: Prussian forces occupy Normandy and
            Maupassant retreats with his regiment to Paris, narrowly
            escaping capture.

1871   18 January: Maupassant is stationed at Rouen when the
            Armistice is signed and sees nothing of the siege of Paris
            (March) or the Commune (May).
            November: Demobilized. War having ruined the family
            business, he is unable to continue his studies.

1872   20 March: Becomes an unsalaried minor civil servant. He
            has no money and complains of loneliness.

1873   1 February: Secures a permanent appointment at 1,600
            francs a year at the Admiralty, where he remains until
            1878, when he transfers to the Ministry of Education. In
            the summer of 1880, he is granted successive periods of
            leave until 11 January 1882, when, confident at last of
            being able to live by his pen, he ceases to be a government
            employee.
            To relieve the boredom of his life, he spends weekends
            boating and chasing girls, and continues writing poems,
            plays, and prose, but without success.

1874   Begins a lasting friendship with Flaubert, his friend and
            literary mentor.

1875   Publication of *La Main d'écorché*, his first published short
            story.

1876   Becomes part of the new 'Naturalist' coterie headed by
            Zola.

1877   August: Leave of absence granted by the Ministry for a
            health visit to Switzerland. Though fit and robust, he is
            bothered by eye trouble, stomach-pains, and headaches.

1878   Though he manages to sell a few poems and stories,
            Maupassant's literary ambitions are far from realized.

1879   19 February: *Histoire du vieux temps*, a verse comedy,
            performed in Paris. It is well received by the critics.

1880   14 February: Maupassant accused of publishing an obscene
            poem. Flaubert writes a letter in his defence.
            16 April: Publication of *Les Soirées de Médan*, a collection
            of stories about the Franco-Prussian War, by 'Zola's young

men'. Maupassant's contribution, *Boule de Suif*, is admired by Flaubert and hailed as a masterpiece.

8 May: Death of Flaubert.

Summer: Maupassant begins writing articles and stories for newspapers. He resorts to ether, first as a pain-killer, and later experiments with its hallucinatory effects.

1881   Divides his time between Paris, Normandy, the Midi. He begins his travels—to North Africa and Italy—to research commissioned newspaper articles. Publication of *La Maison Tellier*, the first of some thirty collections of stories.

1882   Begins to be lionized by high society and embarks on a number of discreet love affairs.

1883   January–February: Maupassant buys *La Louisette*, a small yacht, the first of a number of boats which symbolize his success.

25 February–6 April: serialization of *Une Vie*, the first of his six novels, which brings him international recognition.

19 March: Dr Landholt relates Maupassant's symptoms to syphilis.

1884   Shares his time between Cannes, Étretat, and Paris. Publication of *Sur l'eau*, the first of his three travel books.

1885   6 April–30 May: *Bel-Ami*, one of his most popular novels, serialized in *Gil Blas*.

Takes an increasingly personal interest in mental illnesses, as exemplified by the work of the neurologist Charcot. Maupassant's valet, Tassart, becomes aware of his master's occasionally disturbed states.

1886   19 January: Marriage of Hervé who is set up by Guy as a horticulturalist at Antibes.

August: Brief visit to England where Maupassant meets Henry James.

1887   Summer: Maupassant writes to *Le Temps* protesting at proposals to construct Eiffel's planned tower which he regards as a triumph of modern vulgarity.

Autumn: Having broken with *Le Gaulois* in 1885, Maupassant severs his connection with *Gil Blas*, which can no longer afford to pay the rates he now commands. His income rises from 40,000 francs in 1885 to 120,000 by 1888.

1888   July: Is treated for his worsening physical and mental symptoms at Aix-les-Bains.
       October—March: Further travels to North Africa.

1889   August: Hervé's behaviour becomes erratic and he enters an asylum. His condition continues to deteriorate into madness.
       13 November: Death of Hervé.
       December: Maupassant threatens noisy neighbours with legal action.

1890   30 May: Maupassant quarrels with his publisher over the use of his portrait for advertising purposes.
       23 November: Inauguration of a monument to Flaubert at Rouen. Although he looks well, his friends are privately shocked at his condition.

1891   4 March: First performance of *Musotte* after a difficult period of rehearsal during which Maupassant upsets the director and the actors.
       Summer: Still working hard against medical advice, he embarks on health cures in the South of France. His condition worsens.

1892   1–2 January: Maupassant unsuccessfully attempts suicide and is transferred to the clinic of Dr Blanche at Passy, where he is diagnosed as suffering from syphilitic paresis. There is no medical record of his decline.

1893   6 July: Death of Maupassant, a month before his forty-third birthday.
       8 July: Zola delivers the oration at his funeral.

1897   24 October: Unveiling of a bust of Maupassant in the Parc Monceau in Paris.

1900   June: Monument to Maupassant erected at Rouen.

Mademoiselle Fifi
and Other Stories

Shepherd's Leap

The coast from Dieppe to Le Havre forms a single uninterrupted line of cliffs, a hundred metres high on average and sheer as a wall. From time to time, this great stretch of white rock dips sharply and then a little narrow valley, its steep sides covered with short grass and salt rushes, runs down from the ploughed fields above towards a shingle beach, where it ends in a gully indistinguishable from the bed of a torrent. Nature made these valleys but storm rains put the gullies there, cutting into what remained of the cliffs and scooping out watercourses which lead clear down to the sea's edge and provide humans with a point of access.

Sometimes a village nestles in these small valleys, where the wind rushes in off the open sea.

I spent the summer in one of these notches in the coastline. I had lodgings in the house of one of the locals. It faced the sea and from my window I could see a large triangle of blue water framed by the green slopes of the valley. Sometimes it was flecked with white sails which scudded by in the distance, caught in a noose of sunshine.

The path down to the sea followed the ravine bottom then suddenly squeezed between two walls of marl and turned into a kind of deep rut, before emerging on to a fine stretch of pebbles which had been rolled, smoothed, and polished by the timeless caress of the waves.

This deep, narrow cleft is known as 'Shepherd's Leap'.

This is the tale which tells how it came to be so called.

They say that once the village was ruled by a young priest of austere and violent temperament. He had left his seminary filled with hatred for all who live by nature's laws rather than in accordance with the laws of his God. Inflexibly hard on

himself, he behaved towards others with unrelieved intolerance.
One thing more than all the rest roused him to anger and
loathing: love. Had he lived in towns and gone among civilized,
sophisticated people who draw delicate veils of fine feeling and
tenderness over the crude acts which nature decrees; if only he
had given confession in the gloomy naves of tall, elegant
churches to faltering, perfumed women whose sins are apt to
seem diminished by the grace of their fall and the idealistic
trappings which sanitize the grossness of the physical embrace,
then he would not perhaps have felt such insane disgust, such
uncontrolled fury when confronted by the unclean tumblings of
ragged peasants in muddy ditches or on the straw of some barn.

He set them and their like on a level with the beasts of
the field: they knew nothing of love and merely coupled like
animals. And he hated them for the coarseness of their souls,
the easy, filthy satisfaction of their instincts, and the loathsome
glee shown by the old whenever they still talked of those
unspeakable pleasures.

It may be too that, despite himself, he was tormented by the
pangs of unslaked appetites, secretly torn perhaps between the
struggle of his sickened flesh and a despotic, chaste mind.

But anything to do with the flesh roused his anger and drove
him to a pitch of uncontrollable rage. His violent sermons,
bristling with furious threats and allusions, made the girls and
young men snigger and splutter as they slyly nodded and
winked at each other across the church. And when mass was
over, the blue-smocked farmers and their black-cloaked wives,
returning to their poor cottages, where a thin plume of blue
smoke curled up from the chimney into the sky, would say:
'The curé don't mince 'is words. 'E won't stand no nonsense
with carryin' on.'

Once even, and for no reason at all really, his temper flared
violently and he completely lost control. He was visiting a sick
parishioner. As he made his way into the farmyard, he noticed
a gaggle of children, some from the farm and others belonging
to neighbours, crowding round the dog's kennel. They were
watching something with rapt attention, curious, not moving,
not speaking. The priest strode up to them. The something was
the bitch giving birth to a litter. Outside the kennel, five pups

were swarming around their mother, who was licking them lovingly, and just as the curé craned forward over the heads of the children, a sixth little puppy made its appearance. As it did so, the watching gang erupted with delight and started shouting and clapping their hands: 'One more! that be one more!' It was a game to them, a natural game which had nothing impure about it; they observed the birth as if they had been watching apples fall off a tree. But the man in the black cassock, rigid with indignation and quite beside himself, raised his large blue umbrella and began thrashing the children with it. They took to their heels. Left alone with the bitch, which was still in labour, he set about her uncontrollably. Held fast by her chain, she could not get away and as she struggled and whined, he jumped on her, trampling her beneath his feet, forcing her to give birth to one last pup before he finally stamped the life out of her. He left the bleeding corpse where it lay among the new-born whimpering, clumsy puppies who were already beginning to feel about for her dugs.

He would go walking, by himself, covering great distances, striding along with a wild look about him.

One May evening, as he was returning from a long walk, following the cliff-top on his way back to the village, he was overtaken by a tremendous storm. Not a house in sight, only the bare coast, which the sudden squall riddled with arrows of water.

Out to sea, white horses creamed the running swell, and the large black clouds racing in from the horizon made the rain fall even harder. The wind roared and gusted, flattening the early crops, buffeting the drenched priest, making his sodden cassock cling to his legs, filling his ears with noise and his exalted heart with tumult.

He bared his head and, setting his face into the storm, slowly pushed on to where the way led down to the village. But he was caught by a squall of such violence that he could make no headway against it. Suddenly he made out, just by a sheep-pen, an itinerant shepherd's hut.

It was shelter and he made towards it at a run.

The dogs, lashed by the storm, did not stir as he approached.

He reached the wooden shanty, not much more than a kennel
on wheels, which the men who stand guard over flocks each
summer haul from one grazing-ground to the next.*

Above a stool which served as a step, the low door stood
open, revealing the straw inside.

The priest was about to enter when, in the darkness, he
made out a couple of lovers locked in each other's arms.
Quickly, he swung the door shut and secured it. Then backing
into the shafts, his lean frame bent and straining, pulling like a
horse and gasping for breath under the waterlogged cloth of his
cassock, he set off at a trot towards the steep slope, the slope
of death, dragging the two young people who had been caught
embracing and were now beating on the walls with their fists,
thinking no doubt that it was all a joke played on them by some
passer-by.

When he reached the top of the slope, he released the flimsy
shanty, which began to roll down the steep incline.

It gathered momentum quickly, careering wildly, accelerating
as it went, bounding and lurching like some animal and
beating the ground with its shafts.

An old beggarman huddling in a ditch saw it flash past above
his head and heard hideous screams coming from inside the
wooden box.

Suddenly it lost a wheel, wrenched off by a crashing jolt,
turned on its side, then went on its way again, hurtling like a
ball, just as an uprooted house might have slithered down from
the top of a mountain. Reaching the lip of the last ravine, it
took off, described an arc, and plunged into the gorge below,
where it smashed like an egg.

The bodies of both lovers were recovered, broken, pulver-
ized, with every bone shattered, but still locked together, their
arms wrapped around each other's necks, embracing in their
terror as in their lust.

The curé would not allow their corpses into the church and
refused to say a blessing over their coffins.

And on the following Sunday, during his sermon, he spoke
heatedly of God's Seventh Commandment,* threatening anyone
in love with the power of an avenging, mysterious hand and

quoting the terrible example of the two unfortunates, taken in sin, who had been killed.

As he left the church, two policemen arrested him.

An exciseman sheltering in a lookout post had seen everything. He was sentenced to hard labour.

And the farm labourer from whom I had the story added gravely:

'I knowed 'im, I did. 'E were a hard man right enough, but 'e jes' couldn't abide goin's-on.'

Mademoiselle Fifi

The Major, Count de Farlsberg, the Prussian commandant, was reading the last of his mail, lying back in a deep, tapestry-covered armchair, with his feet, still encased in riding-boots, propped up on the elegant marble mantelpiece in which his spurs, in the three months that he had occupied the Château d'Urville,* had made two deep grooves, which grew deeper by the day.

Steam rose from a cup of coffee on an inlaid occasional table stained by liqueurs, scarred by cigar burns, and scored by the penknife of the victorious officer, who from time to time left off sharpening his pencil with it and used it to jot down figures or doodle patterns on its tasteful surface, as the whim of his wandering thoughts took him.

When he came to the end of his correspondence and finished going through the German newspapers which his post orderly had just brought him, he got to his feet. Then, after throwing three or four enormous green logs on to the fire—for these conquering heroes were prepared to chop down every last tree on the estate to keep warm—he went and stood by the window.

It was raining as it rains only in Normandy, as though great gouts of water were being sprayed by some angry, giant hand, a slanting downpour, dense as a thick curtain, impenetrable as a wall of sloping bars, a lashing, splashing deluge which drenched everything in its path, genuine diluvian rain such as falls only around Rouen, the chamber-pot of France.

The officer stared for some time at the waterlogged parkland and, in the distance, at the swollen Andelle,* which had overflowed its banks. He was drumming a Rhenish waltz on the window-pane with his fingers, when a sound made him turn round: it was his second-in-command, Baron de Kelweingstein, who had the rank of acting captain.

The Major was a giant of a man, with broad shoulders and a long fan-shaped beard which unfurled over his chest, a tall, solemn figure who suggested a military peacock, but a peacock which had its tail fully opened on its chin. He had blue, cold, languid eyes. On one cheek, he carried a sabre scar received in the war against Austria.* He had the reputation of being as decent a sort as he was a courageous officer.

The Captain was a short, fat, brick-faced man, tightly buttoned up in his straining uniform. He wore his bright ginger beard cropped extremely short, in a flaming stubble which in certain lights lent his whole face a phosphorescent sheen. Having had two teeth removed one night when out on the spree, though he could not remember quite how, he spoke in a thick splutter and was not always easy to understand. There was a bald spot just on the top of his head, like the tonsure of a monk, a patch of bare scalp encircled by a shock of short, auburn, gleaming curls.

The Major shook his hand and swallowed his cup of coffee (the sixth that day) in a single gulp and listened to his subordinate's routine report. Then both wandered over to the window and agreed that things had come to a pretty pass. The Major, a man of quiet habits, with a wife back home, took it all in his stride. But Captain Baron de Kelweingstein, a seasoned rake who patronized all the brothels he could find and was a notorious womanizer, chafed at being forced for the last three months to live in compulsory continence in this remote posting.

There was a timid knock. The Major barked 'Enter!' and a private, the usual Teutonic automaton, appeared in the doorway, announcing by the mere fact of his presence that lunch was ready.

In the mess, they found three lower-ranking officers: a lieutenant, Otto de Grossling, and two sub-lieutenants, Fritz Scheunaubourg and the Marquis Wilhem d'Eyrik, who was very short and fair, arrogant and very hard on the men, without mercy for the conquered French and liable to go off like a gun at any moment.

Since his arrival on French soil, he had always been known to his comrades as Mademoiselle Fifi, a nickname prompted by his foppish appearance, his trim figure—he looked as if he

wore corsets—and his pale face, against which an incipient
moustache barely showed at all, but also by the habit he had
adopted, whenever he wished to express his utter contempt for
people and things, of using on every conceivable occasion the
French expression 'Fi, fi donc', which he pronounced with a
slight mincing hiss.

The dining-room of the Château d'Urville was a long, regal
room hung with cut-glass mirrors, now starred with bullet
holes, and tall Flemish tapestries, now slashed by sabres and
hanging down in places, which bore ample witness to the
manner in which Mademoiselle Fifi occupied his idle moments.

On the walls hung three family portraits, a knight in full
armour, a cardinal, and a judge, all of whom were now
provided with long clay pipes to smoke, while in her gold frame
tarnished by time, a noble lady in a tight bodice disdainfully
sported an enormous moustache, which had been added in
charcoal.

The officers ate their lunch more or less in silence, amid the
wreckage of the room darkened by the storm clouds outside.
The place wore a depressing air of defeat, and the old oak
parquet was filthy, like the floor of a tavern.

When it was time to smoke and, now that they had finished
eating, to drink, they fell to talking about how bored they were,
as they did every day. Bottles of cognac and liqueurs passed
from hand to hand. And all of them, lolling in their chairs,
sipped at their drinks while keeping one side of their mouths
permanently clenched on the long curved stems of their pipes,
which invariably ended in porcelain bowls, which, also invariably, were decorated in a manner calculated to delight a
Hottentot.

When their glasses were empty, they replenished them with
gestures of weary resignation. But Mademoiselle Fifi always
smashed his, whereupon an orderly immediately replaced it
with another.

They were enveloped in a cloud of acrid smoke and seemed
about to slide into a somnolent, morose, alcoholic daze, the
cheerless, drunken torpor of men with nothing to do.

But all at once, the Baron sat up straight. He was angry; he had had enough. He swore: 'Hell and damnation! Things can't go on like this. We've got to think up something to do, for God's sake!'

Lieutenant Otto and Sub-Lieutenant Fritz, two Germans admirably endowed with heavy, humourless German faces, said: 'But what, Captain?'

He thought for a moment and then said: 'What shall we do? Well, we'll have a party, if the CO doesn't object.'

The Major took his pipe out of his mouth: 'What sort of party, Captain?'

The Baron pulled up his chair: 'I'll look after the arrangements, sir. I'll send Old Faithful into Rouen and he can bring us back some girls. I know where to get hold of them. We'll organize a dinner party here. We've got everything we need and at least we'll have one good night of it!'

Count de Farlsberg shrugged his shoulders and smiled: 'You're crazy, my friend.'

But the other officers were on their feet, crowding round their CO, pleading with him: 'Let the Captain have his way, sir. This place is so dull.'

In the end, the Major gave in: 'Very well,' he said. The Baron at once sent for Old Faithful who was an elderly NCO who had never been known to smile but carried out all orders, any orders, given by his superior officers with alarming efficiency.

He stood there, his face registering no expression, while he received his instructions from the Baron. Then he left the room. Five minutes later, a large army transport-wagon, drawn by four horses, with a miller's tarpaulin stretched over the top, set off at a gallop through the driving rain.

Immediately, a surge of excitement seemed to put new life into the men. Slumped shoulders straightened, faces brightened, and there was animated talk.

Although the rain was coming down as furiously as ever, the Major remarked that the gloom was lifting, and Lieutenant Otto had no hesitation in stating that the sky would clear soon. Mademoiselle Fifi did not seem to know where to put himself. He got up then sat down again. With pale, cruel eyes, he looked round for something to break. Suddenly, his gaze fell on the lady with the moustache, and the pretty blond thug drew his revolver.

'You won't be seeing any party, you old hag,' he said. And without getting out of his chair, he took aim. Two bullets one after the other shot the eyes out of the portrait.

Then he shouted: 'Time to lay a mine!' All conversation stopped immediately, as though they had all just found something new and absorbing to do.

Mine-laying was Mademoiselle Fifi's invention, his way of wreaking havoc and his favourite pastime.

When the Château had been evacuated, there had been no time for its rightful owner, Count Fernand d'Amoys d'Urville, to remove or hide anything, except his silver, which was buried in a hole in a wall. As he was very rich and lived on a very lavish scale, the great drawing-room through which the dining-room was reached had, before the owner had left in a hurry, looked like a gallery in a museum.

On the walls hung valuable paintings, drawings, and water-colours, while on cabinets and shelves and in elegant glass cases were countless knick-knacks, oriental vases, statuettes, Dresden figurines, Chinese grotesques, old ivories, and Venetian glass, which filled the huge room, crowding into it a population of priceless, outlandish exhibits.

There were hardly any left now. Not that there had been any pilfering, for Major Count de Farlsberg would never have stood for it. But from time to time, Mademoiselle Fifi laid a mine. And on days when that happened, all the officers enjoyed five minutes of first-class entertainment.

The little Marquis scuttled off to get what he needed from the drawing-room. He returned with a very dainty Chinese *famille rose* teapot, which he filled with gunpowder. Into the spout he carefully pushed a long fuse, lit it, and went back to replace this infernal device in the room next door.

He reappeared within moments, shutting the door behind him. All the Germans stood waiting, with smiles of childish expectation on their faces. When the explosion rocked the Château, they all rushed into the room.

Mademoiselle Fifi was first in and stood clapping his hands delightedly in front of a terracotta figure of Venus, the head of which had finally been blown off. Everyone picked up shards of porcelain, fascinated by the strange shapes of the jagged fragments, inspecting the new damage, and arguing about whether this or that piece of wreckage was the result of the previous detonation or not. The Major cast a fatherly eye over the enormous drawing-room which was littered with the debris of art treasures and looked as if Nero had been allowed a free run of it with a machine-gun. He was first to leave, remarking with bluff good humour: 'That was a pretty good show!'

But such a pall of fumes had wafted into the dining-room, where it mingled with the tobacco smoke, that everyone choked. The Major opened a window, and all the officers, who had returned for a last glass of cognac, crowded round.

Damp air blew into the room, bringing with it a smell of waterlogged earth and a fine spray which settled on their beards. They stared out at the huge trees bending before the gusting storm, the wide valley veiled in mists spawned by the overflowing, low, pewter clouds, and, in the distance, the church steeple, which rose like a grey spike into the driving rain.

All the time they had been there, its bell had not rung. Its silence represented the only resistance the invaders had encountered in the area. The parish priest had made no trouble about finding billets and feeding Prussian soldiers; indeed, on a number of occasions, he had been prepared to drink a bottle of beer or claret with the enemy's commanding officer, who regularly used him as a friendly go-between. But he drew the line at ringing his bells: he would have preferred to be shot than allow it. It was his way of registering a protest against the invasion, a peaceful, silent protest, the only kind becoming to a priest, he said, for a priest was a man of love and not a man of blood. Everyone for thirty miles around spoke admiringly of the heroic stand taken by the Abbé Chantavoine, who dared not only to acknowledge but also to proclaim a state of national mourning by maintaining the stubborn silence of his church.

All the villagers, taking their lead from his resistance, were ready to follow their shepherd anywhere and take the consequences, for they felt that his tacit protest salvaged their country's honour. The farming community was convinced that by acting in this way they had served France better than Belfort and Strasbourg,* that they had set an equally fine example, and that the name of their village would be immortalized. This apart, they collaborated wholeheartedly with the Prussian invader.

The Major and his officers laughed among themselves at such toothless courage. But as the entire area was compliant and most accommodating, they were prepared to tolerate its passive patriotism.

The little Marquis Wilhem was the only one of the company who wanted to force the bell to be rung. He was infuriated by his superior's policy of deferring to the priest. Every day, he pleaded with the Major to let him ring the bell, a single 'ding-dong', just the one, for a laugh. Whenever he asked, he purred like a cat, used feminine wiles, and spoke in the honeyed tones of a mistress determined to get her way. But the Major remained firm and, to relieve his feelings, Mademoiselle Fifi would go off and lay a mine in the Château d'Urville.

The five men remained huddled together where they were for a few moments, breathing in the damp air. Then Lieutenant Fritz, with a thick leer, said: 'The ladies do not haf good weather for their liddle drive.'

Thereupon they separated, each man going about his duties, with the Captain having a great deal to attend to by way of preparations for the dinner.

When they reassembled at nightfall, everyone burst out laughing on seeing how smartly turned out they all were: buttons gleaming as though for a ceremonial inspection, hair slicked down and perfumed, faces scrubbed and shining. The Major's hair seemed less grey than it had that morning. The Captain had shaved, keeping only his moustache, which lit a flame under his nose.

In spite of the rain, they kept the window open and from time to time one of them would amble over and listen. At ten minutes past six, the Baron reported the distant sound of wheels. They all rushed to look, and soon the heavy wagon hove into sight, still going at a fair lick, with its team of four horses mud-spattered, steaming, and blowing hard.

Five women got down on to the Château steps, five good-looking girls carefully chosen by a friend of the Captain's to whom Old Faithful had delivered his officer's card.

They had not needed to be asked twice, for they were sure of being paid handsomely. They knew exactly what to expect of Prussians, having had three months of dealing with them, and they reacted to men as they did to things in general. 'Couldn't refuse, not in our line of work,' they told each other as they drove along, doubtless to silence any secret gnawings of whatever conscience they had left.

They were shown directly into the dining-room. Now brightly lit, it looked even more dismal, depressing, and dilapidated. The table, groaning with food, expensive china, and the silver which had been found in the wall where the owner had hidden it, made the place look like an inn where robbers carouse after a good day's looting. The Captain, beaming, took charge of the women with practised ease, running an expert eye over them, giving them kisses, sniffing them out, sizing them up as whores. The three subalterns each wanted to choose their own, but he put his foot down, saying that he would decide who got which, for it had to be done fairly, by rank, so that seniority would be respected.

Then, to avoid arguments, disagreements, and any hint of partiality, he lined them up by height and, turning to the tallest of the girls, said in his most commanding voice:

'Name?'

Raising her voice, she answered: 'Pamela.'

He barked: 'Number one, name of Pamela, assigned to the CO!'

He kissed Blondine, the second girl, indicating that she was his, then gave Amanda, a fat girl, to Lieutenant Otto. Eva, who was known as 'Tomato', went to Sub-Lieutenant Fritz, and the smallest, Rachel, a very young brunette with eyes like two blots of black ink, a Jewess whose turned-up nose was the exception confirming the rule which states that all her race have hooked noses,* was allocated to the youngest officer, the dapper Marquis Wilhem d'Eyrik.

They were all pretty, bouncing girls, with more or less standard-issue faces, their entirely predictable clothes and war-paint having been imposed on them by the daily requirements of their calling and the house-style of the brothel where they worked.

The three younger men wanted to take their girls upstairs at once, hypocritically offering to find them clothes-brushes and soap and water so they could get cleaned up. But the Captain in his wisdom would not hear of it, saying they were sufficiently tidy to sit down to dinner and adding that if they went up with one girl they would only want to exchange her for another when they came down, which would make things difficult for the other couples. His greater experience carried the day. Consequently, they settled for much kissing and fondling and bided their time.

All at once, Rachel choked, coughing so hard that her eyes watered: smoke emerged from her nostrils. Pretending to kiss her, the Marquis had blown a lungful of tobacco smoke into her mouth. She did not lose her temper and said nothing, but she glared at her lord and master, and anger glinted deep in her dark eyes.

They sat down to dinner. Even the Major looked as though he was enjoying himself. He put Pamela on his right and Blondine on his left and, unfolding his napkin, declared: 'Captain, this was a capital notion of yours! Capital!'

Lieutenants Otto and Fritz, behaving as formally as if dining with society ladies, rather intimidated the girls on either side of them. But Baron de Kelweingstein was in his element. He beamed, he told dirty jokes, and, with his halo of flaming red hair, looked as if he had been set on fire. In his guttural French, he addressed suggestive compliments to the ladies, sweet nothings which he had picked up in inns and taverns: expelled through the hole left by his two missing teeth, they reached the girls in a spray of saliva.

Not that they took much of it in. Light seemed to dawn only when he spluttered obscene words and coarse expressions mutilated by his accent. Whereupon, all together, they began laughing like banshees, collapsing on to their partners' laps, repeating words which the Baron promptly began mangling deliberately, to hear them say obscenities. They complied with gusto, for the first bottles of wine had gone to their heads. Then remembering who they were and what they had come for, they started kissing moustaches to the left of them and moustaches to the right of them, pinching arms and shrieking at the tops of their voices. They drank out of everybody's glass and sang ditties in French and snatches of German songs which they had picked up in the course of their daily dealings with the enemy.

Soon even the men, intoxicated by so much female flesh exposed to their view and their hands, went wild, shouting and smashing the china. Meanwhile, from behind their chairs, soldiers waited on them impassively.

Only the Major retained a measure of dignity.

Mademoiselle Fifi had sat Rachel on his knee, but only pretended to join in the fun. One moment, with wild abandon, he would kiss the jet-black curls on the nape of her neck, inhaling the honeyed warmth of her body and the fragrance of her flesh through the narrow gap between her dress and her skin. But the next, gripped by uncontrolled fury and his urge to destroy, he would pinch her so hard through her clothes that she cried out. Sometimes too, he would pull her close to him, so close that they might have been one, and plant a lingering kiss on the cool mouth of the Jewess, but then bit her lip so hard that a trickle of blood ran down the young woman's chin and on to the front of her dress.

Once more she looked him straight in the eye and, wiping away the blood, she murmured: 'You'll pay for that.' He laughed a cruel laugh: 'That's all right by me,' he said.

By now they had reached the dessert, and champagne was being poured. The Major got to his feet and, in the voice he would have used to propose the health of Queen Augusta,* drank to 'The Ladies!'. There followed a whole series of toasts in dubious taste expressed in the language of bar-room and barracks, punctuated by obscene jokes which sounded even coarser in their fractured French.

They all rose to the occasion and to their feet one after the other, making great efforts to be clever and trying hard to be funny. The women, now so drunk they could scarcely stand, eyes glazed and mouths drooling, clapped and cheered the speeches.

The Captain, wishing no doubt to lend the proceedings a more suitably flirtatious note, raised his glass once more and cried: 'To our victories on the field of Love!'

Thereupon, Lieutenant Otto stood up, big as a Black Forest bear, eyes ablaze and sodden with drink. Suddenly overcome by a fit of alcoholic patriotism, he bawled: 'To our victories over the French!'

Although they were by now all throughly drunk, the women went suddenly quiet. Rachel, trembling with anger, turned to the little Marquis and said: 'You wouldn't dare say that to some of the Frenchmen I know.'

But the Marquis, now merry in his cups, still holding her on his lap, merely laughed: 'Maybe. But I've never seen any Frenchmen like those. As soon as we show up, they just run away!'

Beside herself with rage, she hissed at him: 'You're a lying bitch!'

For an instant, he stared at her with his pale eyes, the eyes he used on paintings before shooting them up with his revolver. But then he laughed. 'Come on, then, tell us all about them. Would we be here if they had any guts?' And, warming to his theme, he went on: 'We are their masters! France is ours now!'

She jumped off his knee and sat down heavily on her own chair. He stood up, held out his glass half-way across the table, and repeated: 'France is ours, and all the French people, and the woods, the fields and all the houses in France!'

The other officers, all quite drunk, carried away in a sudden burst of bullish, martial hysteria, grabbed their glasses yelling 'Long live Prussia!' and downed them in one.

The women, reduced to silence and very scared, did not say a word in protest. Even Rachel said nothing, for there was nothing she could say.

Then the little Marquis, balancing his glass, which had been recharged with champagne, on the head of the Jewess, added: 'Not forgetting all the women in France!'

She stood up so quickly that the glass overturned, spilled the wine on to her black hair like holy water at a christening, and fell to the floor where it shattered. Her lip trembled and with a look of fury she defied the officer who was still laughing. In a voice choking with anger, she stammered: 'It's a lie . . . a dirty lie . . . for a start, you can't have the women of France!'

He sat down so that he could laugh in comfort and, affecting a Paris drawl, said: 'That's rich, it really is. So what are you doing here then, sweetie?'

Disconcerted, she said nothing for a moment, her wine-dulled wits too sluggish to take in what he had said. But when she grasped his meaning, she grew even more indignant and retorted impetuously: 'Me? I'm not a woman. I'm a whore. Whores are all Prussians deserve!'

Before she had finished speaking, he slapped her hard across the face. He had his arm raised to do it again but, beside herself with rage, she picked up a small silver-bladed dessert knife from the table and, moving so quickly that no one realized at first what she was doing, she stabbed him with it in the throat, in the hollow where the neck meets the chest.

He was cut off in the middle of a word which stuck in his gullet. He stood there with his mouth open, with a terrible look on his face.

Then all the officers began bellowing and got to their feet. There was uproar. But Rachel tripped Lieutenant Otto with her chair and sent him sprawling. She ran to the window, opened it before they could catch her and disappeared into the night and the rain which was still falling.

Two minutes later, Mademoiselle Fifi was dead. Fritz and Otto unsheathed their sabres and were all for killing the other women, who were now clinging desperately to their knees. Not without difficulty, the Major prevented a massacre and had the four terrified girls shut up in a room, where two soldiers mounted guard over them. Next, as though deploying his men in battle order, he organized the search for the fugitive, confident that she would be recaptured quickly.

Fifty men, urged on by threats of what would happen if they failed, were dispatched into the grounds. Two hundred others combed the woods and searched the houses in the valley.

The table was cleared in moments and the body laid out on it. The four officers, rigid with shock and suddenly sobered, their faces wearing the hard expressions of front-line soldiers, stood at the windows, trying to see through the gloom.

The rain continued to fall in torrents. The darkness was full of the sound of water, a constant wash of water falling, flowing, dripping, splashing.

Suddenly a shot rang out, then, from much further off, another. For the next four hours came the sound of rifle-fire, sometimes close at hand and sometimes distant, and orders being shouted to sections to regroup, and strange-sounding passwords shouted in guttural voices.

All units returned the next morning. Two soldiers had been killed and three others wounded by their comrades in the heat of the chase and the confusion of the night search.

They had not found Rachel.

The local people were subjected to a rule of terror. Houses were ransacked and the district was thoroughly combed, scoured, and turned upside down. It was as though the Jewess had been spirited away without trace.

When the General was informed, he ordered the incident to be hushed up, so that a bad example would not be set for the rest of the army, and he disciplined the Major, who then punished his subordinates. The General had said: 'Fighting this war does not mean having a good time and consorting with prostitutes.' Count de Farlsberg was furious and decided to make the whole area pay.

Since he needed an excuse for taking limitless reprisals, he sent for the priest and ordered him to ring the church bell for the burial of the Marquis d'Eyrik.

Against all expectation, the priest proved to be meek, humble, and throughly respectful. And as the body of Mademoiselle Fifi, borne by soldiers, preceded, surrounded, and followed by an escort marching with guns loaded, left the Château d'Urville and headed for the cemetery, the church bell rang for the first time, tolling a funeral knell to a sprightly rhythm, as if it was being stroked by a friendly hand.

It rang again that evening, and the next day too, then every day. It rang as often and as long as anyone could have wished. Sometimes even at night it would start ringing all by itself, stirring for no apparent reason, and, as if smitten by an odd burst of glee, it would despatch two or three faint reverberations into the darkness. The local population said it was bewitched, and no one, save the priest and the verger, ever went near the belfry any more.

Actually, there was a wretched girl living high in the bell-tower, afraid and alone, to whom the two men secretly brought food.

She stayed there until the German troops had gone for good. One evening, the priest borrowed the baker's *char-à-banc* and himself drove his captive to the outskirts of Rouen. There the priest embraced her. She got down and hurried back on foot to the bawdy house and her madam who had thought she was dead.

Some time later, she was taken away from there by a fair-minded patriot who admired her for the brave thing she had done. Subsequently, he came to love her for herself, married her and made a respectable woman of her, as respectable in fact as many another.

Call it Madness?

Am I mad? Or just jealous? I cannot tell. But this I do know: I have suffered torments. That I am guilty of committing an act of folly, of madness, I cannot deny. But are not jealousy, the kind that stops the breath, and love, exalted, betrayed, and doomed, and the terrible pain I still bear, are not these enough to drive a man to crimes and acts of madness without his being truly criminal either by temperament or design?

Oh, I have suffered! How I have suffered! Suffered unendingly, intensely, agonizingly. I loved that woman impulsively, frenziedly . . . Or did I? Did I really love her? No, no! She possessed me body and soul, she overwhelmed me, trapped me in her coils. I was and am her thing, her toy. I belong to her smile, her lips, her glance, to the lines of her body and the shape of her face: I wilt in the glare of her physical presence. But Her, the woman within, the being inside that body, I hate, despise, and loathe. I have always hated, despised, and loathed her. For she is false-hearted, bestial, unclean, impure. She is the Daughter of Perdition, the lusting, deceitful animal which knoweth not a soul, in whom thought never circulates freely like life-giving air. She is the beast that crouches within the human spirit. And yet she is less than this: she is but a body, a marvel of sweet, swelling flesh wherein dwelleth Infamy.

Those first days of our intimacy were strange and delightful. In her ever-open arms, I drained myself in a frenzy of insatiable desire. Her eyes opened my lips, as though they made me thirst. They were grey at noon, greenish in the dusk, and blue at sunrise. I am not mad: I swear that her eyes were all three colours.

When we loved, they were blue, the blue of bruises, with huge, restless pupils. Sometimes when her body writhed, her lips would stir and part and expel the glistening pink tip of her tongue which quivered like the tongue of a reptile. Then her heavy eyelids would open and she would look up at me in that passionate, spent way which filled me with panic and rage.

When I held her close, I would gaze at those eyes and tremble, torn between the urge to kill the foul creature and my endless need to possess her body.

When she walked across my bedroom, the sound of each footfall started tumults inside me. When she undressed, casting off her clothes and stepping vile and radiant out of the underwear lying crumpled on the floor around her, I would experience in my bones, in my arms and legs and across my heaving chest, a feeling of boundless, pusillanimous weakness.

One day I sensed she had grown tired of me. I saw it in her eyes as she woke. Each morning it was my habit to lean over her and wait for that first look of the day. I waited for it, full of rage, hate, and contempt for the sleeping creature whose slave I was. But when the pale blue of her eyes was unveiled, the liquid blue of water, still languid and full of sleep, still bruised by all the loving, the effect on me was like that of a sudden flame which scorched me and stoked my lust higher. But on that day, when her eyes opened, I saw a dull indifference in them: the absence of desire.

Oh yes, I saw it, I knew, I sensed it! All at once I understood! It was all over, over for good. My intuition was amply confirmed with each hour, each second, that passed.

When I held out my arms or my lips to her, she would turn away petulantly and say: 'Oh, leave me alone!' or 'You are disgusting!' or again 'Can't I have a moment's peace?'

That made me jealous. I was consumed with jealousy. But I was also cunning and suspicious: I pretended that nothing had changed. It was obvious to me that soon she would begin all over again, that there would be another man to rekindle her desire.

I waited and I watched. She would not have tried to deceive me openly. But she continued cold and unresponsive. Sometimes she said: 'Men disgust me,' which was true.

I grew jealous of her. Jealous of her indifference, of the nights she spent alone; jealous of the way she moved, of her thoughts, which I sensed were uniformly vile; jealous of all the things I deduced about her. And when, as still happened occasionally, she had on waking the old melting look in her eyes which used always to follow our passionate nights of love, as though some vestige of lust still lurked in her and stirred her desire, at such moments I felt I should choke with rage. I shook with anger and felt an urge to strangle her, to pin her to the bed with my knee and squeeze her throat until she confessed all the shabby, secret workings of her heart.

Am I insane? I am not.

And then one evening I sensed that she was happy. I sensed that she was inhabited by a new love. I was sure of this, quite sure. She trembled, as though eager to feel my arms about her. Her eyes flashed, her hands were hot, her whole body tense: she exuded an aura of passion which drove me to distraction.

I pretended I did not understand what was happening, but the alertness of my eye was like a net thrown around her.

Even so I did not learn anything new.

I waited a week, a month, a whole season. She opened like a flower in a burst of incomprehensible sensuality. She found satisfaction in the joys of an embrace which eluded me.

And then suddenly I guessed! I am not out of my mind. On my oath, I am not mad!

How can I say it? How can I explain? What words can I find to express something so loathsome and incomprehensible?

This is how I came to know the truth.

One evening, the evening I have already mentioned, she had been out riding. She came back, cheeks glowing, chest heaving, weak-legged and hollow-eyed, and collapsed on to a chair in front of me. I had never seen her like that! It was love! There was no mistaking it!

My mind was in a whirl. I could not bear to see her and turned my head away to look out of the window. Through it I observed a groom heading for the stables, walking her tall frisky horse by the reins.

She too watched the mettlesome, prancing animal. When it disappeared, she promptly fell asleep.

I lay awake thinking all night and felt that I was uncovering mysteries I had never even suspected. Who will ever probe the depths of the perversions of female sexuality? Who will ever understand the improbable caprices of women and their strange ways of satisfying their even stranger fantasies?

Each day at dawn, she set off at a gallop across the fields and into the wood. And each day she would return as limp as after a night of love.

I had understood! I became jealous now of her skittish, galloping horse; jealous of the wind which caressed her cheek as she rode full tilt; jealous of the leaves which kissed her ears as she sped by and of the drops of sunlight which fell through the branches on to her head; jealous of the saddle which carried her, the saddle which she gripped between her thighs.

Here was what made her happy, excited her, appeased her hunger, drained her, and returned her to me jaded and so faint she could barely stand.

I swore I would be avenged. I was gentle and full of attentions. I held out my hand to her as she dismounted after her furious rides. The horse grew angry and tried to kick me. She patted his arched neck. She kissed his quivering nose but did not wipe her lips afterwards. And the smell of her, sticky with sweat as though she had just emerged from a warm bed, mingled in my nostrils with the acrid, animal smell of the horse.

I waited for the right day, the right moment. Each morning, she rode along the same track, which led through a copse of birches and into the wood.

I went out before first light with a length of rope and my pistols hidden under my jacket, exactly as though I were going off to fight a duel.

I made my way quickly to her favourite track. I slung the rope between two trees and then hid in the long grass.

I listened with my ear pressed to the ground. I heard the sound of galloping hooves when she was a long way off. Then I saw her appear at the far end of the vaulted tunnel formed by the spreading leaves. She came on at breakneck speed. Oh, I had made no mistake: here was my answer! She seemed to glow with rapture: there was high colour in her cheek and wildness

in her eyes. The exhilarating momentum of her headlong flight
excited her to heights of frantic, solitary pleasure.

The animal struck the rope with his forelegs and rolled over,
his bones broken. I caught her in my arms—I am as strong as
an ox. When I had laid her on the ground, I went over to Him.
He was watching us. Then, though he still tried to bite me, I
placed the barrel of a pistol in his ear. Then I shot him . . . as I
would have shot another man.

Suddenly I was myself felled, my face gashed by two strokes
of a riding crop. Since she was about to set about me again, I
let her have my other bullet in the stomach.

Tell me, am I mad?

Two Friends

Paris was cut off. Paris was starving. Paris hung by a thread. Sparrows were rare on the rooftops. The rat population in the sewers had thinned. People were eating anything.*

One bright January morning, as he was strolling dejectedly along the outer Boulevard, with his hands in the pockets of his National Guard trousers* and nothing at all in his belly, Monsieur Morissot, a watchmaker by profession forced into retirement for the duration, stopped short on encountering a fellow warrior who turned out to be an old friend. It was Monsieur Sauvage, a fishing acquaintance.

Each Sunday before the war, Morissot had set out at first light with a bamboo rod in his hand and a tin box strapped to his back. He caught the Argenteuil train, got out at Colombes, and then walked the rest of the way to Marante Island.* The moment he reached the place of his dreams, he began to fish. He would fish until it got dark.

Each Sunday, he would meet up with a fat, cheerful little man, Monsieur Sauvage, a haberdasher in the rue Notre-Dame-de-Lorette,* also a very keen fisherman. They had often spent half the day sitting side by side, rod in hand, dangling their legs over the water. They had taken to each other at once.

Some days, they never spoke. On others they would chat. But they got on famously without any need for words, for their tastes were similar and their feelings identical.

On spring mornings, at about ten o'clock, when the returning heat of the sun raised a light mist which hung over the placid surface of the river and drifted downstream on it, and the two fanatical anglers felt the warmth of the new season on their backs, Morissot would say: 'It's grand here, isn't it?' and Monsieur Sauvage would answer: 'No place like it.' It was all they needed to say to understand and respect each other.

In the autumn, towards the end of the day, when the sky, blood-red in the setting sun, cast the reflection of vermilion clouds on the water, turned the whole river crimson, set the horizon ablaze, made the faces of the two friends glow like fire, and gilded the already tawny trees which rustled in the first chill of winter, Monsieur Sauvage would smile at Morissot and say: 'What a sight!' And, without taking his eyes off his float, Morissot would reply wonderingly: 'I'll say. It's a bit better than the view you get on the Boulevard!'

Now, as soon as they recognized each other, they shook hands warmly, so pleased to be together again in such altered circumstances. Monsieur Sauvage sighed and said: 'What a carry-on!' Morissot gave a groan and answered glumly: 'And look at this weather! It's the first fine day we've had this year!'

He was right. The sky was clear blue and full of light.

They began walking along together, each thinking wistful thoughts.

Morissot broke the silence: 'Remember the fishing? Those were the days!'

Monsieur Sauvage asked: 'When do you think we'll be able to go again?'

They went into a little café and drank a glass of absinthe together. Then they set off again through the streets.

Suddenly Morissot stopped and said: 'Fancy another?' Monsieur Sauvage was amenable: 'I won't say no,' he said, and they went into another café.

By the time they left they were rather the worse for wear, as fuddled as anyone who has drunk too much on an empty stomach can be. It had turned mild. A pleasant breeze played on their faces.

The warm air had affected Monsieur Sauvage and made him quite drunk. He stopped and said:

'What if we went now?'

'Where?'

'Fishing, of course.'

'But where?'

'Our island, where else? The French have got their forward positions down Colombes way. I know Colonel Dumoulin. They'll let us through easy.'

Morissot felt a thrill of excitement: 'Right you are. Count me in.'

They each went home to fetch their tackle.

An hour later, side by side, they were striding out along the main road. They reached the house the Colonel was using as his base. He smiled when he heard what they wanted but readily agreed to it. They set off again armed with a pass.

Soon they had left the forward positions behind them. They walked through Colombes, which was deserted, and eventually emerged on the edge of the small vineyards which run down to the Seine. It was then about eleven o'clock.

On the far side of the river, the village of Argenteuil looked quite dead. The rising ground of Orgemont and Sannois dominated the landscape. The wide plain which runs clear away to Nanterre was empty: nothing moved among its cherry trees or in the grey fields.

With one finger, Monsieur Sauvage pointed to the high ground and whispered: 'That's where the Prussians are!' Suddenly apprehensive, the two friends stood rooted to the spot as they looked out across the deserted countryside.

The Prussians! They had never actually seen Prussians in the flesh, but for the last two months they had felt their presence, all around Paris, destroying France, looting, murdering, starving the population, invisible and irresistible. A kind of ominous fear was now spliced into the hatred they felt for that faceless, all-conquering race.

Morissot stammered: 'What if we run into them?'

Monsieur Sauvage replied, his cocky Parisian humour reasserting itself despite the circumstances:

'We'll tell 'em we got other fish to fry!'

But they were reluctant to advance across open country, for they felt intimidated by the silence all around them.

In the end, Monsieur Sauvage took the plunge: 'Come on, let's go. But careful, mind.' They made their way down through a vineyard, bent double, crawling on hands and knees, making the most of the cover provided by the vines, eyes peeled and ears cocked.

Then all that separated them from the river was one stretch of open ground. They took it at a run. As soon as they reached the bank they crouched down in the dry reeds.

Morissot put his ear to the ground to check if he could hear anybody moving around in the vicinity. He heard nothing. They had the place completely and entirely to themselves.

They reassured each other that all was well and started fishing.

Directly in front of them, Marante Island, now deserted, hid them from the opposite bank. The small building which had been the restaurant was shut up and looked as though it had been abandoned for years.

Monsieur Sauvage caught the first gudgeon, Morissot the second, and then with hardly a pause they were pulling out their lines each with a little silver creature wriggling on the end. The fishing there was quite miraculous.

They put the fish carefully in a fine-meshed net in the water close to where they stood. A feeling of utter bliss crept over them, the bliss which comes from rediscovering a favourite pleasure which has long been denied.

The friendly sun warmed their backs. They stopped listening. They stopped thinking. The rest of the world had ceased to exist. They were fishing.

Suddenly a muffled roar, which seemed to come from somewhere beneath their feet, made the earth shake. The big guns were opening up again.

Morissot turned his head and above the river bank to his left saw the massive silhouette of Mont-Valérien.* High up its bulk it sported a white plume—a wreath of smoke from the shot it had just fired.

Immediately, a second puff of smoke was released from the top of the fortress. Instants later, there was the boom of a second detonation.

Others followed and at rapid intervals the hill belched forth its lethal breath, expelling milky-white vapours which rose lazily into the windless sky and formed into a cloud high above it.

Monsieur Sauvage said with a shrug: 'They're off again, then.'

Morissot, who was keeping a careful eye on the feather of his float as it dipped time after time, was, though a man of peace, suddenly filled with fury at the madmen who were fighting each other so senselessly. 'They must be off their heads,' he growled, 'to go around killing èach other like that.'

Monsieur Sauvage said: 'They're worse than animals.'

Morissot, who had just pulled another fish off his hook, said: 'It'll go on being the same, you know, as long as there's governments.'

Monsieur Sauvage stopped him: 'The Republic would never have declared war . . .'

Morissot broke in: 'With kings you got war abroad. With the Republic you got war on your own doorstep.'

And they launched into a friendly argument, sorting out the great political issues with the solid good sense of decent men of limited outlook, and ending up in complete agreement on one point: people would never be free. And all the while, Mont-Valérien kept pounding away, its shells demolishing French houses, destroying lives, killing people, putting an end to so many dreams and expectations and hopes of happiness, opening wounds which would never heal in the hearts of wives, girls, and mothers far away in other lands.

'That's life,' declared Monsieur Sauvage.

'Or death, you should say,' retorted Morissot and he laughed.

Then both of them gave a start of panic as they sensed a movement at their backs. Turning round, they saw four men standing right behind them, four large, armed men with beards, in uniform, like servants, wearing flat caps: they had guns which were pointing straight at them.

The fishing-rods dropped from their hands and floated off down river.

In moments, they were seized, tied up, marched off, and bundled into a boat which took them across to the island.

Behind the building they had assumed was abandoned they saw a score of German soldiers.

A kind of hairy giant straddled a chair smoking a large porcelain pipe. He asked them in excellent French: 'Well, gentlemen. Had a good day's fishing?'

At this juncture, a private arrived with the net full of fish which he had taken care to bring along, and dumped it at the officer's feet: 'Aha! I see you weren't doing too badly. But that's not why you've been brought here. Listen to me now and don't be alarmed.'

'The way I see it, you're a couple of spies sent to keep an eye on me. I capture you and shoot you. You were pretending to fish as a cover for what you were really up to. You have fallen into my hands. It's too bad. But that's war for you.'

'Still, since you must have got out here through your own lines, you obviously know the password which will get you back. Tell me the password and I'll let you live.'

The two friends stood side by side, ashen-faced, their hands shaking slightly. They said nothing.

The officer went on: 'Nobody will ever know and you will report back as if nothing had happened. The secret will be yours to keep. If you refuse, you die. At once. What's it to be?'

They stood motionless and said nothing.

The Prussian gestured towards the water and went on calmly: 'Just think. In five minutes you'll be at the bottom of the river. Five minutes! I imagine you have families?'

Mont-Valérien continued its pounding.

The two anglers went on standing there, saying nothing. The German gave an order in his own language. Then he moved his chair so that he would not be too close to the prisoners. A dozen men took up position at twenty paces, with rifles at the order.

'I give you one minute,' said the officer, 'and not a second more.'

Then he got up suddenly, approached the two Frenchmen, took Morissot by the arm, led him to one side and whispered: 'Quick, the password. Your comrade will never know. I'll make it look as if I felt sorry for you.'

Morissot said nothing.

The Prussian then took Monsieur Sauvage to one side and put the same proposition to him.

Monsieur Sauvage did not answer.

Then once more they were standing shoulder to shoulder.

The officer barked orders. The soldiers raised their rifles.

Just then, Morissot happened to glance down and saw the net full of gudgeon which still lay in the grass a few feet away.

The sun glanced on the still wriggling jumble of fish and

made them gleam. At this, his spirit gave way. His eyes filled
with tears despite his efforts to hold them back.

He stammered: 'Well, cheerio, Monsieur Sauvage.'

Monsieur Sauvage replied: 'Cheerio, Monsieur Morissot.'

They shook hands, shaking all over but unable to control
their trembling limbs.

The officer shouted: 'Fire!'

Twelve shots rang out together.

Monsieur Sauvage slumped forward and collapsed face
down. Morissot, who was taller, spun round, staggered and fell
across the body of his friend. Blood spurted through the holes
in the front of his tunic.

The German barked a new set of orders.

His men dispersed but returned with ropes and stones which
they tied to the feet of the two dead men. Then they carried
them to the bank.

And all this time, Mont-Valérien kept up its pounding. But
now there was a mountain of smoke hanging over its head.

Two soldiers picked up Morissot by the head and feet.
Another two got hold of Monsieur Sauvage the same way. They
swung the corpses backwards and forwards for all their worth
and, with one last heave, released them. The two bodies,
weighed down by the stones, described a curve before falling
into the river feet first.

They made a splash. The water foamed, surged and then
became still. Little wavelets journeyed to both banks.

A few streaks of blood floated on the water.

The officer, as unemotional as ever, muttered: 'And now the
fish get their turn.'

He walked back towards the house.

He noticed the netful of gudgeon in the grass. He picked it
up, examined its contents, smiled, and bawled: 'Wilhelm!'

A soldier wearing a white apron came running. Throwing
him the dead anglers' catch, the Prussian gave another order:
'Fry these little chaps up for me. While they're still alive. They
should be delicious.'

Then he went back to smoking his pipe.

At Sea

The following report recently appeared in several newspapers:

Boulogne-sur-Mer, 22 January: From a correspondent. News of a horrific tragedy has shocked local fishermen here already severely demoralized by similar disasters over the last two years. A fishing-vessel, commanded by its owner, Captain Javel, attempting to make port, was driven too far west on to the breakwater of the harbour wall where it broke up. In spite of the efforts of the lifeboat and the use of rocket-launched life-lines, four crewmen and the cabin boy were lost. The bad weather shows no signs of letting up. Further losses are feared.

Who is this Captain Javel? The brother of the Javel with one arm?

If the poor mariner who was washed overboard and now perhaps lies dead in the wrecked timbers of his shattered boat is indeed the man I'm thinking of, then eighteen years ago he was also involved in another tragedy, which was as awesome and simple as disasters at sea always are.

The elder Javel was then skipper of a trawler.

Now the trawler is the very best kind of fishing-boat there is. Built to withstand any weather, broad-beamed, bobbing like a cork on the surging waves, always at sea, continually buffeted by the grim, salt winds of the English Channel, she works the sea tirelessly, bent under taut sail, dragging a great net slung over the side which drags the bottom of the sea, scouring and scooping up any creatures lurking under rocks: flatfish which cling to the sand, great lumbering crabs with hooked claws, and lobsters with pointed whiskers.

When the wind is fresh and the sea choppy, the boat begins to fish. The net is slung on a long wooden iron-clad boom

which is lowered by means of two hawsers paid out by windlasses fore and aft. As it drifts with wind and current, the boat
drags the trawl-net with it, plundering and devastating the sea
bed.

On board, Javel had with him his younger brother, four
crew, and a cabin boy. He had sailed out of Boulogne in fine,
clear weather to lay his drag-net.

Soon, however, the wind got up and a sudden squall forced
the trawler to run before it. She got as far as the English coast.
But the raging sea tore at the cliffs and flung itself at the land,
making it impossible to enter harbour. So the small boat
headed back out to sea and made for the coast of France. But
the storm continued unabated, making the breakwaters im-
passable and shrouding the approaches to all ports with spray,
thunder, and danger.

The trawler put about again, running on the backs of the
waves, pitching and tossing, shuddering, huge seas breaking
over her decks, battered by walls of water, but in good heart for
all that, for she was used to heavy weather which sometimes
kept her out for five or six days toing and froing between the
two neighbouring countries and unable to land in either.

Eventually, the gale decreased. Since they were in open
water, though there was a heavy swell running, the skipper
ordered the drag-net to be broken out.

The cumbersome tackle was lowered over the side, and two
men in the bow and two in the stern began feeding the ropes
holding it through the windlasses. Suddenly it touched bottom.
At the same instant, a huge sea made the boat heel over and
the younger Javel, who was in the bow directing operations,
was thrown off balance and trapped his arm between the rope,
which had momentarily gone slack under the impact, and the
wooden barrel of the windlass over which it was being paid out.
He made desperate efforts to free it, using his other hand to lift
the hawser. But the net was already trawling and the taut rope
was immovable.

Rigid with pain, he gave a shout. The other hands all came
running. His brother left the helm. They heaved on the rope in
an attempt to free the arm which was being crushed. They

could not budge it. 'We got to cut it,' said one sailor, and from his pocket took a large knife. With a couple of strokes, it could save young Javel's arm.

But cutting the rope would mean losing the net, and the net was worth money, a lot of money—1,500 francs. And it belonged to Javel senior, who was a man who aimed to keep what was his.

In an agony of indecision, he shouted: 'No! Don't cut it. Wait, I'll bring her head round.' And he ran to the wheelhouse and put the helm hard over.

The boat barely responded, inhibited by the drag of the net, which absorbed its momentum, and borne along by the force of drift and wind.

Young Javel was now on his knees, teeth clenched, eyes bulging. He did not speak. His brother returned, still afraid one of the sailors would use his knife, and said: 'Hang on! Don't cut it! We'll let go the anchor!'

The anchor was dropped, and all its chain with it. Then they began turning the boat on the capstan to reduce the tension on the ropes holding the drag-net. Eventually they slackened and released the arm which now hung lifelessly in the blood-stained cloth of its sleeve.

Young Javel looked numb. They removed his jersey and were horrified by what they saw—a pulp of mangled flesh spurting blood as fast as though it were being evacuated by a pump. The man took one look at his arm and said: 'It's buggered.'

The haemorrhage spread a pool of blood on the deck. One of the crew yelled: 'He's goin' to be drained dry. We got to tie that artery up tight.'

They found a length of twine, thick, brown, tarred twine, and, looping it around the arm above the break, pulled it as tight as they could. The spurting slowed and finally stopped altogether.

Young Javel stood up, his arm dangling uselessly at his side. He took hold of it with his other hand, lifted it, turned it this way and that and shook it. It was completely shattered. Every

bone in it was broken. Only the muscles still joined it to his
body. He stared at it grim-faced and thoughtful. He sat down
on a furled sail. His shipmates said he should keep the wound
wet to prevent gangrene setting in.

They left a bucket within reach and every few minutes he
dipped into it with a tumbler and bathed the ghastly mess by
trickling fresh water over it.

'You'd be more comfy below,' said his brother. He went. But
an hour later he came back up on deck. He did not like being
on his own and besides he preferred fresh air. He sat down on
the sail again and bathed his arm some more.

The fishing was good. Broad-backed, white-bellied fish
littered the deck around him, twitching in the spasms of death.
He stared at them, bathing his mangled arm all the while.

As they were about to put back to Boulogne, the wind suddenly
picked up again. The tiny vessel resumed its headlong flight,
pitching and reeling wildly, jolting and jarring the injured
man.

Darkness fell. The heavy weather continued until first light.
As the sun rose, they made out the coast of England again, but
as the sea was moderating, they headed back to France, beating to
windward.

Towards evening, young Javel called to his comrades and
showed them spots of black, ugly signs perhaps that the arm
which no longer belonged to him was beginning to go bad.

The sailors all had a look and said what they thought:

'Could be gangrene,' suggested one.

'It ought to have sea-water on it,' declared another.

So they brought a bucket of sea-water and poured it over the
wound. The injured man's face turned grey. He gritted his
teeth and winced but did not cry out.

When the pain had subsided, he turned to his brother and
said: 'Give us your knife.' His brother gave him the knife.

'Lift my arm up. Hold it straight and keep it like that.'

His brother did what he asked.

Then he began to cut. He worked carefully, deliberately,
slicing through the remaining tendons with the razor-sharp

blade. And soon all that was left was a stump. He heaved a deep sigh and said: 'Had to be done. I'd a been a goner for sure.'

He seemed relieved and breathed deeply. Then he resumed pouring water on what was left of his arm.

That night the weather remained foul and they were unable to make land.

When it got light, young Javel picked up his severed arm and stared at it for some time. Gangrene had set in. His mates came and had a look too. They passed it round, prodded it, turned it over and held it to their noses.

His brother said: 'Time you chucked the thing over the side.'

But young Javel shouted angrily: 'I'll do no such thing! I don't want to! I can do what I like with it! It's my arm!'

He took it back and put it carefully between his feet.

'That'll not stop it going off,' said his brother. Then the crippled Javel had an idea. When they were out for long periods at sea, they packed their catch in barrels of salt to prevent it going bad.

He asked: 'How'd it be if I bunged it in the pickling-water?'

'Now there's a notion,' said the others.

They emptied one of the barrels which contained the last few days' haul and placed the arm at the bottom. They tipped salt over it and then put the fish back one by one.

One of the sailors joked: 'As long as we don't sell it with the rest of the catch!'

Everyone laughed, except the Javel brothers.

The wind was still strong. They headed into it and tacked about within sight of Boulogne until ten next morning. All this time, the injured man continued to bathe his arm.

From time to time he got up and walked the length of the boat and back.

At the wheel, his brother watched him, shaking his head.

They finally sailed into port.

The doctor examined the wound and said it was on the mend. He dressed it properly and ordered complete rest. But Javel refused to take to his bed until he had reclaimed his arm, and he hurried back to the quayside to find the barrel which he had marked with a cross.

His mates emptied it for him and he picked up the arm, perfectly preserved in the brine. It was wrinkled but otherwise in good condition. He wrapped it in a towel he had brought for the purpose and went home.

His wife and children carefully inspected this fragment of their father, feeling the fingers, poking out grains of salt from under the nails. Then they sent for a carpenter who measured it up for a miniature coffin.

The next day, the whole of the crew of the trawler walked to the cemetery behind the severed arm. The two brothers, side by side, led the procession. The parish sexton carried the corpse tucked under one arm.

Young Javel never went back to sea. He got some job or other in the docks and when later on he talked about his accident, he would always add in a confidential whisper: 'If my brother had been willing to cut the line, I'd still have my arm to this day. No doubt about it. But he wasn't the sort who could ever let go of anything that belonged to him.'

The Tribulations of Walter Schnaffs

Ever since arriving on French soil with the invading Prussian army, Walter Schnaffs had considered himself the most unhappy of mortals. He was fat and found marching painful, for he was always short of breath and suffered agonies with his feet, which were very flat and very sweaty. Besides, he was a man of peace and goodwill, neither magnanimous in victory nor bloodthirsty in battle. He was the father of four children on whom he doted, and the husband of a young wife with blonde hair whose affectionate, attentive care and kisses he missed terribly with each passing night. He was a man who liked going to bed early and getting up late, lingering over good food and drinking beer in beer-gardens. He was, moreover, of the opinion that everything that is sweet in this life ends when we die. In his heart he felt a terrible hatred, as instinctive as it was conscious, for cannon, rifles, revolvers, sabres, and the bayonet—especially the bayonet, for he knew he lacked the skill and speed it required for the defence of his enormous paunch.

And when at night, rolled up in his greatcoat, he lay on the bare earth by the side of his snoring comrades, his thoughts would turn to the wife and family he had left behind and to the dangers littering his path ahead: if he got himself killed, what would become of the children? who would feed them and bring them up? Even as things were, they weren't particularly well off, in spite of the money he had borrowed before leaving to ensure they had something to tide them over.

When the fighting had started, he felt his legs go so weak that he would have dropped where he was if he had not reflected that the whole army would simply have marched over him. The whine of bullets raised the hair on the back of his neck.

For months now, he had been living in a state of panic and terror.

His battalion was advancing on Normandy. One day he was sent out on a reconnaissance detail with a small detachment, with orders simply to scout out an area of terrain and then rejoin the unit. The countryside seemed quiet enough; there was nothing to suggest they would meet with any organized opposition.

The Prussians were making their way unguardedly down through a valley rutted with deep ravines when suddenly a crashing volley of shots stopped them in their tracks and left a score of men dead or wounded. A group of partisans* suddenly emerged from a copse no bigger than a man's hand and charged with fixed bayonets.

At first, Walter Schnaffs did not move, so surprised and bewildered that the thought of running away did not even occur to him. Then he was seized by an irresistible urge to be somewhere else. But he knew that he moved like a tortoise compared with the lean Frenchmen who, leaping like a herd of goats, were even now bearing down on him fast. Then he spotted a wide ditch, not six feet from him, filled with bushes with their dried leaves still on them. Without pausing to wonder how deep it was, he dived in feet first, just as if he had been jumping off a bridge into a river.

He shot like an arrow through a thick layer of creepers and prickly brambles which scratched his face and hands, and landed heavily on the seat of his trousers on a bed of stones.

He looked up immediately and saw the sky through the hole he had made. The tell-tale hole could easily give him away and he crawled cautiously on all fours along the bottom of the ditch under the canopy of tangled branches, moving as quickly as he could to put the maximum distance between himself and the fighting. Then he stopped and sat crouching, like a hare in tall dry grass.

For some time yet he went on hearing shots, shouts, and groans. Gradually the noise of battle grew fainter and finally died away. Everything grew silent and peaceful once more.

Suddenly something moved just next to him. He gave a terrified start. It was a small bird which had perched on a branch and made the brittle leaves rustle. Walter Schnaffs's heart went on thumping for more than an hour.

Night was coming on, filling his hole with shadow. Then the warrior started thinking. What was he to do? What would become of him? Rejoin his unit . . . ? But how? Which way had they gone? And if he did manage it, it would mean going back to the terrible life of worry, fear, fatigue, and sheer torture he had been leading since the beginning of the war! Not that! He could not face it any more! He would never have the necessary stamina to endure the marching and cope with the ever-present dangers!

But what was he going to do? He could hardly stay down a hole and hide until the end of hostilities. That was out of the question. If he could have got by without eating, he would not have minded the prospect too much. But he had to eat. Every day.

And so here he was, all alone, fully armed, in uniform, in enemy country, far from the comrades who could defend him. Shivers of fear ran up and down his back.

All at once he thought: 'If only I'd been taken prisoner!' and he was filled by a sudden longing, an urgent, burning longing to become a prisoner of the French. He would be saved. He would have enough to eat, a roof over his head. He would be safe from the bullets and the sabres, with nothing to fear whatsoever, in a beautiful, securely guarded prison. To be a prisoner! What bliss!

His mind was made up instantly:

'I shall surrender!'

He stood up, determined to put this plan into operation without delaying another moment. But he did not move, suddenly assailed by awful thoughts and new terrors.

Where could he surrender? How could it be done? Which way was it? And his mind began to fill with horrible images of death.

He would be running terrible risks if he went wandering off by himself through the countryside in a spiked helmet.

What if he met up with some of the local farmers? Seeing a defenceless Prussian soldier who had lost his way, they would kill him like a stray dog! They would hack him to pieces with pitchforks and picks and scythes and shovels! They would beat him to a jelly, make mincemeat of him, with the ferocity of defeated men who will be revenged!

What if he ran into the partisans? The partisans were lawless, undisciplined, wild men. They would shoot him for a laugh, to while away an idle hour, for the fun of seeing the expression on his face. He imagined he had already been stood up against a wall facing the barrels of twelve rifles, with the small, black holes in the ends of them peering beadily at him . . .

What if he came across the French army itself? The advance guard would take him for an enemy scout, some daring and resourceful trooper out on a lone reconnaissance, and they would shoot at him. He could already hear shots loosed off at will by snipers from their cover in the bushes while he, standing in the middle of a field, was scythed down, riddled with bullets. He could feel the bullets thudding into his body.

He sat down again in despair. There seemed no way out of his predicament.

It was now pitch dark. The night was silent and black. He sat absolutely still, starting at all the faint, inexplicable sounds which always fill the Dark. A rabbit, thumping the ground outside its burrow, nearly prompted Walter Schnaffs to run for his life. The hooting of owls played havoc with his nerves, filling him with sudden fears as painful as any wound. He opened his eyes wide in an effort to see through the gloom. And all the time he kept hearing the sounds of approaching footsteps.

Interminable hours and torments of the damned later, he noticed through the ceiling of branches that the sky was lightening. He felt a huge surge of relief flood over him. The tension went out of his arms and legs, which suddenly relaxed. His heart stopped pounding, his eyes closed, and he slept.

When he woke, he estimated that the sun had probably reached its highest point. It must be midday, then. No sound disturbed the dismal silence of the countryside. And then Walter Schnaffs became aware that he was ravenously hungry.

He yawned and his mouth watered at the thought of sausage, juicy canteen sausage. Cramp gnawed at his stomach.

He stood up, tried a couple of steps, felt the weakness in his legs, and sat down again to think. For another two or three hours, he went through all the arguments for and against, switching sides from one minute to the next, in two minds, unhappy, torn between the most extreme alternatives.

In the end, he settled on a notion which seemed both logical and feasible. He would keep watch for a solitary villager to pass by, unarmed and carrying no potentially lethal tools. He would make straight for him, give himself up, and give him to understand clearly that he was surrendering.

He took off his helmet, for the spike might give him away and, taking infinite care, poked his head over the edge of his hole.

No solitary passer-by was visible anywhere. Some way off to his right, a small village sent smoke—smoke from fires in kitchens!—curling into the sky. Away to his left, at the end of an avenue of trees, he could make out a large chateau with turrets to either side.

He waited till evening, suffering agonies, but saw nothing but rooks flying and heard nothing except the rumbling of his stomach.

Another night fell on him.

He stretched out at the bottom of his lair and slept the feverish, nightmarish sleep of the ravenous.

Another dawn broke above his head. He resumed his watch. But the fields remained as deserted as the day before. Then the mind of Walter Schnaffs was struck by a new fear, the fear that he would starve to death! He pictured himself lying face up, with both eyes closed, in the bottom of his ditch. Insects, all manner of insects would come crawling towards his corpse and start eating him, tucking in all over his body, burrowing under his clothes to get their teeth into his cold flesh. And with its sharp beak, a big black crow would peck out his eyes.

At this, he panicked completely, imagining he was about to faint from hunger, convinced that he had lost the use of his legs. He was about to make a wild dash for the village, resolved to stop at nothing and take the consequences, when he observed three farm-workers going off to their fields with their pitchforks over their shoulders, and he ducked back down into his hiding-place.

But when evening had darkened the land, he clambered out of the ditch and set off, head well down, apprehensive, with his heart racing, towards the distant chateau, preferring to try there rather than the village, which he imagined was as fearful a place as a den of tigers.

There was light in the ground-floor windows. One was actually open and from it emerged a powerful smell of roast meat which immediately wafted up the nose and down into the belly of Walter Schnaffs. It made him wince and catch his breath, and it drew him irresistibly, filling him with the courage of desperation.

And all at once, without pausing to think of what he was doing, he was standing, helmet and all, silhouetted in the window frame.

Inside, eight servants were eating their dinner round a large table. Suddenly, one of the housemaids dropped her glass, slack-mouthed and with eyes like chapel hat-pegs. The others turned to see what she was looking at.

What they saw was the Enemy!

God in Heaven! The Prussians were attacking the chateau!

First, there was an almighty shout, a single cry made up of eight yells uttered in eight different keys, a ghastly, ear-splitting scream of terror. Then there was uproar as everyone leaped to their feet, a great deal of pushing, general confusion, and panic as they all made a rush for the door at the far end of the room. Chairs were overturned. Men knocked women off their feet and trod on them as they fled. In two seconds flat, the room was completely empty, deserted, with its table still laden with food in the middle, under the nose of a dazed Walter Schnaffs, who still stood framed in the window.

After a brief hesitation, he clambered over the sill and bore down on the plates. His hunger, stoked to new heights, made him shake like a man with the ague. But still he held back, paralysed by fear. He listened. The whole house seemed to vibrate. Doors banged. Running feet drummed on the wooden floor above his head. The Prussian went on listening anxiously, alert to every confused sound. Then he heard a series of thuds at the foot of the walls outside, like the sounds made by bodies landing in soft earth: it was the occupants jumping down from the first floor.

Then the hubbub and commotion ceased and the chateau fell silent as the grave.

Walter Schnaffs sat himself down in front of a plate which had survived unscathed, and began to eat. He ate in great mouthfuls, as though afraid he would be interrupted before he had time to pack enough away inside him. He used both hands to stuff food into his mouth, which opened wide like a trap-door. One after another, great gobbets of dinner were dispatched into his stomach. His neck swelled as they went down. From time to time he paused, ready to burst, like a clogged pipe. When this happened, he would reach for the cider jug and clear his gullet as though he were flushing out a blocked drain.

He emptied every plate, dish, and bottle. Then besotted by food and drink, stupefied, red in the face, rocked by hiccoughs, feeling muzzy, and his lips still sticky, he undid the buttons of his uniform so that he could breathe more easily: he would have been quite incapable of putting one foot in front of the other. His eyes closed and his thoughts became fuddled. He lowered his heavy head on to his arms, which lay crossed on the table, and quietly lost all notion of things and events.

The last phase of the moon dimly lit the sky over the trees in the chateau grounds. It was the cold hour before dawn.

In the bushes, silent, flitting shadows swarmed. From time to time a moonbeam picked out the glint of a shaft of steel in the gloom.

The black bulk of the chateau loomed up in the silence. Just two windows on the ground floor were still lit.

All at once a booming voice yelled:

'Forward! Give 'em all you've got, lads! Up and at 'em!'

Within moments, doors, shutters, and windows yielded to a wave of charging men, who overran the house, wrecking and destroying as they went. Within moments, fifty soldiers armed to the teeth burst into the kitchen, where Walter Schnaffs was sleeping peacefully. They pointed fifty rifles against his chest, knocked him off his feet, rolled him round the floor, seized him, and bound him hand and foot.

He gasped with panic, too dazed to understand, bruised, clubbed, and out of his mind with fear.

Then a portly officer, wearing a great deal of gold braid, planted one foot on his stomach and bawled:

'You are my prisoner! Surrender!'

The Prussian made out only one word, 'prisoner', and groaned: 'Ja, ja, ja.'

He was hauled to his feet, tied to a chair, and examined with intense interest by his captors, who were all puffing like grampuses. Several had to sit down, drained by the excitement and their exertions.

He was smiling: he could smile now that he was quite sure that at last he had been taken prisoner!

Another officer appeared and reported:

'The enemy have cleared out, Colonel. Seems like several were wounded. But we've taken the chateau.'

The fat Colonel was mopping his brow. He stopped and bellowed: 'Victory!'

And in a small business memo-book which he now produced from his pocket, he wrote:

'After putting up desperate resistance, the Prussians were forced to withdraw, taking their dead and wounded with them, estimated at fifty men. Several prisoners taken.'

The young officer said:

'What orders should I give, Sir?'

The Colonel replied:

'We shall fall back to avoid a counter-offensive by superior enemy numbers and artillery support.'

And he gave the order to fall back.

The column reformed in the gloom under the walls of the chateau, then moved off. Walter Schnaffs, completely surrounded, with his hands tied, and held by six warriors each holding a pistol in his hand, moved off with them.

Scouts were sent ahead to reconnoitre the road. The main column advanced cautiously, halting from time to time.

At daybreak they arrived at La Roche-Oysel. The daring attack had been carried out by the town's very own National Guard.

The entire population, anxious and apprehensive, had turned out to meet them. When they saw the prisoner's helmet, a great roar went up. Women waved their arms. Old ladies wept. One very old man threw his crutch at the Prussian. It hit one of his guards on the nose.

The Colonel bellowed:

'Keep the prisoner under close guard!'

Eventually, they reached the Town Hall. The prison was opened up. Walter Schnaffs was bundled inside and his hands untied.

Two hundred armed men mounted guard outside the building.

Ignoring the symptoms of indigestion which had been bothering him for some time, the Prussian, deliriously happy, began to do a jig. He danced wildly, swinging his arms and lifting his knees high. And as he danced, he whooped and yelled in a frenzy until finally he collapsed exhausted at the foot of a wall.

He was a prisoner! He was saved!

And that is how the Château de Champignet was retaken from the enemy who had occupied it for a mere six hours.

Colonel Ratier, a draper, who had led the attack at the head of the National Guard of La Roche-Oysel, was later decorated.

Miss Harriet

There were seven of us in the break, four women and three men, one of whom rode on the driving-seat next to the coachman. With the horses slowed to a walk, we were climbing the steep road which snaked up the long hill.

We had left Étretat* at dawn to visit the ruins at Tancarville and were still half asleep and numbed by the sharp morning air. The women especially, unaccustomed to being up and out at hours when men go hunting, could hardly keep their eyes open; they let their heads loll or gave great yawns, oblivious to the beauty of the new day.

It was autumn. Bare fields stretched away on both sides of the road, yellow with a harvest stubble of oats and wheat which covered the ground like a bristly beard. Smoke seemed to rise out of the mist-covered land. Skylarks sang high above our heads and birds chirruped in the bushes.

At last, the sun rose ahead of us, glowing red on the lip of the horizon. And as it climbed, brightening by the minute, the countryside seemed to wake, smile, shake itself, and cast off its shift of white mist, like a girl rising from her bed.

The Count d'Étraille, who was sitting on the driver's seat, called out: 'Look! A hare!', and he pointed to a patch of clover to our left. The hare, almost completely hidden by the greenery, made off, with only its ears showing. It scuttled across a ploughed field, stopped dead, scampered away wildly, switched direction, stopped again, apprehensive, alert to danger, uncertain which way to turn next. Then it was off again, bobbing away with powerful thrusts of its back legs, before disappearing into a large field of beet. All the men woke up as they followed the hare's progress.

René Lemanoir said: 'But we're neglecting the ladies this morning,' and, turning to the lady next to him, the pretty

Baronne de Sérennes, who was finding it hard to keep awake, he whispered: 'You must be thinking about your husband. Don't worry. He won't be back till Saturday. That's not for another four days yet.'

She replied with a sleepy smile: 'You are silly!' Then, shaking herself awake, she added: 'Come on, say something entertaining. How about you, Monsieur Chenal, you're supposed to be a bigger lady-killer than the Duke de Richelieu.* Tell us a story, something romantic, one of your affairs. Anything will do.'

Léon Chenal, an elderly painter who had once been very strong and handsome, very proud of his physique and very much the ladies' man, stroked his long white beard and smiled. After thinking for a while, he suddenly became very serious.

'You won't find it a very amusing tale, ladies. I'll tell you about the saddest love affair I ever came across. I wouldn't ever wish any friend of mine to be the cause of such a passion.'

I

'I was twenty-five at the time and was on a sketching-tour of the Normandy coast.

'When I say a "sketching-tour", I mean wandering about aimlessly with a knapsack on your back from one inn to the next, your excuse being that you are drawing landscapes and making studies from nature. I know nothing finer than this wandering life, which takes you this way and that. You are free, with no constraints of any kind, no worries, no anxieties, and tomorrow can look after itself. You take any road you like, for you have no one to direct you except your fancy, no guide other than the pleasure of looking. You stop because a stream has caught your eye, because the smell of fried potatoes outside some hostelry is so good. Sometimes your mind is made up for you by the scent of clematis or the welcoming glance of a serving-girl at an inn. You should never look down on country matters. Those girls have feelings and senses too, and firm cheeks and cool lips, and their rough kisses taste as strong and sweet as wild fruit. Love, from whatever quarter, should always be respected. A heart that quickens when you appear, an eye that sheds a tear when you go away, these are such rare, such sweet, such precious things that they should never be despised.

'I have had trysts in ditches where the primroses grow, behind byres where the cows lay sleeping, and in the straw of barns still warm from the heat of the day. I have memories of coarse grey linen over supple, rough flesh, and can think back fondly to candid, spontaneous caresses more delicate in their clumsy honesty than the refined pleasures afforded by the most charming, sophisticated ladies of fashion.

'But what there is to like best of all in this aimless gadding-about is the countryside, the woods, sunrise, dusk, and moonlight. They are the painter's honeymoon with the earth. You are alone, close to her, in an unhurried, tranquil communion of souls. You lie down in a field on a bed of daisies and poppies and there, wide-eyed in the clear bright sunshine, you stare into the distance at the small village with its pointed steeple as it strikes noon.

'You sit down beside a spring which wells up through the roots of an oak in the middle of a thatch of fine, tall grass shining with life. You kneel, lean forward, and drink the cold, clear water, which wets your moustache and your nose, you drink with a sensation of physical pleasure, as though you were kissing the spring, mouth to mouth. Sometimes you find a pool in one of these little streams and you dive in, naked, and like some cool, delicious caress, you feel the quick, darting tremble of the current against your skin, which tingles from head to foot.

'On hilltops you are cheerful, melancholy on the banks of ponds, uplifted when the sun sinks into a sea of bleeding clouds and casts red reflections into rivers. And when evening comes, under a moon sailing across the canopy of heaven, you think of many strange things which would never enter your head in the white heat of day.

'Well now, I was wandering in this way through this same part of the world we have come to this year when one evening I reached the little village of Bénouville,* on the cliffs between Yport and Étretat. I had come from Fécamp along the coast, where it forms a high, straight wall with chalky escarpments which drop sheer into the sea. Since morning, I had been walking over the short turf of the links, as fine and springy as a carpet, which grows to the very edge where the salt wind blows in off the open sea. And singing at the top of my voice as I went, striding out with a will, perhaps watching the slow, turning flight of a gull as it traced the white curve of its wings on the blue sky, or maybe looking out at the brown sail of a fishing-boat against the green sea, I had spent a blissful, carefree day.

'I was directed to a small farm which let rooms to travellers, an inn of sorts run by a peasant woman in one of those square, typically Norman settlements which are enclosed by a double row of beeches.

'Leaving the cliff path, I made my way to the place, which was surrounded by tall trees, and knocked at the door of old Madame Lecacheur's house.

'She was an elderly country-woman, very wrinkled and not exactly hospitable. Indeed, she gave the impression that she was not glad to see travellers and that she regarded them with suspicion.

'It was May. The apple trees were in bloom. Over the inn yard, they formed a roof of scented flowers which let fall a rain of pink petals which fluttered down steadily on to the grass and on to anyone who walked under them.

'I asked: "Madame Lecacheur? Do you have a room for me?"

'Surprised that I should know her name, she answered: "That's as maybe. All the rooms is taken. Still, might as well go and look."

'Five minutes later we had come to an arrangement and I dumped my knapsack on the beaten-earth floor of a rather basic room. The furniture consisted of a bed, a couple of chairs, a table, and a ewer. It was next to the kitchen, which was big and smoky. Guests took their meals there with the farmhands and the landlady, who was a widow.

'I washed my hands and went out into the kitchen. The old woman was cooking a chicken for dinner in the large open fireplace. The cooking-pot, black with smoke, hung over the fire.

'"So you have other guests staying here?" I said.

'Crossly she replied: "I got a Englishwoman, getting on a bit. She's got the other room."

'For an extra five sous a day, she agreed to let me have my meals by myself outside in the yard when it was fine.

'And so a table was set for me by the door and I set about chewing my way through the stringy legs of a Normandy chicken, washing it down with still cider and munching coarse white bread, which, though four days old, was excellent.

'And then the wooden gate into the road opened and an odd-looking woman headed towards the house. She was very thin and very tall and so tightly wrapped in a red-checked tartan shawl that anyone would have thought she had no arms but for one long hand which stuck out at thigh level, holding the kind of white parasol holiday-makers carry about with them. Her face had an embalmed look to it and, framed by dangling ringlets of rolled grey hair which bounced with every step she took, it reminded me for some reason or other of a kipper done up in curling papers. She walked past me quickly, with her eyes averted, and swept into the house.

'This strange apparition made me smile. Here, obviously, was the other guest, the Englishwoman getting on in years whom my landlady had mentioned.

'I did not see her again that day. The next morning, as I was settling down to paint in the delightful valley you all know which runs down to Étretat, I happened to glance up and my eye caught something peculiar sticking up on the top of a hill, like a pole with a flag on it. It was her. When she saw me, she disappeared.

'I went back for lunch at noon and sat down to eat with the others, with a view to getting to know this eccentric old woman. But she did not respond to the usual civilities and ignored my attentions. I stubbornly went on filling her glass with water and passed plates to her with enthusiasm. A slight, barely perceptible nod of the head and a word in English spoken so quietly that I could not catch it, were all the thanks I got.

'In the end I gave up, though I could not get her out of my head.

'Three days later, I knew as much about her as Madame Lecacheur herself.

'Her name was Miss Harriet. Looking for some out-of-the-

way village to spend the summer in, she had fetched up at
Bénouville six weeks before and gave no sign of wanting
to move on. She never spoke at mealtimes, and always ate
quickly, while reading a short Protestant tract. She gave these
little booklets away to all and sundry. Even the local priest had
got four delivered to him by a small boy who had been paid two
sous for taking them. Sometimes, in bad French, she would
declare unexpectedly to our landlady, quite out of the blue: "I
love the Lord more than anything in the world. I marvel at Him
in His creations, I worship Him in the fullness of nature, I
carry Him everywhere in my heart." And so saying, she would
hand the woman, who never knew what to say, one of her
pamphlets, which were intended to convert the entire universe.

'She was disliked in the village. The schoolteacher had said:
"She's an atheist", and as a result a cloud of disapproval hung
over her. When consulted by Madame Lecacheur, the priest
said: "She's a heretic. But God seeketh not the death of the
sinner and I believe her to be a person of the strictest moral
character."

'These words "atheist" and "heretic", though no one knew
what they meant exactly, bred suspicion in people's minds.
Furthermore, they claimed she was rich and said she had spent
her life travelling the world because her family had turfed her
out. And why had they turfed her out? Because she had turned
against God, that's why.

'And truth to tell, she was one of those fanatical women of
principle, an entrenched Puritan, the sort England produces in
large numbers, one of those straight-backed, unbearable old
maids who are seen in the dining-rooms of hotels throughout
Europe, spoil Italy, poison Switzerland, make the lovely towns
of the Mediterranean quite uninhabitable, and wherever they
go import their peculiar fads, the morals of fossilized virgins,
ghastly clothes, and that faint odour of rubber which makes you
suspect that at night they are put away in a box.

'Whenever I glimpsed one in a hotel, I always fled, like a
bird that spots a scarecrow in a field.

'But this particular specimen struck me as being so removed
from the normal run that I found her strangely attractive.

'Madame Lecacheur, who was not very bright and instinctively hostile to anything that did not have good country dung on its boots, felt something like hatred for the fanatical way the old spinster carried on. She had found a word for her, a contemptuous word naturally, though how it formed on her tongue or how it had been dredged up from the opaque, mysterious workings of her brain, I cannot tell. She would say: "That woman be a Demoniac." The word, applied to this prim, soulful old lady, struck me as being irresistibly funny. I myself got into the habit of never calling her anything else but "The Demoniac" and could always raise a smile just by saying the word aloud whenever I saw her.

'I would ask old Madame Lecacheur: "And what's our Demoniac been up to today, then?"

'And, looking shocked, she would reply:

' " 'Tis not everyone would believe it, but she been and found a toad with a smashed leg and she've took it to her room and she've set it down in her basin and put a bandage on it like it was 'uman. 'Tain't natural!"

'On another occasion, as she was out walking under the cliffs, she bought a large fish which had just been landed, simply so that she could throw it back into the sea. And the fisherman, although he had been paid handsomely, swore violently at her, angrier than if she had stolen the money out of his pocket. A month went by and still he could not mention the episode without losing his temper and cursing. No doubt about it: Miss Harriet was a Demoniac, all right. It had been a stroke of genius on Madame Lecacheur's part to have found such a word for her.

'The stable-lad, who was known as "Sapper" because he had seen military service as a young man in Africa, had a different view of her. He would say with a leer: "She be an old girl now, but I do reckon she wor a fast one in 'er day."

'What if the "old girl" had known?

'Céleste, the chit of a maid, was never keen to wait on her, though I never understood why. Perhaps it was simply because Miss Harriet was a foreigner, belonged to another race, spoke a different language, practised a different faith. Not that it mattered: she was a Demoniac and that was enough.

'She spent her days wandering through the countryside,

looking for God and worshipping Him in nature. I came across
her one evening on her knees in a thicket. Something red had
caught my eye through the leaves. I pulled the branches back
and Miss Harriet stood up quickly, disconcerted at having been
observed like this. She stared at me with panic in her eyes,
like an owl disturbed in the middle of the day.

'Sometimes, when I was working among the rocks, I would
suddenly see her appear on the edge of the cliff above, looking
like a semaphore signal. She would look out eagerly over the
wide sea shining like gold in the sun and at the crimson fires of
the broad sky. At other times, I would catch sight of her in the
bottom of a valley, marching along briskly with her springy
English stride; and I would set off towards her, feeling somehow drawn to her, just for a sight of the inspired look on her
gaunt, rather silly face, which shone happily with a deep, inner
joy.

'I would also often come across her beside a farm, sitting
on the grass under an apple tree, with her little volume of
Scriptures open on her knee and her eyes staring blankly into
the distance.

'For I too had no wish to leave the place. I felt attached to it,
bound by countless loving threads to its wide, rolling landscapes. I was comfortable in my secluded lodgings, far from
everything, close to the Earth, the good, wholesome, beautiful,
green earth which some day we shall all make richer with our
bodies. And I must also admit that a hint of curiosity kept me
at Madame Lecacheur's. I would have liked to get to know the
strange Miss Harriet and find out what goes on in the lonely
hearts of these wandering English spinsters who are getting on
in years.

II

'We became acquainted in an odd way. I had just finished a
study which to my mind was conceptually rather daring, and so
it was. Fifteen years later, it sold for ten thousand francs. As a
matter of fact, it was simpler than two-and-two-makes-four and
broke all the academic rules. The entire right side of the

canvas showed a rock, a gigantic rugged block festooned with brown, red, and yellow seaweed. Over it sunlight flowed like oil. The light came from the sun, which was not seen since it was hidden behind me, and it fell squarely on the face of the rock, setting it ablaze with golden fire. That was it: a foreground of dazzling light, incandescent, quite magnificent.

'On the left side was the sea, not a blue or slate-grey sea, but a jade sea, greenish, milky, and metallic, beneath a pewter sky.

'I was so pleased with what I had done that I hopped and skipped with it all the way back to the inn. I wanted the whole world to see it at once. I remember I showed it to a cow by the side of the path, yelling:

'"Take a look at this, old girl. You won't see many more like it."

'When I reached the house, I immediately shouted for my landlady at the top of my voice:

'"Shop! Anyone at home? Madame Lecacheur, come here and feast your eye on this!"

'She appeared and looked dully at my masterpiece, incapable of making head or tail of it and not knowing whether it was supposed to be an ox or a house.

'Miss Harriet came in and passed behind me just as I was holding out my canvas at arm's length to show my landlady. The Demoniac could not help seeing it, for I positioned it in such a way that it could not fail to catch her eye. She stopped dead, looking startled, indeed quite thunderstruck. It seems it was "her" rock, the one she always sat on to think her thoughts undisturbed.

'She gave a very English "Ooh!", with such gratifying emphasis that I turned to her with a smile and said:

'"It's my latest study, Miss Harriet."

'She stood there entranced, ridiculous but rather touching too, and murmured:

'"The way you understand nature is so . . . thrilling!"

'And I confess I blushed, better pleased by the compliment than if it had come from a queen. I was enslaved, conquered, vanquished. I tell you, I could have kissed her!

'I sat next to her at dinner as usual. For the first time, she

talked, pursuing her line of thought aloud: "Ooh, I do so love
nature!"

'I passed her the bread, water, wine. Now she accepted them
with her embalmed little smile. And I began talking about
landscapes.

'After the meal, we stood up together and went out through
the courtyard. Then, drawn no doubt by the blazing fire
which the setting sun had lit on the sea, I opened the gate
leading to the cliffs and we set off, side by side, like two
happy people who have just learned to appreciate and understand each other.

'It was a warm, soft evening, one of those evenings which
make you glad to be alive, when body and soul are at peace.
Everything is a pleasure, a delight. The warm, scented air,
saturated with the smell of grass and the tang of seaweed, wafts
its wild perfumes into your nostrils, plants the sea's kiss on
your tongue, and fills your spirit with its pervasive sweetness.
By now, we were walking along the cliff edge, high above the
endless sea, which broke in tiny waves a hundred metres
below. And with mouths open and lungs filled, we breathed the
cool breeze from across the ocean which blew lingeringly over
our hands and faces, salty from the long caress of the rolling
waves.

'Wrapped up tightly in her tartan shawl, baring her teeth to
the wind, she watched entranced as the huge sun slid slowly
towards the sea. Dead ahead, far, far away, as far as the eye
could see, a fully-rigged three-master was silhouetted against
the burning sky, while closer to us a steamship sailed by,
uncoiling a ribbon of smoke and in its wake spreading an
endless hazy trail over the wide sweep of the horizon.

'The crimson globe continued to sink slowly. Soon it touched
the water, just behind the becalmed schooner which was out-
lined in the centre of an incandescent ball in a frame of fire.
Imperceptibly it slipped away, consumed by the sea. We
watched as it foundered, dimmed, and disappeared. And then
it was gone, leaving only the mark of the tiny ship on the gold
cloth of the distant sky.

'Miss Harriet gazed in rapture at the burning death of the
day. It was clear that she was moved by a wild desire to reach
out and embrace the sky, the sea, and the wide horizon.

'She murmured: "Ooh! I do love it all . . . so very much!"

'I saw a tear in her eye. She went on:

' "I would like to be a little bird and fly up into God's heaven!"

'She stood there, as I had often observed her, erect on the cliff-top, her face as red as her crimson shawl. I felt an urge to get out my sketch-book and draw her. She looked like a caricature of Ecstasy.

'I looked away so that I would not smile.

'Then I talked to her about painting, just as I would have done with a friend. I spoke of tone and values and strength of line and colour, using all the technical terms. She listened with attention and understanding, trying to guess the meaning of the obscurer words and catch my drift. From time to time, she would say: "Ooh! I understand! I do understand! How terribly thrilling!"

'We walked back to the inn.

'When she saw me next morning, she rushed up to me and shook me by the hand. At that moment, we became firm friends.

'She was really a very decent old stick with a spring-loaded heart that was forever shooting off enthusiastically in all directions. She was slightly unhinged, like all women of fifty who have never married. She seemed pickled in a kind of sour innocence and yet in her heart of hearts had retained something that was youthful and combustible. She loved nature and animals with an ecstatic, over-fervid intensity, like wine left to keep too long, loved them with all the sensual passion she had never given to a man.

'To be sure, she could not see a bitch suckling its pups, a mare running across a meadow with its foal at its side, a bird's nest full of newly hatched, cheeping fledglings, mouths gaping, heads huge and bodies all naked, without feeling a thrill of flushed excitement.

'Poor, sad, lonely hearts who wander through hotel dining-rooms, poor, ridiculous, pathetic creatures that you are, I have loved you every one since the day I met Miss Harriet!

'I soon became aware that there was something she wanted to say to me but did not dare to and I found her bashfulness rather amusing. When I set off each morning, with my paintbox on my back, she would walk with me as far as the end of the village, not saying anything but visibly anxious and making an effort to find the words to begin. Then all at once she would turn away and march off quickly with that ungainly stride of hers.

'Finally one day she plucked up courage:

'"I would very much like to see how you do your painting. Would you mind? I'm awfully curious to know."

'And she blushed as though she had said something tremendously *risqué*.

'I took her to the bottom of the Petit-Val,* where I had begun a large-scale study.

'She stood behind me, paying close attention to each of my brush-strokes.

'All at once, afraid perhaps that she was a bother to me, she said "Thank you" and went.

'But before long she became more at ease and would go out with me every day, with evident pleasure. She took a folding seat with her under her arm, and would not hear of letting me carry it. She sat next to me. She would sit there for hours, without moving or speaking, her eyes on every movement of my brush. Whenever I managed to get the right effect un-expectedly with a squeeze of paint applied quickly with the knife, she could not hold back an involuntary "Ooh!" of surprise, delight, and admiration. For my canvases, she felt a mixture of emotion and respect, an almost religious awe for such reproductions by the hand of man of a small part of God's creation. She regarded my studies as the equivalent of sacred paintings; and sometimes she spoke to me of God and tried to convert me.

'But her God was a weird being, a kind of village sage with few weapons at His disposal and precious little power, for she always thought of Him as immensely saddened by the injustices committed in His sight—as if He couldn't have prevented them.

'On the other hand, she was on excellent terms with Him, even to the point, it seemed, that He confided His secrets and troubles to her. She would say: "It's God's will" or "It's not God's will", like a sergeant telling a conscript: "Colonel's orders."

'She thoroughly deplored my ignorance of the will of heaven and tried her best to enlighten me. Every day in my pockets, in the hat I had left lying on the ground, in my paintbox, in the shoes I had left outside my door the night before to be cleaned, I would find copies of her slim religious tracts, which had clearly been delivered to her straight from Paradise.

'I treated her like an old friend, frankly and cordially. But soon I detected a slight change in her manner. At first, I did not give it a second thought.

'When I was working, either in the bottom of my little valley or in some quiet lane, I would suddenly catch sight of her walking towards me with those rapid, swinging strides of hers. She would sit down abruptly, breathing hard as though she had been running or was gripped by some deep emotion. Her face would be very red, red like only the English of all peoples know how. And then, for no reason, she would turn pale, her cheeks became like putty and she looked as though she were about to faint. But as I watched, her face would gradually regain its normal colour and she would begin to talk.

'Then without warning she would break off in mid-sentence, get up, and run away so quickly and so queerly that I wondered if I had done something to offend or upset her.

'After a while, I came round to thinking that this was how she behaved normally, but that at the start of our acquaintance she had probably toned her manners down a little in my honour.

'When she got back to the farm after walking for hours on the windswept coast, the long hair which she wore in dangling ringlets at either side of her head had frequently uncurled and hung down slackly as if the spring in them had snapped. Previously, this had not bothered her and she had sat down to dinner regardless, with her hair undone by her sister, the wind.

'But now she always went to her room to twist up her side curls which I called her "corkscrews". And whenever I said, teasing her with a harmless familiarity which always shocked her: "You are lovelier than starlight today, Miss Harriet," her cheeks would turn pink, the pink of youth, the pink of a girl of fifteen.

'But then she reverted to her old prickly ways and stopped coming to watch me paint. I thought: "It's a phase, it'll pass."

But it didn't pass. When I spoke to her now, she replied either with studied indifference or with barely concealed irritation. She was rude, impatient, and tense. I never saw her except at mealtimes, and we hardly spoke. I truly thought I must have offended her in some way. One evening I asked her: "Miss Harriet, why aren't you nice to me like you used to be? Did I do something that's upset you? You're making me very miserable."

'In an angry voice which was really very funny, she replied: "I haven't changed a bit towards you. It's not true to say I have. It's a lie!", and she ran off to her room, shutting the door behind her.

'At times she would shoot me strange looks. Many a time since, I have thought that condemned prisoners must look exactly as she did when they are told they have just one day left to live. There was a crazy gleam in her eye, a promise of something half-mystical and violent. And there were other things besides: feverishness and frustration, a thwarted, helpless yearning for some unrealized but impossible dream! But I sensed too that inside her a titanic struggle was taking place between her heart and an unknown power which she was determined to control. But then again, perhaps it was something else . . . But what? What could it be?

III

'The answer, when it came, was a shock.

'For some time, beginning at dawn each day, I had been working on a picture on this subject:

'A deep, steep-sided ravine between two high shoulders covered with brambles and trees winds its way into the distance: a wilderness shrouded in the milk-white mist which sometimes hangs over such valleys at break of day like cotton wool. And through this dense but transparent mist can be seen, or rather sensed, two approaching figures, a young man and a girl. They are embracing, locked in each other's arms, she craning her head up to him and he bending down to her, and their lips meeting.

'The first rays of the sun, glancing through the trees, cut through the dawn mist, infusing it with pink which glows behind the country lovers, catching their shadowy outline in a shaft of silvery light. It was good, if I say it myself, very good indeed.

'I was working on the hill above the Étretat glen. Luck had smiled on me, for I had just the shroud of mist I needed.

'All at once, a figure loomed up just before me, like a ghost: it was Miss Harriet. When she saw me, her first impulse was to run away. But I shouted to her: "Don't go, Miss Harriet. Come here. I've got a little picture for you."

'She came almost reluctantly. I handed her my sketch. She said nothing but stood quite still and stared at it for some time. Suddenly she began to cry. She sobbed uncontrollably as people do who have fought long and hard against the tears but can hold out no longer and give way to them, though without entirely abandoning the struggle. I jumped up, disconcerted by the spectacle of her distress, which I did not understand. I took her hands in mine. It was a spontaneous gesture of affection, the instinctive gesture of a true Frenchman, who acts first and thinks afterwards.

'She left her hands in mine for a few moments and I could feel them tremble, as though her nerves were stretched to breaking-point. Then she pulled them away quickly, or rather jerked them free.

'I knew what that tremor meant, for I had felt it before: there was no mistaking it. Ah! the trembling of a woman in love, whether she is fifteen or fifty, humbly born or the highest lady in the land, finds my heart so unerringly that I always know what it signifies.

'With all her poor being, she quivered, shook, flinched. And I knew. She walked away before I could say a word, leaving me speechless, as though I had just witnessed a miracle, and feeling as guilty as if I had committed a crime.

'I did not go back for lunch. Instead, I went walking on the cliffs, not knowing whether to laugh or cry, thinking that what had happened was both funny and sad, feeling quite foolish and wondering if she was unhappy enough to go out of her mind.

'I wondered what I should do.

'I concluded that my best course would be to take myself off and I made up my mind there and then to pack up and leave.

'After roaming around until it was time for dinner, feeling a little sad and rather thoughtful, I went back to the inn for the evening meal.

'We all sat down round the table as usual. Miss Harriet was there. She ate solemnly, without speaking, and not raising her eyes from her plate. And she wore her usual expression and behaved as normal.

'I waited until the end of the meal and then turned to the landlady and said:

' "By the way, Madame Lecacheur, it won't be long now before I shall be leaving you."

'Surprised and upset, she said in her slow country voice: "Whatever do you mean? Thinkin' of leavin' us? And with me just gettin' used to your ways!"

'I sneaked a glance at Miss Harriet: her face registered nothing. But Céleste the maid was looking in my direction. She was a big girl of eighteen, with red cheeks, fresh-faced, strong as a horse, and clean, which is a rarity. I had kissed her a couple of times when there was nobody about. I stayed in many inns and it was an old habit, nothing more.

'So dinner ended.

'I went outside and smoked my pipe under the apple trees, walking up and down in the yard. All the thoughts that had been running through my head all day, the bizarre discovery I had made that morning, the grotesque, fervent passion I had aroused, the memories which came back to me now in the light of what I had found out, pleasant but disturbing memories, and maybe too the way the maid had looked at me when I had announced my departure, the combination of all these jumbled sensations excited me now. I felt a surge of physical well-being, the tingle of kisses on my lips and that tell-tale rush of blood which drives a man to do something stupid.

'Night was falling and the shadows gathered beneath the trees. I saw Céleste trotting down to the hen-house at the far end of the yard to lock up. I ran after her, moving so quietly that she would not hear me. As she straightened up after

shutting the flap through which the chickens came and went, I
grabbed her and smothered her fat moon-face with kisses. She
struggled, but she giggled too. She was used to this sort of
thing.

'What all of a sudden made me let her go? Why did I turn
round with a start? How did I sense there was someone behind
me?

'It was Miss Harriet. She was just coming back and had seen
us. She stood rooted to the spot as if she had seen a ghost.
Then she vanished into the night.

'I went inside feeling ashamed, uneasy, and far more dismayed at having been taken unawares like this than if she had
caught me doing something criminal.

'I slept badly, feeling tense and restless, unable to get
depressing thoughts out of my head. I thought I heard someone
crying but I must have imagined this. Several times too I had
the impression that someone was moving about the house and
that the outside door had been opened.

'At last, just before daybreak, overcome by fatigue, I slept.
It was late when I woke and I did not leave my room until
lunchtime, still feeling very uncomfortable and not knowing
what sort of face I should put on.

'Miss Harriet had not been seen. We waited for her. She did
not appear. Madame Lecacheur went to her room, but she was
not there. She had probably gone out before first light as she
often did, to see the sunrise.

'No one found this at all unusual and we began eating in
silence.

'It was hot, very hot, one of those sultry, broiling days when
no leaf stirs. The table had been taken outside and set up
under an apple tree. From time to time, Sapper had to go down
to the cellar to refill the cider-jug because we were all so
thirsty. Céleste brought the dinner from the kitchen. There was
a lamb stew with potatoes, fried rabbit, and salad. Then she
brought us a bowl of cherries, the first of the season.

'Thinking they should be washed and cooled, I asked
Céleste to go and draw me a bucket of very cold water.

'Five minutes later, she came back and said the well had
dried up. She had let out all the rope and the bucket had

touched the bottom but it had come up empty. Madame Lecacheur decided to see for herself, went over and peered into the well. She came back and said she could see something in the shaft that shouldn't be there. Most likely a neighbour with a grudge had dumped a couple of trusses of hay in it.

'I decided I would take a look too, thinking I might have a better idea of what it was, and I leaned over the parapet. I could make out something white but couldn't tell what it was. I had an idea. I suggested we should let down a lantern on the end of a rope. The yellow light danced on the stone sides as it dropped down slowly. All four of us were leaning over the opening, for Sapper and Céleste had joined us. The lamp stopped short above a shapeless heap. It was black and white, looked very odd and left us all baffled. Then Sapper said:

' " 'Tis a horse. I can see the hoof on 'im. Mos' likely fell in last night after gettin' loose from the meadow."

'But all at once, my blood ran cold. I saw a foot, then a leg sticking up. The rest of the body and the other leg were under water.

'Barely whispering but shaking so uncontrollably that the lantern bobbed wildly above the shoe, I stammered:

' "It's a woman . . . there's a woman down there . . . it's Miss Harriet!"

'Only Sapper remained unruffled. He had seen worse than that in Africa!

'Madame Lecacheur and Céleste began screaming and fled.

'The body had to be brought up. I tied a rope securely around Sapper's waist and let him down very slowly on the pulley, watching as he descended into the darkness. In his hands, he carried the lantern and another rope. Soon his voice, which seemed to come from the centre of the world, floated up: "Stop!" I saw him drag something clear of the water. It was the other leg. Then he roped the two feet together and called up again: 'Haul away!'

'I pulled him up. But I felt the strength drain from my arms and my muscles go slack. I was afraid I would release the rope and let him fall. When his head appeared over the rim, I said: "Well?", as if I was expecting him to bring greetings from the woman who was lying down there, at the bottom.

'We both clambered on to the rim of the well and, facing

each other, leaned over the opening and set about hauling up the body.

'Madame Lecacheur and Céleste watched from a distance, hiding behind the wall of the house. When they saw the drowned woman's black shoes and white stockings emerge from the well, they vanished.

'Sapper got hold of the ankles and we dragged that poor, proper old maid clear in the most undignified fashion. Her head was an appalling sight, black and blue and badly lacerated. Her long grey hair had come undone, uncurled forever, and hung down, dripping water and covered in slime. Dismissively, Sapper said:

' "My stars, she be no more'n a bag o' bones!"

'We carried her back to her room. Since the two women did not put in an appearance, I laid her out with the stable-lad's help.

'I washed her sad, bruised face. As I did so, one eye half-opened and looked up at me with the blank, cold, unnerving stare of the newly dead which seems to come from beyond the land of the living. I tidied her dishevelled hair as best I could and with my clumsy hands arranged it differently over her forehead in a way which looked peculiar. I removed her sodden clothes and, feeling as despicable as if I had been desecrating a holy temple, I gradually uncovered her shoulders, breasts and her long arms, which were no thicker than matchsticks.

'Then I fetched flowers, poppies, cornflowers, daisies, and fresh scented grasses, and laid them on the bed where she lay.

'Then, since I was now the only person there, I went through the formalities. A letter I found in her pocket, written at the last moment, requested that she should be buried in the village where she had spent her last days. A terrible thought struck me. Was it not on my account that she wanted to be laid to rest here?

'Towards evening, women from round about arrived to view the body, but I refused to let them in. I wanted to be alone with her. I stayed with her all night, keeping vigil.

'By the light of the candles, I gazed upon her. Poor, unhappy woman, a stranger among strangers, who had died so far from home and in such cruel circumstances. Had she left friends or relatives somewhere? What had her childhood,

indeed her whole life, been like? Where had she come from,
all alone, wandering helplessly like a dog that has been
disowned? What secret suffering and despair had been shut
away inside that unlovely body which she had dragged about
with her all her life like some shameful deformity, encasing her
in a ridiculous shell which had cheated her of affection and any
chance of love?

'How unfortunate some people can be! I felt that this poor
creature had been singled out by the eternal injustice and
implacability of nature! It had all ended for her before perhaps
she had ever known the consolation which sustains even those
who have nothing: the hope of being loved just once in their
lives! Why else had she hidden herself away as she had?
Had she been running away from other people? Why had she
loved every thing, all living creatures except men, with such
passionate tenderness?

'And I saw why she had believed in God: she had hoped to
be compensated in the next life for her unhappiness in this.
Now she would return to dust and live again as a plant. She
would flower in the sun, be food for cows, make seeds for birds
to eat, and, made flesh of their flesh, would live again in
human bodies. But what people call the soul had died at the
bottom of that well. Her sufferings were over. She had given
her life for other lives which she would help to bring into the
world.*

'The hours went by in sombre, silent vigil. A lifting of the
gloom heralded the new day; then a crimson shaft of sunlight
crawled to the bed and dropped a bar of flame on the sheets
and on to her hands. It was the time of day she had loved best.
The birds had woken and were singing in the trees.

'I flung open the window and pulled back the curtains so that
the whole of heaven could see us. I leaned over the icy body, I
raised her battered face in both hands and then, slowly, with
no sense of fear or revulsion, I pressed a long, lingering kiss on
those lips which had never been kissed before . . .'

Léon Chenal stopped. The women were crying. The Count
d'Étraille, on the driving-seat, was heard several times blowing
his nose. Only the coachman was still dozing. And the horses,

without the feel of the whip to urge them on, had slowed and were not pulling at all. The break was barely moving, as if suddenly made heavier by a weight of sadness that had just been taken on board.

A Duel

The war was over. The Germans had occupied France. The whole country lay gasping like some vanquished wrestler pinned beneath the knee of the victor.*

From Paris, a city racked with panic, hunger, and despair, the first trains had begun to leave. They headed for the newly drawn frontiers, crawling at a snail's pace through field and village. The first passengers stared out of the windows at the devastated plains and the burnt-out villages. Outside the doors of houses still left standing, Prussian soldiers wearing their black, brass-spiked helmets straddled chairs and smoked their pipes. Others talked or did chores as though they were members of the family. When the travellers passed through towns, they could see whole regiments drilling in public squares, and above the rumble of the wheels the barking of orders reached them from time to time.

Monsieur Dubuis, who had served in the National Guard in Paris throughout the whole of the siege, was travelling to Switzerland to join his wife and daughter, who had prudently been packed off abroad before the invasion.

Famine and hardship had in no way reduced the size of his paunch, the paunch of a wealthy, peace-loving man of business. He had endured the recent horrors with heavy-hearted resignation and bitter words for man's inhumanity. Now that he was nearing the frontier and the war was over, he was seeing Prussians at close quarters for the very first time, though he had done his duty on the ramparts and stood guard on many a freezing night.

With a mixture of trepidation and anger, he gazed at the heavily armed, bearded men who behaved on French soil exactly as though they were at home, and inside him he felt a kind of flush of helpless patriotic fervour and simultaneously the overriding need, the new instinct to tread warily, which has not deserted us since.

In his compartment, two Englishmen, who had come to see it all for themselves, gazed about them with unperturbed, inquisitive eyes. They were both fat men too and they chattered in their own language, occasionally consulting their guidebook, from which they read aloud as they tried to identify the places it mentioned.

The train was standing in the station of a small town when a Prussian officer, his sabre rattling, suddenly clambered up the two steps and got into their compartment. He was tall, wore a tight-fitting uniform and sported a fiery-red beard which reached up to his eyes. His long moustache, paler in colour, projected beyond each side of his face, which it divided into two halves.

Immediately the Englishmen began staring at him with smiles of gratified curiosity, while Monsieur Dubuis pretended to read a newspaper. He cowered in his corner, like a thief confronted by a policeman.

The train set off again. The Englishmen went on talking to each other, trying to pick out the exact sites where battles had been fought. All of a sudden, as one of them pointed with one arm towards a village on the horizon, the Prussian officer, stretching his long legs and leaning back in his seat, said in French:

'I haf killed twelf Frenchmans in det willage. I haf made more than hundred prisoner.'

The Englishmen, highly intrigued, promptly asked:

'Oh! And what is the name of the village?'

The Prussian replied: 'Pharsbourg.'*

Then he went on: 'I take Frenchmans and I smack their heads!'

And he looked straight at Monsieur Dubuis and laughed arrogantly through his beard.

The train went on its way. It passed through many occupied hamlets. German soldiers could be seen on the roads, on the edges of fields, standing guard at gates or chatting outside cafés. They swarmed over the land like locusts in Africa.

The officer held up one hand:

'If I had been commandant at that time, I take Paris, burn everything, kill all the peoples. France kaput!'

Politely, the Englishmen merely said:

'Oh really?'

He went on:

'In twenty years, all Europe, all, belong to us. Prussia over all!'*

The Englishmen, visibly uncomfortable, said nothing. What could be seen of their faces between their long side-whiskers seemed made of wax. Then the German officer began to laugh. Still sprawling in his seat, he began to scoff. He scoffed at France, which had been humbled, and he insulted his enemies, who had been brought to their knees; he scoffed at Austria, which had already been crushed;* he scoffed at the stout but hopeless resistance put up in the French provinces; he scoffed at the mobile guard* and their ineffectual artillery. He said that Bismarck would build a whole new city out of the iron salvaged from captured French cannon. And then he put his boots up on the seat next to Monsieur Dubuis's leg. Monsieur Dubuis, scarlet with rage, looked the other way.

The Englishmen seemed to have lost interest, as though they had suddenly been transported back to their island home, far from the unpleasantness of the world outside.

The Prussian took out his pipe and looking the Frenchman in the eye said:

'You hef tabak?'

Monsieur Dubuis replied:

'Sorry, no.'

The officer went on:

'I wish you to go buy tabak when the train is stopping next.'

And he began to laugh again:

'I vill give you tip.'

The train whistled and dropped its speed. They rolled into the smoke-blackened remains of a station and came to a complete stop.

The German opened the compartment door and taking hold of Monsieur Dubuis's arm, said:

'Go fetch tabak for me. Quick-quick.'

The station was occupied by a detachment of Prussians.

Other soldiers, standing in a line behind the wooden fence, looked on. The engine whistled and was about to set off. All at once, Monsieur Dubuis leaped out on to the platform and, ignoring the gesticulations of the station-master, jumped into the next compartment.

He had it all to himself! He unbuttoned his waistcoat, for his heart was beating wildly, and, breathing hard, he wiped his forehead.

The train stopped at another station. Suddenly the officer appeared outside the door and got in. The two Englishmen, intrigued, followed promptly. The German sat down opposite the Frenchman and, still laughing, said:

'You hef not fetch tabak.'

Monsieur Dubuis replied:

'That's so.'

By now the train was moving.

The officer said:

'I cut off your moustaches and put moustaches in mein pipe.'

He reached out his hand towards Monsieur Dubuis's face.

The Englishmen, as impassive as ever, stared with expressionless eyes.

The German had grabbed a twist of hair and was pulling hard when Monsieur Dubuis knocked his arm away with the back of his hand and, seizing him by the collar, pushed him back on to his seat. Then, beside himself with anger, the veins on his temples standing out, and a red mist descending over his eyes, he throttled his man with one hand while, with the other, now a tightly clenched fist, he began punching him furiously in the face. The Prussian struggled, tried to draw his sabre and attempted to get his arms around his opponent, who was lying on top of him. But Monsieur Dubuis had him pinned down under the vast weight of his paunch and went on hitting him: he hit him again and again without pausing to rest or catch his breath or even knowing where his punches were landing. There was blood. The German, half-choking, his breath coming in hoarse retches, spat out teeth and made vain efforts to shrug off the fat, raging man who was battering him.

The Englishmen had left their seats and came nearer to get a better view. They stood there delightedly, curious to know how it would all turn out, and ready to take bets for and against both combatants.

Suddenly, Monsieur Dubuis, quite exhausted by his efforts, got to his feet and went back to his place without a word.

The Prussian made no move to attack him but remained where he was, too bewildered to stir, stunned by surprise and dizzy with pain. When he had got his breath back, he said:

'If you vill not gif me satisfaction with the bistol, I kill you.'

Monsieur Dubuis replied:

'Agreed. I am at your disposal.'

The German went on:

'Here is Strasbourg arriving. I find two officers to be my seconds. I hef time to do this before the train leave.'

Monsieur Dubuis, who was puffing as loudly as the engine, said to the Englishmen:

'Would you act as my seconds?'

They answered in unison:

'Rather!'

The train stopped.

In less than a minute, the Prussian had found two comrades who provided pistols, and the group headed for the ramparts.

The Englishmen kept glancing at their watches, putting their best foot forward, hurrying through the preliminaries, with one anxious eye on the time so that they would not miss their train.

Monsieur Dubuis had never held a pistol before. He was placed at a distance of twenty paces from his adversary. He was asked:

'Are you ready?'

As he answered: 'Ready!', he was aware that one of the Englishmen had opened his umbrella as protection against the sun.

A voice ordered:

'Fire!'

Without more ado, Monsieur Dubuis fired wildly and was amazed to see the Prussian facing him stagger, throw up his hands and fall flat on his face. He had killed him.

One of the Englishmen let out an 'I say!' vibrant with delight, satisfied curiosity, and gratified impatience. The other, who still had his watch in his hand, grabbed Monsieur Dubuis by the arm and led him off at the double back to the station.

The first Englishman high-stepped as he ran, with fists clenched and elbows tucked well into his body.

'One, two! one, two!'

Paunches notwithstanding, all three cantered along abreast, looking for all the world like cartoon characters in a comic paper.

The train was about to leave. They jumped into their compartment. Then the Englishmen took off their travelling caps, waved them in the air and shouted three times in rapid succession:

'Hip, hip, hooray!'

Then both of them in turn gravely offered their right hands to Monsieur Dubuis, after which they returned to their places in their corner and sat down side by side.

A Vendetta

The widow of Paolo Saverini lived alone with her son in a tumbledown shack on the ramparts of Bonifacio.* The town, built on a projecting spur of the mountain and jutting out in places above the sea, looks out towards the lower-lying coast of Sardinia, across the intervening strait, which bristles with reefs. At its foot, on its land-facing side, circling it almost completely, runs a deep fault in the cliffs, like some gigantic passageway. This serves as its harbour. Where it ends the first houses begin. Through it, steering a long, circuitous course, come the small Italian and Sardinian fishing-boats and, once a fortnight, the asthmatic old steam-packet which provides a regular service to Ajaccio.

Against the white of the mountainside, the huddled houses show whiter still. Clinging to the rock high above the awesome channel, where few boats venture, they look like wild birds' nests. The wind, never still, scourges the sea and batters the bare, eroded coast, where the grass grows sparsely. It roars into the channel, lashing the land on either side. The patches of white foam surging round the black snags of the innumerable rocks which rise everywhere through the waves, look like tattered sails bobbing on the surface of the water.

All three windows of the widow Saverini's house, which was built into the sheer side of the cliff, looked out across this wild, desolate vista.

She lived there alone, with her son, Antoine, and Spitfire, a large, gaunt bitch, a variety of sheep-dog, with a long, coarse coat. When the young man went hunting, he used her as his retriever.

One evening, after an argument, Antoine Saverini was foully murdered—basely done to death with one treacherous thrust of a knife by Nicolas Ravolati, who escaped to Sardinia the same night.

When his old mother saw the body of her son, which bystanders brought home to her, she did not weep but stood for some time, without moving, staring down at him; then, stretching out her wrinkled hand over his corpse, she swore that he would be avenged. She would not let anyone stay with her and shut herself up with the body and the howling dog. The animal went on howling. It stood at the foot of the bed with its head craning towards its master and its tail between its legs. It remained as still as the old woman, who now bent over her son's body with glazed eyes and wept large, silent tears as she looked at him.

Lying on his back, in his rough wool jacket, which was holed and torn over the chest, the young man looked as if he were asleep. But there was blood everywhere: on his shirt, which had been ripped open by onlookers who had done what they could for him, on his waistcoat, on his breeches, on his face and his hands. Clots of blood had congealed in his beard and hair.

The old woman began talking to him. At the sound of her voice, the dog stopped its howling.

'There, there, my own, my poor boy, he'll pay for this. Sleep now, sleep, you shall have your vengeance, do you hear? Your ma swears it. And you know your ma is always as good as her word.'

And slowly she leaned forward and pressed her cold lips to his dead mouth.

Then Spitfire started howling again, a howl that was long, unvarying, harrowing, terrible.

The woman and the dog stayed where they were until morning.

Antoine Saverini was buried the next day. Soon the people of Bonifacio stopped talking about him.

He had left neither brothers nor close male cousins, so there was no one to pursue the vendetta. Only his mother, who was old, thought about it.

From dawn to dusk, she could make out a white speck on the coast on the other side of the strait. It was a tiny Sardinian village, Longosardo,* where Corsican bandits hide up when the police get too close. They are virtually the only inhabitants of the place, which lies across the water from their own country, and there they stay until it is safe for them to return home and go back to the maquis. It was in this village, she knew, that Nicolas Ravolati had gone to ground.

All day long she would sit all alone at her window, staring out at the speck and dreaming of revenge. How was she to manage it by herself? She was not strong any more and had not long to live. But she had given her word, she had taken an oath over the body. She could not forget. She had no time for waiting. What could she do? She could not sleep at night; rest and peace of mind eluded her; stubbornly, she went on looking for a way. The dog dozed beside her. Sometimes, it would look up and howl into the distance. Ever since its master had died, it would often howl like this, as though it were calling to him, as though the spirit of this inconsolable dumb animal had also stored a memory which nothing could erase.

Then one night, just as Spitfire began to howl once more, an idea came to the old woman. It was vindictive and brutal, the idea of a primitive savage. She thought it over until morning. Then, getting up at first light, she went to church. There she prayed, lying full-length on the stone floor, prostrating herself before God, asking for his help and support, begging him to give her poor wasted body the strength she needed to avenge her son.

Then she went home. In her back yard, there was a broken old barrel which she used for collecting rain-water from the roof. This she turned on its side, emptied, and secured to the ground with stakes and stones. When she had finished, she chained Spitfire in this makeshift kennel and went into her house.

For the rest of the day she paced restlessly around her room, never taking her eye off the Sardinian coast. The murderer was there, over the water.

All day long and all through the night, the dog howled. Next morning, the old woman put water in its dish but nothing else—no meat or bread.

That day went by. Spitfire, weak from hunger, slept. The next morning, its eyes were bright, its coat unkempt, and it jerked frantically on its chain.

And still the old woman gave it nothing to eat. The animal, crazed with hunger, went on barking, though now it was hoarse. Another night passed.

When the sun rose, the widow Saverini went round to her neighbour's and asked if they would let her have two trusses of straw. She took some old clothes which had once been her husband's and stuffed them with the straw so that they looked like a man's body.

She fixed a stake in the ground in front of Spitfire's kennel and tied the guy to it so that it looked like a real man standing up. Then she made a head for it out of old rags.

The dog stared at the straw man in surprise and, though it was ravenous, stopped barking.

The old woman went to the butcher's and bought a long string of black pudding. When she got home, she lit a woodfire in the yard next to the kennel and set the sausage to cook on it. Spitfire went wild, jumped up and down in a frenzy and foamed at the mouth, but never took its eyes off the pan. The smell of cooking went straight to its belly.

Then the old woman took the soggy, steaming mess and put it on the straw man, like a halter. She tied it on with string, taking her time, allowing the juices to soak in. When this was done, she untied the dog.

With one vicious bound, the animal went for the straw man's throat and began tearing it out with its front paws on the shoulders. It dropped on all fours with a piece of the sausage in its jaws, then leaped up again, sank its fangs into the string, bit off lumps of food, dropped to the ground again and jumped ravenously for more. It ripped the face to pieces with its teeth and reduced the whole neck to tatters.

The old woman watched, without moving or speaking, but there was a gleam in her eye. Then she tied the animal up again, gave it nothing to eat for another two days and then repeated the same strange drill.

For three months, she put it through its paces, training it to earn its dinner with its teeth. She stopped chaining the dog. But now she could set it on the straw man with a simple command.

She had trained it to savage it and tear it to pieces even

when there was no food hidden inside the neck. Afterwards, as a reward, she always gave it the rest of sausage she had cooked for it.

Whenever the dog saw the straw man, it stiffened, turned to its mistress, who hissed 'Get him!' and pointed with her finger.

When she judged the time was right, the widow Saverini went to confession one Sunday morning and took communion with ecstatic fervour. Then she dressed in men's clothes, so that she looked like any other old, ragged vagabond, and agreed a price with a Sardinian fisherman, who ferried her and her dog over the strait to the other side.

With her she had a large piece of sausage in a canvas bag. Spitfire had eaten nothing for two days. The old woman kept letting the dog smell the food to make it even more ravenous still.

They walked into Langosardo village. The old woman limped into a baker's and asked where Nicolas Ravolati lived. He had gone back to his old trade, which was carpentry. He was alone in the back of his shop. He was working.

The old woman pushed the door open and called:

'You there! Nicolas!'

He turned. The old woman untied her dog and cried:

'Get him! Tear him to pieces! Kill!'

The dog went for him in a frenzy and got him by the throat. The man locked his arms round it, struggled and wrestled it to the ground. For a few moments, he writhed, beating the floor with his heels, and then became still. Spitfire went on savaging his neck, tearing great strips off it.

Two neighbours who had been sitting on their doorsteps later recalled having distinctly seen a ragged old man leave the shop with a thin black dog. The dog had been eating something that was a dirty brown colour which its master gave it as they walked along.

By evening, the old woman was home again. That night she slept soundly.

The Model

Curved like a crescent moon, the little town of Étretat, with its white cliffs, white pebbly beach, and blue sea, basked in the bright sunshine of a hot July day. Both horns of the crescent ended in natural arches of eroded rock which jutted out into the glassy sea. The smaller, on the right, was supported on a midget's foot, and the larger, on the left, by the leg of a giant. And the Needle, standing almost as tall as the cliffs, broad at the base and tapering at the top, aimed its sharp point at the sky above.

On the beach, a crowd of people sat by the water's edge, watching the bathers. On the terrace of the Casino, another crowd, sitting and strolling under the luminous sky, showed up like a floral garden, ablaze with women's dresses and bursting with red and blue parasols embroidered with large silk blooms.

On the promenade at the far end of the terrace, other people—the quiet, placid people—went their sedate way, far from the bustle of the well-dressed, smart throng.

A young man, a painter, who was well known, indeed famous, Jean Summer, was walking gloomily by the side of a small invalid carriage in which a young woman—his wife— was sitting. It was a type of Bath chair and was being pushed by a manservant. The invalid, who was severely disabled, gazed dejectedly at the joyous sky, the balmy sunshine, and the happy crowds.

They did not speak. They did not look at each other.

'Let's stop for a moment,' the woman said.

They stopped and the painter sat down on a folding chair which his man put up for him.

People passing behind the unmoving, silent couple looked at them pityingly. His legendary devotion was the talk of the

place. He had married her despite her disability, touched by
her love for him, people said.

No distance away, two young men were sitting on a capstan,
talking and staring idly out to sea.

'. . . no, it's simply not true. I tell you I know Jean Summer
very well.'

'In that case, why did he marry her? She was already
crippled before their marriage, wasn't she?'

'She certainly was. He married her . . . for the same reason,
dammit, that men always marry—stupidity!'

'But there must be more to it than that?'

'More to it? But there isn't any more to it! If a man acts like
an idiot, it's because he is an idiot! Anyway you know as well
as I do that painters tend to specialize in absurd marriages.
They invariably marry their models and cast-off mistresses,
which are damaged goods by any standards. Why do they do it?
Who can tell? You'd think it would be the opposite. All that
close contact with so-called models, a particularly silly breed
of woman, should by rights put them off that sort for life. But
no. They make them pose and then they marry them. You
should read Alphonse Daudet's marvellous little book *Artists'
Wives.** It's so true and very cruel.

'With that couple over there, fate moved in an unusual and
really quite appalling way. The girl played a game, a game
with tragic consequences. You could say she staked everything
on a single throw. Was she sincere? Was she really in love
with Jean? You can never tell in these cases. Who can ever say
for sure to what extent women are calculating or genuine in the
things they do? They are always sincere—but only in the sense
that they invariably act upon their feelings, which are constantly
changing. They are passionate, shameless, devoted, admirable,
or wicked, as their elusive moods take them. They lie all the
time, automatically, unconsciously, uncomprehendingly, and
yet at the same time they respond with total honesty to feelings
and emotions which they express in violent, unexpected, totally
baffling, irrational ways that upset the way we men think, our
more cautious habits, and all our selfish calculations. Because
their actions are sudden and unpredictable, we will always find
them inscrutable and enigmatic. We are forever asking

ourselves: "Are they sincere? Or are they playing a game?"

'The truth is that they are sincere and insincere at the same time, because it is in their nature to be both—to extremes—and yet to be neither.

'Just think of the ploys even the most honest of them use to get us to do what they want. Their methods are complicated and simple—so complicated that we can never work them out beforehand, and simple because the moment we realize we've fallen into the trap we kick ourselves and say: "How on earth did she twist me round her little finger so easily?"

'And they always win, old man, Especially when they've made up their minds they want to get married.

'But anyway here is Summer's story.'

'The girl was a model, of course. She sat for him in his studio. She was pretty and knew how to dress. By all accounts her figure was divine. He fell in love with her the way a man falls in love with any reasonably attractive woman he sees on a regular basis. He got it into his head that he loved her with all his being. Now that is a curious phenomenon. Once a man wants a woman, he is quite capable of believing that he cannot live without her for the rest of his life. He may be perfectly aware it's all happened to him before. He may know that once he's had his way with her he'll get bored. He may realize that if he's going to spend the rest of his life with her, then what is needed is not just crude animal passion, which fades quickly, but a compatibility of soul, temperament, and feeling. But the important thing is to work out whether the spell that binds you is the result of physical attraction, plain sensuality, or a deeper affinity of minds.

'Anyhow, he believed he was genuinely in love with her. He made a mountain of promises about being faithful and took her to live with him.

'She was really very sweet. She had the gift many Paris girls have for being smart and flippant. She prattled, she chattered, she said silly things which sounded clever because she put them so amusingly. She had a stock of graceful movements calculated to charm the eye of a painter. When she raised her arms or bent down or got into a carriage or offered you her hand, every gesture was always perfectly right and perfectly fitting.

'For three months, Jean did not notice that basically she was indistinguishable from any other girl who models.

'They rented a house at Andrésy* for the whole summer.

'I happened to be there one evening when the first doubts took root in my friend's mind.

'It was a glorious night and we decided to take a turn by the river. Moonbeams struck the broken water like a rain of light and scattered in yellow fragments in the eddies and currents of the broad, sluggish, unceasing stream.

'We walked along the bank feeling a little light-headed and vaguely excited, as sometimes happens on such romantic evenings. We felt as though we could have done great things and fallen in love with the figments of our poetic imaginations. We felt strange joys, desires, and aspirations stir within us. We did not speak but surrendered to the calm, exhilarating cool of that wonderful night, the cool of moonlight which pierces and suffuses the body and washes over the mind in a fragrant flood of sweet content.

'Suddenly, Josephine (Josephine was her name) gave a loud yell:

'"Oooh! Did you see that? A great big fish jumped over there!"

'Without bothering to look or take in what she had said, he murmured: "Of course, darling."

'She snapped back crossly: "No you didn't. You were looking the other way."

'He smiled: "So I was. It's so peaceful here I'm not really thinking about anything."

'She did not reply. But a moment later, feeling the need to talk, she asked:

'"Are you going to Paris tomorrow?"

'He said: "I really couldn't say."

'She lost her temper again:

'"I suppose trudging about not talking is your idea of fun. People talk, you know, unless they're totally brainless."

'He did not answer. Feeling, with the perverse instinct

women have for these things, that it would annoy him, she began singing that insufferable little song, "I was a-looking up aloft",* which has been grating on people's ears and minds for the past two years.

'He murmured: "Oh do shut up!"

'She answered furiously: "Why do you want me to be quiet?"

'He replied: "Because you're ruining the scenery."

'Then there came the scene, the hateful, stupid scene, the startling accusations, the unwarranted recriminations, and, inevitably, tears. No holds were barred. In the end, they turned for home. He had let her have her say without answering back, dazed by the beauty of the evening and stunned by her hail of inanities.

'Three months later he was struggling desperately to free himself from the unbreakable, invisible bonds which such relationships invariably weave around our lives. But she would not let go and nagged him constantly and made his life a misery. They quarrelled morning, noon, and night. They called each other names. They even came to blows.

'Finally, he decided it was time to end it and make a clean break, whatever the cost. He sold all his paintings and borrowed money from friends. In this way he raised 20,000 francs (he was still relatively unknown). One morning, he put the money on the mantelpiece with a farewell letter.

'He took refuge in my flat.

'At about three in the afternoon, there was a ring at the door. I went to see who it was. A woman leaped at me, pushed me aside, rushed past and ran up to my studio. It was Josephine.

'When he saw her, he stood up.

'With a gesture of considerable dignity she tossed the envelope containing his banknotes on the floor at his feet and said curtly:

' "There's your money. I don't want it."

'She was very pale and trembling and was evidently in such a state that she might do anything. But I saw that he too turned pale, pale with anger and frustration, in a mood which could easily turn ugly perhaps.

'He asked: "What do you want?"

'She replied: "I won't be treated like a whore! You begged and pleaded until you got your way. I never asked you for anything. Keep me with you!"

'He stamped his foot: "This is too much! If you think you can . . ."

'I grabbed him by the arm: "Don't say any more, Jean! Leave this to me."

'I walked over to where she stood and quietly, patiently, I tried to talk sense to her. I ran through all the usual arguments that are always wheeled out in these situations. She listened without moving a muscle, but just went on staring straight ahead of her, stubborn and silent.

'In the end, not knowing what else I could say and sensing that it was all about to end badly, I scraped up one last argument. I said:

'"He still loves you. But his parents want him to get married . . . You know how it is."

'This got a reaction: "Ah! I see! Now I understand . . ."

'Then she turned to him and said:

'"Are you . . . are you really going to be . . . married?"

'He replied without hesitation: "Yes."

'She took one step forward: "If you go through with it, I shall kill myself. Do you hear?"

'He said with a shrug: "Go ahead. Kill yourself."

'Though half-strangled by powerful emotions, she managed to articulate two, maybe three times:

'"What did you say . . . ? What did you say . . . ? Say that again!"

'He said it again: "Go ahead. Kill yourself, if that's what you want."

'Still frighteningly pale, she went on:

'"Don't push me too far. I'll throw myself out of the window."

'He began to laugh, crossed to the window, opened it and, bowing like a man stepping aside to allow others to go first, declared:

'"It's this way. After you!"

'For a moment. she held him in a fixed, blazing, crazed stare. Then, gathering herself as though she were about to jump over a hedge in the country, she ran past me, past him, cleared the balcony railing and disappeared.

'I shall never forget the effect of that open window on me after I had seen her body go through it and fall. In that second, it looked as wide as the sky and as empty as space. I stepped back instinctively, not daring to look down, as though I might fall out of it myself.

'Jean, aghast, stood there without moving.

'They carried the poor girl back. Both her legs were broken. She will never walk again.

'Her lover, beside himself with guilt and perhaps feeling that after all he did owe her something, took her back and married her.

'And that's the whole story, old man.'

Evening was coming on. The young woman felt cold and said she would like to go. The servant started to push her Bath chair towards the village. The painter walked beside his wife. They had not spoken a word to each other for an hour.

Mother Savage

I

I had not been back to Virelogne for fifteen years. But one autumn, I returned for a spot of shooting on the estate of my friend Serval, who had finally managed to rebuild his chateau, which the Prussians had destroyed.

It was a part of the country I liked enormously. There are lovely places the world over which can strike the eye as possessing a special sensual charm, and there are people who fall physically in love with them as with a person. Those of us who are vulnerable to the sense of place store sweet memories of certain springs or woods or lakes or hills which once were familiar sights and touched our hearts as deeply as the happiest things that have happened to us. Sometimes our thoughts will even return unbidden to a forest glade, a stretch of river-bank, or an orchard white with blossom which, though glimpsed but once on some carefree day, are indelibly imprinted on our hearts, like those pictures we have of women, observed on some spring morning walking along a street in frothy white dresses, who left our minds and bodies aflame with unforgettable, unsatisfied desire and an intimation of the happiness which might have been ours.

I loved the whole area around Virelogne. It was dotted with copses and criss-crossed by brooks which sank into the ground like veins carrying blood to the earth. There you could fish for shrimp, trout, and eel. What bliss! There were places where you could swim. You often saw snipe there, in the tall grass which grew on the banks of the narrow streams.

I was walking along, nimble as a goat, keeping an eye on my two dogs foraging ahead of me. A hundred yards to my right, Serval was beating for game in a field of lucerne. I skirted the

trees which mark the limits of Saudres Wood and saw the ruins
of a cottage.

I suddenly remembered it as it had been the last time I saw it,
in 1869, neat, clothed in vines, with chickens strutting outside
the door. Is there anything sadder than a house that has died, a
skeleton that will not lie down, a crumbling, eery ruin?

I also remembered the nice woman who had asked me in one
day when I was very tired and given me a glass of wine. Serval
had told me all about the people who lived there. The father, an
inveterate poacher, had been killed by the gendarmes. The son,
whom I had seen myself, was tall and thin and was also said to
be a scourge of local game. They were called the Savages.

Was that their real name or a nickname?

I called out to Serval. He came, striding along on his long
legs.

I asked him: 'What's become of the people who lived there?'
And he told me this tale.

II

When war was declared, the son, who was then thirty-three,
enlisted, leaving his mother alone in the house. People were not
unduly sorry for the old woman, though, because they knew she
had money.

She lived by herself in her lonely cottage on the edge of the
woods far from the village. She was not afraid, for she was made
of the same stuff as her menfolk, a tough old lady, tall and thin,
who rarely smiled: she wasn't the sort you could stop and joke
with. Country women never laugh much anyway, they leave that
to the men. Their outlook is dreary and limited, for their lives
are bleak and cheerless. Farm workers go to taverns now and
then and at least learn how to have a rowdy good time. But
their wives remain sullen and unrelentingly grim of visage.
Their facial muscles never learn the movements which produce
laughter.

Mother Savage continued to live in her cottage very much as
before. Soon the snow came. She would walk to the village once
a week to buy bread and a little meat. Then she would go

back home directly. Since there was talk of wolves, she took to
going out with a rifle slung over one shoulder, her son's. It was
rusty and its butt was rubbed smooth with the action of his hand.
Mother Savage made an odd sight, a tall, slightly hunched figure
trudging through the snow with the rifle-barrel projecting above
the black bonnet which encased her head and trapped the
white hair no one had ever seen.

One day the Prussians arrived. They were billeted on the local
people according to means and available accommodation. The
old woman, who was known to have money, was given four.

They were four strapping young men with fair skins, blond
beards, and blue eyes, who still looked well-fed despite the
hardships they had already endured and still managed to remain
easy-going, despite being in conquered territory. Living alone
with an old lady, they went out of their way to be helpful
and, whenever they could, spared her the heavy work and
unnecessary expense. Each morning, in the hard glare of the
snow, all four could be seen in their shirt-sleeves, getting
washed at the well, splashing water liberally over their white and
pink Northern skins, while old Mother Savage came and went,
getting the dinner ready. Afterwards, they cleaned the kitchen,
scrubbed the floor, chopped wood, peeled potatoes, did the
washing, and went about the household chores exactly like four
devoted sons helping their mother.

But the old woman kept thinking about her own son, her
tall, gaunt son with his hooked nose, brown eyes, and thick
moustache which grew like a bush of black hairs on his upper
lip. Every day she asked each of the soldiers billeted on her:

'Do you know where the French Regiment's gone to? The one
my boy's in? It's the Twenty Third Infantry.'

They replied: 'Nein. Not know. Know noddink.'

But they too had mothers at home and, understanding her
worry and anxiety, went out of their way to be nice to her. For
her part, she grew quite fond of her four enemies, for country
people know little of patriotic hatred which is the preserve
of the well-to-do. The humble——those who pay the most
because they have nothing, because any new burden weighs
heaviest on them; those who are slaughtered in their thousands
because, as the most numerous class, they make natural

cannon-fodder; those who suffer most cruelly from the horrors and hardships of war because they are the weakest and least able to resist—the humble know nothing of the bellicose zeal, the prickly sense of honour and the so-called political manœuvring which in six months bring two warring nations, the winner no less surely than the loser, to their knees.

Of Mother Savage's four Germans, local people said:

'Mark you, them four have got theirselves a cosy billet.'

One morning when the old woman was at home by herself, she saw a man walking across the fields towards the cottage. Soon she could make out who it was: the man who delivered the post. He gave her a letter. She got the glasses she used for sewing out of their case and read it:

Dere Madame Savage,

I am writting to give you bad news. Yore son Victor was killed yesterday by a cannon-ball it jest about cut him in two. I was by him. We was always next in line in the Company. He always said I was to write and let you know straight off if anything happened to him.

I took his watch out of his pocket so I could bring it back when the war is over.

Cheerio and all the best.

césaire rivot (Cpl) 23rd Infantry.

The letter was dated three weeks earlier.

She did not cry. She just stood, not moving, so shocked and dazed that for the moment she felt nothing. 'So now Victor's gone and got himself killed,' she thought. Gradually, tears welled up in her eyes and grief filled her heart. Then other thoughts came one by one, painful, harrowing thoughts. Never again would she be able to kiss her boy, her great lump of a boy! The gendarmes had killed the father and now the Prussians had killed the son! . . . Cut in two by a cannon-ball! It seemed that she could see the horrible thing happening: his head blown off, the eyes still open, while he went on chewing the end of his bushy moustache as he always did when he was angry.

What had they done with his body, afterwards? If only they had brought her boy back to her, as they had done with her husband, with the bullet in the middle of his forehead.

She heard the sound of voices. It was the Prussians returning from the village. Hurriedly she pushed the letter into her apron pocket and, having had time to dry her eyes, greeted them calmly, looking very much her usual self.

They were all smiles and looked very pleased with themselves. They had brought back a fine rabbit, doubtless stolen, and made signs to indicate to the old lady that there was something good to eat.

Immediately she busied herself with preparing the meal. But when she came to kill the rabbit, her courage failed her, though it was not the first she had killed, by any means. One of the soldiers killed it instead, clubbing it with his fist behind the ears.

When the animal was dead, she skinned it and tore the red body free. But the sight of the sticky blood, the blood that smeared her hands, warm blood which she could feel growing cold and congealing, made her shake all over. And all the time she could see her boy cut in two, no less red and raw than the still-quivering body of the rabbit.

She sat down at the table with the Prussians but could not eat, not so much as a mouthful. They devoured the rabbit and paid no attention to her. She watched them out of the corner of her eye, not speaking, turning an idea over in her head, her face so expressionless that they noticed nothing.

All at once she asked: 'I don't even know your names and you been here a whole month.' With some difficulty, they finally grasped what she wanted and told her their names. But that was not enough. She made them write them down on a piece of paper, with the addresses of their families and then, perching her glasses on her long nose, stared at their foreign handwriting. She folded the paper and put it in her pocket, on top of the letter which told of the death of her son.

When the meal was over, she said to the men:

'I'm going to do something for you.'

And she began carrying straw into the hay-loft where they slept.

They were puzzled by what she was doing. She explained that it was so they wouldn't feel the cold so much. They helped her. They stacked bales as high as the thatched roof and built themselves a large room with four walls made entirely of cattle-fodder, warm and sweetly scented, where they would sleep like kings.

At supper, one of them became concerned when he saw that Mother Savage again ate nothing. She said she had cramps in her stomach. She lit a blazing fire and warmed herself by it. The Germans went up to the hay-loft, climbing the ladder they used each night.

As soon as they had lowered the trapdoor, the old woman removed the ladder, opened the outside door without a sound and went for more bales of straw. She filled the kitchen with them. She walked barefoot through the snow, moving so quietly that no one heard her. From time to time, she stopped and listened to the loud, uneven snores of the four sleeping soldiers.

When she judged that her preparations were complete, she threw a bundle of straw on to the fire. When it caught, she spread it over the rest. Then she went outside again and watched.

Within seconds, a searing light completely filled the inside of the cottage, which turned into an inferno, a vast, incandescent furnace. Light from it spurted through the narrow window and cast a brilliant glare upon the snow.

There was a loud yell from the top of the house. It was followed by the bellowing of shouting men, a ghastly scream of panic and terror. The trapdoor inside collapsed and a great gout of fire leaped into the loft, ate through the thatch of the roof, and rose into the sky like the flame of an immense torch. The whole cottage blazed.

Inside, all that could be heard now was the crackle of the fire, the noise of walls buckling and beams collapsing. Suddenly the roof fell in and in the billowing smoke the burning carcass of the house sent a huge shower of sparks into the air.

Lit by the glow, the ground outside, white with snow, gleamed like a lake of silver stained with red.

Far away a bell began to toll.

Old Mother Savage stood before her gutted home, gun at the ready, the gun that had been her son's, in case any of the men got out alive.

When she saw that it was all over, she threw the gun into the blazing ruin. It exploded loudly.

People began to arrive. Local people. And Prussians.

They found her sitting on the trunk of a tree. She had an air of quiet satisfaction about her.

A German officer who spoke French like a native asked her: 'Where are the soldiers who were quartered here?'

With one thin arm, she pointed to the smouldering heap. The fire was dying now. She replied in a firm voice: 'In there!'

The crowd pressed round her. The Prussian said: 'How did the fire start?'

She said: 'I lit it.'

No one believed her. They assumed that the tragedy had turned her wits. But then, with everyone standing round and listening, she told the whole story from start to finish, from the time the letter had been delivered to the final screams of the men who had gone up in smoke along with her home. She omitted no detail of what she had felt and done.

When she had finished, she took two pieces of paper out of her pocket and, so that she could tell them apart in the fading light of the fire, she put on her glasses once again. Holding up one, she said: 'This one says how Victor died.' Then she held up the other and, with a nod in the direction of the glowing embers, added: 'And this one's got their names on, so you can write to their families.' Calmly, she offered the white paper to the officer, who now had her by the shoulders. She continued:

'You got to write and tell them how it happened. Tell their families it was me, Victoire Simon, Mother Savage, that did it! And don't you forget.'

The officer shouted orders in German. She was seized and made to stand against one wall, which was still hot, of her home. Twelve men formed up quickly in front of her at a range of twenty yards. She did not move. She knew what would happen. She waited.

An order rang out. It was instantly followed by a prolonged volley of rifle fire. One belated shot went off by itself after the others.

The old woman did not fall: she subsided as though her legs had been scythed from under her.

The Prussian officer strode across to where she lay. She had been virtually cut in two. In her hand, she clutched her letter. It was soaked in blood.

My friend Serval added:

'The Germans took reprisals. They razed the local chateau, which belonged to me.'

But I was thinking of the mothers of the four fine lads who had been burned to death here. And of the fearsome heroism of that other mother who had been lined up against this wall and shot.

I bent down and picked up a stone. It had the blackness of fire still on it.

The Little Keg

Monsieur Chicot, proprietor of Épreville's* only tavern, reined in his dog-cart outside the farm belonging to old Madame Magloire. He was a big man, forty years old, with a hearty manner, a red face, and a pot belly. People said he was a sly one.

He hitched his horse to the gatepost and walked into the farmyard. He owned a piece of land adjoining the old woman's property, which he had wanted to get his hands on for some time. He had offered to buy it a score of times, but Madame Magloire stubbornly refused to sell.

'I was born here,' she said, 'and here I shall die.'

He found her peeling potatoes outside the front door. She was seventy-two years old, thin as a lath, wizened and bent, but she could do a good day's work as well as any chit of a girl. Chicot gave her a friendly pat on the shoulder and sat down on a stool beside her.

'Hello, Ma. You been keeping well?'

'Pretty fair. And yourself, Monsieur Prosper?'

'A few aches and pains. Otherwise, mustn't grumble.'

'Well that's all right then.'

After this, she did not speak again. Chicot watched as she finished what she was doing. Her fingers, hooked, gnarled, and hard as a crab's legs, cradled the greyish tubers firmly and twirled them round and round while, with the blade of an old knife which she held in the other hand, she removed long swathes of peel. And when each potato showed waxy white all over, she dropped it into a bucket of water. Three bold hens one after the other made straight for the peelings at her feet then made off quickly, bearing away their spoils.

Chicot seemed awkward, uncertain, anxious, as though there was something on the tip of his tongue which would not come out. Eventually he took the plunge:

'Listen, Ma . . .'

'I'm listening.'

'About the farm. Are you still set against selling up?'

'Sell? Never! And don't you go thinking otherwise. My mind's made up. So you needn't start on about it.'

'The thing is I got this arrangement worked out. It would suit us both down to the ground.'

'What's this arrangement, then?'

'It goes like this. You sell it to me but you still get to keep it. Are you with me? Listen, I'll tell you how it would work.'

The old woman stopped peeling her potatoes and stared at the innkeeper. Her eyes were bright and alert beneath their scaly lids.

He went on: 'It'd be like this. Every month, I give you 150 francs. You got that? Every month regular I'll come in the cart and fetch you 30 écus.* Beyond that, it'll all be exactly the same as now. No difference at all. You can stay put. You won't have to bother your head about me. You won't owe me a penny piece. All you have to do is take my money. How does that suit?'

He beamed at her good-humouredly.

The old woman looked at him with suspicion, trying to see the snag. She asked:

'That's what I get out of it. But what about you? This plan of yours, don't it mean you get your hands on the farm?'

He replied: 'Don't worry your head about that. You can stay here for as long as the Good Lord spares you. This is your place and your place it stays. But you'll have to sign a paper, a proper legal paper, saying that when you go I get the property. You got no family, except for them nephews of yours you got no time for. So how does that suit you? You hang on to the farm for the rest of your days and I give you 30 écus a month. It's all clear profit for you.'

The old lady was taken aback, uneasy but tempted. She said:

'I don't say no. But I shall have to get my thinking-cap out. Come back one day next week an' we'll talk it over again. I'll tell you what my answer is then.'

Whereupon Chicot drove off, as happy as a king who has just subdued an empire.

Madame Magloire was left with her thoughts. She did not sleep that night. For four days she remained in a fever of indecision. She felt sure there was something in the plan that was not to her advantage, but the thought of the 30 écus every month, thirty round, shiny coins cascading into her lap, dropping from the sky above, and with nothing for her to do to earn them, made her ill with greed.

So she went to see the notary and put her problem to him. He advised her to accept Chicot's proposition but to ask for 50 écus rather than 30, since the farm was worth at the very least 60,000 francs.

'If you live another fifteen years,' the notary said, 'even at the higher figure all he'd be paying for it would be 45,000.'

The old woman felt weak at the knees at the prospect of 50 écus a month. But she was still suspicious, fearing all manner of unexpected difficulties and hidden traps, and she stayed asking questions until evening, unable to bring herself to leave. In the end, she gave instructions for the deed to be drawn up and went home with her head swimming, as though she had drunk a gallon of young cider.

When Chicot came for her answer, she made him wait for it, saying no, she did not want to sign, but all of a tremble inside, in case he would not agree to give her the 50 écus. He pressed her and in the end she laid down her conditions.

He gave a mortified start and refused point-blank.

So to talk him round, she began working out how long she probably had to live.

'Just five or six years at most, that's all I got left, most likely. I'm going on seventy-three now and none too spry. Last night, I really thought my time had come. Didn't have the strength to set one foot in front of the other. I had to be put to bed.'

But Chicot was not going to be had so easily.

'Don't give me that! Sound as the church bell, that's what you are. You'll live another ten years and more. You'll see me off yet, and that's a fact.'

The rest of the day was spent arguing. But since the old woman would not budge, the innkeeper agreed in the end to give her the 50 écus.

They signed the deed the next day. For doing so, old Madame Magloire insisted on being primed with a small gratification, a matter of 10 écus to oil the wheels.

Three years passed. The old woman remained as fit as a fiddle. She did not seem to get a day older and Chicot was at his wits' end. He felt as if he had been paying out for years and years, that he had been had, diddled, ruinated. From time to time he called to check how she was, rather as a farmer will go out into his fields in July to see if his corn is ready for cutting. She always met him with a gleam of spite in her eye. It was as if she was gloating, revelling in the clever way she had outmanœuvred him. He never stayed long and climbed back into his dog-cart muttering:

'Die, damn you, die!'

He did not know what to do. Each time he saw her, he would have gladly throttled her. He hated her with the savage, sly hatred of the peasant who knows he has been swindled.

He racked his brains for a way out.

Then one day he called to see her. He was rubbing his hands just as he had done the day he had come to put his proposition to her.

He chatted for a few minutes. Then he said:

'Listen, Ma, why don't you drop by the inn for a bite to eat next time you're in Épreville? There's been talk. People are saying how you and me have fallen out. Now that grieves me no end. It wouldn't cost you a penny, mind. I'm not so tight-fisted I'd grudge you the price of a spot of dinner. Come as often as you want. Don't be shy! I'd be happy to see you.'

Madame Magloire did not need to be asked twice. The next day but one she had to go to market and Célestin, her farm-hand, drove her in her trap. Bold as brass, she told him to leave the horse in Monsieur Chicot's stable and then went to claim the dinner which had been promised her.

Beaming, the innkeeper gave her a royal welcome and brought chicken, black pudding, sausage, a leg of lamb, and a plateful of bacon and cabbage. But she ate almost nothing: as a girl, she had been raised frugally and had always lived on a diet of soup and bread and butter.

Disheartened, Chicot pressed her. She did not drink wine either. She would not have coffee.

He said: 'But you will have a glass of something to finish, won't you?'

'Go on then. I won't say no.'

He bawled to the far end of the bar:

'Rosalie! Bring the brandy! The three star! The good stuff!'

The serving-girl appeared with a tall bottle. It had a label in the shape of a vine leaf.

He filled two small glasses.

'Get your tongue round that, Ma, it's a corker.'

The old woman raised her glass and took small, slow sips, to make it last. When it was empty, she tilted it so that not a drop would go to waste. She said:

'I'll not deny it, it's a grand drop of stuff.'

The words were hardly out before Chicot was pouring her another. She tried to say no but it was too late, and she lingered over it as she had with the first.

He tried to persuade her to have a third but she refused. He insisted:

'Oh go on, it's like mother's milk. I can sup ten or a dozen glasses of the stuff and not feel it. Goes down like nectar. It don't lie heavy on the stomach and it don't give you a headache. It's like as if it evaporates on the tongue. Does you a power of good!'

Since she was sorely tempted, she let herself be persuaded. But only half a glass, she said.

Then, in a burst of generosity, Chicot cried:

'Look, since you like it, I'll give you a little keg of it. Just to show we're still good friends.'

The old woman did not say no and went home feeling slightly woozy.

The next day, the innkeeper drove into the yard of Madame Magloire's farm. From his dog-cart he produced a small keg bound with iron hoops. He said he wanted her to taste what was it in so she would see for herself that it was the same as she had sampled already. When they had drunk three tots a-piece, he went away, saying:

'And when it's all gone, mind, there's more where that came

from. Don't be shy. I'm not bothered about the money. The sooner it's gone, the better pleased I'll be.'

Then he climbed into the dog-cart.

He was back four days later. The old woman was sitting by her door, cutting up bread for the soup.

He said good morning, standing as close as he could get so that he could smell her breath. He detected a strong whiff of alcohol. His face brightened.

'Aren't you going to offer me a drop of that brandy, then?' he said.

They drank two or three friendly glasses.

Soon, it was being said everywhere that Madame Magloire had taken to drink. She was found lying on the floor of her kitchen, in the yard outside, in lanes roundabout, and had to be carried home, as dead to the world as a corpse.

Chicot never went to see her now and whenever anyone mentioned her, his face turned sad and he would sigh:

'It's a terrible thing, taking to the bottle at her age. Still, when you get old, there's not much else left. Mark my words, it'll all end in tears!'

And it did. She died the following winter, around Christmas, after collapsing, drunk, in the snow.

Monsieur Chicot inherited the farm. He said:

'Poor old stick! If she'd only kept off the drink, she'd have been good for another ten years.'

The Dowry

No one was surprised when lawyer Simon Lebrument married Mademoiselle Jeanne Cordier. Lawyer Lebrument had just bought the practice of the notary, Monsieur Papillon. Now that took money, and Mademoiselle Jeanne Cordier was rich to the tune of 300,000 francs in cash and bearer-bonds.

Monsieur Lebrument was a good-looking man who cut quite a dash, or as much dash as any provincial lawyer can cut, and dash was not a plentiful commodity in Boutigny-le-Rebours.

There was grace in Mademoiselle Cordier's movements and a bloom on her cheek. The grace was perhaps a little stiff and the bloom a little faded, but she was undeniably handsome and attractive, and eminently presentable.

The wedding was the talk of Boutigny-le-Rebours.

The couple drew admiring looks from everyone and after the ceremony, they took their new-found conjugal bliss off to the house where they would spend their married life. Instead of making a splash, they had decided on a brief honeymoon in Paris after first spending a few days together, just the two of them.

Those few days together were delightful, for lawyer Lebrument brought to his first close relations with his wife quite remarkable qualities of tact, delicacy, and timing. His motto was: 'Everything comes to him who waits.' He was both patient and enterprising and success came quickly and was complete.

Four days later, Madame Lebrument worshipped her husband. She could not do without him. She had to have him by her every minute of the day so that she could snuggle up and kiss him, stroke his hands, fiddle with his beard, tweak his nose, and so on and so forth. She would sit on his knee, pull both ears and say: 'Open your mouth and close your eyes.'

And he would open his mouth obediently, half close his eyes, and get a great big loving, lingering kiss which sent shivers up and down his back. He did not have enough kisses or lips or hands—there simply was not enough of him—to lavish on his wife from morning to night and night to morning.

When that first week had sped by, he said to his young wife:

'If you like, we'll go to Paris on Tuesday. We'll pretend we aren't married. We'll go to restaurants and theatres and music halls, the lot.'

She jumped for joy.

'Oh yes! Yes! Yes! Let's go. Let's go as soon as we can!'

He went on: 'And just in case we forget, remind your father to have your dowry ready. I'll take it with us and I can settle up with Monsieur Papillon when we're there.'

'I'll tell him first thing in the morning,' she said.

Then he took her in his arms for a further instalment of the billing and cooing she had grown so fond of in the past week.

On the following Tuesday, both in-laws went to the station with their daughter and son-in-law to see them off to Paris.

The father-in-law said: 'I really think it most unwise of you to be taking so much money with you in a briefcase.'

But the young lawyer merely smiled: 'No need to worry on that score, papa, I'm used to carrying large sums about with me. Why, in my job I sometimes have nearly a million francs on me. This way we'll avoid endless formalities and delays.'

The guard shouted: 'All aboard for Paris!'

They made a dash for a compartment which was occupied by two old ladies.

Lebrument whispered in his wife's ear:

'Damn! That's a bore! Now I won't be able to smoke.'

She whispered back:

'It's a bore for me too, but it's not the smoking I'll miss.'

The train whistled and set off. The journey lasted an hour, during which they hardly spoke, for the old ladies remained awake.

When they got outside the Gare Saint-Lazare, Monsieur Lebrument said to his wife:

'If you like, darling, we can go and have lunch on the

Boulevard first and then make our way back slowly, collect the luggage and have it sent on to the hotel.'

She agreed at once: 'Oh yes! Do let's go for lunch in a restaurant. Is it far?'

He said: 'It's a fair way. But we'll catch a bus.'

She was surprised: 'Why not take a cab?'

He chided her gently, with a smile:

'That's no way to save money! A cab for a five-minute ride is 30 centimes a minute. Do you always intend to have everything you want?'

'You're right,' she said, feeling rather ashamed.

A large omnibus drawn by three horses trotted by. Lebrument hailed it:

'Driver! I say, driver!'

The heavy vehicle halted. Pushing his wife in front of him, the young lawyer said hurriedly:

'You go inside. I'm going on top so I can at least get one cigarette smoked before my lunch.'

She did not have time to answer. The conductor grabbed her by the arm to help her up the steps and bundled her inside, where she collapsed in a bewildered, flustered heap on a seat from which she could see her husband's legs through the rear window disappearing up the steps on to the top deck.

She sat motionless between a fat man who reeked of pipe-smoke and an old woman who smelled of dog.

All the other passengers sat silently in rows. There was a grocer's boy, a factory girl, an infantry sergeant, a gentleman wearing gold-rimmed spectacles and a silk hat with huge brims turned up like the gutters on a roof, two self-important, sour-looking women whose manner seemed to proclaim 'We may be in a bus but we're really above this sort of thing', two nuns, a girl with no hat, and an undertaker's mute. They looked like a collection of caricatures, a museum of grotesque figures, a series of cartoons of the human face, and virtually indistinguishable from the line of comic dolls and aunt sallies who have balls shied at them at fairgrounds.*

The jolting of the bus made their heads roll gently from side to side, shook them up, and made their flaccid cheeks wobble.

The vibration of the wheels was hypnotic and they all looked torpid and half asleep.

Madame Lebrument sat limply in her seat.

'Why didn't he come with me?' she wondered. She felt vaguely depressed. Really, he should have been able to do without that cigarette!

The nuns signalled to the conductor to stop and they got off one behind the other, leaving behind the musky smell of old robes.

The bus set off and then stopped again. A cook got in, red in the face and out of breath. She sat down and put her shopping-basket on her knee. A strong whiff of washing-up water spread through the bus.

'It's further than I thought,' thought Jeanne.

The undertaker's mute got out and his seat was taken by a cab-driver who was evidently no stranger to stables. The girl with no hat was replaced by a street-porter whose feet spoke eloquently of his many comings and goings.

Jeanne began to feel very peculiar, rather sick and ready to burst into tears for no reason at all.

More people got off and others got on. The omnibus continued on its way through the interminable streets. It halted at stops and then set off again.

'What a long way it is!' Jeanne said to herself. 'I hope he hasn't forgotten or gone to sleep. He's been tired out these last few days.'

Gradually all the passengers got off. She was left quite by herself. The bus-conductor shouted:

'Vaugirard!'*

Since she made no move, he repeated:

'Vaugirard!'

She looked at him. She knew that the word was meant for her, since there were no other passengers. The man said it a third time:

'Vaugirard!'

She asked: 'Where are we?'

He answered roughly: 'Good God, this is Vaugirard. I been telling you, over and over.'

'Is it far to the Boulevard?' she said.

'Which one?'

'The Boulevard des Italiens, of course.'

'We passed it ages ago.'

'Really? Would you be so good as to tell my husband.'

'Husband? What husband?'

'He's upstairs.'

'Upstairs? There ain't been anybody up top for ages.'

She gave a start of panic.

'What? But that's not possible! He got on when I did. Go and look. He must be there!'

The conductor's tone changed:

'Look, darlin', give it a rest! So you missed a trick. There's plenty more where he came from. Now hop it! You'll get another pick-up on the street.'

Tears welled up in her eyes. She insisted:

'You're wrong! I tell you, quite wrong! He was carrying a large briefcase under his arm.'

'A big briefcase? Oh yes, I remember him. Got off at the Madeleine,' said the bus-conductor and he began to laugh. 'Looks as if he's gorn and given you the slip all right!'

The omnibus had reached the end of the line. She got off and though she knew it was pointless, her eye was instinctively drawn to the top deck of the bus. It was quite, quite empty.

She began to cry and, not realizing that people could hear and were staring, she said out loud:

'What's to become of me?'

The station inspector came over:

'What's goin' on here, then?'

The bus-conductor said waggishly:

'This lady's husband hopped off the bus and left her in the lurch.'

The inspector said:

'Is that all? She'll be all right. Now get that bus moving.'

He turned and went away.

She began walking wherever her legs took her, too flustered and frightened even to take in what was happening. Where could she go? What was she to do? What had happened to him? How could such a mistake have happened—had he forgotten? made a miscalculation? lost his memory?

She had two francs in her pocket. Who could she turn to? Then suddenly she remembered her cousin Barral, a deputy chief clerk at the Admiralty.

She had just enough for her cab-fare. She told the driver to take her there. She caught him just as he was leaving for the office. Like Lebrument, he was carrying a briefcase under his arm.

She leaped out of the cab.

'Henry!' she cried.

He stopped in amazement:

'Jeanne? What on earth are you doing here? And by yourself! What are you up to? Where have you been?'

Her eyes brimming with tears, she stammered:

'My husband . . . He's disappeared!'

'Disappeared? Where?'

'On a bus.'

'A bus? I say!'

And she told him the whole story through her sobs.

He heard her out, thought for a moment, and then asked:

'He didn't seem at all strange this morning?'

'No.'

'I see. Did he have much money with him?'

'Yes, he had my dowry.'

'Your dowry? The whole lot?'

'Yes, all of it. He was going to make the payment for the practice this afternoon.'

'Oh dear. Listen, coz, I'd say that your husband, even as we stand here talking, is well on his way to Belgium.'

For a moment, she could not take it in. She stuttered:

'My husband . . . ? How do you mean . . . ?'

'I mean he's run off with your money. It's as simple as that.'

She just stood there, choking. She hissed:

'So . . . he's . . . he's a rotter!'

Then, faint with shock, she collapsed against her cousin's waistcoat and sobbed.

People were stopping and beginning to stare. He guided her gently through the front door of the building where he lived and, supporting her around the waist, helped her up the stairs. When his startled maid opened the door, he said:

'Sophie, run round to the restaurant and bring back lunch for two. I shan't be going to the office today.'

The Bequest

Monsieur and Madame Serbois were sitting disconsolately at opposite ends of the table, finishing lunch.

Madame Serbois, dainty and fair, with a pink complexion, blue eyes, and a very affectionate manner, ate slowly, head bent, as though in the grip of sombre, tenacious thoughts.

Monsieur Serbois, tall and vigorous, with side-whiskers and the look of a government minister or a successful businessman, seemed on edge and preoccupied.

After a while, as though he were talking to himself, he said:

'Really! It's most extraordinary!'

His wife asked: 'What is, dear?'

'The fact that Vaudrec did not leave us a penny-piece.'

Madame Serbois blushed bright red. She blushed quite suddenly, as though a pink veil had been drawn over her skin, starting at the throat and working up to cover her entire face.

'Perhaps a will was deposited with the lawyer. We don't know anything yet.'

Even so, she seemed to know.

Serbois reflected: 'Yes, that's possible. After all, he was the best friend we both had. He was always here and dined with us every other day. Oh I know he was always giving us presents, it was as good a way as any of repaying our hospitality. But when a person has people like us for friends, he ought to remember them in his will. I'm positive that if I had been as ill as he was, I would have left him a little something, even though my legal heir is you.'

Madame Serbois lowered her eyes. As her husband set about carving the chicken, she blew her nose. She blew it as people do when they are crying.

He went on: 'Well I suppose there might be a will with the lawyer and a small legacy for us. I wouldn't want much,

something to remember him by, that's all, a keepsake, just
something to show that he was really fond of us.'

At this, his wife said in a faltering voice: 'If you like, after
lunch we'll go and see Monsieur Lemaneur in his office. We'll
know where we stand then.'

He declared: 'Fine. That's all right by me.'

He had tied his napkin round his neck to avoid dripping
gravy down his front. With his handsome whiskers showing
black against the white linen, he looked like a talking severed
head, the head of a butler in a rather good house.

When they walked into the offices of the lawyer, Monsieur
Lemaneur, the clerks all looked up. When Monsieur Serbois
was satisfied that he had their attention he gave his name,
though everyone knew perfectly well who he was. The chief
clerk stood up with noticeable alacrity. His deputy beamed.

Husband and wife were ushered into the presence of
Monsieur Lemaneur.

He was short, bulbous, rotund: every part of him was round.
His head looked like a cannon-ball screwed to a globe which
was supported on a pair of legs so short and fat that they also
looked spherical.

He greeted them, motioned them to sit and, giving Madame
Serbois a slightly knowing look, said:

'I'm glad you came. I was just about to write and ask you to
call so that I could inform you of the testamentary dispositions
of Monsieur Vaudrec which concern you.'

Monsieur Serbois could not stop himself from exclaiming:
'Ah! I knew it!'

The lawyer went on:

'I shall now read out the will. It's not very long.'

He picked up a document from his desk and read:

I, the undersigned, Paul-Émile-Cyprien Vaudrec, being sound in
mind and body, hereby set out my last wishes.

Since death may come and take us at any time, I have, before I am
duly gathered in, taken the precaution of writing my will, which is to
be given into the keeping of Monsieur Lemaneur.

Being without direct heirs, I bequeath my entire estate, to wit,
stocks and shares to the value of 400,000 francs, together with

land and property currently valued at approximately 600,000 francs, to Madame Claire-Hortense Serbois, without encumbrances or conditions. I ask her to accept this gift from a dead friend as a proof of his devoted, profound, and respectful affection.

Paris, 15 June 1883

Signed: VAUDREC

Madame Serbois sat quite still, with her head bent, while her husband looked in astonishment from the lawyer to his wife and back again.

'Naturally, Monsieur, your wife will require your consent before she can accept the legacy.'*

Monsieur Serbois got to his feet: 'I shall require time to reflect,' he said.

The lawyer, with an unpleasant sneer, bowed deferentially: 'My dear sir, I understand the scruples which could well give you pause, for people are sometimes prone to draw uncharitable conclusions. Perhaps you would like to return tomorrow with your answer? Shall we say the same time?'

Monsieur Serbois bowed: 'Very well. Until tomorrow, then.'

He took his leave stiffly and formally, offered his arm to his wife, who was as red as a beetroot and kept her eyes stubbornly fixed on the ground, and swept out of the office with such presence that the clerks were thrown into a panic.

When they reached home, Monsieur Serbois closed the door and said grimly:

'You were Vaudrec's mistress!'

'How could you think . . . ?'

'Don't deny it! No man leaves all his money to a woman unless . . .'

She had turned deathly pale and her hands shook slightly as she tried to retie the ribbons of her hat to prevent them trailing on the ground.

She thought for a moment, then said:

'Look, you are being foolish, extremely foolish . . . only a little while ago you yourself were saying you hoped he'd . . . well, leave you something.'

'I did and he could jolly well have left something to me . . . to me, see? Not to you!'

She looked at him, staring deep into his eyes in the oddest, most searching way, as if she were trying to see something there, a glimpse of the mysterious essence of the human personality which no one can ever know, though we may sometimes have a sudden sense of it at odd moments, unguarded, unconstrained, careless moments, which are like doors left open to reveal the hidden workings of the soul within.* Choosing her words, she said:

'But it strikes me that . . . if . . . that people would have thought it just as . . . strange if he had bequeathed such a large sum of money to . . . you.'

With the petulance of a man cheated of his expectations, he snapped:

'Why should they think that?'

She said: 'Because . . . ' and stopped, looking away as though too embarrassed to go on.

He was now pacing from one end of the room to the other. He said:

'You're not going to accept, of course?'

She answered without emotion:

'It's out of the question. So there's no point in waiting until tomorrow. We might as well let Monsieur Lemaneur know at once.'

Serbois halted in front of her and for a few seconds they stood eye to eye, very close, each trying to see and know the truth, to understand and unmask the other, to probe the inner recesses of each other's minds. It was a silent, urgent, questing moment, such as occurs between two human beings who live together but because they know so little of each other, are reduced to suspicions, unspoken questions, and endless watching.

With his face close to hers, he suddenly hissed:

'Come on, admit you were Vaudrec's mistress.'

She shrugged: 'Don't be stupid . . . I'm fairly sure Vaudrec was in love with me. But he was never my lover, never.'

He stamped his foot: 'You're lying. It doesn't add up.'

Calmly she said: 'Maybe. But that's how it was.'

He started walking up and down again. Then he stopped and said:

'If you're telling the truth, why did he leave all his money to you?'

She replied casually: 'It's simple. As you said, we were his only friends. He spent as much time here as he did in his own house. So when he came to write his will, he naturally thought of us. Then as a compliment to a lady, he put my name on the paper, because it was my name that would instinctively have come to mind, a reflex. When he used to bring a present it was always for me, never for you. He used to give me flowers, and on the fifth of every month would come with a trinket or something for me, because we had met him one fifth of June. Correct me if I'm wrong. He hardly ever gave you anything. He wouldn't have dreamed of it. Mementoes and keepsakes are for wives, never for husbands. Well, it was to me he offered his last present, not you. There. It's really quite straightforward.'

She was so calm, so unruffled that Serbois hesitated:

He went on: 'All the same, it would look very bad. Everybody will believe the worst. We can't accept.'

'In that case, we'll say no. It'll mean that we'll be a million out of pocket, that's all.'

He began talking not directly to his wife but the way people talk when they are thinking aloud:

'A million . . . ! out of the question . . . reputation in ruins . . . can't be helped . . . he should have given half to me, then everything would have been all right . . .'

He sat down, crossed his legs, and began fiddling with his whiskers, as he always did when he was doing some serious thinking.

Madame Serbois had opened her sewing-box. She took out her embroidery and as she began working on it she said:

'I don't want the money. You sort it out.'

He did not speak for a while. Then he said hesitantly:

'Look, perhaps there is a way out. You must make half the legacy over to me by deed of covenant. We have no children, so it would be perfectly legal. That would stop the tongues wagging for sure!'

She said gravely: 'I don't see how that would stop anybody's tongue wagging.'

Suddenly he lost his temper: 'Are you stupid or what? We'll

say that we inherited half each. It's true, after all. We don't
have to tell everybody that you were the sole beneficiary.'

She gave him another piercing look: 'As you wish. I'm
willing.'

He got up and resumed his pacing. He seemed to be hesitating again, though his face lit up:

'No . . . perhaps it would be best to turn it down . . . it would
be more dignified . . . still, if we did as I said, nobody could
point the finger . . . Even the most pernickety would have to
shut up and go along with it . . . Yes, it's the answer . . .'

He halted in front of his wife: 'Listen, angel, if you like I
could go back and see Monsieur Lemaneur by myself. I'll ask
him what he thinks and explain it all to him. I'll tell him you
prefer it this way, for the sake of decency, so that people
won't gossip. The moment I accept half the bequest, it'll be
quite obvious that I'm sure of my ground, that I'm fully in
the picture, and that I'm satisfied that nothing underhand or
dishonest has been going on. It's as if I were to tell you: "If I,
your husband, can accept, you can too." As things stood, it
wouldn't have been decent to accept.'

Madame Serbois said simply: 'As you wish.'

He went on in a great flow of words: 'Oh yes! It all becomes
simple if we split the bequest. We have come into money left
us by a dear friend who did not wish to distinguish between us
or treat us differently or to appear to be saying: "In death,
I prefer this one or that one, exactly as I did in life." And
you can be absolutely sure that if he'd given the matter any
thought, then that is exactly what he would have done. But he
didn't think. He didn't foresee the implications. As you very
rightly pointed out, it was to you he always gave presents
and it was to you he wished to leave one final token of
remembrance . . .'

She stopped him with a hint of impatience: 'Oh all right! I've
got the point. There really is no need for all these explanations.
Why don't you just go round and see the lawyer?'

He turned red, feeling foolish all of a sudden, and stammered: 'You're right. I'm going.'

He picked up his hat, crossed to where she was sitting, and
held out his lips to kiss her.

'Shan't be long, darling,' he murmured.

She tilted back her head and he kissed her on the brow. His long side-whiskers tickled her cheeks.

Then he was gone, highly pleased with himself.

Madame Serbois dropped her embroidery into her lap and began to cry.

Monsieur Parent

I

Little George, on hands and knees, was making mountains out of the sand of the path. He scooped it up in both hands, piled it up into pyramids, and then stuck a chestnut-leaf in the top.

His father sat on an iron bench, watching him in rapt, fond attention, seeing only him, though the little park was crowded.

All along the circular path which runs by the side of the pond as far as Trinity Church* and back, thus completing a full circuit of the green, other children were similarly engaged on their fledgling games, while their bored nurses looked on callously and mothers chatted to each other without taking their eyes off their noisy brood for an instant.

Nannies advanced gravely, two by two, with the long, brightly coloured ribbons on their bonnets streaming out behind them, carrying small white bundles done up in lace. Between hoop-races, small girls, bare-legged in short dresses, conversed earnestly. The park attendant in his green tunic wandered through the swarm of noisy infants, constantly going out of his way to avoid knocking sand pies over, taking care not to step on hands, doing nothing to disrupt the ant-like labours of these pretty little grubs of humanity.

The sun was about to dip behind the roofs of the rue Saint-Lazare and bathed the swarm of shrieking, well-turned-out children in its bright, level rays. The chestnut-trees were illuminated by its golden radiance, and the three fountains playing in front of the great west door of the church seemed to run with liquid silver.

Monsieur Parent gazed at his son crouching in the dirt of the path. He watched every little thing he did with doting eyes, and his pursed lips seemed to blow kisses at every movement George made.

But glancing up at the clock on the church tower, he saw he was five minutes late. He got to his feet, took the little unbreeched boy by the arm, shook the dirt off his dress, wiped his hands, and led him off in the direction of the rue Blanche. He walked quickly, anxious to be home before his wife got back; and the toddler, who could not keep up, struggled along at his side.

His father bent down and picked him up in both arms and, quickening his step again, began to breathe heavily as the road grew steeper. He was forty, prematurely grey, and a little overweight; he carried before him the paunch of a carefree bachelor but held himself uneasily, like someone who has been unmanned by life.

A few years earlier, he had married a young woman whom he loved tenderly. But now she rode roughshod over him, treating him with the authority of an all-powerful tyrant. She was forever telling him off for the things he did and did not do, shrewishly finding fault with his most insignificant actions, his habits, his simple pleasures, his tastes, the way he behaved, his swelling waistline, and the placid sound of his voice.

All the same, he still loved her, but he loved the child she had given him more. George, now three, had become his greatest joy and the principal object of his affections. Monsieur Parent had a modest private income, did not work, and managed on his 20,000 francs a year; and his wife, whom he had married without a dowry, never stopped complaining about her husband's idleness.

He reached his house at last, set the boy down on the bottom step, wiped his forehead, and began climbing up the stairs.

On the second floor, he rang the bell.

An elderly housekeeper who had raised him, one of those domineering servants who rule families with a rod of iron, opened the door. Anxiously he asked:

'Has the mistress returned?'

The servant gave a shrug:

'Since when has Monsieur known Madame be back before half past six?'

He answered awkwardly:

'Well that's all right, then. Gives me time to change. I'm awfully hot.'

The servant gave him a look of waspish, pitying contempt. She said peevishly:

'No need to tell me, I can see for myself that Monsieur has got himself all hot and bothered. Monsieur has been running. Carried the boy I shouldn't wonder. And all that hurry to be back so he can wait for Madame to get home at half past seven. You won't catch me being ready on time. I make the dinner for eight and it's too bad on them that has to wait for it. Meat's no good if it's burnt to a cinder.'

Monsieur Parent pretended not to hear. He murmured:

'Fine, excellent. George needs his hands washed, he's been making sand-pies. I'm off to get changed. Tell the maid she's to give the lad a good scrubbing.'

And he went straight into his room. Once inside, he pushed the bolt home so that he could be by himself, alone, undisturbed. He was so used now to being bullied and browbeaten that he felt safe only behind locked doors. He did not dare think, reflect, or work anything out in his mind unless he felt protected by the turn of a key against the hostile eyes and the insinuations. Collapsing on to a chair to recover a moment before he put on a clean shirt, it occurred to him that Julie was turning into an additional menace in his household. She hated his wife, that much was clear to see. But she positively loathed his friend Paul Limousin, who had remained that rare thing, a close, regular family friend who had been the inseparable companion of his bachelor days. It was Limousin who poured oil on troubled waters and stood as a buffer between Henriette and him, defended him energetically, sometimes sharply, against the undeserved nagging, the withering scenes, and all the squalor of his daily existence.

But for almost six months now, Julie had been free with malicious remarks and comments about her mistress. She passed judgement on her constantly, and every day said over and over: 'If I was Monsieur, you wouldn't catch me being led by the nose like that. But there you are . . . there's no helping it . . . folks can't change their natures.'

One day in particular she had been quite rude to Henriette, who had not reacted save to tell her husband that evening: 'Any more cheek out of her and I'll send her packing.' But it seemed that she, who was scared of nothing, was afraid of the old servant. Parent put her forbearance down to her consideration for the maid who had brought him up and closed his mother's eyes.

But enough was enough, things could not go on as they were much longer, and he felt weak-kneed at the thought of what would happen. What should he do? Dismissing Julie seemed to him so awesome a move that he dared not let his mind dwell on it. To side with her against his wife was equally impossible. Another month would not go by now before things between them became absolutely unbearable.

He sat there with his arms dangling, vaguely trying to find ways of settling the whole business, and not succeeding. Then he murmured: 'Fortunately I've got George . . . If I didn't have him I'd be so miserable.'

It occurred to him that he might ask Limousin for his advice; he made up his mind to do so; but then the memory of the animosity between his housekeeper and his friend made him afraid that Limousin would advise him to dismiss her. And he slipped back into his slough of anxiety and uncertainty.

The clock struck seven. He started. Seven o'clock and he hadn't changed yet! Panic-stricken, breathing hard, he undressed, washed, put on a clean shirt, and hurriedly threw on his clothes, as though there were people in the next room waiting for him for some extremely important occasion.

Then he went to the drawing-room, feeling easier now that he had nothing to fear.

He glanced at the paper, looked out of the window, then sat down on the sofa. A door opened and his son, washed and combed, came in with a smile on his face. Parent took him in both arms and hugged him tight. First he kissed him on the hair, next on his eyes, his cheeks, his lips, and finally his hands. He tossed him into the air, and held him aloft at arm's length. Then he sat down again, winded by his exertions. Sitting George on one of his knees, he bounced him up and down, playing gee-gees.

The boy, in raptures, laughed, waved his arms about,

shrieked with delight. And his father laughed too and roared with pleasure, his paunch wobbling, enjoying himself even more outrageously than the child.

He loved him with all his weak, resigned, battered heart. He loved him crazily, impulsively, smothered him with wild kisses, loved him with all the shamefaced tenderness hidden away inside him which had never been allowed out, not even on his wedding night, for his wife had always proved cool and reserved.

Julie appeared in the door. Her face was pale, her eyes blazed and in a voice shaking with irritation announced:

'It's half past seven.'

Parent gave the clock a worried, resigned look and murmured: 'So it is. Half past seven.'

'I've made the dinner. It's ready. Now.'

Seeing the clouds gather, he tried to ward off the storm:

'But I thought you said when I got back that you wouldn't have it ready until eight?'

'Eight! . . . Whatever are you thinking of? You're not going to start letting the boy have his dinner at eight, are you? Dinner at eight is all very well, of course. But making him eat at eight o'clock will ruin the lad's stomach. It wouldn't be so bad if there was only his mother to consider! Now there's one that takes real good care of him, I don't think! A fine mother she's turned out, I must say! Makes you grieve to see mothers like her!'

Quivering with anguish, Parent felt he had to put a rapid end to the scene which threatened:

'Julie,' he said, 'I won't have you talking about your mistress like this. Do you understand? And don't forget in future.'

The old servant, choking on her surprise, turned on her heel and left the room, slamming the door with such violence that glass in the chandelier rattled. For a few seconds, it was as though a faint, indefinite tinkle of tiny unseen bells rang through the still air of the drawing-room.

George, startled at first, now began to clap his hands with delight and, puffing out his cheeks, went 'bang!' with all the strength of his lungs, to imitate the noise of the slammed door.

His father started telling him stories. But with his mind on other things, he kept losing the thread of his tale, and the little boy, who quickly got lost, stared up at him with great round eyes.

Parent could not stop looking at the clock. He had the impression he could see the hands move. He would have liked to stop the clock, make time stand still until his wife got home. He was not cross with Henriette for being late but he was afraid of her, afraid of Julie, afraid of what might happen. Another ten minutes was all it would take to precipitate an irretrievable disaster—arguments and violent outbursts—which he did not dare even imagine. The mere thought of the quarrel, the raised voices, insults whistling through the air like bullets, the two women standing toe to toe, glaring straight into each other's eyes and screaming hurtful insults at each other, all this made his heart beat faster, made his mouth as dry as a walk in the hot sun, turned him limp as a rag, so limp that he felt too weak to hold his son up high and bounce him on his knee.

The clock struck eight. The door opened and Julie reappeared. Her look of irritation had gone and had been replaced by an air of callous, cold determination which was even more frightening.

'Monsieur,' she began, 'I served your mother till the day she died, and I also raised you from the time you were born until now! I think it could be said that I've always been devoted to the family . . .'

She paused, waiting for an answer:

Parent stammered:

'Oh, absolutely, Julie.'

She went on:

'You know I have never done anything because I stood to gain by it but always acted in your best interests. I've never gone behind your back and I never told you lies. Nor did you ever have any cause to find fault . . .'

'Of course not, Julie.'

'Well, things can't go on any longer the way they are. Because I'm so fond of you, I never said anything before and left you not knowing. But it's all got out of hand and too many people roundabout think you're a laughing-stock. You can do what you like, but it's common knowledge. So it's come down to this: I've got to tell you, though a fat lot of good it'll do me. If Madame comes home as she does at all hours, it's because she gets up to all sorts.'

He sat there in bewilderment, not understanding. All he could manage was to stutter:

'Not another word! . . . You know I forbade you to . . .'

She interrupted him with iron determination:

'No, Monsieur, I've got to tell you everything now. Madame has been carrying on with Monsieur Limousin for ages. I seen them myself plenty of times kissing in corners. The truth is that if Monsieur Limousin had been rich, it wasn't you that Madame would have married. If you remember how the marriage came about, you'd see through the whole thing from start to finish . . .'

Parent was on his feet, ghastly pale, stammering:

'Be quiet . . . be quiet . . . or . . .'

She went on:

'No, it's all got to come out. Madame married you for your money. She was unfaithful from the word go. They fixed it up between them, don't you see? Just think a minute and you'll see it all. Then since Madame wasn't happy once she'd married you, who she didn't love, she's given you a hard time, so hard that it's broken my heart to see it . . .'

He took two steps towards her, fists clenched, repeating: 'Be quiet! . . . be quiet!' for he could find nothing to say in reply.

The old servant stood her ground. She seemed determined to hold nothing back.

Just then, George, at first startled then frightened by their snarling voices, began to wail. He stood behind his father, with his face screwed up and his mouth open, and howled.

The noise his son made provoked Parent beyond measure and gave him the courage of anger. He rushed at Julie, arms raised, ready to strike her with both fists, yelling:

'You wicked old hag! You'll turn the boy's wits!'

He was almost on her when she shouted back right at him:

'Go on, hit me if you want, hit an old woman who raised you. But that won't alter the fact that your wife is deceiving you or that your son isn't yours at all . . . !'

He stopped in his tracks and let his arms drop. He stood

face to face with her, so stunned that he was entirely at a loss
to understand what he was hearing.

She went on:

'You only got to look at him to know who his father is. He's
the image of Monsieur Limousin. You only have to look at his
eyes and his forehead. A blind man could see it . . .'

But he grabbed her by the shoulders and started shaking her
for all his worth, stammering:

'Serpent . . . you . . . you . . . serpent! Get out, you viper!
Get out or I'll kill you. Get out! Out!'

And with a desperate lunge, he bundled her into the
adjacent room. She fell over the dinner table which had been
laid, knocking over the wine glasses, which smashed. She got
to her feet, and, keeping the table between herself and her
employer, while he ran round it trying to get his hands on her,
she flung terrible words in his face:

'All you've got to do is go out . . . tonight . . . after
dinner . . . and then come straight back . . . you'll see . . .
you'll see if I'm telling lies . . . Just try it . . . you'll see . . .'

She got to the door which led to the kitchen and fled. He ran
after her and clambered up the back stairs to her room, where
she had locked herself in. He beat on her door and screamed:

'You will leave this house at once!'

She answered through the door:

'You can count on it. I'll be gone in an hour.'

He came back down the stairs slowly, clutching the banister
to prevent himself falling. He returned to the drawing-room,
where George was still sitting on the floor, crying.

Parent collapsed on to a chair and stared at the child in
bewilderment, totally at a loss to understand what was going
on. He felt stunned, dazed, witless, as though he had just
fallen on his head. He could barely recall the appalling things
his housekeeper had said. But imperceptibly, like cloudy water
settling, his mind stopped racing and cleared. And then her
ghastly disclosures began to gnaw at his heart.

Julie had spoken so categorically, with such strength of
feeling, with such confidence and conviction that he could not
doubt her sincerity, though he could not believe that she had
drawn the right conclusions. She could have been mistaken,

blinded by her loyalty to him, carried away by her instinctive hatred of Henriette. Yet even as he tried to reassure and convince himself that this was so, countless little memories came back to him: words his wife had spoken, something in the way Limousin had looked, a host of trivial, unnoticed, almost unseen things, her comings and goings after hours, the fact that both of them were often out of the house at the same times, and even insignificant but odd gestures which he had not noticed or understood at the time, now assumed alarming proportions and clearly indicated that something was going on between them. Everything that had happened since his engagement suddenly surfaced in his memory, which in his distress had been thrown into turmoil. He went back over everything, unusual inflexions of their voices, the suspect way they had behaved. And the vulnerable mind of this easy-going, good-hearted man, racked by doubt, now turned what would otherwise have been no more than suspicions into certainties.

With the obstinacy of desperation, he sifted through five years of marriage, trying to remember everything, month by month, day by day. And each disturbing recollection he stumbled across punctured his heart like the sting of a wasp.

He had stopped thinking of George, who had stopped crying now and was sitting on the carpet. Becoming aware that no one was paying any attention to him, he started crying again.

His father sprang to his feet, picked him up and smothered him with kisses. At least he still had his son! What did the rest matter! He held him in his arms, held him close, with his mouth pressed against that fair hair, comforted, consoled, stammering: 'George . . . my son . . . my own darling little George . . .' But all at once he recalled something Julie had said . . . Yes, she had said that his son was really Limousin's . . . But that could not be, it was absurd! No, he could not believe it, he could not believe it for a single moment. It was one of those odious, unspeakable lies which sprout in the vile minds of servants! Over and over he said: 'George . . . darling George.' The little boy, now that he was suitably fussed over, stopped crying again.

Through both their clothes, Parent felt the warmth of the boy's little chest next to his. It filled him with love and strength and joy. The pleasant warmth of the child's body soothed him, gave him strength, was his salvation.

He held the boy away from him a little, moved by a passionate urge to gaze at that pretty, curly head. He studied it greedily, distractedly. What he saw made him feel slightly drunk and he went on repeating: 'Oh George! . . . my own little George! . . .'

But then he thought: 'But supposing he really does look like Limousin after all?'

Inside him, he felt something strange and very distressing, a stabbing, violent sensation which made his blood run cold and spread to every part of his body, as though all his bones had suddenly been turned into icicles. What if the boy really did look like Limousin! . . . and he went on staring at George, who was now laughing happily. He stared with dazed, misty, stricken eyes. He stared at his forehead, his nose, mouth, and cheeks, wondering if he might discover in them some trace of Limousin's forehead, nose, mouth, and cheeks.

His thoughts became confused, as happens in madness. His son's face changed as he looked, assumed peculiar expressions and formed unlikely similarities.

Julie had said: 'A blind man could see it.' Was there something so very obvious, then, something quite incontrovertible? But what? The forehead? Yes . . . that was it! But Limousin's forehead was narrower. The mouth, then? But Limousin wore a full beard! How could anyone see if there was a connection between the little boy's chubby chin and the hairy jowls of a grown man?

Parent thought: 'I can't see it, can't see for looking; I'm too upset; I couldn't see it now if it stood out a mile . . . Better wait. I must have a proper look tomorrow morning when I get up.'

Then he thought again: 'But if he looks like me, I'm saved! Saved!'

With two bounds he was across the room: he wanted to examine his child's face next to his in the mirror.

He held George in the crook of his arm so that their faces were together and, totally bemused by now, began talking to himself. 'Yes . . . we've got the same nose . . . the same

nose . . . perhaps . . . I'm not sure . . . and the same look about
the eyes . . . No we haven't, his eyes are blue . . . So . . . Oh
God! . . . Oh God! . . . I'm going out of my mind . . . I don't
want to see any more . . . I'm going off my head!'

He retreated far from the mirror, to the other end of the
room, fell into one armchair, set the boy down on another, and
began to cry. He wept in great despairing sobs. George became
frightened when he heard his father sobbing and immediately
began to wail.

The doorbell rang. Parent jumped, as though he had been
struck by a bullet. He said: 'That's her . . . What am I going to
do . . . ?' And he ran to his room and shut himself in so that he
would at least have time to dry his eyes. But a few seconds
later, a second ring of the doorbell made him jump again. He
remembered that Julie had gone and no one had told the maid.
So there was no one to open the door! What was to be done? He
went himself.

But all of a sudden, he felt bold, determined, prepared to
play unfairly and ready for a fight. The terrible shock of it all
had made him grow up in an instant. And now he wanted to
know the truth. He wanted to know with the anger of the timid
man, the determination of the mild-mannered man who has
been goaded beyond endurance.

But he was trembling! Was it fear? Yes . . . Perhaps he was
still scared of her? Who can tell how courageous a coward may
be when pushed too far?

Reaching the door on tiptoe, he stopped and listened. His
heart was beating furiously. It was the only sound he could
hear: its loud, dull thudding inside his chest. That, and the
piercing voice of George, who was still crying in the drawing-
room.

Suddenly, the sound of the doorbell just above his head
rocked him like an explosion. He reached for the lock and,
breathing hard and feeling faint, turned the key and opened the
door.

His wife and Limousin stood facing him at the top of the
stairs.

With a look of surprise in which there was a faint trace of
irritation, she said:

'So you've taken to answering the door now, have you? What's happened to Julie?'

His throat was dry and his breath came quickly. He tried to answer but the words did not come.

She went on:

'Cat got your tongue? I asked you where Julie was.'

At last he stammered:

'She . . . she . . . she's gone!'

His wife began to get angry:

'What do you mean, gone? Where's she gone? Why?'

He was beginning to pull himself together and felt within him a flicker of hate for the overbearing woman standing before him.

'That's right, gone for good . . . I sent her packing . . .'

'You told her to go? Julie? Are you out of your mind?'

'I told her to get out because she had been impertinent . . . and because . . . because she was rough with the boy.'

'Julie was?'

'That's right.'

'What was she impertinent about?'

'About you.'

'About me?'

'Yes. Because the dinner had got burned and because you hadn't come home.'

'What did she say?'

'She said . . . nasty things about you, things I had no business hearing and didn't want to hear.'

'What things?'

'There's no point in repeating them.'

'I want to know what they were.'

'She said it was pitiful for a man like me to be married to a woman like you, unpunctual, untidy, slovenly, a bad home-maker, a bad mother, and a bad wife . . .'

The young woman had stepped into the hall, followed by Limousin, who, confronted by the unexpected turn of events, said nothing. She slammed the door shut, threw her cape over the back of a chair, and bore down on her husband, beside herself, spluttering with rage:

'What did you say? . . . You said that I'm . . .'

He was very pale but very calm. He answered:

'I didn't say anything, dear. I merely repeated what Julie said, since you wanted to know. And may I remind you that I sent her packing precisely for the things she said.'

She shook with a furious desire to pull out his beard and scratch his cheeks with her nails. In his voice, his tone, his whole attitude, she sensed revolt, though there was nothing she could say. She tried to regain the initiative by saying something blunt and hurtful.

'Have you had dinner?' she asked.

'No, I waited.'

She shrugged impatiently.

'It's quite absurd to keep dinner waiting after seven-thirty. You might have guessed I'd been held up, that there were things I had to do, errands to run.'

Suddenly, she felt an urge to tell him how she had spent her time, and briefly, arrogantly, she explained that having to go far, really far out of her way, miles, to the rue de Rennes in fact, to pick out some bits and pieces for the house, she had bumped into Limousin on the way back, on the Boulevard Saint-Germain, it was then well after seven, and she had asked him to give her his arm and take her for a bite to eat in a restaurant she didn't dare to go into by herself, though she felt faint with hunger. That was how she had had dinner, with Limousin, if, that is, if you could call it dinner. For in their hurry to get back, all they'd had to eat was a little soup and half a chicken.

Unruffled, Parent said:

'And quite right too. Look, I'm not complaining.'

Limousin, who had remained silent up to this point, almost completely hidden behind Henriette, now stepped forward and held out his hand, murmuring:

'Feeling all right?'

'Parent took the proffered hand and shook it limply:

'Yes, fine.'

But the young woman had seized upon a word in her husband's last remark.

'Complaining? What have you got to complain about? Anyone would think you have something on your mind . . .'

He apologized:

'No, not at all. I only wanted to say that I wasn't the least worried by the fact that you were late and that I didn't hold it against you.'

This sent her into a huff, for she was looking for any excuse for an argument.

'Me, late? Anybody'd think it was one in the morning and that I often stay out all night.'

'Not at all, darling. I said "late" because there doesn't seem another word for it. You were supposed to be back at half past six and you get back at half past eight. I think that qualifies as late. I understand, really I do; it didn't come as any sort of . . . er . . . surprise to me. But . . . well it's hard for me to use any other word for it.'

'But the way you say it makes it sound as though I'd been out all night . . .'

'Not at all.'

She realized that he had no intention of putting up a fight and was about to go to her room when she finally became aware that George was howling. With an anxious look on her face, she asked:

'What's the matter with George?'

'I told you. Julie was rough with him.'

'What did that dreadful woman do to him?'

'Oh nothing much. She pushed him and he fell down.'

She wanted to see her child and rushed into the dining-room, but stopped short when she came upon the table covered with spilt wine, broken decanters, shattered wine-glasses and upset salt-cellars.

'What on earth is all this mess?'

'It was Julie. She . . .'

She cut him short in a fury:

'This really is the limit! Julie calls me a hussy, beats my baby, breaks my crockery, turns my house upside down, and you seem to think it all quite natural.'

'Not at all . . . I did dismiss her.'

'Did you now! . . . So you dismissed her. You should have had her arrested. When this sort of thing happens, normal people send for the police!'

He stammered:

'But, dear . . . really . . . I couldn't do that . . . there was no cause to . . . Believe me, it was all terribly difficult . . .'

She shrugged her shoulders with boundless contempt.

'Do you know something? You'll always be a jelly, a sorry specimen, a miserable little man with no will, no spirit, no go! Oh Julie must have spun you some pretty tales for you to make up your mind to kick her out. I'd love to have been there for a minute, just one minute.'

Opening the drawing-room door, she ran to George, picked him up, and held him tightly in her arms while she kissed him. 'George, what's the matter, my darling pretty chick?'

Now that he was being fussed over by his mother, he stopped crying. She repeated:

'What's the matter, then?'

George, who had observed events with the uncertain eyes of a frightened child, replied:

'Zulie thmack daddy.'

Henriette turned and looked at her husband. At first, she was totally nonplussed. But then a wild urge to laugh flitted across her face, spread with a tremor over her delicate cheeks, lifted the corners of her lips, flared the wings of her nose, and finally exploded in her mouth in a clear burst of delight, a cataract of glee, which swelled and soared like birdsong. She punctuated her laughter with little cries of malice which squeezed past her white teeth and made Parent wince, as if he had been bitten.

'Oh! . . . Ha ha ha . . . Ha ha ha . . . she sma-a-a-cked you! Ha ha ha . . . that's rich . . . it's so funny! . . . Did you hear, Limousin? Julie smacked him . . . thmacked . . . Zulie thmacked my husband! Ha ha ha! What a scream!'

Parent spluttered:

'No, no! It's not true . . . It wasn't like that . . . It's the other way round. It was I who pushed her into the dining-room . . . pushed her so hard she knocked the table over. The boy didn't see properly. It was me that smacked *her*!'

But Henriette was crooning to her son:

'Say it again, my pet. Was it Julie who smacked daddy?'

He answered:

'Yeth. Zulie did.'

Then another idea struck her. She said:

'But he can't have had his dinner! Have you had anything to eat, darling?'

'No, mummy.'

She rounded furiously on her husband:

'You must be mad, quite mad. It's half past eight and George has not had his dinner yet!'

Feeling quite lost in the scenes and the arguing, crushed by the debris of his life, which had collapsed about his ears, he made excuses:

'But, my dear, we were waiting for you. I didn't want to have dinner without you. You get home late every day and I assumed you'd be back at any minute.'

She tossed her hat, which until now she had kept on her head, on to an armchair and said crossly:

'Really, it is intolerable that one should have to depend on people who haven't a clue, can't add up two and two and get four, and are quite incapable of doing anything without being told. I take it, then, that if I had got back at midnight, the boy wouldn't have got anything to eat at all! As if you couldn't have had the sense to know that once it got to seven-thirty, I must have been held up, delayed, detained . . .'

Parent had begun to tremble, feeling anger well up inside him. But Limousin stepped in and, turning to the young woman, said:

'You're being very unfair, Henriette. Parent could not possibly have guessed that you'd be back quite so late. It's never happened before. Besides, how did you expect him to cope all by himself after he'd sent Julie packing?'

But Henriette replied angrily:

'Well he'll have to cope now, for I have no intention of helping him. Let him sort it out!'

And without more ado she went to her room, having already forgotten that George had not eaten.

When she had gone, Limousin set to, giving his friend a helping hand. He swept up and removed the broken glasses which littered the table, reset it, and sat the boy on his high-chair while Parent went off in search of the maid, who would give him his dinner.

She arrived looking very surprised, for she had been working in George's nursery and had heard nothing.

She brought the soup, an incinerated leg of lamb, and mashed potatoes.

Parent was sitting by the child's side, his mind in a whirl, his wits scattered to the four winds by the disastrous turn of events. He fed his son, tried to eat something himself; he cut up his meat, chewed it, and swallowed it with difficulty, as though his throat had seized up.

But gradually there formed deep within him a compulsive urge to stare at Limousin, who was sitting opposite him, rolling bread into little pellets. He wanted to see if he looked like George. But he did not dare raise his eyes. He screwed up his courage, however, and suddenly peered up at the face which he knew well, though it seemed to him that he had never really seen it before, so different did it appear from the way he remembered it. Every few moments, he glanced up quickly at that face, attempting to identify the smallest contour, feature, or characteristic that he could recognize; and then he would look at his son, hoping it would seem that all he was doing was feeding him.

Two words buzzed in his ears: 'His father! His father! His father!' They throbbed inside his brain in time to each beat of his heart. Yes, this man, who was now coolly sitting across the table from him, was perhaps the father of his son, George, dear little George! Parent stopped eating: he could not go on. An agonizing pain, such as makes people cry out, roll on the ground, and bite the furniture, tore through his insides. He felt as though he could take his knife and bury it in his stomach. It would put him out of his misery. He would be saved. It would all be over and done with.

Could he go on living now? Could he bear to go on getting up each morning, eating at mealtimes, raking the roads, going to bed and sleeping at night with that one thought permanently drilled into his head: 'Could George be Limousin's son?' No, no! He would not have the strength to put one foot in front of the other, or dress, or think of just nothing, or talk to people! Every hour, every minute of every day, would he not wonder, would he not try to find out, to guess, to uncover the awful truth? He would not be able to see his little boy, his darling little boy, without experiencing unbearable agonies of doubt, without being stricken to the depths of his soul, without feeling an ache in the very marrow of his bones. He would have to go on living here, he would have to remain in this house, living closeted with a little boy whom he would love and grow to hate! Oh yes, in the end, he would surely come to hate him. It would be torture! If he knew for sure that Limousin was the father, perhaps he might resign himself and make the best of his unhappiness and pain. But not knowing was intolerable!

Not knowing, always wondering and suffering eternally, how could he go on for ever hugging a child who was the flesh of another, taking him for walks into town, carrying him in his arms, feeling that soft hair brush against his lips, loving him, and at the same time have one thought constantly in his head: 'Perhaps he's not mine'? Would it not be better if he never saw him again, deserted him, abandoned him in some street? Or perhaps he should go away, far away, so far that he would never hear anything more about him ever again?

He gave a start when he heard the door open. His wife was back.

'I'm hungry,' she said. 'How about you, Limousin?'

Limousin hesitated before answering:

'I'll say!'

She rang for the lamb to be brought back.

Parent was wondering: 'Did they really have dinner? Or did they make themselves late because they had been making love?'

They were both eating heartily. Henriette, who had calmed down, laughed and joked. Her husband now began watching her too, glancing up at her, then averting his eyes. She was wearing a pink dressing-gown edged with white lace. Her blonde head, cool neck, and plump hands protruded from her pretty, perfumed, pert wrap, which was like a shell trimmed with foam. What had she been doing all day with this man? In his mind's eye, Parent saw them together kissing and whispering words of passion! Why couldn't he know for sure? Why couldn't he tell by watching them as they sat side by side across the table from him?

What a ninny they must have thought him, if he had really been taken in from the day he had married her! Was it right that a man, a good man, should be toyed with in this manner simply because his father left him a little money? Why weren't such things visible in people's hearts? How was it that there was never anything to give decent persons any inkling of the deceitful actions of the wicked? Why was it that the voice which told lies was the same as the voice which spoke words of love? Why was the two-faced gaze of the deceiver impossible to distinguish from a look of sincerity?

He continued to spy on them, hoping to detect a gesture, a word, or some inflexion of the voice. Suddenly he thought: 'I'll catch them at it tonight.'

'Oh Henriette,' he said. 'Since I've given Julie her marching-orders, I'm going to have to think now, today, about finding a replacement. I'll go this moment and see if I can get somebody for tomorrow morning. I may be a little late getting back.'

She answered: 'All right. I shan't be stirring from here. Limousin will keep me company. We'll wait for you to get home.'

Then, turning to the maid, she said: 'You can put George to bed and clear away. Then you can go to bed.'

Parent stood up. He swayed on his feet. He felt giddy and unsteady. He muttered: 'Be back soon,' and made his way to the door, clinging to the wall for support, for the floor was heaving like the deck of a ship.

When George had been borne away in the arms of the maid, Henriette and Limousin moved to the drawing-room. The moment the front door closed, he said:

'Really! You must be mad, going for your husband like that!'

She turned to face him:

'You know, I'm beginning to find that this new habit of yours of making out that Parent is some kind of a martyr, has got beyond a joke.'

Limousin threw himself into an armchair, crossed his legs and went on:

'But I don't make out that Parent's a martyr. Not at all. But I do think that it is pretty silly, in our position, for you to be nagging at him from morning till night.'

She took a cigarette from the mantelpiece, lit it, and replied:

'But I don't nag him. On the contrary. It's just that he gets on my nerves. He's such a fool. I treat him the way he deserves.'

Limousin resumed, with a note of impatience in his voice:

'But what you're doing is stupid! But there, women are all the same. Put it like this. Here you have a very decent chap, too decent, his wits softened by his trusting, unselfish good nature, someone who never interferes, doesn't suspect a thing, leaves us free as air to do whatever we want. And you go out of your way to annoy him and ruin everything.'

'You know something?' she said. 'You make me sick! You're a coward, like all men. You're scared of the idiot!'

He jumped to his feet angrily: 'Me, scared? But tell me, I'd like to know what he ever did to you and what you've got against him. Does he make you unhappy? Does he knock you about? Does he run after other women? No. The way you make his life hell just because he's such a decent sort is simply revolting: you've only got your knife into him because you're deceiving him.'

She went close to Limousin, looked him in the eye, and snarled:

'You're hardly in a position to accuse me of deceiving anybody! Who do you think you are? What a twisted mind you've got!'

He defended himself rather shamefacedly: 'But I'm not accusing you, darling. I only meant that you should go a little easier on your husband because neither of us can afford to get on the wrong side of him. I'd have thought you could see that!'

They stood toe to toe, he tall, dark, with heavy side-whiskers and the rather vulgar manner of a ladies' man who is very aware of his good looks, and she pretty, pink, and fair, a part flirtatious, part respectable Parisienne who had been born in the back of a shop and raised in the front to catch the eye of passers-by and, having duly hooked one, had married him, an unsuspecting man who fell in love with her after seeing her each day in the doorway of her shop as he went out in the morning and returned home in the evening.

She said: 'And what you don't see, stupid, is that I hate him precisely because he married me—bought me I should say— and because everything he says and does and thinks gets on my nerves! Every minute of the day he irritates me with his stupidity, which you call his good nature, and that ponderous way he has with him, which you think of as his trusting soul. But basically the reason is that I'm married to him and not to you! I feel he's always there between us, though I suppose he doesn't really get in our way much. And besides . . . Oooh! He can't really be so stupid he doesn't suspect! He could at least be a tiny bit jealous. There are times when I could scream at him: "Are you blind, you great booby? Can't you see Paul is my lover!"'

Limousin said with a laugh: 'Meanwhile, it would be as well to say nothing if you want things to stay the way they are.'

'Oh, I shan't spoil anything. There's nothing to be afraid of with a clown like him. No, but I really can't believe you have no idea of just how loathsome and irritating I find him. You always give the impression that you actually like him. When you shake his hand it always looks as if you mean it. Sometimes men can be very unpredictable.'

'It doesn't always pay to show all your cards, my sweet.'

'We're talking about feelings, not cards. You men are all the same. When you deceive another man, you like him all the better for it. But the minute a woman deceives a man, she hates him.'

'I don't for the life of me see why anyone should hate some decent chap simply because you've gone off with his wife.'

'You don't see? Really! You could at least have the decency to try, though none of you ever do. But it's no good talking. It's the sort of thing you have to feel: saying it isn't enough. Perhaps it oughtn't to be said anyway . . . But you wouldn't understand, so it's quite pointless. Men have no subtlety.'

And as sweetly contemptuous as any hardened woman of the world, she put both hands on his shoulders and pouted her lips; he lowered his head to meet them, drew her close and their mouths met. They were standing directly in front of the mirror above the fireplace, and a second couple, identical to them in every detail, kissed behind the clock on the mantelpiece.

They had heard nothing, not the sound of the key in the lock nor the creak of the door. But all at once, with a sudden shriek, Henriette pushed Limousin away with both hands, and they both saw Parent watching them, deathly pale, fists clenched, with no shoes on and his hat over his eyes.

He stared at them in turn without moving his head, his eyes darting quickly from one to the other. He looked deranged. Then, without saying anything, he threw himself at Limousin, grabbed him with both hands as if to throttle him, and sent him sprawling into the corner of the room with such force that Limousin, losing his footing and with arms flailing wildly, cracked the back of his head against the wall.

When she realized that her husband was about to kill her lover, Henriette flung herself on Parent, got hold of him by the neck and, digging her delicate pink fingers into his throat, squeezed so hard, with the strength of desperation, that blood oozed under her nails. She bit him on the shoulder as though intent on tearing him to pieces with her bare teeth. Half-strangled and fighting for breath, Parent released Limousin and turned his attention to his wife, who had him by the neck. Seizing her by the waist, he flung her clear across the room with one heave.

But then, having the quick-cooling anger of the weak and the short-lived violence of the faint of heart, he remained where he was, between them, panting, exhausted, not knowing what to do next. All his uncontrolled rage had been spent by his exertions, like the fizz from an uncorked bottle of champagne. His unaccustomed outburst had left him breathless.

As soon as he could speak, he stammered:

'Now go . . . the pair of you . . . At once . . . Get out!'

Limousin remained in his corner, not stirring, stuck fast to the wall, too dazed as yet to take in what was happening and too scared to move a muscle. Henriette, leaning straight-armed on an occasional table, head craned forward and hair undone, with the front of her dressing-gown open exposing her naked breasts, crouched like a wild animal waiting to pounce.

In a firmer voice, Parent repeated:

'Get out! This minute . . . Go!'

Seeing that he was over the worst of his anger, his wife
rallied, straightened up, took a couple of steps towards him,
and, with something of her customary self-assertion returning,
said:

'Are you off your head? What on earth has got into you?
What do you mean by attacking us in this disgraceful way . . . ?'

He turned to face her, raising one fist as though he would
strike her dead, and spluttered:

'Oh! . . . That's the last straw! That caps the lot! I . . . I . . . I
heard . . . everything . . . ! Everything, do you hear . . . ? You
are despicable! . . . Despicable, the pair of you! . . . Get out of
my house, both of you . . . ! Now! Before I kill you! Get out!'

She realized that it was all over, that he knew, that she
would not be able to claim she was innocent: all that was left
now was to admit defeat. But she had recovered all her old
insolence, and her loathing for her husband, exacerbated by
the situation, made her bold and defiant. Out of sheer bravado,
she said in a clear, confident tone:

'Come on, Limousin, Since I've been turned out of here, I'll
go home with you.'

But Limousin did not move. Parent, seized by a new fit of
anger, began screaming:

'Out! Get out! . . . You are despicable! Go, or else I'll . . .'

He picked up a chair and swung it round his head.

At this, Henriette crossed the room quickly, grabbed her
lover by the arm, yanked him away from the wall, to which he
seemed attached, and dragged him to the door, repeating:
'Come away! You can see he's mad! Come on, will you!'

As she was about to go, she turned to face her husband,
trying to think of something to do or say that would cut him to
the heart before she left the house. Then an idea struck her,
one of those cruel, lethal ideas into which women distil all
their venom.

In a determined voice, she said: 'I want to take my baby with
me.'

Totally taken aback, Parent stammered: 'Your . . . baby?
How dare you talk of your son . . . ? How dare you ask to have

your son... after... after what... I don't believe this!
You've got a nerve! Now get out, you slut, just go!'

She came back towards him, a smile lurking at the corners
of her mouth, sensing that she had already got her own back,
or as good as. Defiantly, she faced him:

'I want my baby. Anyway, you've no right to keep him seeing
he's not yours. Do you hear? Don't you understand? He isn't
yours! He's . . . Limousin's!'

His mind in a whirl, Parent screamed: 'You're lying! You're
a lying bitch!'

But she went on: 'You stupid fool! Everybody knows except
you. I tell you, Limousin is his father. One look is enough to
see it . . .'

Parent retreated before her, his legs weak. Then he turned
abruptly, picked up a candle, and rushed into the next room.

He emerged again almost at once carrying little George
wrapped in the blankets from his bed. Having been woken
suddenly and feeling frightened, he was crying. Parent bundled
him into his wife's arms and without another word pushed her
out roughly, towards the stairs, where Limousin was waiting
prudently.

Then he shut the door behind them, double-locked and
bolted it. He had only just reached the drawing-room when he
collapsed full-length on to the floor.

II

From that day Parent lived alone, totally alone. For the first
few weeks after the separation, the novelty of his new life left
him little time to brood. He reverted to his bachelor ways,
roaming through the town and eating in restaurants. He had not
wanted any scandal and arranged for an allowance to be paid to
his wife through their lawyers. But gradually the memory of his
little boy began to haunt his thoughts. Often of an evening
when he was by himself at home, he would suddenly imagine
he could hear George calling 'Daddy!' His heart would pound
and he would leap out of his chair and rush to open the
landing-door just in case by some chance his son had returned.

Why not? He could easily come back, like dogs or homing pigeons. Why should a child have fewer instincts than a dumb animal?

Then, realizing he was mistaken, he would go back to his chair and think about the boy. He would think about him for hours on end, for whole days together. It was not simply a mental fixation but also—and even more strongly—a physical compulsion, a need of his senses and sinews, to kiss and hold and touch him, to sit him on his knee, to bounce him up and down and make him turn somersaults in his arms. He became frustrated when he thought of the playful cuddles of the old days. He felt those little arms round his neck, that little mouth giving him a great big kiss on his beard, the tiny curls brushing his cheek. His need for affectionate contacts, of which he was now deprived, for delicate, warm, pretty skin to kiss, obsessed him like desire for a woman he had loved and lost.

In the street, he would suddenly burst into tears at the thought that he could have had his little George with him skipping along on his little legs just as he always used to when he took him out for a walk. He would go home then and, head in hands, would sit sobbing until it got dark.

Or again, he would ask himself the same question over and over every day: 'Was he, or was he not, George's father?' But it was especially at night that he turned this idea round and round in his head. No sooner was he in bed than he began on the same series of despairing arguments and counter-arguments.

After his wife's departure, he had had no doubts at first: of course the boy was Limousin's. But gradually he had come to be less sure. Clearly, no reliance could be put on Henriette's word. She had defied him in an attempt to make him utterly miserable. But if the pros and cons were weighed, there was every chance that she had been lying.

There was only Limousin who could perhaps give him the true story. But how could he find out? How could he be questioned? How could he be made to admit the truth?

And sometimes Parent would get up in the middle of the night determined to find Limousin and beg him on bended knee, ready to give him anything he asked if only he would put an end to his unbearable uncertainty. But then he would get back into bed in despair, thinking that the lover would probably lie to him too! Obviously he would lie to prevent the real father taking back his son.

So what was there he could do? Nothing!

He kicked himself for having brought matters to a head the way he had, for not having stopped to think and bide his time, for failing to wait and dissemble for a month or two, so as to see how the land lay for himself. He ought to have given the impression that he suspected nothing and left them to give themselves away naturally. All it would have taken would have been for him to see how the other man kissed the boy and he would have guessed the truth and known! A family friend does not kiss like a father. He could have spied on them from behind doors! Why hadn't he thought of that? If Limousin, alone with George, had not immediately picked him up, hugged him close, and kissed him eagerly, and had instead just left him to play by himself and taken no interest and not bothered with him, then there would have been no room for doubt: it would have been clear that he was not, did not believe and did not feel that he was the boy's father.

The upshot would have been that he, Parent, could have sent the boy's mother packing but would have kept his son, and he would have been happy, cloudlessly happy.

He tossed and turned in his bed, bathed in perspiration, racked with misery, and tried to recall how Limousin had behaved with the boy. But he could remember nothing, absolutely nothing, not a gesture or a look, not a suspicious word or a kiss. There was too the fact that the mother had not paid much attention to the boy. If her lover had been the father, then surely she would have loved him more?

So he had in all likelihood been parted from his son through revenge and cruelty, to punish him because he had found them together.

He resolved that he would go to the courts first thing the next morning and make a legal application for George to be returned to him.

But no sooner had he made up his mind that this was what he would do than he was overcome by the certainty that the opposite was true. The moment Limousin had become

Henriette's lover, had been truly loved by her, that is from the very start, she must surely have given herself to him with the mad abandon, the passion which invariably makes women mothers. And was not the cold reserve she had always shown in her intimate relations with him, her husband, an additional obstacle to her having conceived a child by him?

So what he would be doing would be to make a formal application to take home, keep by him and care for, the child of another man. He would never be able to look at him or kiss him or hear him say 'daddy' without being struck, destroyed, by the thought: 'This is not my son!' He would be condemning himself to unremitting torture, to a life of misery! No! Better by far to remain as he was, to live alone and grow old alone and die alone.

And so each day, each night, brought a return of his unbearable uncertainties, of sufferings which nothing could assuage or allay. Above all, he feared the darkness which came with evening, the desolation of dusk. It was then that he felt, as it were, a rain of sorrow in his heart, a flood of despair which rose as the shadows gathered, engulfing him and filling him with panic. He feared his thoughts as others fear evil men, and fled before them like a hunted animal. And he feared nothing more than his empty apartment, so gloomy now and forbidding, and the deserted streets, lit at intervals by occasional gas-lamps, where the odd passer-by, heard from afar, turns into a dangerous prowler who makes you slow or quicken your step according to whether he is walking towards you or approaching from the rear.

At such moments, despite himself, Parent would instinctively make for the blazing, busy streets. The bright lights and the people drew him, occupied his mind, and made his head spin. When he was tired of wandering aimlessly through the eddying swirls of humanity and saw the crowd start to thin and the pavements begin to empty, his fear of solitude and silence guided him to some bustling café full of lights and men drinking. He was drawn to such places like a moth to a candle. He would sit down at a small round table and order a beer. He drank slowly and felt anxious each time a customer got up to leave. He would have liked to take him by the arm and ask him to stay a little longer, for he dreaded the moment when the waiter, standing before him, would say bad-temperedly: 'Time, sir! Drink up!'

For every night he was the last to leave. He saw the tables being brought in from the terrace outside and all the gas-lights go out one by one, till only two remained, his and the one over the bar. With sinking spirits, he watched as the woman at the cash-desk counted her money and locked it away in a drawer. And then he would leave, turned out by waiters who muttered: 'Bleedin' awkward customer. Anybody'd think he'd got no home to go to.'

Alone in the empty street, he would begin to think about little George and start racking his brains, forcing himself to think of a way of discovering whether he was or was not the father of his son.

And so he got into the habit of going to cafés, where rubbing shoulders with other drinkers brings a man up against a crowd he recognizes by sight but never talks to, where thick clouds of pipe-smoke dull all care, and strong beer slows the brain and steadies the nerves.

He spent all his waking hours in the café. As soon as he got up, he would head straight there to have somebody to look at and something to think about. Gradually, because he could no longer be bothered to move, he began taking his meals there. Around noon, he banged a saucer on the marble-topped table and the waiter would immediately bring a plate, a glass, a napkin, and the day's lunch, When he had finished eating, he would sip his coffee, with one eye fixed on the bottle of cognac which by and by would supply a good hour's mindless oblivion. He began by wetting his lips with the alcohol, appreciating the flavour, as yet merely relishing the taste of the brandy with the tip of his tongue. Then, head back, he let it trickle drop by drop into his mouth, allowing the strong spirit to wash over his palate, his gums, and the rubbery inside of his cheeks, so that it mingled with the fresh saliva of his watering mouth. When the mixture was suitably diluted, he swallowed it contemplatively, feeling it dribble down the back of his throat and sink to the pit of his stomach.

In this way, for over an hour after each meal, he would

regularly down three or four small glasses, which imperceptibly induced a state of somnolence. His head drooped over his stomach, he closed his eyes and dozed. He woke half way through the afternoon and immediately reached for the glass of beer which the waiter had placed in front of him while he was asleep. When he had finished it, he would raise himself up on the red plush seat, hitch up his trousers, pull down his waistcoat to cover the expanse of white which had appeared in the gap between the two, smooth the collar of his jacket, drag his cuffs out of his sleeves, and then resume his perusal of the newspapers, which he had already read that morning.

He read them again from the first line to the last, including the advertisements, the jobs-wanted section, the births, marriages, and deaths, the share prices, and what was on in the theatre.

Between four and six he went for a stroll along the Boulevards, to take the air, he said, after which he returned to the seat which had been kept for him, and ordered his absinthe.

He would then chat with the regulars he had got to know. They discussed the day's big news, items from the paper, and what was happening on the political front. This took him up to dinner. The evening passed like the afternoon until closing-time. For him, this was a dreadful moment, the moment of going home to the darkness, to his empty bedroom so full of painful memories, horrible thoughts, and despair. He never saw anything now of his old acquaintances or of his relatives or of anyone who might remind him of the old days.

Because his apartment had turned into a kind of hell, he took a room in a large hotel, a good room on the mezzanine from which he could watch people pass by. He no longer felt alone in such a cavernous, public lodging: he could feel the swarming presence of others all around him. He could hear voices through the walls; and when the old anguish returned and tormented him more cruelly than he could bear as he stood between his turned-down bed and his lonely fire, he would step out into the wide corridors and, like a patrolling sentry, walk past all the closed doors, despondently noting the two pairs of shoes left outside each: the pretty little boots of women snuggling up to stout male shoes. And he thought that their owners were probably all happy and sleeping cosily side by side or locked in each other's arms in their warm beds.

And so five years went by, five desolate years, with nothing to mark them except from time to time a couple of hours of love duly bought and paid for.

And then one day, as he was taking his customary stroll between the Madeleine and the rue Drouot,* he caught sight of a woman. Something about her struck him. With her were a tall man and a boy. All three were walking in front of him. He wondered: 'Where have I seen these people before?' and suddenly he recognized a gesture of a hand: it was his wife— his wife, with Limousin and his son, his little George.

His heart beat so fast he almost choked. But he did not stop. He wanted to see them and he set off in their wake. Anyone would have taken them for a family, an ordinary middle-class family. Henriette leaned on Paul's arm, talking to him in a low voice, occasionally turning her head to look at him. At such moments, Parent could see her profile, made out the familiar graceful line of her cheek, the movements of her lips, her smile, and the caress in her eyes. But his attention was drawn by the child. How big he was! How strong he looked! Parent could not see his face for the long blond hair which hung down in curls over his collar. Yet this bare-legged, strapping boy marching along like a little man at his mother's side was his George!

Then, when they stopped to look in a shop window, he had a good view of all three. Limousin was grey and looked older and thinner. On the other hand, his wife, though as attractive as ever, had put on weight. George was quite unrecognizable—so different from the old days!

They set off again. Parent continued to follow and then put on a spurt which would take him past them so that he could turn and come back and see them close to from the front. When he passed the boy, he felt a wild urge to gather him in his arms and make off with him. He brushed against him as if by accident. The boy turned and glared, annoyed by his clumsiness. Parent fled, stricken and pursued by that glare, which he felt like a physical hurt. He fled like a thief, terrorized by the appalling fear that he had been noticed and recognized by his wife and her lover. He ran all the way to his café without stopping and collapsed, panting, on to his usual seat.

That evening, he drank three absinthes.

For four months, the wound left by the encounter stayed open in his heart. Each night he saw the three of them, happy and contented, father, mother, and son, strolling along the Boulevard before going home to dinner. This new image replaced the old. But the effect was quite different: he had a new mental picture now and he also felt a new kind of torment. His little George, the George he had once loved and cuddled so much, vanished into a distant past which was over and done with, and another George formed in his mind's eye, a kind of brother to the first, a sturdy boy with bare legs, who did not know him from Adam! This thought hurt him deeply. The love his son had shown him was dead; there was now no bond between them. This other boy would never have held out his arms when he saw him; there had even been something hostile in the way he had looked at him.

But gradually he returned to an even keel; the mental torture subsided; the vivid visual memory of the encounter which haunted his nights became blurred and intermittent. He began to live again more or less as most people do, like the men with nothing better to do who drink their beer at marble-topped tables and wear out the seats of their trousers on the shabby plush seats of cafés.

He grew old amid the pipe-smoke and grew bald in the light of the gas-lamps. He came to regard his weekly bath, his fortnightly visit to the barber, or buying new clothes or a new hat as red-letter days. When he walked into his café wearing a new hat, he would always, before sitting down, peer at himself at length in the mirror. He would put it on and take it off several times in succession, try it on this way and then that, and in the end always asked his friend, the lady at the till, who had been watching with interest: 'Think it suits me?'

Two or three times a year he went to the theatre. In the summer, he would spend the occasional evening in a music-hall on the Champs-Élysées. He came away with tunes in his

head which played on in the recesses of his memory for weeks
on end: he would even hum them and beat time with one foot
as he sat with his glass of beer.

The years went by slowly, monotonously, and quickly
because they were empty.

He never felt that they were passing him by. Unresisting and
unconcerned, he slid towards death in his seat at a table in a
café. There was only the large mirror against which he leaned
the back of his head, which grew balder with each passing day,
to reflect the ravages of time, which passes, flies, and devours
mortal man. O frailty!

He never, or scarcely ever, thought now of the tragic events
on which his life had foundered, for twenty years had passed
since that terrible evening.

But the life he had made for himself had sapped his
strength, undermined his constitution and drained his vitality.
The proprietor of the café, the sixth since he had started
patronizing the establishment, would often say: 'You should
shake yourself a bit, Monsieur Parent. You oughter get a bit of
air, get yourself out into the country. Take it from me, you ain't
been your old self this last month or two.'

When Monsieur Parent had gone, the café owner shared his
thoughts with the lady at the till. 'Poor old Monsieur Parent's in
a bad way. It don't do nobody any good being stuck in Paris all
the time. See if you can't get him to take a little trip out now
and then, down by the river, where he can get a nice bit of fish
for his dinner. He'll take it from you. Won't be long now before
summer's here. It'll buck him up.'

Every day, the lady at the till, feeling genuinely sorry and
concerned for her most regular customer, would tell Parent: 'Go
on, dear, take the plunge. Get some fresh air. It's reely nice is
the country when the weather's lovely. If it was me, I'd go and
live there permanent if I could!'

And she would tell him her dreams, the simple, romantic
dreams that fill the heads of all those poor working-girls who,
trapped from one year's end to the next behind some shop
window, watch the noisy, unnatural life of the streets glide past
while they imagine the quiet, slow life of the countryside—a
life spent beneath spreading trees, in the bright sun which

shines down on meadows, deep woods, clear streams, on cows
lying in the grass and on all the different kinds of flowers that
bloom free—blue, red, yellow, purple, mauve, pink, white: all
the sweet, fresh, fragrant flowers of nature which can be picked
on walks and gathered into huge bunches.

She enjoyed talking to him neverendingly about her never-
ending, unrealized and unrealizable longings. While he, a poor
old man who had run out of hopes, enjoyed listening to her. He
got into the habit of sitting next to the counter to chat with
Mademoiselle Zoé and talk to her about the country. And so,
little by little, he acquired a vague fancy to go and see, just
once, if it was really as nice beyond the city walls as she said it
was.

One morning he asked her:

'Any idea where a chap could get a decent lunch out of
town?'

She answered:

'Why not try the Terrace at Saint-Germain.* It's reely nice
there.'

He had been there for walks long ago, when he was engaged.
He decided to go back.

He chose a Sunday, for no particular reason, except that
people usually go out on Sundays, even people who do nothing
all week.

So one Sunday morning, he set off for Saint-Germain.

It was early July, a hot, dazzling day. From his seat next to
the door of his compartment, he watched as the trees and the
odd-looking houses on the outskirts of Paris flashed by. He felt
rather miserable and regretted having succumbed to such a
novel whim and disrupted his normal routine. The countryside,
constantly changing but always remaining the same, made him
feel weary. He was thirsty and every time the train stopped he
felt like getting out and making a bee-line for the inevitable
café he saw behind the station, where he could drink a couple
of glasses of beer and then take the first train back to Paris that
came along. Besides, the journey seemed terribly long. He
could sit still for days on end as long as he had the same
unmoving things to look at. But he found that it made him
restless and tired to be constantly on the move, to see every-

thing around him shift, while he himself remained perfectly
still.

The Seine caught his interest, however, each time he
crossed it. He caught sight of skiffs scudding beneath the Pont
Chatou,* with bows pulled half out of the water by the powerful
strokes of bare-armed oarsmen, and he thought: 'Those chaps
are having a grand time of it!'

The long ribbon of the river, winding away from each side of
the Pont du Pecq, stirred somewhere deep within him an idle
whim to go walking along its banks. But then the train hurtled
into the tunnel just before Saint-Germain station and moments
later drew up at the platform.

Parent got out and, with steps weighed down by lassitude,
walked off, with his hands behind his back, towards the
Terrace. When he reached the iron balustrade, he paused and
looked at the view. The wide plain stretched away at his feet as
limitless as the ocean. It was very green and sprinkled with
large villages as crowded as towns, and criss-crossed by white
roads. Patches of forest turned into woodland here and there
and the lagoons around Le Vésinet shone like silver plates.
The distant hills of Sannois and Argenteuil rose up out of a
faint, bluish haze which obscured all detail. The sun shone
down hot and fierce on the land, which rolled away beneath
a shroud of early-morning mist; the dampness of the sun-
drenched earth rose as thin wisps of steam, and warm, moist
river-breath blew from the Seine, which lay in endless coils
over the plain, sidling past the villages and skirting the hills.

A warm breeze, laden with the smell of grass and rising sap,
fanned his cheek, entered his lungs, made his heart lighter and
his head clearer, and sent the blood coursing through his
veins.

Taken by surprise, Parent inhaled deeply and he gazed
wide-eyed at the sheer size of the plain. He muttered: 'It really
is nice here.'

He walked on for a few steps and then stopped again to look.
He had the impression that he was seeing things that were
new and undiscovered. Not things which he could see with
the naked eye, but intuitions of things: experiences he had
never had, joys which he had only half-glimpsed, joys he

had never felt. A whole new horizon of life whose existence
he had never suspected now suddenly opened up before him
as he stared out across the limitless land.

The wretched drabness of his existence suddenly loomed up
in the pitiless glare which lit the view before him. He saw the
twenty dreary, cheerless, desperate years he had spent in
cafés. He might have travelled, as others did, and gone away,
far away, and seen foreign peoples and uncharted lands across
the sea. He might have taken an interest in the arts and
sciences, which other people find so absorbing. He might have
learned to love life in all its countless forms, the mystery of life
itself, with all its delights and sorrows, endlessly changing,
always inexplicable, and invariably fascinating.

But now it was too late. He would go from one glass of beer
to the next until the day he died, without family or friends,
without hope and without an interest in the world. He was
overcome by a feeling of utter desolation and felt a sudden urge
to get away from there, to hide, to rush back to Paris, to his
café and his apathy. All the thoughts, dreams, and desires
which lie dormant in the stagnant recesses of the subconscious
mind had suddenly awakened, stirred by the sun which beat
down on the plain.

He sensed that if he remained there any longer by himself,
he would go mad, so he hurried off to the Hôtel Henri IV* to
get some lunch, dull his mind with wine and brandy, and find
somebody, anybody, to talk to.

He sat down at a table for one in the garden which looks out
over the landscape below, ordered his lunch, and asked for it
to be brought at once.

Others also out for the day began to arrive and sat down at
tables nearby. He felt better; he was no longer by himself.

Three people were having lunch under the trees just across
the way. He had glanced at them several times without really
seeing them, the way people do when they look at strangers.

Suddenly, a woman's voice struck him so forcibly that he felt
the shock of it in the pit of his stomach.

The voice had said: 'George can carve the chicken.'

And another voice answered: 'Yes, mother.'

Parent looked up and at once knew, knew instinctively, who

these people were, for he would never have recognized them. His wife had grown white-haired and quite stout and had turned into a dignified, respectable old lady; she was eating with her head forward to avoid dropping food on to her dress, though she had arranged a napkin down her front. George had grown up and was a man. He sported a beard or rather the straggly, nondescript, curly fuzz which upholsters the cheeks of young men. He was wearing a top hat, a white twill waistcoat, and—doubtless for effect—a monocle. Parent stared at him in astonishment! Was that George, his son? Surely not. The young man was a stranger; there could not be anything between them any more.

Limousin had his back turned and was eating, hunched over his food.

But the three of them seemed happy and contented. They ate in well-known restaurants in the country. Their existence had been calm and peaceful, based on family life in a comfortable, warm home full of those little insignificant things which make it good to be alive—little acts of loving kindness, tender words exchanged by people bound by genuine affection. This was how they had lived, courtesy of Parent, on his money, after deceiving him, robbing him, and ruining his life! They had sentenced him, an innocent, trusting, decent man, to the pain of loneliness, to a life lived in streets and cafés, to every kind of mental torture and the direst physical misery! They had turned him into a useless, lost creature with no place to go to, a wretched old man with neither joy nor hope of joy, who expected nothing more of people or of life. For him, the world was an empty place because there was nothing in it to love. He could travel to far-off lands or roam the streets at home, he could call at every house in Paris and see inside every room, but he would never open a door and see the long-lost, much-loved face of a woman or child light up when he walked through it. This idea, that he could ever open a door and find someone behind it to kiss, went round and round inside his head.

And it was all the fault of these three wicked people—his ignoble wife, his despicable friend, and the tall blond boy with the arrogant airs.

For now he hated the boy as much as the others! So he was Limousin's son after all! Would Limousin have kept and loved him if it were not so? It was obvious that he would have dropped mother and child in next to no time if he had not been certain the boy really was his. Who brings up other people's children?

And here they were, sitting next to him: the three wreckers who had caused him such pain.

Parent watched them, his anger mounting and his temper rising as he recalled all his past suffering, anguish, and despair. But what made him angriest of all was their look of bovine self-satisfaction. He wanted to kill them, throw his soda-water syphon at them, split the skull of Limousin who, as he ate, kept lowering his head on to his plate and then straightening up again.

It was obvious their lives would go on as before, without worries or care of any kind. Oh no! It was more than he could bear! He would have his revenge! And he would have it here and now, for he had them in the palm of his hand. But how was he to manage it? He thought hard. But his mind ran to horrible deeds, the kind which feature in cheap novelettes, but came up with nothing feasible. Meanwhile, he drank glass after glass to keep his anger primed and screw up his courage, so that he would not miss this opportunity. Another as good might never come his way again.

Then out of the blue, there came an idea, a savage idea. He stopped drinking and began to think it through. A smile parted his lips and he muttered: 'Got them! I've really got them! We'll see if I haven't!'

A waiter asked him: 'What would you like to follow, sir?'

'Nothing. Just coffee. And cognac. Your best.'

He went on watching them as he sipped his brandy. There were too many people in the restaurant for his purposes. So he would wait and when they left he would follow them, for they were sure to take a turn along the Terrace or in the woods. When they had gone some way, he would catch them up: that was when he would take his revenge! Sweet revenge! And none too soon either, after twenty-three years of suffering. They had no idea that the sky was about to fall on their heads!

They were quietly finishing their lunch, chatting safely among themselves. Parent could not make out what they were saying, but their gestures indicated that they were quite relaxed and unworried. His wife's face made him feel especially angry. She had acquired airs and the well-padded look of the sanctimonious, unbending bigot who has girded on the sword of principle and the buckler of virtue.

Eventually they paid the bill and stood up. It was then that he had his first view of Limousin. He could have passed for a retired diplomat, for he looked a very important person indeed, so splendid were his white, lissom side-whiskers, which hung well down over the lapels of his frock-coat.

They left the restaurant. George was smoking a cigar and wore his hat jauntily over one ear. Parent immediately followed them out.

They began with a turn round the Terrace. They admired the view unenthusiastically, as is the way with people who have lunched well. Then they walked into the woods.

Parent rubbed his hands. He continued to follow them but did not get too close, keeping out of sight to avoid attracting their attention too soon.

They walked slowly, enjoying the greenery and the pleasant, warm air. Henriette took Limousin's arm and walked by his side, head high, safe in the knowledge that she was a respectable wife and proud to be so. With his cane, George slashed at the leaves and from time to time leapt across the ditch by the side of the path, as nimbly as an eager young stallion which might at any moment gallop away into the trees.

Parent gradually closed the gap, panting with excitement and fatigue, for he hardly ever walked anywhere now. Then he was level with them. But all at once he felt afraid, confusedly, inexplicably afraid, and he passed them intending to turn and meet them face to face.

He walked on, his heart pounding, feeling their presence behind him. He kept telling himself: 'Right, this is the moment. Get a grip on yourself! Do it now!'

He turned round. But the three of them were sitting on the grass under a large tree. They were still talking.

He made up his mind and walked quickly back towards

them. He stopped in front of them, in the middle of the path and, his voice halting and breaking with emotion, stammered:

'It's me! I'm here! You weren't expecting to see me, were you?'

All three stared at this man who looked as if he might be quite deranged.

He went on:

'Anybody'd think you didn't recognize me. Well, take a good look. I am Parent, Henri Parent. You weren't expecting to see me, were you? You thought it was all over and done with. You thought you'd never see me again. Well, you were wrong. I'm back. And now we're going to have it all out.'

Henriette, shocked and startled, hid her face in her hands, murmuring: 'Oh my God!'

Seeing that some stranger was somehow threatening his mother, George had got to his feet, ready to grab him by the collar.

Limousin was thunderstruck and stared in fear at this ghost from the past, who, pausing briefly to catch his breath, went on:

'That's right, we're going to have it all out. At last, the time has come! You deceived me, you condemned me to a living hell and you thought I'd never catch up with you!'

But the young man seized him by the shoulders and pushed him away:

'You must be off your head! What do you want? Clear off and be quick about it before you feel the back of my hand!'

Parent replied:

'I'll tell you what I want. I want you to know the truth about these two . . .'

But George, infuriated, was shaking him and was about to start using his fists. Parent went on:

'Let me go, will you? I'm your father . . . Look at them for yourself and then tell me they don't know who I am!'

Disconcerted, the young man let go of him and turned to his mother.

As soon as the hands holding him relaxed, Parent advanced towards her:

'Go on! Tell him who I am! Tell him that my name is Henri

Parent. Tell him I'm his father because he is George Parent, because you are my wife, because all three of you live on my money, the allowance of 10,000 francs I have been paying you ever since I kicked you out of my house. And tell him why I kicked you out of my house. Because I found you with this despicable. vile snake who was your lover! Tell him what I was like, an ordinary decent man who you married for his money and deceived from the very start. Tell him who you are and who I am . . .'

He spluttered and ran out of breath, so enraged was he.

The woman gave a piteous cry:

'Paul, stop him! Make him stop! Make him be quiet! Stop him saying all these things for my son to hear!'

Limousin was also on his feet now. He said very quietly:

'Silence, man! Hold your tongue! Don't you realize what you are doing?'

Parent went on furiously:

'I know exactly what I'm doing. And there's more. There's something I should like to know, something that has been torturing me for twenty years.'

Then he turned to George, who, quite bewildered, was leaning against a tree, and said:

'Listen here, boy. When she walked out on me, she didn't think deceiving me was enough: she wanted to drive me to despair. You were all I had. And she took you away with her, swearing that I was not your father, that the real father was this man here! Was she lying? I have no idea, but I've been asking myself that question for twenty years.'

He went up to her, a tragic, terrible figure, and, pulling away the hand which hid her face, demanded: 'Well? I insist that you tell me here and now which of us is the father of this young man. It is him or me? Your husband or your lover?'

Limousin leaped on him but Parent threw him off and, bristling with rage, snarled:

'You're brave enough today—braver than on the day when you ran away down the stairs because I was going to kill you! If she won't say, you tell me. You must know as well as she does. Well say: are you the boy's father? Come on! Out with it!'

He turned back to his wife.

'If you won't tell me, then at least tell your son. He's a man now. He's entitled to know who his father is. I don't know the answer. I've never known! So I can't tell you, my boy.'

He was now quite beside himself and his voice grew shrill:

'Come on . . . Answer! . . . She doesn't know herself! I bet even she doesn't know! . . . That's it . . . She doesn't know! . . . My God! She was doing it with both of us . . . ! So nobody knows, nobody at all! . . . How could anyone know . . . ? So you'll never know either, my boy, no more than I do . . . Come on . . . ask her . . . go on, ask her . . . You'll see she doesn't know . . . Nor do I . . . nor does he . . . nor do you! Nobody knows! . . . So you can choose . . . that's it, why not just choose . . . it's either him or me . . . Take your pick . . . There's no more to be said . . . there's an end to it . . . But if she does decide to tell, you will come and let me know, won't you? I'm at the Hôtel des Continents . . . I'd rather like to know . . . Good afternoon to you. All the very best and so forth . . .'

And with arms waving and still talking to himself, he walked off under the tall trees, through the clear cool air heavy with the smell of rank vegetation. He did not turn round to look at them but kept straight on, buoyed up by his anger and sustained by a feeling of exhilaration, with his mind still full of one thought only.

Suddenly he was aware that he was standing outside the station. A train was about to leave. He got in. As he sped along, his anger cooled, he collected his wits and returned to Paris, astonished at his own daring.

He felt sore and weary, as though every bone in his body had been broken. Even so, he decided to call in at his café for a beer.

When she saw him walk through the door, Mademoiselle Zoé was surprised and asked:

'Back already? Feeling tired?'

He answered: 'Yes . . . tired . . . so tired . . . You know how it is if you're not used to getting out and about . . . But that's the finish, I shan't be going back to the country ever again. I'd have been better off staying in town. From now on, I shan't be venturing far from here.'

Try as she might, she could not get him to tell her about his

little outing, though she would have dearly liked to hear all
about it.

That night, for the first time in his life, he got completely
drunk, so drunk that they had to carry him home.

This Business of Latin

This business of Latin* that people have been going on and on about lately until we're all heartily sick of it, reminds me of a story which happened when I was a boy.

I was in my last year of school in a crammer in a large town in central France, Robineau's Academy, which was famous in the area for its teaching of Latin.

For ten years, Robineau's Academy had obtained much better examination-results than the town's grammar school and all the secondary schools in the area, and its continuing success was generally attributed to one lowly assistant master, Monsieur Piquedent, or rather Old Piquedent.

He was one of those men with grey hair who are neither old nor young, whose age is a mystery and whose life story an open book to the most casual observer. At twenty he had got a job as an unqualified, very junior master in the first school that would have him, so that he could continue to study for his degree and possibly go on afterwards to a doctorate. But he had got so stuck in the dismal schoolteaching rut that a very junior master he had remained all his life. But he had never lost his love of Latin, indeed he was obsessed by it, almost unhealthily so, as if by some unwise passion. He continued to read and reread the Latin poets, prose-writers, and historians, reinterpreting, finding new meanings, and writing commentaries on them with a doggedness verging on mania.

One day he got the idea of making all the pupils in his class give their answers entirely in Latin. He persisted with this notion until they could keep up a conversation with him as easily as they could in their own tongue.

He listened to them as the conductor of an orchestra listens to musicians rehearsing, and he was forever banging his desk with his ruler, saying:

'Lefrère, Lefrère, you are perpetrating a howler! Can't you remember the rule . . . ?'

'Plantel, that turn of phrase is irretrievably French, not Latin. You must get the feel of the language. Pay attention, listen to me . . .'

At the end of one school year, pupils of Robineau's Academy walked off with all the prizes for prose composition, unseen translation and Latin diction.

The following session, the headmaster, a small man as sly as the grinning, grotesque monkey he so closely resembled, inserted the following into the prospectus and advertising-matter and also had it painted over the door of the Academy:

Specialization in Latin Studies.
Five First Prizes Awarded in all Five Classes in the Academy.
Two Distinctions in Public Examinations open to all
Grammar and Secondary Schools in France.

For ten years, Robineau's Academy continued to carry all before it. My father, tempted by its success rate, sent me as a day-boy to the Academy run by Robineau, whom we used to call Robinetto or Robinettino, and arranged for me to have special lessons with Old Piquedent at five francs an hour, of which the teacher got two and the headmaster three. I was eighteen at the time and in my last year.

These extra lessons were held in a small room which overlooked the street. But instead of talking to me in Latin, as he did in class, Old Piquedent now started telling me his troubles in French. Having no family or friends, the poor old boy took a liking to me and poured out his heart.

For ten or fifteen years, he had never once spoken like this to another person.

'I'm like an oak-tree in a desert,' he said, ' "sicut quercus in solitudine." '

He did not get on with the other teachers and had no friends in town, for he had never had time to make any.

'Never free, not even at night, and nights are hardest. I've always dreamt of having a room with my own furniture, my books, my bits and pieces of belongings, things other people can't touch. But I don't have anything I can call my own, except the coat and trousers I stand up in. Not even my own mattress or pillow. I don't have four walls where I can shut myself away, except this room, when I come to give a lesson. Can you conceive of what that means? A grown man who lives his life without having the right or the time to be alone in a room, any room, to think and reflect and work and dream? My boy, happiness is a key, the key of a door you can lock behind you. It's the only real happiness there is.

'Here I stand all day in front of a class of ghastly boys who can't sit still, and at night I'm on dormitory duty with the same little horrors who won't stop snoring. I sleep in public, in a bed with no privacy, at the head of two rows of other beds occupied by boys I'm supposed to keep in order. I can never be alone, never! If I go out, I find the streets are full of people. When I'm tired of walking about, I go into a café which is full of men smoking and playing billiards. I tell you, it's like being in prison.'

'Why don't you leave and try something else, sir?'

He exclaimed: 'But what, dear boy? What else? I can't make boots or hats and I'm no carpenter or baker or barber. All I know is Latin and I've no letters after my name so I can't make any sort of money out of the only thing I have to sell. If I had a doctorate, I could ask a hundred francs for what I currently let them have for five—and they wouldn't get such good lessons either, for just having a degree would be enough to maintain my reputation.'

Sometimes he would say:

'The only peace I ever have is the time I spend with you. Don't be afraid that you're missing anything. I'll make it all up in class: I'll get you to talk twice as often as the others.'

One day I screwed up my courage and offered him a cigarette. At first he stared at me in dismay and glanced towards the door:

'What if somebody came in, old chap?'

'Very well, let's smoke by the window, then,' said I.

We leant on our elbows at the window overlooking the street, with secretive hands curled like sea-shells around the thin tubes of tobacco.

Opposite us was a laundry. Inside, four women in loose white overalls were pressing linen spread out in front of them with heavy, hot flat-irons which raised clouds of steam.

A fifth woman, a girl, leaning to one side to counteract the weight of the large basket she carried in one hand, suddenly emerged from the shop on her way to deliver shirts, handkerchiefs, and sheets to customers' houses. She paused in the doorway as though weary before she began. Then she glanced up, smiled when she saw us there smoking, and, with her free hand, blew us a sarcastic kiss, with all the jaunty cheek of a working girl. Then she walked off slowly, shuffling her shoes.

She was about twenty, small-boned, a little on the thin side, pale and rather pretty. Her manner was pert, and, beneath a mass of untidy fair hair, she had mocking eyes.

Old Piquedent, moved by the sight, muttered:

'That's not a woman's work. That's a job for a horse.'

And he spoke with feeling of the plight of the poor. He had the fanatical convictions of an idealistic socialist and he spoke of the hardships of the workers with a catch in his voice and phrases borrowed from Jean-Jacques Rousseau.*

The next day we were leaning out of the same window. The same girl spotted us and, putting her thumb to her nose and wiggling her fingers, called up in a funny little voice: 'Careful you don't strain your brains!'

I threw her a cigarette, which she lit at once. The four other women ran to the door of the laundry and held out their hands so that they could have cigarettes too.

In this way an exchange of friendly banter became a regular feature of each day between these women in the street outside, who worked so hard, and the two of us in school, who hardly worked at all.

The way Old Piquedent behaved was hilarious. He was afraid of being seen—it was more than his job was worth—and he went through a repertoire of shy, silly antics, exactly like some bashful swain in a play, to which the women reacted by shooting him showers of kisses.

A rather cruel idea was beginning to form in my mind. One day, as I entered the room where we always met, I whispered to Old Piquedent:

'You won't believe this, sir, but I ran into her! You know, the short one with the basket. I spoke to her!'

Slightly disconcerted by my tone of voice, he asked: 'What did she say?'

'She said . . . now what did she say? . . . ah yes! She said she thought you're very good-looking! Do you know what I think? . . . I think she fancies you!'

I saw him turn pale. He went on:

'Nonsense, it's a joke. Such things don't happen when you're my age.'

I said gravely:

'Why not? You *are* good-looking.'

I sensed that my little lie had got to him but I did not follow it up.

However, each day I pretended that I had met her and talked to her about him. In the end, he was completely taken in and became terribly earnest and began returning her kisses with passionate interest.

Now it so happened that one morning, on my way to school, I did actually meet her. I went straight up to her and spoke as if I had known her for ten years.

'Hello. How are you?'

'Oh fine, thanks.'

'Want a cigarette?'

'I can't. Not in the street.'

'You can smoke it later.'

'Oh, all right then.'

'Listen. I imagine you know?'

'Know what?'

'The old gent, my teacher . . .'

'Old Piquedent?'

'That's right, Old Piquedent. So you know his name?'

' 'Course I do. So?'

'Well, he's in love with you.'

She shrieked with laughter and said: 'Get away with you!'

'It's no joke. He spends every lesson talking about you. I bet he wants to marry you!'

She stopped laughing. The prospect of getting married

makes any girl turn serious. Then with a sceptical look she repeated:

'Get away!'

'It's true! Honestly!'

She picked up her basket, which she had set down between her feet.

'Well, we'll see,' she said.

And away she went.

When I got to school, I took Old Piquedent to one side:

'You've got to write to her. She's really gone on you.'

So he wrote a long, respectful love-letter full of fine phrases and finer periphrases, dripping with metaphors and similes, philosophical *pensées*, and donnish cooings, a masterpiece of unintentional humour which I undertook to deliver to the girl.

She read it. She looked grave and visibly affected. Then she murmured:

'Don't he write lovely! Anybody can tell he passed exams and that! Does he really want to marry me?'

I answered shamelessly:

'Does he want . . . ? He can't think of anything else!'

'In that case, he'd better ask me out this Sunday. We could have a meal down on the Île des Fleurs.'

I promised she would be invited.

Old Piquedent was very moved by everything I told him about her. I added:

'She loves you, sir. She strikes me as a decent sort. I hope you're not planning to lead her on and then abandon her.'

He answered firmly:

'Of course not. I too am a decent sort.'

I confess that in all this I had no particular plan of any kind. To me, it was all a joke, a schoolboy lark, nothing more. I saw how foolish and innocent the old boy was and had found his weak spot. I was just having a bit of fun and never wondered how it would all end. I was eighteen and had a long-standing reputation in school as a confirmed practical joker.

Anyway, it was agreed that Old Piquedent and I would take a cab to the ferry at Queue-de-Vache. There we would meet up with Angèle, and the two of them would climb aboard my boat, for I was a big boating-man in those days. I would row them out to the Île des Fleurs and all three of us would have lunch together. I had insisted on being there too, to enjoy the fruits of my plotting, and in agreeing to this the old boy showed just how naïve he was, for by having me along he was inviting competition.

When we got to the ferry, where my boat had been moored since morning, I could make out in the grass, or more accurately above the tall reeds that lined the river bank, an enormous red parasol, which sprouted like a monstrous poppy. Under the parasol, our little laundress was waiting for us, dressed in her Sunday best. I was amazed: she was really pretty, if a little pale, and quite presentable, if slightly common.

Old Piquedent removed his hat and bowed. She held out her hand and they both looked at each other without saying a word. Then they got into my boat and I took the oars.

They sat side by side in the stern.

The old boy was first to break the silence:

'It's a lovely day for a row on the river.'

She murmured:

'I'll say!'

She trailed her hand in the river, skimming the water with her fingers, which left a thin, transparent wake, like a glass wave, which broke against the side of the boat with a low, lapping, pretty splash.

When we were sitting in the restaurant, she found her tongue and ordered her lunch: whitebait, chicken, and salad. Afterwards, she insisted on showing us round the island, which she knew well.

By this time she was in high spirits, a little forward and even ready to poke fun.

The question of love had not come up until dessert. I'd stood a bottle of champagne and Old Piquedent was tight. She was well away too and kept calling him: 'Monsieur Piquenez.'

All of a sudden, he said:

'Raoul has, I think, told you how I feel?'

Immediately, she became as sober as a judge.

'Yes.'

'And do you feel the same?'

'A girl never answers questions like that.'

Stirred to the core and breathing hard, he spoke with feeling:

'Might there come a day when you would entertain a feeling of sympathy in respect of my person?'

She smiled:

'You old silly. I think you're very sweet.'

'In short, my dear, do you think that at a later date, we might . . . ?'

She hesitated a second. Then, in a voice that trembled, she said:

'You mean you'll marry me? 'Cos get this straight: there's nothing doing otherwise.'

'Of course, Angèle!'

'Then you're on, Monsieur Piquenez!'

And that's how two silly people plighted their troth, and all through the fault of a schoolboy joker. Not that I believed it was serious. Perhaps they didn't either. But then she seemed to have second thoughts:

'You know, I haven't got a penny to my name.'

He stammered, as drunk as Silenus:*

'It's all right. I've got 5,000 francs saved up.'

She cried in triumph:

'So we could start a little business?'

He looked startled and said:

'What sort of business?'

'How do I know? We'll see what. With 5,000 francs we can do all sorts. You don't want me coming to live in that school of yours, now do you?'

He had not thought that far ahead and, quite at a loss, he stuttered:

'What sort of business? It's not easy. All I know is Latin.'

So she put her mind to work on the problem, and ran through all the occupations she had ever fancied.

'You couldn't set up as a doctor?'

'No, I'm not qualified.'

'Or a chemist?'

'I'm not qualified for that either.'

She gave a cry of delight. She had found the answer.

'In that case we'll buy a grocery business! Oooh, lovely!

We'll buy a grocer's shop. Not too big, of course. You can't get much for 5,000 francs.'

At this, he mutinied:

'Out of the question! I can't be a grocer! I'm . . . I'm . . . too well known . . . All I know . . . is Latin!'

But she held a glass of champagne to his lips. He drank it and said no more.

We got back into the boat. It was dark now, black as the ace of spades. But I could see enough to observe that their arms were round each other's waists and that they kissed more than once.

But it all turned out catastrophically. Wind of our little escapade got out and Old Piquedent was sacked. And my father, who was outraged, took me away and sent me to see the school year out as a boarder at Ribaudet's School.

I sat my university entrance exams six weeks later. Later on I went to Paris to read law and did not return to my home town for another two years.

On the corner of the rue du Serpent, a shop caught my eye. The window read: 'Piquedent's Imperial Produce'. Under it, for the benefit of the ignorant: 'Groceries'.

I said aloud:

'Quantum mutatus ab illo!'*

He looked up, abandoned the woman he was serving and hurried towards me with hands outstretched.

'Ah! Dear boy! What brings you here? What a surprise! What a splendid surprise!'

A fine-looking woman, amply proportioned, rushed out from behind her counter and threw her arms round me. I hardly recognized her, she had grown so fat.

I asked:

'How are you getting on?'

Piquedent turned away and busied himself weighing goods on his scales:

'Very well, excellent well. This year, I've already made 3,000 francs.'

'What about the Latin, sir?'

'Latin? Latin? Gracious me. Man cannot live by Latin alone!'*

Madame Husson's May King

We had just passed Gisors,* where I had been woken up by the station porters shouting out the name of the place, and was about to go back to sleep, when the train gave a terrific lurch and I was thrown against the fat lady sitting opposite.

A wheel had broken on the engine, which had slewed across the track. The tender and the luggage-van had also been derailed and had come to rest next to the stricken locomotive, which screamed in agony, groaning, hissing, gasping, and spitting, like a horse that has fallen in the roadway and lies there with sides pulsating, chest heaving, nostrils smoking, its whole body convulsed, yet seemingly quite unable to make the smallest effort to get up and walk.

There were no dead or seriously injured, only a few cuts and bruises here and there, for the train had not yet got up full speed after the stop. We gazed in dismay at the great, crippled iron beast which was not going to take us anywhere and would block the line for some while yet since a relief train would have to be sent from Paris.

It was then about ten in the morning and I promptly decided to head back to Gisors and have lunch.

As I walked along the track, I kept thinking: 'Gisors? Gisors? Don't I know someone here? Who can it be? Gisors? Surely I've a friend who lives in town.' Suddenly a name surfaced in my memory: Albert Marambot. He was an old school-friend I hadn't seen in a dozen years at least. He was a doctor and had a practice at Gisors. He'd often written inviting me down. I'd always promised I'd go but never had. This time I'd make the most of the opportunity.

I asked the first passer-by I met: 'Do you know where Doctor Marambot lives?' He replied at once, in a drawling Norman accent: 'Rue Dauphine.' And there indeed, fixed to the door of the house he had pointed out, I saw a large brass plate engraved with the name of my old friend. I rang. But the door was opened by a girl with straw hair and slow movements who half-wittedly repeated: 'Not at home. He's not at home.'

I could hear the rattle of forks and the clink of glasses. I shouted: 'Hey, Marambot!' A door opened and a large, whiskery party appeared. He was holding a napkin and looked cross.

I swear I wouldn't have known him. He looked at least forty-five, and in that split second I had a sudden glimpse of life in the provinces, which slows a man down, clogs his mind, and makes him old before his time. With one flash of intuition, which took less time than it did to hold out my hand to him, I knew everything about him, his way of life, the way his mind worked, and his views on everything. I knew all about the leisurely meals to which he owed that paunch, the after-dinner naps induced by the torpid workings of over-burdened digestive processes generously lubricated with brandy. I could picture the perfunctory manner in which he examined his patients, with half his mind on the chicken roasting on the spit in front of the fire. His culinary conversation, his discussions on the subject of cider, brandy, and wine, or the way certain dishes should be prepared and certain sauces properly thickened, were all revealed to me by the mere sight of his florid, pasty cheeks, the fleshy lips and the dullness of his eyes.

I said: 'You don't recognize me. I'm Raoul Aubertin.'

He opened his arms wide and almost hugged me to death. The first thing he said was:

'I don't expect you've had lunch?'

'No.'

'That's very well met! I was just about to sit down. I've some capital trout.'

Five minutes later I was facing him across the luncheon table. I asked him:

'You're not married?'

'Absolutely not!'

'Do you like it here?'

'I don't get bored. I'm kept pretty busy. There are my

patients and I've got friends. I eat well, feel fit, and I like a joke, and there's hunting. I get by.'

'So you don't find life in a small town too dull?'

'Not at all. The secret is to know how to keep busy. A small town isn't really any different from any big city. Fewer things happen and there aren't the same opportunities for enjoying yourself, but what there is means a great deal more. You know fewer people but you see them more often. When you know all the windows in a road, each of them becomes much more absorbing and intriguing than a whole street of houses in Paris.

'Small towns are very entertaining, very entertaining indeed. Take Gisors. I know it like the back of my hand from its beginnings up to the present day. You have no idea how fascinating its history is.'

'Were you born here?'

'Me? No, I'm from Gournay,* which is the nearest town and its arch-rival. Gournay is to Gisors what Lucullus was to Cicero.* Here, all people care about is appearances, which is why it is said that Gisors is "stuck-up". At Gournay, all they think about is eating, so, as the expression goes, Gournay folk "get stuck in". Gisors despises Gournay, but Gournay just laughs at Gisors. It's a very funny place.'

It suddenly dawned on me that I was eating something which was truly exquisite: soft-boiled eggs coated in a jelly made of meat juices flavoured with herbs and sealed in aspic.

To please Marambot, I smacked my lips: 'This is really very good.'

He smiled. 'It needs two basic ingredients. A good aspic, which is hard to get, and the very best eggs. Good eggs are really difficult to come by, with lots of flavour and that hint of red in the yolk. I keep two separate chicken-runs, one for eggs and the other for the pot. I give my laying-hens special feed. I've got my own ideas about that. In an egg, just as in the flesh of poultry or beef or lamb, in milk, in anything you can think of, you get, and should be able to taste, the goodness from everything the animal has been eating. How much better we would all eat if we only took more trouble with these things!'

I laughed.

'So you've become a gourmet, then?'

'I should say! Only fools aren't. Being a gourmet is like being an artist or a scholar or a poet. As organs go, the palate is as sensitive, cultivable, and honourable as the eye or the ear. To have no palate is to be deprived of an exquisite faculty, to be deficient in the ability to discern the qualities of a dish in exactly the same way as you might be insensible to the qualities of a book or any other work of art. It is to lack a basic sense, a part of the gifts which make us superior to animals; its absence reduces us to the level of the many groups of the sickly, ill-favoured, and frankly stupid people of which the human race is composed; it means in fact that you have defective taste-buds in exactly the same way that you might have slow wits. A man who cannot tell crayfish from lobster or distinguish between herring—an admirable fish crammed with every taste and aromatic essence the sea can offer—and mackerel or pollack, or between a William pear and a Bartlett, is the equivalent of a man who cannot see the difference between Balzac and Eugène Sue*, or tell a Beethoven symphony from a military march composed by some regimental bandmaster, or the Apollo Belvedere from the statue erected in memory of General Blanmont!'*

'And who on earth is General Blanmont?'

'I'm sorry. Of course, you wouldn't know. It's pretty obvious you don't come from Gisors. A moment ago I told you that the denizens of the town are said to be self-satisfied, and never was an adjective better applied. But let's have lunch first and I'll tell you all about our town when I show you around.'

He had halted his flow from time to time to take a sip from a half-filled wine-glass at which he gazed fondly each time he set it down on the table.

With his napkin tied round his neck, cheeks aflame, eyes a-sparkle, and side-whiskers blooming round his busy mouth, he made a comic sight.

He plied me with food until I thought I would burst. Afterwards, when I said I ought to be getting back to the station, he took me by the arm and dragged me off through the streets. The town, which has a pleasant provincial feel to it, is dominated by its fortress, the best-preserved example of seventh-century military architecture in France. It in turn dominates a long, green valley of verdant pastures where ponderous Norman cattle graze and chew the cud.

The doctor said: 'Gisors, population 4,000, stands on the banks of the Eure. It is mentioned in Caesar's *Commentaries*: "Caesaris ostium", which became Caesartium, Caesortium, Gisortium, Gisors. I'll show you the site of the Roman camp. Traces of it are still visible.'

I laughed and said: 'See here, old man, it strikes me you've come down with a strange malady which as a doctor you ought really to look into. It's called parochialism.'

He stopped dead in his tracks: 'But parochialism, old friend, is no more than the natural form of patriotism. If I love my house, my town, and, by extension, my part of the world, it is because here I can still find the old familiar values of the village where I was brought up. But if I love the frontiers of France, if I am prepared to defend them, if I react with anger when I see them violated by our neighbours, it is precisely because I see a threat to my home and way of life, it is because a distant frontier, which I have never seen, is the road that leads to the province where I live. I am Norman born and bred and proud of it. I may dislike the Germans and want revenge for their aggression in the late war, but I do not hate them with the instinctive loathing I feel for the English, who are the true, the hereditary, the natural enemy of the Norman, because the English have many times swept over this land, where once my ancestors dwelt, looting and destroying, because my aversion for that perfidious race was handed down by the father who sired me . . . But here we are: this is the statue of General Blanmont.'

'General *who*?'

'General Blanmont. We had to have a statue—they don't call us Gisors folk proud for nothing! So we dredged up General Blanmont. Just take a look at the books in that window.'

He dragged me off to a bookshop where a display of a dozen or so tomes in yellow, red, and blue wrappers caught the eye.

As I read the titles, I began to giggle. There were:

Gisors, its Origins and its Future, by Monsieur X, Member of Divers Learned Societies;

A History of Gisors, by Abbé A;

Gisors from the Time of Julius Caesar to the Present, by Monsieur B, Gentleman;

Gisors and its Environs, by Doctor C.D.;

The Glories of Gisors, by An Antiquary.

'You see?' Marambot went on. 'Not a year passes, not one, do you hear, without the appearance of yet another history of Gisors. We've got twenty-three to date.'

'Who or what exactly are the Glories of Gisors?' I asked.

'Oh, I shan't mention all of them, I'll just tell you about the most glorious ones. First, we had General de Blanmont, then the Baron Davillier, the renowned ceramicist, who combed Spain and the Balearics and brought to the attention of collectors the splendid craft of the Hispano-Arabic potter.* In the world of letters, a journalist of considerable talent, now dead, Charles Brainne, and among those happily still with us, the highly respected editor of the *Nouvelliste de Rouen,* Charles Lapierre* . . . and many more besides . . . a great many.'

We were making our way down a long, gently sloping street the whole length of which basked in the hot June sunshine which had driven all the inhabitants indoors.

Suddenly, at the far end of this street, a man appeared, a drunk, who staggered as he walked.

He came towards us, head lolling, arms swinging, legs unsteady, in little spurts of three, six, or ten quick steps, each followed by a rest. One such surge of short-lived energy carried him half-way down the street. Then he came to a sudden halt and swayed on his feet, wondering whether to fall down or try another quick dash. Then he moved off in no particular direction and cannoned into a house to which he clung as though trying to climb in through the wall. Then he whirled round suddenly and looked straight ahead, with his mouth open and his eyes blinking against the sunshine, and then, with a thrust of his hips, he pushed himself off the wall and continued on his way.

A small beige-coloured dog, a half-starved mongrel, trailed

behind him, barking. It stopped when he stopped and moved on when he did.

'That', said Marambot, 'is Madame Husson's May King.'

Rather taken aback, I asked: 'Madame Husson's May King? what the dickens is that?'

The doctor began to laugh:

'Oh, it's just a name we have here for drunks. It comes from an old story which has become a local legend of sorts, though every word of it is absolutely true.'

'Is this tale amusing?'

'Very.'

'Then let's hear it.'

'By all means.'

'A long time ago, an old lady lived in the town. She was very virtuous herself and was keen on the cause of virtue in others. Her name was Madame Husson. The names I'm using are real, by the way, not made up. Madame Husson was particularly given to good works, succouring the poor and helping the deserving. She was tiny and scurried rather than walked. She wore a wig made of black silk, was very formal in her manners, unfailingly courteous, and on the very best of terms with her Maker, in the person of Abbé Malou. For Vice, which offended her deeply, she had a constitutional loathing, especially for the particular branch of it which the Church designates as Lust. The idea that children could be conceived before marriage enraged her, drove her berserk, to the point where she would behave in ways that were quite out of character.

'In those days, in the countryside around Paris, it was the custom to give a garland of roses and a small dowry to village maidens of conspicuous virtue,* and it struck Madame Husson that it would be a good idea if Gisors had its own May Queen.

'She shared her thoughts with Abbé Malou, who promptly drew up a list of candidates.

'Now Madame Husson was looked after by a maid, an old woman named Françoise who was every whit as straight-laced as she was herself.

'When the priest had gone, Madame Husson called her maid and said:

' "Françoise, these are the girls the curé has suggested for May Queen. I want you to go round and find out what people think of them."

'Françoise set off on the trail. She gathered every piece of gossip, every tale, every piece of tittle-tattle and scandal she could. So that she would not forget anything, she wrote it all down in the kitchen account-book, alongside the household expenses, and every morning she submitted it to the scrutiny of Madame Husson, who, after settling her spectacles on her thin nose, read the following:

Bread . . . . 4 sous
Milk . . . . 2 sous
Butter . . . . 8 sous
Malvina Levesque was got into trouble last year by Mathurin Poilu.
Leg of lamb . . . . 25 sous
Salt . . . . 1 sou
Rosalie Vatinel was spied in Riboulet woods up to no good with Césaire Piénoir by Madame Onésime who takes in washing on 20 July jest as it was getting dark.
Radishes . . . . 1 sou
Vinegar . . . . 2 sous
Salts of sorrel . . . . 2 sous
By all accounts Josephine Durdent have not done nothing wrong yet but she writes regular to the Oportun boy whose stationed in Rouen he sent her a hat for a present by the carrier's man.

'No girl emerged unscathed from her enquiries, which left no stone unturned. Françoise questioned everybody—neighbours, shopkeepers, the schoolteacher, the sisters in the convent school—and she made a note of every rumour she heard.

'Now, the girl has yet to be born who has never been the subject of old wives' gossip, and it came to pass that not one maiden in the entire district escaped the wagging of slanderous tongues.

'Madame Husson was determined that Gisors' May Queen should be, like Caesar's wife, above suspicion, and she was dismayed, appalled, and outraged as she went through her housekeeper's account-book.

'So the circle of investigation was widened to include the surrounding villages, but the results were negative.

'The Mayor was consulted. His nominees did not measure up. The names put forward by Doctor Barbesol did not fare any better, even though he backed their claims with guarantees of scientific precision.

'One morning, as she returned from the shops, Françoise said to her mistress:

'"I tell you, Madame, if you must have a May-somebody, it'll have to be Isidore. There's nobody else round here."

'Which set Madame Husson thinking.

'She knew Isidore well. He was the son of Virginie the greengrocer. His proverbial chastity had been a running joke in Gisors for a number of years, and afforded an amusing topic of conversation for the townspeople and a source of entertainment for the girls, who loved teasing him. He was turned twenty, tall, clumsy, slow, and timid. He helped his mother in the shop and spent most of his time sitting on a chair outside the door, sorting fruit and vegetables.

'He had an unhealthy fear of girls and lowered his eyes if a woman came into the shop and glanced at him with a smile. His celebrated shyness made him the butt of all the wags in the neighbourhood.

'Rude words, crude jests, and smut brought a blush to his cheek so quickly that Doctor Barbesol had christened him Modesty's Litmus Paper. Did he or did he not know? wondered the neighbours nastily. Was it simply an intuitive sense of secret, shameful mysteries, or a conscious revulsion against the disgusting act ordained by Love which apparently stirred such powerful feelings in the son of Virginie the fruiteress? All the horrible boys in the area ran past the shop shouting obscenities to make him look the other way; the girls took great delight in parading before him while they whispered rude suggestions which drove him indoors. The most brazen of them baited him openly, for fun, for a laugh, saying they would meet him later and making all kinds of wicked propositions.

'All of which set Madame Husson thinking.

'It was quite true: Isidore was an instance of exceptional, manifest, undeniable virtue. No one, not even the most sceptical unbeliever, would have dared accuse Isidore of causing the smallest breach in any moral law you cared to name. Nor had he ever seen the inside of a café, nor ever been observed hanging about on street corners. He went to bed at eight o'clock and got up at four. He was a paragon, a pearl.

'And yet Madame Husson hesitated. The idea of having a May King instead of a May Queen did not seem quite right. It worried her. She decided to consult Abbé Malou.

'He told her:

'"What is it exactly you wish to reward? Virtue, is it not? Pure virtue! So why should you be concerned whether it be found in man or woman? Virtue is eternal. It has neither country nor sex. Virtue is Virtue!"

'Thus encouraged, Madame Husson went off to see the Mayor.

'He gave her his full backing.

'"We shall make it an Occasion," he said. "Next year, if we find a girl as deserving as Isidore, we'll have a May Queen. Besides, we'll show Nanterre how it should be done.* And let's not be too exclusive. We must look with gladsome eye on Virtue in all its forms."

'When the news was broken to Isidore, he blushed bright scarlet but seemed pleased.

'The ceremony was duly fixed for 15 August, Assumption Day and the anniversary of the birth of the Emperor Napoleon.*

'The Town Council had resolved that no expense should be spared for the occasion. A platform was erected on the Couronneaux, a delightful continuation of the ramparts of the old fortress. I'll show you round it later on.

'By a natural reversal of public feeling, Isidore's virtue, hitherto a matter of ridicule, had suddenly become respectable and a source of envy, for it had become known that it would be worth 500 francs to him, plus a post-office savings book, great honour, and more glory than he knew what to do with. The girls now regretted their flightiness, flippant comments, and brazen behaviour. And Isidore, still as modest and shy as ever, now had a faintly complacent air which expressed his inner satisfaction.

'On the eve of the 15th, the whole of the rue Dauphine was already hung with flags and bunting. But I was forgetting! I must tell you the story of how it came to be called the rue Dauphine.

'It seems that during a visit to Gisors, the Dauphine, or rather a dauphine, I don't remember exactly which one, had been kept hanging about for so long by the Mayor and Corporation, who were anxious to show her off, that in the middle of her triumphal progress through the town, she stopped the cortège outside one of the houses in the street and exclaimed: "What a sweet little house! I'd love to see inside! Whose is it?" She was told the name of the owner who was sent for, located, and presented to the Princess, blushing but proud.

'She got out of her coach, went inside, said she wanted to see everything, from top to bottom, and even insisted on being by herself for a few moments in one of the smaller rooms.

'When she emerged, the people, gratified by the signal honour conferred upon a citizen of Gisors, shouted: "Long live the Princess!" But some wag made up a ditty, and thereafter the street took the name of Her Royal Highness, for:

> The Princess thought fit, may God defend her!
> To dispense with churchly splendour
> And to baptise this street, the great King's daughter
> Instead dispensed not holy but royal water.

'But to get back to Isidore.

'The route followed by the procession had been strewn with flowers, as is the custom on Corpus Christi Day, and the National Guard paraded under the orders of its commanding officer, Captain Desbarres, a stiff-backed veteran of Napoleon's Grand Army, who could point with pride, next to the case containing the Cross of Honour conferred upon him by the Emperor in person, to the beard of a Cossack which had been removed from its owner's chin by a single stroke of the Captain's sabre during the retreat from Moscow.

'The men he commanded formed an élite corps, whose glory shone throughout the province: Gisors's Company of Grenadiers was always in demand for every notable occasion within a radius of forty or fifty miles. It is said that once, when King Louis-Philippe* was inspecting the militias of the Eure, he stopped in amazement in front of the Gisors contingent and exclaimed: "And who are these fine Grenadiers?"

' "The company from Gisors," replied the general.

' "I might have known," murmured the King.

'Anyway, Captain Desbarres came with his men, preceded by the band, to fetch Isidore from his mother's shop.

'The band played briefly under his window and then the May King appeared in person at the door.

'He was dressed from head to foot in a white linen suit and on his head he wore a straw hat which sported, by way of a rosette, a sprig of orange-blossom.

'The question of what he should wear had been a source of considerable worry to Madame Husson, and she had hesitated at length between the black coat as worn by boys taking their first communion and this all-white suit. But Françoise, who advised her, persuaded her to go for the white outfit by pointing out that in it the May King would look just like a swan.

'Behind him there appeared his benefactress and sponsor, a beaming Madame Husson.

'As she stepped out, she leant on his arm, and the Mayor took up his position on the other side of the May King. There was a roll of drums. Captain Desbarres bawled: "Present arms!" Then the procession moved off again towards the church, through the vast crowds of people who had flocked in from the neighbouring villages.

'After a short service and a touching address from Abbé Malou, they all processed in the direction of the Couronneaux, where the banquet had been laid out in a marquee.

'Before sitting down, the Mayor said a few words. This is the text of his speech: I learnt it by heart, for it is very fine:

Young man, it was a bountiful Lady, loved by the poor and respected by the rich—I refer to Madame Husson, whom I should like to thank on behalf of the whole locality—who first thought of a happy and most philanthropic scheme for instituting an award which would honour virtue and be an inestimable spur to each and all who live in this beautiful Borough of ours.

Young man, you are the first recipient of this award, the founding laureate of a dynasty of temperance and decency. Your name will forever figure at the head of the roll of merit. But mark: the whole of your life to come must be worthy of this auspicious beginning. Today, as you stand before the gracious Lady who rewards your conduct, before the citizen-soldiers who have paraded under arms to do you honour, before this fervent throng here gathered to applaud you, or rather to applaud Virtue in your person, you offer a solemn pledge to the whole town, to each and every one of us, that you will remain true, until the day you die, to the magnificent promise of your youth.

Never forget, young man: you are the first seed scattered in the field of hope. May you bring forth the fruits which we expect of you!

'The Mayor took three steps forward, flung open his arms, and clasped the sobbing Isidore to his bosom.

'The May King wept openly, though he could not have said why, from a tangle of emotions which included pride and a mixture of vague but not unpleasant feelings.

'Then into one hand the Mayor thrust a silk purse, from which came the clink of gold—500 francs' worth!—and into the other the post-office savings book. And then in a solemn voice he intoned: "Homage and glory and riches be to Virtue!"

'Captain Desbarres shouted: "Hear, hear!" The grenadiers cheered. The crowd applauded.

'Madame Husson wiped a tear from her eye.

'Then they sat down round the table on which the banquet was spread.

'It was an interminable and sumptuous affair. Course followed course. Tawny cider and red wine waited shoulder to fraternal shoulder in their glasses before joining forces in stomachs. The rattle of plates, the sound of voices, and the muted notes of the band formed a steady, deep-throated buzz which rose and scattered into the air, where swallows swooped. From time to time, Madame Husson straightened her black silk wig, which kept slipping over one ear, and chatted with Abbé Malou. The Mayor talked politics excitedly to Captain Desbarres. Meanwhile, Isidore ate and Isidore drank as he had never eaten and drunk before! He helped himself to everything and asked for more, conscious for the first time in his life of how sweet it is to feel the stomach fill with good things which, *en route*, have given such pleasure to the palate. He had discreetly unbuckled the belt of his trousers, which grew uncomfortably tight against the pressure of his swelling stomach. He did not say much and, feeling very conscious of the stains made by a few drops of wine he had spilled down his linen jacket, he stopped chewing from time to time and put his glass to his lips, keeping it there as long as possible, sipping, savouring the taste.

'Then it was time for the toasts, which were numerous and enthusiastically received. The shadows lengthened. They had been at table since midday. Already, delicate, milky-white wisps of mist hung in the valley, casting the light cloak of night over stream and meadow. The sun clipped the horizon. Cows lowed through the haze which shrouded distant pastures. Then it was all over and everyone began making their way back down into Gisors, no longer in good processional order but in straggling knots. Madame Husson had taken Isidore's arm and heaped much urgent and excellent advice on his head.

'They halted outside the greengrocer's and left the May King at his mother's.

'She was not back yet. She had been invited by her family to share the celebrations of her son's triumph and had gone to lunch at her sister's after following the procession all the way to the marquee.

'And so Isidore was left by himself in the shop in the gathering dusk.

'Flushed with wine and pride, he sat down on a chair and looked around him. In the closed space, the carrots, cabbages, and onions exuded a strong smell of vegetables, a pungent, earthy odour over which hovered a sweet, pervasive tang of strawberries and the faint, elusive fragrance of a basket of peaches.

'The May King reached for one and ate it greedily, though his stomach was as swollen as a ripe pumpkin. Then all at once, wildly elated, he began to dance. Something jingled in his coat.

'In surprise, he thrust both hands into his pockets and brought out the purse containing the 500 francs, which in his drunken state he had forgotten. Five hundred francs! A fortune! He poured the coins on to the counter and spread them out with a slow, caressing movement of the open palm of his left hand so that he could see them all together. There were twenty-five of them, twenty-five round discs of gold: gold! Against the wood, they showed up bright in the deepening gloom, and he counted them over and over, placing a finger on each one, muttering: "One, two, three, four, five . . . a hundred; six, seven, eight, nine, ten . . . two hundred." Then he put them back into the purse and returned it to his pocket.

'Who can know, who can tell what awesome struggle took place in the May King's soul between good and evil, how violent the attack launched by Satan, what lures and temptations he threw against this meek and virgin heart? What enticements, visions, and covetous desires did the Evil One invent to charm Virtue's Elect and set him on the road to perdition? The chosen of Madame Husson picked up his hat, the hat which still sported its sprig of orange-blossom, and leaving by the alley at the back of the house, he disappeared into the night.

'Virginie, the greengrocer, informed that her son had gone home, went back to the shop, which she found deserted. Not unduly concerned at first, she waited. But after a quarter of an hour, she made enquiries. Her neighbours in the rue Dauphine had seen Isidore come home but had not seen him go out again. They went looking for him but found nothing. Virginie, who now began to worry, rushed off to the Town Hall. The Mayor could tell her nothing beyond the fact that he had left the May King outside his front door. Madame Husson had just retired to bed when she was told that her protégé had disappeared. She immediately put her wig on, got up again and called in person on Virginie. Virginie, who, like all uneducated souls, had little control over her emotions, sat crying her eyes out in the midst of her cabbages, carrots, and onions.

'The fear was that there had been an accident. But what? Captain Desbarres alerted the police, who organized patrols all around the town. On the road to Pontoise, they found the little sprig of orange-blossom. It was placed on the table around which the authorities were debating what to do next. The May

King must have been the victim of a trick, some organized plot prompted by jealousy. But how had it been done? What means had been used to spirit the innocent lad away? And why?

'Wearying of their fruitless search, the authorities went to bed, leaving a tearful Virginie to keep watch alone.

'And then, the next evening, when the Paris coach got in on its return journey from Paris, the whole of Gisors was astounded to learn that its May King had stopped the driver two hundred metres outside town, had paid his fare with a golden louis, pocketed the change, and got out as cool as a cucumber in the centre of the city.

'Feeling ran high throughout the area. Letters were exchanged between the Mayor and the Chief of the Paris police, but the outcome was negative.

'Day followed day. A week went by.

'Then one morning, Doctor Barbesol, who was up and about early, observed a man in dirty grey clothes sitting in a doorway sleeping, with his head against the wall. He went over to him and saw that it was Isidore. He tried to wake him but failed. The sometime May King was asleep, deeply, solidly, worryingly asleep and the astounded Doctor went off to fetch help to carry the young man to Boncheval's, the chemist's. When they lifted him, he was observed to be lying on an empty bottle. The Doctor sniffed it and declared that it had contained brandy. It was a useful clue to what sort of treatment was required. It was given and proved successful. Isidore was drunk, drunk and dazed by a week of solid drinking, so drunk and so revoltingly filthy that no self-respecting dustman would have gone near him. His lovely white suit had become a dirty-yellow, greasy, mud-spattered rag, torn and quite disgusting, and his person reeked of the sewers, the gutter, and Vice.

'He was cleaned up, given a good talking to, and told to stay at home. He did not go out for four days. He seemed ashamed and truly repentant. The purse with the 500 francs had not been found on him, nor the savings book, nor even the silver watch, a sacred heirloom, which had been left to him by his father the grocer.

'On day five, he ventured out into the rue Dauphine. Inquisitive eyes watched him and he walked past the houses in the street with head bowed and gaze averted. He disappeared from view where the road leaves town and dips down into the valley. But two hours later he reappeared, laughing raucously and cannoning into walls. He was drunk, dead drunk.

'He proved to be quite incorrigible.

'Thrown out by his mother, he became a carter and drove waggons for the firm of Pougrisel, which is still in existence to this day.

'He became well known as an old soak and his fame spread far and wide. Even in Évreux, people talked about Madame Husson's May King, and ever since then drunks hereabouts have never been called anything else.

'A good deed never goes unsung in a naughty world.'

Doctor Marambot rubbed his hands together as he finished his story. I asked:

'Did you know the May King yourself?'

'Oh yes. I had the honour of closing his eyes.'

'What did he die of?'

'An attack of the DTs, what else?'

We were now quite near the old fortress, a pile of ruined walls above which rise the huge Tower of Saint Thomas of Canterbury and the so-called Prisoner's Keep.

Marambot told me the story of the prisoner who, using only a nail, had covered every inch of the walls of his cell with carvings by following the movement of the sunlight as it filtered through the narrow slit of a loophole.

I learnt that Clotaire II had given his patrimony of Gisors to his cousin Saint Romain, Bishop of Rouen; that Gisors ceased to be the capital of all Vexin after the Treaty of Saint-Clair-sur-Epte; that the town is the most crucial strategic point in this part of France and that, because of this natural advantage, it has been taken and retaken many, many times. On the orders of William Rufus, the celebrated engineer Robert de Bellesme built a mighty fortress here which was later besieged by Louis the Fat and subsequently by the Norman barons; defended by Robert de Candos; surrendered by Geoffrey Plantagenet to Louis the Fat; retaken by the English through the treachery of the Templars; fought over by Philippe-Auguste and Richard the

Lion-Heart; burned by Edward III of England; recaptured by the English in 1429; restored at a later date to Charles VII by Richard de Marbury; seized by the Duke of Calabria; occupied by the League; used by Henri IV as a royal palace . . . and so on and so forth.*

Marambot, with great conviction and something approaching eloquence, repeated:

'A nasty piece of work, the English! And hard drinkers with it! They're all May Kings and hypocrites the lot of 'em!'

Then, after a pause, he gestured with his arm to the gleaming thread of the river which wound through the meadows:

'Did you know Henry Monnier* was one of the most assiduous anglers ever to adorn the banks of the Epte?'

'No, I didn't.'

'And Bouffé,* old man, Bouffé made stained glass here.'

'You don't say!'

'But I do. I can't think how you don't know these things.'

Hautot and Son

I

The house, half farm, half manor, was one of those country piles of mixed character which once upon a time were almost semi-feudal manors and nowadays are occupied by wealthy farmers. Outside the main entrance, the dogs, chained to the apple-trees in the forecourt, barked and howled when they saw game-bags slung round the necks of the gamekeeper and the inevitable gang of small boys. In the large kitchen-cum-dining-room, Hautot senior, Hautot's son, the inspector of taxes, Monsieur Bermont, and Monsieur Mondaru, the lawyer, were having a bite to eat and a drop to drink before they set out, for it was the first day of the hunting-season.

Hautot senior, proud of his possessions, was already boasting of the game his guests would find on his estate. He was one of those big, strong Norman types, brick-faced and raw-boned, who can lift a cartload of apples on their shoulders. Half peasant, half squire, rich, respected, influential, and autocratic, he had made his son, César, stay in school until he was fourteen to ensure he got an education, and then had taken him away in case he grew up to be a gentleman with no interest in the land.

César Hautot, almost as tall as his father but more slightly built, was a good son, submissive, contented, and full of admiration, respect, and regard for the wishes and opinions of Hautot senior.

Monsieur Bermont, the tax-inspector, was short and fat. His scarlet cheeks were mottled with delicate networks of purple veins, which showed up like the tributaries and winding courses of the rivers marked on maps in an atlas. He asked:

'What about hares—got any hares?'

Hautot senior replied:

'There are hares a-plenty, especially in the Dips around Le Puisatier.'

'Where will we make a start?' asked the lawyer, a high-living, fleshy, pale-faced man, also on the portly side, who bulged in a hunting-outfit too small for him which he had bought the previous week in Rouen.

'That's where we'll start, in the Dips. We'll drive the partridge down on to open ground and bag 'em from above.'

Hautot senior stood up. They all followed suit, fetched their guns, which stood in the corners of the room, inspected the firing-pins, stamped their feet to work them into their boots, which were rather stiff and not yet softened by their natural body heat. Then they went outside. The dogs, on hind legs, straining at the end of their chains, yelped and whined and beat the air with their front paws.

They set off for the Dips, a shallow valley, or, to be more accurate, a gently undulating stretch of scrub-land which had never been farmed because of the poorness of the soil. It was pitted by gullies and covered with bracken, and provided excellent cover for game.

The hunters spaced themselves out, Hautot senior on the right, his son on the left, and the two guests in the centre of the line. The gamekeeper and the boys with the game-bags brought up the rear. It was that solemn moment before the first shot when hearts beat a little faster and nervous fingers close constantly on triggers.

Suddenly, the long-awaited shot cracked out! Hautot senior had fired. They all halted and saw a partridge peel away from a covey which was making off at top speed and fall into a gully covered in thick undergrowth. The jubilant hunter ran towards it in leaps and bounds, tore through the brambles in his path until he too disappeared into the bushes in search of his bird.

Almost at once there was a second shot.

'The sly old devil!' cried Monsieur Bermont. 'Sounds as if he's disturbed a hare under all that lot.'

They all waited expectantly, their eyes glued on the impenetrable tangle of vegetation.

Cupping his hands round his mouth like a loudhailer, the lawyer yelled: 'Did you get them?' When Hautot senior did not answer, César turned to the gamekeeper and said: 'Go and give him a hand, Joseph. We've got to keep in line. We'll wait here.'

Joseph, a wiry old man, as gnarled as a tree-trunk, with swollen, knobbly joints, walked off quietly and climbed down into the gully, picking his way through the dense undergrowth as carefully as a fox. All of a sudden he shouted:

'Quick! Come 'ere! Looks like there's bin an accident!'

They all ran forward and plunged into the brambles. Hautot was lying unconscious on his side, holding his abdomen with both hands. Through the cloth of his jacket where the shot had torn a hole, long skeins of blood ran on to the grass. Letting go of his gun as he reached for the partridge, which was within arm's reach, he had dropped it. The shock of the fall had discharged the second barrel which had caught him in the stomach. They pulled him out of the gully, removed his clothes, and uncovered an appalling wound, through which his intestines bubbled out. After bandaging him up as best they could, they carried him home and waited for the doctor, who had been sent for, and a priest.

When the doctor arrived, he shook his head gravely and, turning to the son who sat sobbing on a chair, said:

'I'm sorry, my boy, it looks pretty bad.'

But when the doctor had finished dressing the wound, the patient moved his fingers, opened his mouth and then his eyes. He stared straight in front of him, looking vacant and confused, as though sifting through his memory to recall and understand what had happened. Then he murmured:

'Damn! I'm done for!'

The doctor held his hand:

'Rubbish! A couple of days in bed and you'll be right as rain.'

But Hautot went on:

'Done for. Guts shot to pieces. I know.'

Then with urgency in his voice, he said:

'I want to talk with my boy, if there's time.'

Despite himself, young Hautot wept and repeated over and over like a little boy:

'Dad! Oh dad! Poor dad!'

But his father's voice grew stronger:

'Stop snivelling . . . not the time for it. I got to talk to you. Come here, closer, won't take long, then I'll be easy in my mind. The rest of you, leave us please, just for a moment.'

They trooped out, leaving the son alone with his father.

When they were alone, Hautot said:

'Listen, son, you're twenty-four now, old enough to be told certain matters, though come to think of it these things don't warrant all the fuss people make over them. As you know, your mother's been dead these seven years, that's right, and I'm no more than forty-five, because I married when I was nineteen. That's right, isn't it?'

Young Hautot stammered:

'Right enough.'

'So your mother's been dead for seven years and I never married again. Well now, I'm not the kind to remain much of a widower at thirty-seven. Isn't that so?'

The son replied: 'True.'

Hautot, breathing hard, very pale, and his face contorted, went on:

'God, it hurts! Anyway, you appreciate that man was not made to live alone. But I could never bring myself to find someone to take your mother's place. I'd promised her I wouldn't. So . . . you understand, don't you?'

'Yes, dad.'

'So I found myself a girl in Rouen, 18 rue de l'Éperlan,* third floor, second door—I'm telling you all this so you don't forget—a nice lass who was very good to me, affectionate, faithful, a real wife to me. Got the picture?'

'I'm with you.'

'So if I don't make it, I reckon I owe her something, something substantial so she won't ever have to worry about money. Do you follow me?'

'Yes, dad.'

'I tell you she's a fine girl, a real good girl. If it hadn't been for you and your mother's memory, but also because the three of us all lived in this house together, I'd have brought her here and married her for sure . . . Listen . . . listen, boy . . . I could have made a will . . . but I didn't. I didn't want to . . . there

are some things, things like this, that oughtn't to be put in
writing . . . it makes things too hard for the family . . . anyway
it creates all sorts of difficulties . . . messes everything up . . .
creates havoc for everybody! Steer clear of lawyers' papers,
see? Don't have anything to do with them. If I've ended up a
rich man it's because I've always avoided them like the plague.
Are you with me?'

'Yes, dad.'

'There's something else . . . Pay attention . . . You see now
why I never made a will . . . Never wanted to . . . besides, I
know you. You're a good lad, you're not always thinking about
money, not greedy, right? I promised myself I'd make a clean
breast of it when my time came, and ask you to remember the
girl: Caroline Donet, 18 rue de l'Éperlan, third floor, second
door, don't forget. Are you listening? Go there the moment
I pass on . . . and see that she has no reason to regret my
memory . . . You'll have the wherewithal . . . you can afford
it . . . I'll be leaving you plenty . . . Listen, you can't reach her
most weekdays, she works for Madame Moreau in the rue
Beauvoisine. Go on a Thursday. That's when she expects me.
Thursday has been my day for the last six years. Poor lass,
she'll be really upset! . . . I'm telling you all this, son, because
I know you. There are some things you can't tell everybody,
lawyers and priests and the like. But people do them, everyone
knows that, but nobody talks about them. Except when it can't
be helped. So no outsiders in the know, just family, because
families all pull together, see?'

'Yes, dad.'

'Promise?'

'Yes, dad.'

'Swear?'

'Of course, dad.'

'Please, son, I'm asking you, don't forget. It means so much
to me.'

'I won't forget, dad.'

'Go yourself. I want you to take care of everything personally.'

'Yes, dad.'

'That way you'll see . . . you'll see . . . But she'll explain it
all. I can't tell you any more. So on your honour . . . ?'

'Yes, dad.'

'Thanks, son. Now kiss me. Goodbye. My number's up. I can feel it. Tell them they can come in now.'

Young Hautot embraced his father tearfully. Then, as submissive as ever, opened the door, and the priest, in a white surplice, came in, bearing the holy oils.

But the dying man had closed his eyes and would not open them. He would not answer nor would he give any sign that he understood what was going on.

He had talked a great deal and his strength was gone. Besides, he felt his heart lie easy now and wanted to be left alone to die in peace. What need was there to confess to one of God's earthly representatives since he had already made a full confession to his son, who, after all, was family?

Surrounded by friends and farm-hands kneeling at his bedside, he was given the last rites, was purified and absolved. No flicker or movement in his face gave any indication that he was still alive.

He died around midnight, after four hours of convulsive spasms suggestive of atrocious suffering.

II

He was buried on the Tuesday following the Sunday which had marked the start of the hunting-season. When he returned home after laying his father to rest in the cemetery, César Hautot spent the rest of the day in tears. He hardly slept that night and when he woke felt so depressed that he wondered how he could go on living.

All day, however, until night fell, he kept thinking that to obey his father's last wishes, he would have to go to Rouen the next morning and see the girl, this Caroline Donet who lived at 18 rue de l'Éperlan, third floor, second door. So that he would not forget, he said her name and address to himself over and over again, the way some people mutter a prayer, till in the end he was mumbling them compulsively, quite unable to stop or to think of anything else except these words, which kept running round inside his head.

So the following morning, about eight o'clock, he ordered Graindorge to be hitched to the trap and was borne away smartly by the thickset Norman horse along the main road which led from Ainville to Rouen. He had on his black coat and his tall top hat and was wearing his breeches with the stirrup-straps. In the circumstances, he decided it would be inappropriate to protect his best suit by putting on the loose blue overall which bellies out in the wind, preserves the clothes underneath from dust and dirt, and may be slipped off quickly on arrival, the instant the wearer jumps down from the driving-seat.

He drove into Rouen just as it was striking ten and pulled up as he always did outside the Hotel des Bons-Enfants in the rue des Trois-Mares. He had to endure the condolences of its proprietor, the proprietor's wife, and their five sons, for they had heard the sad news, and then was required to describe exactly how the accident had happened, which made him cry. He rejected the offers to help they heaped on him, for they knew he was now a rich man, and he even refused to accept their invitation to lunch, which ruffled their feathers.

He shook the dust off his hat, brushed his coat, and wiped his shoes before setting off in search of the rue de l'Éperlan. He did not dare ask anyone the way for fear of being recognized and awakening suspicions.

In the end, unable to find the street, he saw a priest and, trusting to the professional discretion of a man of the cloth, asked him.

It was only another hundred yards further on, the second turning on the right.

But then he hesitated. Thus far he had carried out the deceased's wishes like a faithful dog. Suddenly he felt thoroughly uncomfortable, embarrassed, and ashamed at the prospect of finding himself, the son, face to face with the woman who had been the mistress of his father. The strict principles ingrained in all of us by centuries of traditional moral training, which underpin our feelings and our desires, everything he had been taught since his catechism classes about loose women, the instinctive contempt in which they are held by men, even men who marry them, his blinkered country puritanism—all this now stirred within him, made him hold back, filled him with shame, and turned his shy cheeks scarlet.

But he thought: 'I made my father a promise. I mustn't go back on it.' So he pushed the half-open door to the house numbered 18, made out a dark staircase, went up three flights, saw one door and then a second, found a bell-pull and rang.

The tinkling of the bell inside the room made him jump. The door opened and he found himself face to face with a young woman who was well dressed, dark, and rosy-cheeked. She stared at him in surprise.

He did not know what to say to her, while she, ignorant of events and expecting his father, made no move to invite him in. They stood looking at each other for perhaps half a minute. In the end, she asked:

'Can I help you?'

He murmured: 'I am Hautot's son.'

She started, turned pale, and said falteringly, as though she had known him for years:

'Ah! You're César Hautot!'

'Yes.'

'And . . . ?'

'I've got a message for you. From my father.'

She said: 'Oh my God!' and then stepped back so that he could come in. He closed the door behind him and followed her inside.

He saw a little boy of four or five sitting on the floor, playing with a cat by a stove from which came the smell of food keeping hot.

'Sit down,' she said.

He sat.

She asked: 'Well . . . ?'

Not daring to speak, he kept his eyes fixed on the table in the middle of the floor, where three places had been laid, including one for the child. He stared at the chair with its back to the fire, the plate, napkin, the two glasses, the bottle of red wine which had been started, and the unopened bottle of white: that was where his father sat, with his back to the fire! They had been expecting him. That was his bread there next to the fork, he knew it was his, because the crust had been removed, for Hautot's teeth had been bad. Then he glanced up and, on the wall, saw the large photograph taken in Paris in the year of the Great Exhibition:* the same photograph hung on a nail above the bed in his father's bedroom at Ainville.

The young woman said again:

'Well, Monsieur César?'

He looked at her. Anxiety had taken the colour from her cheeks and she waited, her hands shaking with fear.

Then he gathered his courage.

'Fact is, dad died on Sunday. He was out shooting. Sunday was the start of the season.'

She was so shocked that she remained absolutely still. After a few moments' silence she said in an almost inaudible whisper:

'But . . . it can't be!'

Then suddenly tears brimmed in her eyes. She covered her face with her hands and began to sob.

The little boy looked up and, seeing his mother crying, began to wail. Sensing that this strange man was responsible for making her sad, he rushed at César, grabbed his trousers in one hand and with the other thumped his leg as hard as he could. Bewildered and deeply moved, César went on sitting there, between the woman who was grieving for his father and the boy who was protecting his mother. Their grief was contagious and he felt his eyes prick with tears. To regain his self-possession, he began to talk.

'Yes,' he said, 'it happened on Sunday morning, about eight o'clock . . .' And he proceeded to tell her everything, as though she were capable of listening. He left nothing out and included the most trivial details with typical peasant literal-mindedness. And all the while, the little boy went on thumping him, though now he was kicking him on the ankle.

When he got to the part where Hautot had talked about her, the woman caught her name and, dropping her hands, asked:

'I'm sorry, I wasn't following you and I want to know everything . . . So would you mind starting again?'

He began again, in the same terms: 'It happened on Sunday morning, about eight o'clock . . .'

He told her the whole story, at length, with pauses, occasionally emphasizing certain details and adding reflections of his own. She listened eagerly, visualizing with a woman's keen intuition every turn of events as he described them, recoiling in horror and exclaiming at intervals 'Oh my God!' The little boy, believing she was all right again now, had stopped hitting César and was holding his mother's hand. He listened too, as though understanding every word.

When his tale was told, César Hautot went on:

'And now the two of us have got to make arrangements so his wishes are respected. Listen, I'm not short of money. He left me well off. I wouldn't want you to have anything to complain about . . .'

She broke in quickly:

'Oh, please, please, not today! I'm too upset . . . Another time, some other day . . . But not now . . . If I accept anything, please understand it's not for myself . . . I swear. It would be for the boy. Anyhow, whatever's coming must be put in his name.'

Rocked to the core, César, guessing the truth, stammered:

'So . . . the boy is . . . his?'

'Why yes,' she said.

César Hautot stared at his half-brother with conflicting feelings as intense as they were painful.

After a long silence, for she had begun crying again, César, acutely embarrassed, went on:

'Well now, Mademoiselle Donet, I must be getting along. When would it be convenient for us to talk it over?'

She cried:

'No, don't go! You mustn't go! You can't leave me here with Émile all by myself! I'd die of grief. I haven't got anybody left now, nobody except my baby. Oh Monsieur César, it's awful, awful! Come on, sit down again. Talk to me some more. Tell me about what he used to do at home all week.'

César, who was used to obeying, sat down.

Pulling up another chair for herself, she sat next to him in front of the range where the pans still simmered, took Émile on her knee, and besieged César with questions about his father—ordinary, revealing little questions which made him feel instinctively that the poor young woman had loved Hautot with every fibre of her being.

Then, obeying his natural train of thought, which tended to run along the same tracks, he returned to the accident and began telling it all over again, supplying all the same details as before.

When he said: 'He had a hole in his stomach big enough for you to have got both hands into', she gave a little half-cry and once more tears welled up in her eyes. Her grief was infectious and César began crying too and, since tears always loosen the sinews of the heart, he leaned towards Émile, whose head was within reach of his mouth, and kissed him on the forehead.

The boy's mother, recovering her breath, murmured:

'Poor lad! He's got no father now.'

'Just like me,' said César.

After this, they fell silent.

But then the young woman's housewifely instinct, which requires her to rise to any occasion, suddenly reasserted itself.

'Have you had anything to eat since this morning, Monsieur César?'

'No, Mademoiselle.'

'Then you must be hungry. You must have something with us.'

'No thank you,' he said. 'I'm not hungry. I've been too upset.'

She said:

'Worry or no worry, life must go on. You mustn't say no. Anyway, you will stay a little longer, won't you? I don't know what I shall do when you're gone.'

He resisted for a while before giving in and, sitting down with his back to the fire, ate a plateful of the tripe that was crackling in the oven and drank a glass of red wine. But he would not let her open the white.

More than once he wiped the mouth of the little boy who dribbled gravy all over his chin.

As he was getting up to go, he asked:

'When would you like me to come back to talk about the business, Mademoiselle Donet?'

'If it's no inconvenience to yourself, Monsieur César, would next Thursday be all right? That way I won't have to take time off work. I always get Thursday off.'

'Next Thursday would suit me fine.'

'You will come for lunch, won't you?'

'Oh I don't know about that. I won't promise.'

'It's just that it's easier to talk when you're eating. And it'll give us more time too.'

'All right. I'll come at twelve o'clock.'

Then he left, but not before kissing little Émile again and shaking Mademoiselle Donet's hand.

III

It seemed a very long week to César Hautot. He had never been alone before and the solitude seemed unbearable. Until now, he had always stayed close to his father, like his shadow. He had gone out to the fields with him, had seen that his orders were carried out, and even if he spent a few hours away from him, always knew they would meet up again for dinner. Evenings they spent sitting smoking their pipes, discussing horses, cattle, or sheep. And the greeting they gave each other every morning was like a symbolic exchange of deep, family affection.

Now César was alone. He wandered aimlessly, watching the men ploughing the autumn fields, expecting at any moment to catch sight of the tall figure of his father waving his arms on the other side of a meadow. To kill time, he called on neighbours, telling the tale of the accident to anyone who had not heard it and sometimes telling it again to those who had. And when he had run out of things to do and things to think about, he would sit down by the side of the road and wonder if life would always be like this.

He often thought of Mademoiselle Donet. He had liked her. He thought her a very proper person, and every bit as kind and honest as his father had said. If there was ever a decent sort, then she most certainly was it. He was determined to act handsomely by her and made up his mind to make her an allowance of 2,000 francs a year, the capital to be settled on the boy. Indeed, he even felt a certain pleasure at the prospect of seeing her again on the following Thursday and making the arrangements with her. The thought of having a half-brother, this little five-year-old who was his father's son, disturbed and irritated him to some extent but it also filled him with a feeling of warmth. This unacknowledged youngster, though he would never bear the name of Hautot, was kin of sorts, a member of the family whom he could acknowledge or not as he thought fit, someone to remind him of his father.

And thus, as he set out for Rouen on Thursday morning, borne along by the rhythmic trot and ringing hooves of Graindorge, he felt more cheerful and more at peace than he had been at any time since the accident had happened.

When he entered Mademoiselle Donet's apartment, he saw that the table had been laid exactly as it had been the previous Thursday, the only difference being that the crust had not been cut off the bread.

He shook the young woman's hand, kissed Émile on both cheeks, and sat down feeling quite at home, although his heart was heavy. He thought Mademoiselle Donet looked thinner and paler. She must have wept a great deal. She now seemed awkward in his presence, as though she was now all too aware of what she had not felt the week before when she had been unsettled by her sudden loss, and she behaved with exaggerated politeness and, in the humility of grief, treated him with touching attentiveness, as though to repay with scrupulous solicitude the kindness he had shown her. They took their time over lunch, discussing the business which had brought him. She did not want so much money. It was too much, far too much. She earned enough to live on. All she wanted was for Émile to have something behind him when he grew up. César stuck to his guns and even threw in a gift of a thousand francs, for her, for her mourning-clothes.

When he had finished his coffee, she asked:

'Do you smoke?'

'Yes, I've got my pipe with me.'

He felt in his pocket. Hell and damnation! He had forgotten to bring it! He was on the point of lamenting its absence when

she offered him one of his father's pipes, which she produced
from a cupboard. He accepted and took it in his hand. He
recognized it, held it to his nose, said feelingly that it was a
very good pipe indeed, filled it with tobacco and lit it. Then he
put Émile astride his knee and played horses with him while
she cleared the table and put the dirty dishes in the bottom of
the dresser to wash when he had gone.

At about three o'clock, he got to his feet regretfully, feeling
quite sad at the thought of leaving.

'Well, Mademoiselle Donet,' he said, 'I must be saying
cheerio. It's been very nice seeing you again like this.'

She stood facing him, flushed and deeply moved. She looked
at him but was thinking of his father.

'Won't we be seeing each other again?' she said.

He answered simply:

'Of course we can. If you like.'

'I'd like that very much, Monsieur César. Shall we say next
Thursday? Would that suit?'

'That would suit me fine, Mademoiselle Donet.'

'You'll come for your lunch, won't you?'

'But . . . if you insist, I won't say no.'

'That's settled, then, Monsieur César. Next Thursday, twelve
o'clock, same as today.'

'Thursday, twelve o'clock it is, Mademoiselle Donet!'

The Grove of Olives

I

When the men of the tiny port of Garandou in Provence, on Pisca Bay, between Marseilles and Toulon, sighted the Abbé Vilbois's boat as he returned from fishing, they made their way down to the beach to help haul her ashore.

The Abbé was alone in the boat. He rowed like a born sailor, with rare vigour, remarkable in a man of fifty-eight. His sleeves were rolled up over a pair of muscular arms; his cassock was hitched up and firmly held between his knees, and the top buttons were undone, exposing his chest. His three-cornered priest's hat lay on the seat beside him, and on his head he wore an old pith-helmet covered in white cloth. He looked like one of those brawny, eccentric men of God, not uncommon in the tropics, who seem more cut out for action than for psalm-singing.

At intervals, he looked over his shoulder to check his bearing. Then he would ply his oars again, pulling with strong, practised, rhythmic strokes, to demonstrate yet again for the benefit of the clumsy sailors of the South how men rowed in the North.

With one last pull, the boat struck the shore, her momentum carrying her over the sand and, it seemed, likely to propel her clear up the beach, with her keel gouging a groove behind her. But she stopped dead, and the five men who had been watching the Abbé in stepped forward. They gave him a warm welcome, happy to see him back, for they liked their curé.

'Catch anything, Father?' said one of them in a strong Provençal accent.

The Abbé Vilbois shipped his oars, took off his sun-helmet and put on his clerical hat, rolled his sleeves down, buttoned

up his cassock, and then, once more wearing the trappings and
dignity of a village priest, he answered proudly:

'Oh yes, a decent haul! Three perch, two eels, and some
rock-fish.'

The five fishermen went alongside and, leaning over the
gunwhale, ran their expert eye over the dead fish—the fat
perch, the flat-headed eels, which looked like horrible sea-
snakes, and the rock-fish, which were purple with zigzag
markings the colour of orange-peel.

One said: 'I'll take 'em up to the lodge for you, Father.'

'Thanks. You're a good lad.'

After shaking them all by the hand, the curé went on his
way, accompanied by one of the men, leaving the others to see
to his boat.

He walked with long slow strides which gave him an air of
strength and authority. Still feeling hot after his hard spell at
the oars, he removed his hat at intervals as he passed through
the gentle shade of the olive trees, to allow the evening air,
still hot but a little cooler now in the light breeze blowing in off
the sea, to fan his wide forehead beneath his crop of short,
straight, white hair. It was more the brow of a soldier than of a
man of the cloth. The village came into sight, perched on an
outcrop in the middle of a broad valley which widened into a
plain and swept down to the sea.

It was one evening in July. The dazzling sun had almost
reached the scalloped tops of distant mountains and cast the
slanting, interminable shadow of the priest across the white
road which was buried under a shroud of dust. Over the fields
that lined it, his three-cornered hat, splayed and misshapen,
trailed a wide, black, playful lozenge which seemed to climb
up every olive trunk it encountered only to jump back down
again and scuttle away between the trees.

From under the Abbé Vilbois's feet rose a cloud of the
powdery dust, as soft and fine as flour, which covers the roads
of Provence in summer. It rose like smoke around his cassock,
coating it, hiding it under a layer of grey which grew whiter as
he walked. He went his way, feeling cooler now, his hands in
his pockets, with the measured, powerful tread of a mountaineer
climbing a slope. He gazed tranquilly at the village, his

village, where he had been curé for twenty years, the living he
had chosen and been given as a mark of great favour, the
village where he hoped to die. The church, his church,
rose out of the flat cone of houses huddling in its shadow, with
its two asymmetrical, square towers built of brown stone
standing up above this pleasant southern valley, their ancient
bulk seeming more like the bastions of a fortress than the bell-
towers of a House of God.

The Abbé was happy. He had caught three perch, two eels,
and a few rock-fish.

It was another little triumph and another one in the eye for
his parishioners who respected him chiefly because he was,
in spite of his age, the strongest man for miles around. These
harmless little vanities were his chief pleasure in life. He was a
crack shot with a pistol and could cut the stem of a flower with
a single bullet. Occasionally, he measured swords with the
tobacconist next door, who was an ex-regimental fencing-
instructor. And he was the best swimmer on the coast.

In fact, he was a man who had once cut quite a dash. He
was the Baron de Vilbois, who had been known in the smartest
circles as a leader of fashion. He had entered the church at the
age of thirty-two as the result of an unhappy love-affair.

Descended from an old Picardy family, staunchly royalist
and catholic, whose sons for centuries had gone into the army,
the law, and the church, he had initially listened to his mother
and seriously considered taking holy orders. But, at his father's
insistence, he decided instead to go to Paris, embark on a
course of legal studies and then later look for some sober
appointment in the law-courts of the capital.

But while he was finishing his studies, his father died
of pneumonia, caught during shooting-expeditions on the
marshes, and his mother, overcome by grief, followed shortly
after. Having unexpectedly come into a large fortune, he gave
up all thought of a career and settled for the leisured life of a
man of considerable means.

Handsome and intelligent, though with an outlook limited by
beliefs, traditions, and principles which were as inbred as the
muscles he had inherited from a long line of Picardy squires,
he was popular, made his mark in the best circles, and enjoyed

life as a somewhat straight-laced young man who was rich and respected.

And then, after seeing her several times at a friend's house, he fell in love with a young actress who, though one of the youngest pupils at the Conservatoire, had just made a highly successful début at the Odéon.*

He fell in love with her as violently and as completely as men do who are born with a temperamental weakness for absolute ideas. He fell in love and always saw her through the romantic role she had played so successfully the very first time she had performed in public.

She was pretty, temperamentally perverse, and had an expression of childish innocence which he called 'her angel face'. She found him easy game and had no difficulty in turning him into the kind of raving, demented, soulful lunatic who is doomed by the glance or skirt of a pretty woman to burn on the pyre of Mortal Passion. He made her his mistress, persuaded her to give up the stage, and for four years loved her with a love which never ceased to grow. There is no doubt that, his name and the tradition of family honour notwithstanding, he would have ended up marrying her, had he not discovered one day that she had been deceiving him for some considerable time with the same friend who had brought them together.

The blow was all the more shattering because she was then pregnant and because he was only waiting for the child to be born to make up his mind to marry her.

When he had tangible proof in the form of letters discovered in a drawer, he called her faithless, false, and despicable with all the brutishness of the semi-savage that he was.

But she was a child of the streets of Paris, as brazen as she was shameless, as sure of her hold over the other man as of him, and as fearless as any working-class girl who climbs the revolutionary barricades out of sheer bravado, and she defied him with insults. And when he raised his hand to strike her, she pointed to her belly.

He stopped and turned pale at the thought that a child of his, who would bear his name, was contained within the tainted flesh, the vile body of this repulsive creature. He leaped on her intending to crush the life out of both of them and thus erase his double shame. She tasted fear, for she sensed that he fully intended to kill her. As she was punched to the ground and saw his foot poised over her swollen stomach ready to stamp out the embryonic life within, she raised her arms to ward off the blow and screamed:

'Don't kill me! It's not yours, it's his!'

He recoiled so dumbfounded, so stunned that his rage hung suspended in mid-air, like his boot, and he spluttered:

'What did you say?'

Beside herself with fear at the murderous intent she saw written in his eyes and his terrifying gestures, she said again:

'It's not yours, it's his!'

Dazed, he whispered through clenched teeth:

'You mean the child?'

'Yes.'

'You're lying!'

And once more he raised his foot threateningly, as though he was about to stamp the life out of her. As he did so, his mistress got to her knees and tried to back away from him, still stammering:

'I tell you it's his! If it was yours, why haven't I had a baby long before this?'

This explanation struck him forcibly; it was self-evidently true. In one of those sudden flashes of insight when all arguments come together with blinding clarity, unambiguous, unanswerable, conclusive, and irrefutable, he was absolutely and utterly convinced that he could not be the father of the brat the slut carried inside her. Relieved of a great burden, absolved and suddenly almost at peace, he gave up all thought of killing the trollop.

In a calmer voice he said:

'Get up and go. I don't want to see you ever again.'

Crushed, she obeyed and went.

He never did see her again.

He too went away. He travelled down to the Midi, heading for the sun, and stopped in a village which stood on a hill in a valley on the Mediterranean coast. An inn there overlooking the sea caught his fancy. He took a room and stayed. He stayed for a year and a half, grieving, desperate, and com-

pletely alone. He lived there haunted by the memory of the
woman who had betrayed him, of her charm, her poisonous
coils, the infernal spell she had weaved about him, yet
yearning too for her presence and her touch.

He wandered through the valleys of Provence, beneath the
sun which filtered through the silver-grey leaves of the olive-
trees, his poor, sick mind still gripped by his obsession.

But old thoughts of God, the zeal of his youthful piety, now
less exalted, slowly revived in his unhappy, lonely heart.
Religion, which he had once considered to be a refuge against
life's uncertainties, now appeared to him as a safe haven for
those whom life has betrayed and tormented. He had not lost
the habit of prayer. Now, in his sorrow, he clung to it and often
at dusk went and knelt in the darkening church lit only by
the flame of the lamp on the altar, the sacred guardian of the
sanctuary and symbol of the Divine Presence.

He laid his troubles before God, his God, and poured out all
his woes. He asked for guidance, pity, help, protection, consolation, and his prayers growing more fervent with each passing
day, he invested them with growing emotional intensity.

His battered heart, consumed by love of a woman, did not
heal but beat on, crying still for affection. And little by little,
through the habit of prayer, by living the life of a hermit and
observing the outward form of his growing piety, by surrendering to the secret communion of saintly souls with the Saviour
who consoles and draws unhappy mortals to Himself, the
mystical love of God entered into him and drove out the carnal.

He resurrected his old plans and resolved to offer the
Church the life, now shattered, which in his youth he had
thought to give pure and without stain.

He became a priest. Through his family and contacts, he
obtained the living of the Provençal village to which fate had
guided his steps. He gave most of his fortune to charitable
causes and, keeping only enough to enable him to help and
succour the needy for as long as he lived, he settled down to a
life devoted to the tranquil duties of piety and the service of his
fellow men.

He was a priest with a literal mind but a kindly disposition,
a kind of religious guide with the outlook of a soldier who

forcibly kept faltering, blind, lost humanity on the straight but
narrow road which leads through the forest of life, where all our
instincts, preferences, and desires are so many paths to lead us
into temptation. But much of the man he used to be still
remained alive within him. He never lost his love of physical
exercise or the taste for the sport of gentlemen, especially
shooting and fencing. He hated women, all women, with the
same fear of danger a child has of the unknown.

II

The fisherman who was walking just behind the priest, being a
man of the garrulous Midi, felt his tongue itch with the urge to
talk. But he did not dare, for the Abbé kept his flock in awe of
him. But in the end, he took the plunge:

'Settled in all right at the lodge, then, have you Father?' he
said.

This 'lodge' was one of those shacks in the country, usually
no bigger than dog-kennels, where people from the towns and
villages of Provence go in summer in search of a breath of air.
The one the Abbé had taken was in a field, not five minutes'
walk from the presbytery, which stood next to the church in
the centre of the parish and was much too cramped and
overlooked.

He did not live outside the village all the time, not even in
summer. He merely went there now and then for a few days, to
be amongst fields and trees and to keep his eye in with his
pistol.

'Oh yes,' said the Priest. 'I'm very comfortable there.'

The low-roofed house came into view among the trees, the
pink of its walls streaked, cross-hatched, lacerated by the
leaves and branches of the intervening olives which grew in an
unfenced grove: it looked as if it had sprouted there by itself,
like a Provençal mushroom.

They could also make out the tall figure of a woman moving
to and fro in front of the door, in the process of laying a place
for one on a small dining-table, making separate journeys with
a plate, a napkin, a piece of bread, and a glass. She was

wearing an Arlésienne cap: a pointed, black cone made of silk or velvet topped by a gleaming mushroom of white material.

When the Abbé was within earshot, he called:

'Hello, Marguerite!'

She stopped to see who it was, then recognizing him said:

'You back already, Father?'

'Yes, and I've brought you quite a catch. Stop what you're doing and grill me a perch, in butter, just in butter, mind.'

The servant who had come to meet the two men inspected the fish, which the sailor was holding, with an expert eye.

'But I've already cooked a chicken and rice.'

'Can't be helped. The fish you eat tomorrow doesn't compare with fresh fish caught today. I'm going to have a little treat. It doesn't happen very often. Anyway, as sins go it's only a small one.'

Marguerite picked out a perch and as she was going off with it, she turned and said:

'A man was here looking for you, Father. He came three times.'

He asked absently:

'A man? What sort of man?'

'To tell the truth, I didn't much care for the look of him.'

'What do you mean? Was he a beggar?'

'Perhaps he was. I don't say he wasn't. But I'd say he was more your hedge-creeper sort.'

The Abbé Vilbois laughed at this old country word for a bad lot, a light-fingered tramp, for he knew Marguerite was nervous by disposition and could not stay at the lodge for long without imagining all day and every day—and especially all night—that they were about to be murdered.

He gave the sailor something for his trouble and the man went away. Then just as he was saying: 'I'm going to wash my face and hands', for he had never abandoned his habits of neatness and cleanliness from the old days, Marguerite shouted to him from the kitchen, where she was scraping the back of the perch against the grain with a knife which brought off the blood-flecked scales like tiny silver coins:

'He's come back!'

The Abbé turned towards the road and saw a man, who from a distance looked down-at-heel, making his way slowly towards the house. He stood and waited for him, still smiling at his servant's fears and thinking: 'Upon my word! She was right. He's a hedge-creeper if ever I saw one.'

The man came nearer, with his hands in his pockets and his eyes fixed on the priest. He seemed in no hurry. He was young and had a full, blond, curly beard. Twists of hair poked out from under a soft felt hat which was so dirty and battered that no one could have said what colour and shape it had once been. He was wearing a long brown overcoat and his trousers were ragged round the bottoms. On his feet he had a pair of rope sandals which gave him the stealthy, noiseless, disquieting, padded tread of a prowler.

When he got to within a few paces of the priest, he removed the wide-brimmed ruin that shaded his eyes, with a somewhat theatrical gesture, revealing a wasted, dissolute, but handsome face. On the crown of his head was a bald patch, the result perhaps of premature ageing or a misspent youth,* for he could not have been more than twenty-five.

The priest also removed his hat at once, sensing as much as deducing that here was no ordinary tramp, no labouring man looking for work, no jailbird just out of one prison and heading for the next and incapable of speaking in anything but the cant of thieves.

'Good day to you, Father,' said the man. The priest gave a curt 'Good day' in reply, reluctant to encourage this ragged, suspicious-looking stranger. The two men stared at each other and, caught in the prowler's scrutiny, the Abbé Vilbois felt uncomfortable and apprehensive, as though he were suddenly face to face with an unknown enemy. He was aware of a vague uneasiness, the kind of disquiet which can stop the breath and make the blood run cold.

After a while the tramp went on:

'Well? Don't you recognize me?'

Taken aback, the priest said:

'Certainly not! I have no idea who you are.'

'So you don't know who I am. Take another look at me.'

'It's no good me looking at you. I never saw you before in my life.'

'Now that's quite true,' said the tramp ironically. 'But I'll show you someone you do know.'

He replaced his hat and unbuttoned his overcoat. Under it, he was bare-chested. A red sash wound round his skinny waist held his trousers up on his hips.

From his pocket he produced an envelope, one of those unlikely envelopes, utterly filthy and stained, which tramps and vagabonds always keep tucked in the lining of their coats to hold their papers, which, authentic or forged, stolen or legal, are the precious guarantors of their liberty in any chance encounter with the police. Out of it he took a photograph, in the letter format which used to be so common. It was brown with age, bent and cracked with much handling, and, having been carried for so long next to his skin, had faded in the heat of his body.

Holding it up next to his face, he asked:

'Do you know who this is?'

The Abbé took two paces forward to get a clearer view and turned pale, rooted to the spot, for it was a photograph of himself which he had had taken for Her in those dim and distant days when he had been in love.

He did not answer, completely at a loss for anything to say.

The tramp repeated: 'Do you know who this is?'

The priest stammered: 'Of course.'

'Who is it?'

'It's me.'

'Are you sure?'

'Of course.'

'Well cop a look at the two of us, the photo and me.'

But the crestfallen Abbé had already looked and he had seen that the two men, the one in the photograph and the grinning tramp standing before him, were as alike as two brothers. But he still could not understand. He stuttered:

'What do you want with me?'

The tramp said with a leer: 'I'll tell you what I want. For a start, I want you to say you know me.'

'But who are you?'

'What am I, more's the point? Ask the first person who comes along. Ask your housekeeper! We'll go down the village and ask the mayor if you like: we'll show him this! He'll have a good laugh, I promise you. So you won't admit that I'm your son, then, Father? Or should I say Pa?'

The old priest raised both arms in a despairing, biblical gesture and moaned:

'It's not true!'

The young man came up very close and stood there, face to face:

'So it's not true, is it? But you're a priest! You got to stop telling lies, see?'

The expression on his face was threatening and his fists were clenched. He spoke with such vehemence and conviction that the Abbé, backing away from him, wondered which of the two of them was making the mistake.

But again he insisted:

'I never had a son.'

The other retorted: 'I don't suppose you ever had a mistress neither?'

Resolutely, the old priest gave his answer, a dignified admission:

'I did.'

'And was this mistress going to have a baby when you booted her out?'

Suddenly all the old anger which had been suppressed twenty-five years before, or rather not suppressed but entombed deep in his lover's heart, now burst through the canopy of faith, pious resignation, and renunciation which the Abbé had raised over it, and, beside himself with fury, he shouted:

'I turned her out because she had deceived me and was carrying another man's child. Otherwise, I'd have killed her and you too.'

Taken aback in turn by the strength of the Abbé's outburst, the young man hesitated before continuing in a more subdued tone:

'Who was it told you that the child was somebody else's?'

'She did, she told me. She defied me.'

Without challenging this statement, the tramp gave a casual shrug, the typical lout's way of settling an argument:

'I reckon Ma must have got it wrong when she was having it out with you, that's the top and bottom of it.'

Pulling himself together after his outburst, the Abbé in turn now started asking questions:

'And who told you that you were my son?'

'She did, just before she died, Father. And of course there was this.'

He held the little photograph under the Abbé's nose.

The Abbé took it. Slowly, lingeringly, and with an ache in his heart, he compared this unknown vagrant with the picture of himself as a young man and all his doubts vanished: this was indeed his son.

His whole being was filled with distress, with an inexpressible, appalling, bitter anguish which was like the feeling of remorse for a crime committed long ago. He understood some of it and guessed the rest. The savage quarrel which had led to their parting came back to him. The faithless, heartless woman had thrown this lie in his teeth to save her life, which was endangered by the man she had wronged. And the lie had worked. A son had been born to her and he had grown into this squalid little hedge-creeper who stank of vice the way goats reek of animal.

He murmured: 'Shall we take a little walk? We'd better talk this over.'

With a leer, the man said: 'Why not? That's what I came for.'

They walked together, side by side, through the grove of olives. The sun had set. The cool of the Provençal dusk spread over the land like a chill, invisible cloak. The Abbé shivered and, glancing up out of habit as though he were observing his congregation during holy service, he saw all round him the tiny silver-grey leaves, trembling between him and sky, of the sacred trees which once, in their dappled shade, had cradled Christ's greatest agony, His one moment of weakness.

A brief, despairing prayer suddenly surged within him, spoken by that inner voice which does not require lips to speak, the prayer of the true believer who turns to his Saviour: 'O Lord, help me!'

He turned to his son and said:

'So your mother is dead?'

A new sorrow swelled within him as he said those words: 'your mother is dead.' He felt the pain of it in his heart, the strange physical ache of a man who has never quite succeeded in forgetting what has been, a cruel echo of the torment he had suffered. But more than this too, since the woman was dead, he felt a stirring of the heady, brief joy of his youthful love, of which nothing now remained but the wound in his memory.

The young man replied:

'Yes, Father, my mother's dead.'

'Has she been dead long?'

'Yes, more than three years.'

A new doubt struck the priest:

'And how is it you didn't come looking for me sooner?'

The man hesitated:

'Can't rightly say. I got . . . prevented. But look, do you mind if I don't say any more now? I'll tell you the whole story later. I'll tell you everything you want to know. But the thing is I haven't had anything to eat since yesterday morning.'

The old priest felt a surge of pity and, holding out both hands, he said:

'Oh, my poor boy!'

The young man took the powerful outstretched hands and felt them close over his own slim, clammy, feverish fingers.

With the sardonic leer which was part of his fixed expression, he said:

'Well now, I think you and me are going to get along just fine.'

The Abbé started walking back to the house.

'Let's go and have a bite of supper,' he said.

Suddenly, he felt a spontaneous thrill of pleasure, which was both puzzling and odd, as he remembered the fish he had caught that very day. With the chicken and the rice, it would make a grand dinner for the poor lad.

The housekeeper, anxious and ready to grumble, was waiting by the door.

'Marguerite,' cried the Abbé, 'clear the table and take it inside. Quick as you can, now. And lay two places. And sharp about it.'

She was quite appalled by the thought that her curé intended to eat his supper with a criminal.

So the Abbé himself started removing the plates and cutlery which had been set out for him and began carrying them into the only downstairs room in the house.

Five minutes later, he was sitting opposite the vagrant in front of a tureen of cabbage soup. From it, into the space between the two men, rose a faint cloud of scalding steam.

III

When their plates were full, the prowler began to gulp down his soup in hurried, greedy spoonfuls. The Abbé did not feel hungry any more and was content to sip a little of the tasty cabbage broth slowly and left the bread where it was at the bottom of his plate.

All at once he said:

'What's your name?'

The man laughed, content now that his hunger was being satisfied:

'Never had no father,' he said, 'so I never had any other name than my Ma's, which I shouldn't think you've forgotten. Still, I got two Christian names, though they don't suit me at all: Philippe-Auguste.'

The Abbé turned pale and in a strangled voice asked:

'Why were you given those names?'

The tramp gave a shrug:

'Can't you guess? After she left you, Ma wanted the other man to think I was his. He believed it too till I was fifteen. But around that time I started looking a bit too much like you and the swine disowned me. So that's why I was given both his names, Philippe-Auguste. And if I'd been lucky enough not to look like anybody in particular or if I'd been the son of some other so-and-so who'd never shown his face, then today I'd have been known as Vicomte Philippe-Auguste de Pravallon, belatedly acknowledged as the son of the Count and Senator of the same name. Instead of which, I'm plain Unlucky Joe.'

'How do you know all this?'

'Because I was there when it all came out. Went at it hammer and tongs they did, believe me! It's that sort of thing that teaches you what life is really like.'

The priest felt oppressed by something more distressing, more painful than anything he had felt and suffered in the last half-hour. He was aware of a choking sensation welling up inside him which he knew would grow stronger and finally kill him, and it came not so much from what he heard but from the way it was said and from the way it sounded in the foul mouth of the dissolute good-for-nothing who told it. Between this man and himself, between his son and him, he began to sense a swamp of moral filth which is deadly poison to some people. Was this really his son? He still could not believe it. He wanted to hear the evidence, all of it. He wanted to know and hear everything, to listen and to suffer. Again he thought of the olive-trees which grew round the house and a second time he murmured: 'O Lord, help me!'

Philippe-Auguste had finished his soup. He asked:

'Is that it or is there any more grub?'

The kitchen was not in the house but in a built-on lean-to, and Marguerite could not hear the curé when he called. So the priest was in the habit of letting her know what he wanted by means of a Chinese gong hanging on the wall behind him.

He reached for the leather-bound hammer and struck the metal disc with it several times. It yielded a sound which started low, then grew louder and more insistent, and turned into the reverberating, piercing, high-pitched, harrowing, horrible screech of beaten brass.

The housekeeper appeared. She was scowling and stared furiously at the hedge-creeper as if somehow she had sensed, with the instinct of a faithful dog, the tragedy which had befallen her master. She was carrying the grilled perch, which exuded a mouth-watering smell of melted butter. The Abbé slit the fish from head to tail with a spoon and, giving the back portion to the son of his younger self, said, with a vestige of pride which had survived his distress:

'I caught it myself this afternoon.'

Marguerite made no move to leave.

The priest continued: 'Bring us some wine, some of that good Cap Corse white.'

For a moment it looked as though she were about to rebel and he was obliged to repeat sternly: 'Get along now, bring two bottles.' For when he offered anyone wine, a rare pleasure, he always stood himself a bottle too.

Philippe-Auguste beamed and said:

'Now you're talking! Good idea. I haven't had a feed like this for a long time.'

The housekeeper returned two minutes later. To the Abbé they seemed like two eternities, for he was now consumed by a burning need, as hot as hell-fire, to know.

The bottles were already opened but the housekeeper remained, with her eyes fixed on the man.

'Leave us,' said the curé.

She pretended that she had not heard.

A harsh note crept into his voice as he repeated:

'I said leave us.'

She went.

Philippe-Auguste was tearing voraciously into the fish. His father watched him, increasingly astounded and dismayed by the uncouth vulgarity writ large on this face which was so like his own. The morsels which the Abbé Vilbois raised to his lips remained in his mouth, for his constricted throat made it impossible for him to swallow. He chewed each mouthful over and over and meantime tried to discover which, of all the questions crowding into his mind, would give him the answer he wanted the most quickly.

At last he murmured:

'What did she die of?'

'Chest. TB.'

'Was she ill for long?'

'Eighteen months or so.'

'How did she catch it?'

'Dunno.'

They both fell silent. The Abbé was left with his thoughts. There were so many things preying on his mind that he would have liked to know long ago, for ever since the day they had gone their separate ways, the day he had almost killed her, he had never heard anything more of her. Of course, he had not wanted to hear anything more, for he had resolutely buried the memory of her and with it all recollection of the days of his happiness. But now that she was dead, he felt a burning need to know everything, a jealous need, a lover's need almost.

He went on:

'She wasn't alone, was she?'

'No. She was still living with him.'

The old priest gave a start:

'With him! With Pravallon?'

'Of course.'

The man who had once been betrayed calculated that the woman who had deceived him had remained with his rival for more than thirty years.

Almost in spite of himself he stammered:

'Were they happy together?'

The young man replied with a leer:

'Oh yes. Of course, they had their ups and downs. It would have worked out all right for them if it hadn't been for me. I always spoiled things.'

'How do you mean? Why?' said the priest.

'I already told you. Because he always thought I was his until I was fifteen or thereabouts. But the old man wasn't anybody's fool. He worked it out all by himself from the resemblance. And then there were scenes. I used to listen to them outside the door. He'd say she'd pulled the wool over his eyes. She'd say: "It's not my fault. When you took me on, you knew I'd been somebody else's mistress." The Someone Else was you.'

'So they used to talk about me sometimes?'

'Oh yes. But they never said your name when I was there till the end, right at the very end, the last few days really, when Ma realized her number was up. They didn't trust me.'

'And were you very young when you realized that your mother wasn't married?'

'Look, I'm not stupid! I wasn't born yesterday! Things like that, well, you get a sense of them once you start seeing how the world goes round.'

Philippe-Auguste kept filling his glass. His eyes grew bright. After going so long without eating, he was getting drunk quickly.

The priest noticed and nearly stopped him. But it struck him that the wine was loosening the young man's tongue and lowering his guard. He reached for the bottle and refilled his glass.

Marguerite brought the chicken and rice. She set it down on the table and again stared at the prowler. Then she turned to the priest and said indignantly:

'Look at him, Father, he's drunk.'

'Will you stop bothering us,' said the priest, 'and go away?'

She went out, slamming the door behind her.

He asked:

'What did your mother say about me?'

'The sort of thing women always say about men they've dumped. She said you was a nuisance, the sort that gets in a woman's way. She said you'd have made life very difficult for her with your ideas.'

'Did she say that often?'

'Yes, and sometimes in roundabout ways so's I wouldn't understand. But I always guessed.'

'And how were you treated at home?'

'Me? Fine to start with but later on it got rough. When Ma saw I was queering the pitch for her, she chucked me out.'

'Really?'

'Yes, really! It was quite simple. When I was sixteen, I got into a few scrapes, like. So the old buggers had me sent to a reformatory to get me out of the way.'

He leant his elbows on the table and cupped both cheeks in his hands. He was more than tipsy now and his brain was clouded by the wine. Suddenly he felt an irresistible urge to talk about himself, the way drunks always tell the most fantastic boastful lies about themselves.

He smiled a pretty smile. There was something feminine and graceful in the curve of his lips, a perverse charm which the priest recognized: he knew it of old. But more, he felt the power of its hateful, seductive spell, which had once been his downfall and his ruin. The son now looked more like his mother but the resemblance lay less in the cast of his features than in the winning but sly look in his eyes and especially in the captivating, hypocritical smile, which seemed like a door which opened only to release the vileness within.

Philippe-Auguste began talking:

'Oh yes, I've had a hell of a life ever since I got out of the reformatory, I can tell you. The sort of life some novelist would

pay good money for. Listen, even old Dumas in *Monte Cristo**
never dreamt up anything half as amazing as the things that
have happened to me.'

He paused with the ponderous gravity of the drunk who tries
to collect his thoughts. Then he went on slowly.

'If you want a kid to turn out well, you shouldn't send him to
reform school, see? No matter what he done. On account of the
other lads he comes up against inside. With me it was just a
lark that went wrong. One night, about nine o'clock, I was out
with three mates. We'd all had a bit to drink. We're walking
along the road just by the ferry at Folac when what do I see but
this coach with all the people in it, the driver and the rest of
the family, fast asleep. They were from Martinon and were on
their way home after eating out in town. I take the horse's
bridle, on to the ferry she goes, and then I shove the whole
thing out into the middle of the river. It made a noise. The old
boy with the reins wakes up, can't see a damn thing and cracks
his whip. Off goes the horse and falls in the drink, coach and
all. Drowned, the lot of them! My mates shopped me. At the
start, they laughed like drains when they saw what I was up to.
We never dreamt it would turn out like that. We thought they'd
just get a ducking, that's all. It would have been a laugh.

'After that I done a lot worse things to get my own back for
being put away for that first stunt, which I didn't deserve,
honest. I won't go into all them other stunts, they're not worth
bothering with. I'll just tell you about the last one because
you'll love it, you really will. I cleaned your slate for you, Pa!'

The Abbé stared at his son in horror. He had stopped eating.

Philippe-Auguste was about to continue.

'No,' said the priest. 'Not now. Wait a moment.'

Turning round, he beat the thundering Chinese gong.

Marguerite appeared immediately.

He spoke to her so roughly that she averted her eyes,
frightened into docility:

'Bring us the lamp and anything else you've got to put on the
table. When you've done that, don't come back unless you hear
the gong.'

She left the room, then returned with a lamp with a white
porcelain base and a green shade, which she set down on the

cloth together with a large wedge of cheese and a bowl of fruit.
Then she went away again.

Steeling himself, the Abbé said:

'Go on. I'm listening.'

Philippe-Auguste calmly filled his plate with cheese and
fruit and his glass with wine. The second bottle was almost
empty, though the curé had not touched it.

Then he took up his rambling story in a voice thick with food
and too much drink.

'Now that last stunt was something! I'd gone back home and
I stayed—though they didn't want me around because they
were scared of me. Scared rigid they were . . . ! Had to keep on
the right side of me. I can get very nasty if I'm crossed,
see? . . . Anyhow . . . they were living together and not together.
He had two places . . . a Senator's mansion and this little love-
nest. But he spent more time in Ma's than in his other house
because he couldn't do without her . . . Now Ma, she was
smart, she had what it takes! She knew how to keep her hooks
in a man! She had him body and soul and kept him that way till
the end. Men can be so stupid! Anyway, I'd come back and
ruled them with fear. I can take good care of myself if I got
to—I know all the angles and dodges and can use my fists an'
all, I ain't scared of anybody. Then Ma got sick and he sent
her off to this beautiful place near Meulan* with grounds all
round it the size of a forest. She was there about eighteen
months . . . like I told you. Then we realized the end was not
far off. He used to come down from Paris every day. He was
pretty cut up, he really was.

'Anyhow, one morning the pair of them had been jawing for
nearly an hour and I was beginning to wonder what they could
be going on about for so long when they called me in. Ma said:

' "I'm dying and there's something I want to tell you, though
the Count thinks I shouldn't"—she always called him "the
Count"—"it's your father's name. He's still alive." '

'Now I'd ask her hundred of times, thousands of times, what
his name was. Hundreds of times. And she'd always refused to
tell me . . . I think I even hit her one day to make her talk, but
it didn't do any good. To make me leave off, she told me you'd
died without leaving a penny. She said you were a bad lot, a

mistake she'd made when she was too young to know better, a maiden's folly, things like that. And she told it so well I fell for it and believed you was really dead.

'Anyway she said: ". . . your father's name."

'The Count was sitting in an armchair and suddenly he butts in. Three times he says:

' "You're wrong, wrong, wrong, Rosette."

'Ma sat up in bed. I can see her now, with those burning cheeks and bright eyes, for she was very fond of me, in spite of everything, and she said:

' "Then do something for him, Philippe!"

'When she talked to him, she said "Philippe" and I was "Auguste".

'He started shouting like a maniac:

' "For a worthless lout like him, never! Do something for a waster, a convicted felon, a . . . a . . ."

'And he called me everything under the sun, as though he'd spent his whole life just thinking up nasty names for me.

'I was starting to get riled but Ma told me to shut up. She told him:

' "Do you want him to starve? I have no money."

'The idea didn't bother him. He replied:

' "Rosette, I've been giving you 35,000 francs a year for thirty years. That's close on a million. Thanks to me, you have lived the life of a rich woman, a woman who has been truly loved and, dare I say, has been happy. I owe nothing to this good-for-nothing who has ruined our last years together. He won't get a penny from me. It's no good arguing. Tell him his father's name if you must. I think you're wrong, but I wash my hands of the whole business."

'Then Ma turns to me. I was thinking: "Right! So now I'm going to get to know who my real father is! And if he's in the money, I'm home and dry!"

'She went on: "Your father, the Baron de Vilbois, is now the Abbé Vilbois, the parish priest of Garandou near Toulon. I was his mistress until I left him for the Count."

'And then she tells me the whole story, only she left out the bit about how she led you up the garden path about who was the father. But that's women for you. They don't tell the truth.'

Blissfully unaware of the effect he was producing, he gave a leer into which all the viciousness of his nature was channelled. He took another drink and went on gleefully:

'Ma died two days . . . yes two days later. Him and me both walked behind the coffin all the way to the cemetery . . . funny thought, that: just him and me and three servants, that's all! He cried like a baby . . . And there we were, standing side by side, just like father and son.

'After we went back to the house. Just the two of us. I was thinking: "I'm going to have to scarper empty-handed." All I had was fifty francs. What could I do to get my own back?

'He took me by the arm and says: "I want a word with you."

'I followed him into his study. He sat down behind his desk and started snivelling. He said he wasn't going to be as hard on me as he told Ma he would. He asked me not to come bothering you—but that's something between just you and me. Then he fishes out this thousand-franc note and hands it over . . . a thousand . . . a measly thousand . . . What good's a thousand francs to the likes of me? I could see he had more notes in his drawer, a great wad of them. The sight of them made me go berserk. I stick out my hand for the note he was holding, but instead of taking his charity I jump him. He fell on the floor and I got him round the neck and squeezed till his eyes popped. When he was almost a goner, I gagged him and tied him up, undressed him, turned him over, and then . . . You was revenged good and proper, I can tell you!'

Philippe-Auguste spluttered and almost choked with glee. His lip did not lose its savage, jubilant curl, in which the Abbé recognized the familiar smile of the woman who once had goaded him beyond endurance.

'What happened then?' he asked.

'What happened then? . . . it was so funny! . . . There was this blazing fire in the grate . . . it was a December that Ma died, freezing cold it was . . . a big coal fire . . . I got the poker . . . put it in till it was red-hot . . . and I made crosses all over his back with it, eight maybe ten, I don't remember exactly how many . . . then I turned him over and done the same on his front. What a laugh, eh? That's the way they used to brand convicts in the old days. He wriggled like an eel but I had him gagged good and proper and he couldn't shout out. Then I took the wad of notes, there was twelve in there and with mine that made thirteen in all, and un unlucky number for me it turned out to be. Then I cleared off. I told the servants the Count was asleep and wasn't to be disturbed till dinner.

'I worked it out he'd keep his mouth shut on account of the scandal, him being a Senator and all. But I was wrong. Four days later, I was arrested in a restaurant. I got three years. That's why I didn't come looking for you before now.'

He took another drink. His speech was so thick now that he was hardly intelligible.

'So here we are . . . Pa . . . 'Ere, my Pa's a Father! That's a good'un! Seems funny having a priest for a dad . . . ! You gotter be nice to your little boy 'cos your little boy's special . . . and 'cos he put one across the old codger, didn't he? He really done him over!'

The same anger which had driven him to the point of madness when confronted by the treachery of his mistress long ago, now rose within him at the sight of this vile excuse for a man.

In the name of God, he had forgiven so many shameful secret sins whispered in the mystery of the confessional. Now in his own, he could feel no pity, no forgiveness. He could not bring himself to call upon the merciful Lord, the ever-present help in time of trouble, for he knew that in this life there is no help from God or man that can save those who have such misfortune visited upon them.

The fires of passion and violence which smouldered deep in his nature, damped down by his priestly calling, now burst into a flame of unquenchable revulsion against this lout who was his son, against his physical likeness to himself and to his despicable mother too, who had created him in her own image, against fate which had shackled him to a worthless wretch for a son, like a convict to a ball and chain.

He saw everything, knew what he had to do in a blinding flash of clarity, shocked out of the pious rest and religious peace in which he had slumbered for twenty-five years.

He knew instinctively that he must take a strong line to

make this scum afraid and strike terror into him with his
opening move. Grinding his teeth in rage and forgetting that
the man was quite drunk, he said:

'Now that you've told me everything, you can listen to me.
Tomorrow morning you will go away. You will live in a place of
my choosing and you will never leave it unless you have my
permission. I shall make you an allowance which will be
enough to live on. It won't be much for I have no money. If you
step out of line just once, this arrangement will be at an end
and you will have me to deal with . . .'

Although he was fuddled by wine, Philippe-Auguste understood the threat, and the criminal in him suddenly came to life.
Between the hiccoughs, he hissed:

'Don't try me, Pa! . . . You're a priest an' I got you where I
want you, see? . . . You'll toe the line, just like them others
had to!'

The Abbé bridled. He was old but his still-powerful muscles
ached to take hold of the monster, bend him like a sapling and
show him that he could not win.

He shook the table and, ramming it against the man's chest,
shouted:

'Be careful! Be good and careful . . . I'm not afraid of you or
anybody!'

Losing his balance, his son, very much the worse for drink,
swayed on his chair. Feeling himself about to fall and realizing
that he was in the priest's power, he stretched out his hand
and, with murder in his eyes, made a grab for one of the knives
on the table-cloth. The Abbé Vilbois saw the movement and
gave the table a heave so violent that his son fell over backwards and landed face up on the floor. The lamp rolled on to
the ground and went out.

For several seconds, the pleasant tinkle of glasses rattling
against each other filled the darkness. It was followed by the
muffled sound of a soft body dragging itself over the tiled floor.
Then everything went quiet.

When the lamp smashed, darkness had settled on the two
men so sudden, unexpected, and impenetrable, that they were
both as stunned as if there had been a dreadful accident.
Philippe-Auguste crouched against the wall and did not stir.

The priest remained in his chair in the blackness, which defused his anger. The dark veil of shadow which enveloped him not only stayed his arm but stilled the fury that raged in his heart. Instead, other thoughts filled his head, thoughts as black and grim as the surrounding gloom.

There was a silence, the oppressive silence of a closed tomb in which no life, no breath stirred. Nor was there any sound from outside, no rumble of distant cartwheels, no barking of dogs, not even the rustle of leaves on branches, the tapping of branches against a wall, or the faintest sigh of the wind.

The silence dragged on a long, long time, maybe an hour. Then suddenly, the gong sounded. Struck by a single hard, sharp, heavy blow, it growled and reverberated. Then there came the loud, puzzling noise of something falling and the sound of a chair being overturned.

Marguerite, who had been listening anxiously, now rushed to the room. But as she opened the door and saw the impenetrable blackness inside, she recoiled in terror. Shaking all over, her heart pounding and her breath coming in great gasps, she called in a whisper:

'Father? Father?'

No one answered. Nothing moved.

'Oh God! Oh God! What have they done? Whatever's happened?'

She did not dare go into the room or go back to fetch a light. She was gripped by a panic-stricken urge to run, to get away and scream, though her legs felt as if they were about to give way beneath her. She called again:

'Father? Father? It's me, Marguerite.'

But through her fear, she felt instinctively that she had to help her master and a surge of the courage which reckons the self as nought and on occasions can make women truly heroic suddenly made her foolhardy in her fear. She hurried away to her kitchen and returned with a lamp.

She paused on the threshold. First she saw the tramp lying against the wall asleep or apparently asleep. Next she made out the broken lamp, then, under the table, the black boots and the black-stockinged legs of the Abbé Vilbois who, falling over backwards, must have struck the gong with his head.

Quaking with fear, her hands trembling, she repeated:

'Dear God! Oh my God! Whatever has been going on here?'

She advanced slowly and hesitantly and then her foot slipped on something greasy and she very nearly fell.

Bending down, she saw, on the red tiles of the floor, a liquid, also red, which made a pool round her feet and spread towards the door in a steady flow. She guessed it was blood.

Mad with terror, she turned and fled, dropping the lamp, not wanting to see any more. She rushed out into the fields and made for the village. She ran, careering into trees, her eyes fixed on the distant lights, screaming.

Her shrill voice soared into the night like the ominous screech of an owl. Over and over she whooped: 'The tramp . . . the hedge-creeper . . . the hedge-creeper . . . !'

When she reached the first houses, startled men appeared and gathered round her. But she waved her arms and gesticulated without answering them, for she was too distraught to make sense.

Eventually, they gathered that something terrible had happened out at the Abbé's lodge and a group of men armed themselves to go to the rescue.

In the middle of the grove of olives, the little pink-washed house had turned black and fused completely into the impenetrable, silent dark of the night. Ever since the lamp glowing in the single lit window had gone out like an eye closing, it had remained sunk in the shadows, lost in the gloom, invisible to anyone who was not a native of the place.

Soon lights approached, skimming the ground, weaving through the trees, drawing nearer. They cast long, yellow pencils of light over the scorched grass. They flickered and bobbed and caught the twisted trunks of the olive trees, transforming them into monsters and coiled, writhing serpents from Hell. Then, fingered by the still distant lights, a faint, whitish shape loomed in the darkness and soon the low, square front of the little house turned pink in the gleam of the lanterns. They were carried by a handful of villagers who escorted two gendarmes, revolvers at the ready, the local gamekeeper, the Mayor, and Marguerite, who, on the verge of collapse, was being half-carried by some of the men.

When they reached the door, which still gaped wide and sinister, they paused uncertainly for a moment. Then the sergeant, taking one of the lanterns, entered resolutely and the others followed.

The servant had told the truth. Blood, already congealed, covered the floor like a carpet. It had spread as far as the tramp, soaking one of his legs and one hand.

Father and son were sleeping, one, with his throat cut, the sleep of the Lord, and the other the sleep of the drunk. The two gendarmes seized the tramp and before he was awake had the handcuffs on him. He rubbed his eyes stupidly, still sodden with drink. When he saw the body of the priest, he looked frightened out of his wits and seemed not to understand.

'Why didn't he run away?' said the Mayor.

'Too drunk,' said the sergeant.

They all agreed, it would never have occurred to anyone to think that the Abbé Vilbois might, just conceivably, have taken his own life.*

Who Can Tell?

I

Praise be! I have at long last decided to set down on paper what has been happening to me! But shall I be able to see it through? Have I the courage? The whole thing is too weird, too inexplicable, too incomprehensible and too crazy!

If I were not quite sure of what I've seen, not absolutely certain that there has been no error in my reasoning, no mistake in my findings, no gaps in the meticulous record of my observations, I should say I have simply been the victim of a hallucination, the plaything of some very unusual optical illusion, After all, who can tell?

I am currently staying in a clinic. But I came here voluntarily, as a precaution, because I was afraid! Only one person knows my story, the resident doctor. I shall now write it all down. Why I want to do this I don't exactly know. To get it out of my system, perhaps, for it weighs on me like some unbearable nightmare.

This is my story.

I've always been a loner, a dreamer, a solitary philosopher of sorts, charitably disposed, not asking much of life, bearing no ill will towards my fellow men and having no quarrel with God. I lived alone—I always have—because of a certain awkwardness which being with others induces in me. How can I explain it? I couldn't even begin. I do not go out of my way to avoid people, talking to them or dining with friends. But when I feel they have been around me for any length of time, even those I've known longest, they weary me, they exhaust me, they grate on my nerves, and I am aware of a growing, nagging urge to see them gone or to go myself and be alone.

This urge is now much more than a mild hankering: it has become an absolute imperative. If I had to spend much longer in the company of these same people, if I were forced not exactly to listen to them but rather to undergo any more of their conversation, it is quite likely that something might happen to me. What? Who can tell? Perhaps I should pass out under the strain? That's probably it!

I like being by myself so much that I cannot bear the idea of having other people around me, sleeping under the same roof. I can no longer live in Paris, because each day I spend there I die a little. I am dying inside. Feeling the vast crowds living, swarming around me even when they are sleeping, is to me physical and emotional torture. For me, knowing that other people are asleep is even more unbearable than hearing them speak. I cannot rest when on the other side of some bedroom wall I know that there are lives temporarily suspended by this regular eclipse of consciousness.

Why do I feel like this? Who can tell? Of course, there may be a simple explanation: I tire very quickly of anything that does not concern my inner life. And there are many like me.

The world is made up of two kinds of human beings. Those who need other people to divert attention from themselves, to keep them occupied and sane, because such people cannot cope with loneliness, which simply exhausts them and leaves them as prostrate as if they had scaled some forbidding ice-bound peak or crossed a desert. And those who on the other hand are wearied, frustrated, hemmed in, constrained by others, but find peace and rest in solitude, where they are detached and free to follow their own thoughts wherever they lead.

What we have here is, of course, a perfectly normal psychological phenomenon. Some people are naturally gregarious while others have a talent for the inner life. Speaking for myself, my external attention-span is short and quickly exhausted, and the moment my limit is reached I begin to experience sensations of unbearable physical and mental stress.

The result has been that I relate strongly, and always have, to inanimate objects, which to me seem as real as people, so that my house became, or rather had become, a world of its own, in which I lived a solitary, busy life surrounded by things—furniture and odds and ends—which to me were as

familiar and comfortable as friendly faces. I had gradually
filled—no, dressed—the house with them, and inside my four
walls I felt contented, fulfilled, and as happy as I would have
been in the arms of a woman whose habitual touch had become
a sweet and agreeable necessity.

I had built my house in spacious grounds well away from the
roads and within reach of a town where I could avail myself, if
I felt so inclined, of the amenities of society. The servants slept
in a separate building at the far end of the walled vegetable-
garden. In the silence of my isolated house, tucked away and
shrouded by the dense foliage of the great trees, the dark
enveloping cloak of night was so restful, so welcome, that each
evening I would spend hours putting off going to bed so that I
might enjoy it for a little while longer.

That evening, there had been a performance of *Sigurd** in
the theatre in town. It is a splendidly atmospheric musical
drama and that was the first time I had heard it. I had enjoyed
it immensely.

I was walking home, with a spring in my step, my head still
buzzing with snatches of the music and my eye still dazzled by
the spectacle I had seen. It was dark, very dark, so dark that
I could hardly see the road, and more than once I almost
wandered off it into a ditch. From the toll-gate to my house is
about a kilometre, perhaps a shade more, and takes twenty
minutes' slow walking. It was one in the morning, one or half
past. Ahead, the sky began to clear and a sliver of moon
appeared, the sickly crescent of the waning moon. In its first
quarter, when it comes up at four or five o'clock in the late
afternoon, it is clear, bright, and polished like silver; but
the crescent which rises after midnight is ruddy, bleak, and
ominous—a moon fit for a Witches' Sabbath. Anyone who is
regularly out and about by night must have made the same
observation. A waxing moon, though it be no thicker than a
thread, emits a faint but cheerful light which lifts the spirit and
casts bold, sharp shadows upon the earth. But a waning moon
gives out a dull, dying glow, so dim that it hardly casts
shadows at all.

In the distance, I made out the dark shape of my walled
garden and I was suddenly aware—though how or why I cannot

say—of being made distinctly uneasy by the thought of going home. I slackened my step. The air was very mild. The tall, massed trees looked like a gravestone beneath which my house was buried.

I opened the gates and started down the long tunnel-like avenue of over-arching sycamores which led towards my house between dense clumps of bushes and skirted lawns where flower-beds showed up clearly in the mitigated gloom like paler ovals of no particular colour.

As I drew nearer to the house, I felt curiously uneasy. I stopped. It was utterly quiet. No breath of wind stirred in the leaves. 'What's the matter with me?' I thought. For ten years I had been returning home like this and had never experienced the faintest twinge of apprehension. I was not afraid. I'm never afraid at night. The sight of a man, a prowler or burglar, would merely have made me furious and I should have gone for him without hesitating. In any case I was armed. I had my revolver with me. But I did not draw it, for I was not going to bow to the fear I felt stirring within me.

What was it? A premonition? The strange precognition which takes possession of a man's mind when he stands on the verge of the supernatural? Perhaps. Who can tell?

As I walked on, I felt my skin creep and by the time I was standing under the shuttered front of my enormous house, I knew I should have to wait a few moments before I opened the door and went in. I sat down on a bench outside the windows of my drawing-room. There I remained, shaking slightly, with my head leaning against the wall and my eyes staring into the blackness of the trees. For the first few moments, I noticed nothing unusual. I was aware of a slight buzzing in my ears, but I often get that. Sometimes, I have the impression I can hear trains going past, bells ringing, crowds marching.

But the buzzing soon became clearer, distinct enough for me to make it out. I had been wrong. It was not the usual pulsating of my arteries which filled my ears with this noise, but a quite specific though very muffled sound which came, and of this I was quite sure, from inside my house.

I could hear it through the wall. It was steady, more a perturbation than a noise, a faint stirring of many objects being moved about, as though all my furniture was being gently shifted, moved about, dragged around.

For some considerable time yet, I could not bring myself to trust what I was hearing. But I pressed one ear to a shutter to get a better idea of the strange disturbance inside and became convinced, absolutely certain, that something abnormal and incomprehensible was happening in my house. I was not afraid, I was . . . how shall I say . . . stunned by the sheer surprise of it all. I did not take the safety-catch off my revolver, for I sensed I should not need it. I waited.

I waited a good long time, unable to decide what I should do, with my mind perfectly clear but feeling desperately apprehensive. I stood there, waiting, listening to the sound which grew louder, at times rising to a pitch of violence before subsiding into a vehement, angry rumbling which radiated a mysterious turbulence.

Then, ashamed of my cowardice, I took out my bunch of keys, selected one, thrust it into the lock, turned it twice, and, with one almighty push, flung the door open with such force that it went crashing back against the wall inside.

It made a bang like a rifle-shot or a loud explosion, which was immediately answered by a terrific din which seemed to come from all over the house. It was so sudden, so terrifying, so deafening that I stepped back several paces and, though knowing that it would be quite useless, drew my revolver from its holster.

Again I waited, but not for long. I could now hear an extraordinary tap-tapping on the stairs, the parquet floors and the carpets, the tap-tapping not of human boots or shoes but of sticks and crutches made of wood and iron which rang out as loud as crashing cymbals. And then, in the doorway, I suddenly caught sight of an armchair, my big reading-chair, absconding at a waddle. Out through the garden it went. Other pieces of furniture followed. First the contents of the drawing room, next the low-slung sofas, dragging themselves along on their stubby legs like crocodiles, then all my chairs, leaping like goats, and my little stools, which hopped and skipped like rabbits.

Imagine how I felt! I slipped into a clump of bushes, where I crouched and stared at my furniture as it marched past, for every item was on the move, one piece after the other, making off quickly or slowly according to size and weight. My piano, my large grand piano, went by like a runaway horse, its insides a-jangle. Smaller items, brushes, glasses, vases, scampered across the gravel of the drive like ants, and on them the moon hung twinkles bright as glow-worms. Curtains and carpets slithered along, spreading like puddles, like octopuses on an ocean bed. I saw my writing-desk emerge. It was a rare eighteenth-century collector's piece and contained all my letters, the record of my romantic past, an old story no doubt but one which has given me much pain. And in it there were also my photographs.

My fear suddenly evaporated. I sprang forward and grappled with it as though I were tackling a burglar or apprehending a woman who was attempting to run away. But it was unstoppable, and though I tried everything, for I was very angry, I could not even slow its progress. As I fought desperately against its awesome power, I fell to the ground in the struggle. It rolled over me and dragged me along the drive behind it. The furniture which followed close on its heels began stepping on me, trampling my legs and bruising them in the process. When finally I let go, the rest swept over my body like charging cavalry over an unhorsed trooper.

Now beside myself with terror, I managed to drag myself off the wide drive and hid once more in the trees so that I could watch the disappearance of my belongings, the most insignificant, smallest, humblest items, objects I never knew I owned.

Then in the distance I heard, from inside my house which now echoed the way all empty houses echo, a tremendous din of doors being closed. The banging started in the attics and worked down through the building until the last, the hall door, which I myself had foolishly opened and thus started the exodus, slammed shut.

At this, I fled too, making off at a run towards town. I did not regain my composure until I was in the streets and met up

with people going home late. I headed for a hotel where I was
known and rang the bell. I had brushed down my clothes with
my hands to remove the dirt and explained that I had lost
my keys including the key to the kitchen garden, where my
servants slept in a separate building, behind the high wall
which protected my fruit and vegetables from the attentions of
marauding visitors.

I settled deep into the bed they gave me and pulled the
covers up to my eyes. But I could not sleep and waited for
daybreak with the sound of my heart pounding in my ears. I
had left orders that my servants were to be alerted at first light
and at seven in the morning my valet beat on my door.

There was a stunned expression on his face.

'Sir, sir, something terrible happened last night!' he said.

'What is it?'

'Somebody has stolen all the furniture, sir, everything, the
whole lot, even the smallest bits and pieces.'

I was most gratified to hear it. Why? Who can tell? I was
now in complete control of myself once more, confident I
could draw a veil over the night's events, say nothing about
what I had seen, keep it hidden, bury it in the back of my
mind like some terrible secret. I answered:

'The men who did this must be the same people who stole
my keys. We must inform the police at once. I'm getting up.
I'll be with you in a couple of minutes.'

The enquiry lasted five months. It came up with nothing.
Not even the smallest of my possessions was ever recovered,
nor was there any trace of the thieves. Lord! If I'd only told
them what I knew! But if I had, it would have been me they
locked up, not the thieves, me, the man who had seen such a
thing!

Oh, I kept my mouth shut all right! But I did not refurnish
my house. There was no point. It would only have happened
again. I did not even want to go back. Nor did I. I have never
seen the place since.

I moved to Paris and put up at a hotel. I consulted various
doctors about my nerves, which, after that terrible night, began
giving me cause for concern.

They prescribed travel. I took their advice.

II

I began with a trip to Italy.* The sun did me good. For six
months I wandered from Genoa to Venice, from Venice to
Florence, from Florence to Rome, from Rome to Naples. I
toured Sicily, a fascinating place with splendid scenery and
historic ruins left by Greek and Norman occupations. Thence
I travelled to Africa and made a leisurely crossing of the
endless, silent, yellow desert, where camels, gazelles, and
nomadic Arabs roam: nightmares have no place in that clear,
limpid air by day or by night.

I returned to France by way of Marseilles and for all the
bright good humour of Provence, the light there was less
intense and it depressed me. Now that I was back in Europe,
I was aware of the unsettling sensation experienced by the sick
man who believes he has been cured but is reminded by a
nagging pain that the cause of his illness has not gone away.

I returned to Paris. Within a month, I was bored with the
place. It was autumn and I decided that before winter came on
I would take a trip through Normandy, which I did not know.

I started at Rouen, naturally, and spent a fascinating,
thrilling week wandering idly through this fine old medieval
town, which is an amazing living museum of gothic survivals.

One afternoon, about four o'clock, I was making my way
along a street that had to be seen to be believed. Down the
middle of it ran a stream known as the Eau de Robec* which
was black as ink. As I stared at the bizarre façades of the
houses, which were all incredibly old, my eye was suddenly
caught by a series of second-hand furniture shops standing in a
row one after the other.

The gruesome junk-dealers who had set up their stall here
had certainly chosen their pitch well, in this ramshackle alley,
beside a sinister stream, beneath the pointed tile and slate
roofs on which weathercocks from a bygone age still groaned.

In the unlit back of each of these shops could be seen
teetering mounds of carved chests, Rouen, Nevers, and
Moustiers chinaware, statuettes, some painted and others
in unvarnished oak, of Christ, the Virgin, and the Saints,

ecclesiastical trappings, chasubles, copes, even chalices, and, notably, a gilt shrine now empty of the Divine Presence. It was astonishing to find such Aladdin's caves in these tall, baggy houses stuffed from attics to cellars with objects of every possible description which seemed to have outlived their purpose, just as they had survived their natural owners, their century, their epoch, and their fashion, yet now stood ready to be bought by later generations as interesting old curios.

My weakness for old bric-à-brac revived in this antiquarian's paradise. I went from shop to shop, stepping briskly over the bridges made of four rotten planks which crossed the evil-smelling Eau de Robec.

And then—God in Heaven!—I almost stopped breathing! In an arched doorway cluttered with all kinds of rubbish which made it look like the entrance to the catacombs of a cemetery where old furniture had been laid to rest, I saw one of my finest wardrobes. I went towards it trembling all over; I shook so much that I did not dare to touch it. I reached out my hand, then hesitated. It was mine, all right: a unique Louis Treize wardrobe which would have been recognizable at a glance to anyone who had ever seen it. Then, looking a little further into the darker back of the shop, I saw three of my armchairs with their petit-point coverings, and, a little further on still, both my Henri II tables, which were pieces so rare that people had come from Paris to see them.

Can you possibly imagine how I felt?

I went in, rigid, almost dead with apprehension, but went I did, for I am no coward. I went like a knight in the dark days of yore entering a magician's castle. As I advanced, I came across all the things that had once been mine—my chandeliers, my books, my pictures, my curtains, my suits of armour, it was all there with the exception of the desk containing my letters, which I could not see.

On I went, down into dark galleries and up to the floor above. I had the place to myself. I called but there was no reply. I was alone; there was no one in the whole vast, rambling labyrinth of a building.

Night fell and in the end I sat down on one of my own chairs in the gloom, for I was determined not to leave. From time to time I shouted: 'Hallo? Hallo? Is there anybody at home?'

I had been there a good hour when I heard the sound of footsteps. They were faint, unhurried, but I could not tell where they came from. I was tempted to clear out but, pulling myself together, I called again and then, in the next room, I saw a light.

'Who's there?' said a voice.

I answered:

'A customer.'

The voice said:

'It's a bit late to be wandering into shops.'

I went on:

'I've been waiting for you for more than an hour.'

'You could have come back tomorrow.'

'By tomorrow I'll have left Rouen.'

I did not dare go to meet him and he did not come to me. Meanwhile, in the light of his lamp, I could see a tapestry showing two angels hovering over dead soldiers on a battle field. That was mine too. I said:

'Well? Are you coming?'

He answered:

'I'm waiting for you.'

I got to my feet and went to him.

In the centre of the room, which was very large, stood a very small man. He was short and enormously fat, like the fat man in a circus, a hideous freak.

He had a thin, straggling, dirty-yellow, patchy beard and not a hair on his head. Not one! As he raised his candle up at arm's length to get a look at me, his skull gleamed like a small moon in the huge room piled high with old furniture. His face was wrinkled and bloated and his eyes were barely visible.

After some haggling, I bought three chairs which belonged to me and handed over a large sum in cash, giving him only the number of my room in my hotel. They were to be delivered there the next morning before nine o'clock.

Then I left. He showed me to the door most politely.

I went straight to the main police station, where I explained that my furniture had been stolen and told them about what I had just found out.

The Inspector immediately telegraphed a request for information to the Public Prosecutor's Office, which had investigated the burglary, and asked me to wait for the reply. It came within the hour and was entirely satisfactory from my point of view.

'I shall have the man arrested and questioned at once,' he said. 'He might have suspected something and moved your effects out of sight. Why don't you go and have dinner and come back in a couple of hours. I'll have him here then and I'll question him again in your presence.'

'That's splendid, Inspector. I really am most grateful.'

I went back to my hotel and made a much better dinner than I expected. Overall, I was pretty pleased: they had got him.

I went back to see the Inspector two hours later. He was expecting me.

'Now then,' he said as I was shown in. 'We can't find this chap of yours. My men haven't been able to lay hands on him.'

I suddenly felt faint.

'But . . . you found the shop all right?' I asked.

'Oh yes. I've even arranged for it to be watched and guarded till he gets back. But as for your man—vanished.'

'Vanished?'

'No sign of him. He spends most evenings with his next-door neighbour, a widow, also a dealer, a rum old hag name of Madame Bidoin. She hasn't seen anything of him this evening and can't tell us a thing. We'll have to leave it until tomorrow.'

I left. The streets of Rouen seemed horribly sinister, disturbing, haunted.

I slept very badly, in fits punctuated by nightmares.

I did not want to appear too anxious or eager, so I waited until ten o'clock the next morning before putting in an appearance at the police station.

The antique-dealer had not shown up. His shop was still closed.

The Inspector said:

'I've taken all the necessary steps. The Prosecutor's Office is fully in the picture. We'll both go round to this shop of yours and open it up. Then you can identify whatever belongs to you.'

We drove there at once. A number of policemen plus a locksmith were stationed outside the shop. The door was open.

As I went in, I saw no sign of my wardrobe, my chairs, my tables or any of the pieces which furnished my house, nothing!—though the evening before I had not been able to put one foot in front of the other before stumbling across one or other of my possessions.

The Chief Inspector was puzzled and a look of suspicion came into his eyes.

'Don't you see', I said, 'how oddly it all ties in? First the dealer disappears and now the furniture's gone.'

He smiled: 'You're right. It was a mistake to buy back those chairs yesterday and pay him cash. It tipped him off.'

I went on:

'But what I can't understand is how all this space, which was crammed with all my things yesterday, is now filled by all this other stuff?'

'Well,' said the Inspector, 'he had all night and I imagine he had accomplices too. There are sure to be doors communicating to the adjoining buildings. Don't worry, sir, I shall be taking a close personal interest in the case. The thief won't stay free for long now we've got his base.'

⁂

But oh my beating, racing, pounding heart!

⁂

I stayed in Rouen for two weeks. The man never showed up. The devil take him! Who could ever outwit or trap a man like him?

Then one morning, exactly a fortnight later, I received a strange letter from my head gardener, whom I had left in charge of my house, which had stood empty since the night of the robbery:

Dear Sir,

I am writing to inform you that something happened here last night that nobody can fathom, not the police nor us neither. All the furniture has come back, all of it, even the smallest bits and pieces. The house is now exactly the same as it was before the robbery. It's enough to turn your wits. It happened on Friday night last. The drive is all churned up as if everything had been dragged from the gates all

the way to the front door. It looked just the same as the morning after
it all disappeared.

> Awaiting your return, I remain
> Your obedient servant,
> Philippe Raudin.

No, no, no! it's out of the question! I shall never go back there!
   I took the letter round to the Inspector in Rouen.
   'Hm! A very clever restitution. We'll keep our heads down.
We'll get your man one of these days.'

But they didn't get him. They've never caught him and now I'm
scared of him, as afraid as if a dangerous animal has been let
loose on my trail.
   He cannot be traced! They'll never trace the monster with
the moon skull! He'll never go back to the shop. There's no
reason why he should. I'm the only man alive who could
identify him and that I won't ever do!
   I won't! I won't! I won't!
   And even if he did turn up, if he reappeared in his shop,
who can prove that my furniture had ever been there? There's
only my evidence against him and I have a suspicion that my
word is beginning to be doubted.
   I felt that life was becoming absolutely impossible. I could
not go on any longer without telling somebody about what I had
seen. I could not go on living like ordinary people, with the
fear that similar things might happen again at any moment.
   So I came here to consult the specialist who runs this clinic
and told him the whole story.
   After questioning me at length, he said:
   'Would you be willing to stay here for a while?'
   'I'd be glad to.'
   'You're not short of money?'
   'No, Doctor.'
   'Would you like private rooms away from the main
buildings?'
   'Yes I would.'
   'Do you want to see visitors?'
   'No, Doctor, I don't want to see anybody. The man . . . the

man from Rouen . . . would be quite capable of following me
here, to even the score.'

And so I have been living here alone, quite alone, for three
months. I feel safe, more or less. There's only one thing I'm
afraid of . . . Suppose the antiques dealer went mad . . . and
they brought him here, to the asylum . . . Even prisons are not
safe places.

EXPLANATORY NOTES

SHEPHERD'S LEAP

First published in *Gil Blas*, 9 March 1882; reprinted in *Le Père Milon* (1899). The story was incorporated into *Une vie* (chap. X), Maupassant's first novel, which appeared in 1883.

6   *to the next*: Romantic writers were much given to commending these mini-caravans, which they saw as a symbol of freedom and love. 'I never yet did see a shepherd's travelling coop,' confessed Chateaubriand (*Les Martyrs*, Bk. X), 'without thinking it would suffice for me if you were there.' The most famous example, however, appears in Vigny's poem *La Maison du berger* (1844): it has four wheels, stands no higher than his mistress's eye, and sleeps two.

  Seventh Commandment: more accurately, the ninth (Exodus 20: 17). Though Maupassant spent four years at a Catholic school at Yvetot, his knowledge of the later commandments was clearly shaky.

MADEMOISELLE FIFI

First appeared in *Gil Blas*, 23 March 1882, and a few weeks later gave its name to Maupassant's second collection of tales.

8   *château d'Urville*: though there is an Urville 11 km west of Cherbourg and another 20 km south of Caen, the chateau of this name is an invention, as are the names of the characters in the story. The names Maupassant gives to places and people are frequently fictitious, if resonant to a French ear, and in these notes only the more significant references are explained.

  the Andelle: the Andelle rises near the spa town of Forges-les-Eaux, 40 km east of Rouen, and flows into the Seine near Pont-de-l'Arche. Maupassant set a number of his war stories in the area between the Andelle and Rouen, for it was from this quarter that a force of 25,000 Prussians arrived in Rouen on 6 December 1870.

9   *the war against Austria*: which marked the end of Austrian domination and the emergence of Prussia as a political and

military power. The war ended with the Prussian victory at
Sadowa in 1866.

14 *Belfort and Strasbourg*: on 3 November, Belfort, in the Jura,
began a gallant resistance against the German invader which
lasted until 16 February 1871. The defence of the town was
commemorated in Bartholdi's 'Lion of Belfort' (1880). On 9
August 1870, the Prussians laid siege to Strasbourg, which held
out for almost two months.

15 *all her race have hooked noses*: like many others, Maupassant
was mildly infected by the current mistrust of the Jewish
influence in French public life which, in the run-up to the
Dreyfus affair (1894–9), was rabidly denounced by Edouard
Drumont in *La France juive* (1886). Maupassant's anti-Semitism
did not run very deep and is most apparent in novels like *Bel-Ami*
(1885) and *Mont Oriol* (1887), which reveal a certain hostility to
wealthy Jews. His occasional anti-Jewish sentiments have been
exaggerated by association with the notorious film of *Bel-Ami*
made in 1942 by the German propaganda-machine in Occupied
France. In 'Le Père Judas' (1883), he shows the cruel effects of
anti-Semitic feeling in a peasant milieu, and here, the fact that
Rachel is a Jewess makes her patriotism all the more telling.

17 *Queen Augusta*: Princess Augusta of Saxe-Weimar (1811–90)
married Frederick-William, the seventh King of Prussia, in
1829. She became Empress Augusta when her husband,
henceforth William I, accepted the imperial crown of Germany,
on 18 January 1871.

CALL IT MADNESS?

First published in *Gil Blas*, 23 August 1882; reprinted in the second
edition of *Mademoiselle Fifi* (1883).

TWO FRIENDS

First published in *Gil Blas*, 5 February 1883, and included the same
year in the second edition of *Mademoiselle Fifi*.

27 *eating anything*: this tale is set during the last days of the siege
of Paris, which had begun on 19 September 1870 and ended
after the armistice of 28 January 1871. Trees in the parks were
felled for fuel and animals in the zoo were slaughtered for food.

And when they had gone, reported J. Cheney (*A Ramble Round France*, London, 1885), 'gentlemen have been glad to eat sausage made from the entrails of a dog' and 'animals of a more questionable description were consumed. Rats, for instance, were in great demand, and the *Journal Officiel* stated that the use of them had become unavoidable, and gave directions about the amount of cooking necessary to render them wholesome. By the end of the siege a fat rat cost six-and-eightpence.'

27 *National Guard trousers*: the Garde nationale was a military force independent of the regular army, raised locally for local peace-keeping duties in times of unrest. Recruits were aged between 25 and 50 and it was on them that Gambetta had counted in 1870 to defend France's towns and cities. In the event, National Guardsmen, well-meaning, untrained, and often rather elderly for active service, proved ineffectual. Maupassant usually presented them in a ridiculous light as grocers playing at soldiers, blazing away at anything that moved. At the beginning of 'Boule de suif', he reports that National Guardsmen from Rouen 'had been out on cautious patrols in the surrounding woods, sometimes shooting their own sentries and preparing for action whenever a rabbit stirred in the undergrowth'. In the early days of the siege of Paris, they manned the ramparts in assorted garb and later certain battalions were equipped with brown or green uniforms. It is difficult to say exactly of what colour or cut Monsieur Morissot's trousers were, but it is clear that Maupassant intends him to be a comic spectacle.

Marante Island: Argenteuil is 10 miles west of Notre Dame. Maupassant clearly has the nearby Île de Colombes in mind. He knew the area well: it was on the Seine west of Paris that as a young man he had spent many weekends boating.

rue Notre-Dame-de-Lorette: runs from the rue Pigalle to the rue St Lazare in the 9th *arrondissement*.

30 *Mont-Valérien*: the fort of Mont-Valérien, overlooking Suresnes, on the highest hill in the Paris area, was by now (January 1871) the Prussian headquarters. Cheney notes: 'At Mont Valérien were two immense cannon, called Joséphine and Valérie, the thunder of which could be heard throughout Paris . . . The bombardment is said to have passed through three stages; in the first the forts only were fired at, in the second the town, in the third, and worst, what were called incendiary shells were thrown, and they not only burst, but set fire where they fell.'

AT SEA

First published in *Gil Blas*, 12 February 1883; reprinted the same year in *Contes de la Bécasse*.

THE TRIBULATIONS OF WALTER SCHNAFFS

First published in *Le Gaulois*, 11 April 1883; reprinted in *Contes de la Bécasse* (1883).

41 *group of partisans*: the Garde nationale mobile was not part of the regular army but an emergency force which had seen service notably during the revolutions of 1830 and 1848. It was modelled on partisan groups ('francs-tireurs') first formed in 1792. In 1867, new companies appeared, their ranks being filled by young men who had avoided conscription. They worked with the regular army at times but retained near-absolute operational freedom, which reduced their usefulness. At the start of 'Boule de suif', Maupassant described their retreat from Rouen: 'Units of *francs-tireurs* with vainglorious names— "Avengers of the Defeat", "Citizens of the Grave", "Companions of Death"—trudged by in turn, looking for all the world like bandits.' The Mobile Guard played a notable role after the fall of Sedan in September 1870 and during the siege of Paris and the Commune of May 1871. What the *moblots* lacked in discipline and training they made up with courage, and they were particularly feared by the Prussians.

MISS HARRIET

First published as 'Miss Hastings' in *Le Gaulois*, 9 July 1883; extensively revised before publication in 1884 in the collection to which it gives its name. The text used for the translation is that of the revised version.

49 *Étretat*: as a boy, Maupassant had spent many summers at Étretat and always wrote of it lyrically: see, for example, the opening page of 'A Model'. Tancarville overlooks the Seine estuary, 45 km to the south-east. The ruins in question were of a castle which once belonged to a tutor to William the Conqueror.

50 *Richelieu*: the Duke de Richelieu (1696–1788), Marshal of France, was one of the most brilliant soldiers and courtiers of his age but also one of the most debauched. History, however,

has treated him kindly, and he is remembered as a dashing rake of great wit and charm.

51 *Bénouville*: a village 4 km east of Étretat.

60 *Petit-Val*: one of two valleys which lead down to the break in the cliffs occupied by Étretat.

68 *to bring into the world*: Maupassant's mechanistic view of nature denies the religious beliefs on which Miss Harriet based her faith in an afterlife. For Maupassant, the only immortality we can hope for is in the new forms of life which will grow out of our decomposing bodies.

A DUEL

First published in *Le Gaulois*, 14 August 1883; reprinted in *Le Colporteur* (1900).

70 *knee of the victor*: the Armistice was signed on 28 January 1871 and peace terms were ratified by the French Assembly on 1 March, by which time life in the capital had begun to return to normal.

71 *Pharsbourg*: perhaps Phalsbourg, near Saverne, in the Vosges, which had put up stout resistance against the Prussians.

72 *Prussia over all!*: the echoes of 'über alles' are clear. What was later, in 1919, to be adopted as the German national anthem grew out of a popular nationalist song composed in 1841.

already been crushed: see note to page 9.

mobile guard: see note to page 41.

A VENDETTA

First published in *Le Gaulois*, 14 October 1883; reprinted in *Contes du jour et de la nuit* (1885). It is one of Maupassant's Corsican tales, which exploit the island's popular image, first promoted by Balzac and Mérimée, of lawlessness and revenge.

76 *Bonifacio*: a small fishing-village on the southernmost tip of Corsica.

77 *Longosardo*: a fishing-village of some 500 inhabitants on the northern coast of Sardinia which, being Italian, afforded a safe and accessible haven for refugees from French justice.

Explanatory Notes 245

THE MODEL

First published in *Le Gaulois*, 17 December 1883; reprinted in *Le Rosier de Madame Husson* (1888).

82 *Artists' Wives*: a collection of stories published in 1874. Alphonse Daudet (1840–97), principally remembered as a humourist, reflected the anti-feminism of his times. The view of woman as the destroyer of male artistic creativity was a literary commonplace. After Wenceslas Steinbock marries in Balzac's *La Cousine Bette* (1846), his promise as a sculptor is ended prematurely; Zola's *L'Œuvre* (1886) demonstrates the incompatibility of marriage and art, etc. Maupassant's dim view of women had been confirmed by his reading of Schopenhauer and Herbert Spencer.

84 *Andrésy*: 24 km from Versailles, south of Pontoise, where the Oise joins the Seine.

85 *I was a-looking up aloft*: a popular waltz from an operetta, *Les Cloches de Corneville*, which was first performed at the Folies-Dramatiques on 19 April 1877.

MOTHER SAVAGE

First published in *Le Gaulois*, 3 March 1884; reprinted in *Miss Harriet* (1884).

THE LITTLE KEG

First published in *Le Gaulois*, 7 April 1884; reprinted the same year in *Les Sœurs Rondoli*.

96 *Épreville*: 6 km inland from Fécamp on the road to Goderville.

97 *écus*: the écu, or crown, first struck in the thirteenth century, remained in circulation until the time of the Revolution when the coinage of the ancien regime was replaced by the metric franc. The écu, which had been worth 3 livres, survived in name only until the end of the nineteenth century when it was the notional equivalent of 5 francs.

THE DOWRY

First published in *Gil Blas*, 9 September 1884; reprinted in *Toine* (1885).

104 *at fairgrounds*: Maupassant the strict realist here dismisses the cruder depiction of life by caricaturists like Honoré Daumier (1808–79) and Gavarni (1804–66). But as an exponent of the short story, Maupassant himself was prone to caricature: see his account of the spherical lawyer on page 110.

105 *Vaugirard!*: in the 15th *arrondissement*, just west of Montparnasse. Madame Lebrument's omnibus, a number 10, has travelled south from the Gare Saint-Lazare, along the Boulevard de la Madeleine, over the Seine, and reached its terminus in the rue Blomet.

THE BEQUEST

First published in *Gil Blas*, 23 September 1884. It was never reprinted in volume form, though it was incorporated, with few alterations, into *Bel-Ami* (II, chap. vi), which Maupassant was currently writing.

111 *accept the legacy*: the Napoleonic code of civil law allowed married women few legal rights: in law, it was said, their position was indistinguishable from that of children and mad persons. They were not allowed to bequeath or inherit property, manage their own money, make decisions regarding their own children, and so on, without the prior approval of father, husband, brother, or a duly appointed male guardian. Their position changed slowly: French women did not vote until 1946, and only in 1965 were wives free to open a separate bank-account.

112 *the soul within*: a reflection of Maupassant's interest in psycho-analysis, which was then beginning to get to grips with the subconscious mind.

MONSIEUR PARENT

Written in the autumn of 1885 but never serialized. It first appeared in January 1886 in the collection of tales to which it gave its name.

116 *Trinity Church*: in the rue Saint-Lazare, built in hybrid Renaissance style by Théodore Ballu (1817–85) between 1863 and 1867. Subsequent mentions of the rue Saint-Lazare and the rue Blanche indicate that Monsieur Parent lives in the 9th *arrondissement*, a part of Paris Maupassant knew well for having shared a flat with his father there in the 1870s.

145 *Madeleine . . . rue Drouot*: Monsieur Parent's constitutional takes him along the Boulevard de La Madeleine, and past the Paris Opera in the Boulevard des Capucines and the fashionable cafés of the Boulevard des Italians.

148 *Saint-Germain*: Saint-Germain-en-Laye, 16 km west of Paris, stands on a hill above the Seine. French Kings built a royal palace there in the twelfth century. A Renaissance chateau, completed by Henri IV (Louis XIV was born there in 1638) was pulled down in 1776 except for the Pavillon Henri IV, which subsequently became a hotel. The celebrated Terrace runs north from the Pavillon for 2½ km before entering the Forêt de Saint-Germain, a former royal hunting-ground with extensive walks. The commanding view was compared by James II to that from the Terrace at Richmond.

149 *Pont Chatou*: the first of two railway bridges—the second is the Pont du Pecq of a few lines further on—which cross the final loop of the Seine before Saint-Germain. Chatou was a favourite boating-haunt of Maupassant's.

150 *Hôtel Henri IV*: see note to page 148.

THIS BUSINESS OF LATIN

First published in *Le Gaulois*, 2 September 1886; reprinted in the posthumous collection, *Le Colporteur* (1900).

158 *This business of Latin*: in the aftermath of Jules Ferry's reform of primary education in the early 1880s, enthusiasm for vocational training undermined the status of dead languages in the secondary syllabus. The publication of Raoul Frary's *La Question du Latin* (1885) had prompted a lively debate in which Maupassant participated in his regular newspaper-columns. He agreed that secondary schools were not unlike prisons (the atmosphere of Robineau's Academy in this tale draws on his memory of the school he had attended at Yvetot). Yet as a competent Latinist himself, he believed in the civilizing value of the classics, though only to boys of good family, since he believed the lower classes to be incapable of advanced study. Maupassant, who had no children, enjoyed the luxury of regarding education as a thorough bore.

161 *Jean-Jacques Rousseau*: Rousseau (1712–78), originator of child-centred education, was widely regarded as a precursor of Marx: the *Social Contract* (1762) opens with the rousing

declaration that 'Man was made free by Nature and is everywhere in chains.' To Rousseau, Maupassant much preferred
the sardonic and cynical Voltaire and had no sympathy with
democracy, which he viewed as government by the ignorant and
the rule of vulgarity. He scoffed at its principles and missed no
opportunity to mock idealists who held them.

165 *Silenus*: chief Satyr and perhaps the son of Hermes or of Pan. If
discovered in a drunken sleep, he could be made to sing or
prophesy. He was represented as a paunchy, hairy old man,
always drunk and carrying a wineskin, usually supported by
other satyrs or seated on a donkey.

166 *Quantum mutatus ab illo!*: 'How changed the man since that
time.'

by Latin alone: in *Le Gaulois* of 4 January 1882, Maupassant,
with comparable irony, had quoted the dedication to *Le
Bachelier* (1881) by Jules Vallès (1883–5): 'To those who,
suckled on Greek and Latin, have died of hunger.'

MADAME HUSSON'S MAY KING

First published in *La Nouvelle Revue*, 15 June 1887; reprinted as the
title story of *Le Rosier de Madame Husson* (1888).

167 *Gisors*: a market town about half-way between Paris and Rouen.
Its origins were Merovingian, not pre-Roman, though during the
Middle Ages it produced more history, as Saki's Arlington
Stringer remarked of Cyprus, 'than could be consumed locally'.
The etymology supplied by Albert Marambot on page 171, how-
ever, is an invention: Gisors is not mentioned in Caesar's
Commentaries.

169 *Gournay*: Gournay-en-Bray lies 26 km north of Gisors.

what Lucullus was to Cicero: the Roman general Lucullus
(c. 110 BC–AD 57) kept a lavish table and his feasts were
celebrated. The image of the orator Cicero (106–43 BC) was
altogether more severe.

170 *Balzac and Eugène Sue*: Maupassant greatly admired the novels
of Honoré de Balzac (1799–1850), though in his view the
'Comédie humaine' catalogued mass psychology in a general
way which he found unsympathetic: he himself preferred to
use a 'microscope'. Eugène Sue (1804–57) was the first mass-
circulation novelist. *The Wandering Jew* (1844–5) and *The*

Mysteries of Paris (1842–3), serialized in the cheap newspapers of the 1840s, were melodramatic, ill written, but marked by a powerful if sensational imagination. Maupassant thought him vulgar.

170 *General Blanmont!*: the most famous image of the god Apollo is the Apollo Belvedere in Rome, which represents the most noble intellect with consummate masculine beauty. It stands seven feet high. It was discovered in the ruins of Antium in 1495 and was purchased by Pope Julius II, who placed it in the Belvedere of the Vatican. General Marie-Pierre-Isidore Blanmont (1770–1846) saw active service in the armies of Revolutionary France, of Napoleon, and of the Restored monarchy, and retired in 1832 after a career spanning forty years. He is commemorated by a marble statue, by Antoine Desboeufs (1793–1862), which was erected near the chateau in 1851.

172 *the Hispano-Arabic potter*: Jean-Charles, Baron Davillier (1823–83), 'the Christopher Columbus of Hispano-Arabic porcelain' as Maupassant called him, bequeathed his important collection to the Louvre. In *Le Gaulois* (23 March 1883), Maupassant wrote: 'Baron Davillier, who has just died, possessed the capacity for fine discernment in artistic matters to a singular degree. This was his greatest distinction and one which will guarantee the immortality of his name to the collectors of the future.'

Charles Lapierre: the journalists Charles Brainne (1825–64) and Charles Lapierre (1828–88), a friend of Flaubert's, had both married daughters of Henri Rivoire, proprietor of the Catholic newspaper *Le Nouvelliste de Rouen*. Maupassant dedicated *Une Vie* to Madame Brainne and was a regular visitor to her house in Paris. He was also on friendly terms with Lapierre, who became the newspaper's editor.

173 *conspicuous virtue*: an old custom revived at the end of the eighteenth century when it was condemned by liberal thinkers as a relic of feudalism and little more than a variant of the *droit du seigneur*. The custom survived longer at Nanterre and Saint-Denis than elsewhere. The nearest British equivalent is the crowning of the May Queen.

176 *show Nanterre how it should be done*: see note to page 173.

. . . Emperor Napoleon: the choice of this date, acceptable to both right and left, reveals the political astuteness of the town's Mayor.

177 *King Louis-Philippe*: Louis-Philippe (1773–1850), King of France between the revolutions of 1830 and 1848, the period of the 'bourgeois monarchy'.

184 *and so on and so forth*: these stultifying details, listed with satirical intention, are confirmed in Charpillon, *Gisors et son canton* (Les Andelys, 1867), though Maupassant is more likely to have found them in local guide-books, which, in the age of the train, were published in large numbers for the new tourist-trade. Most accounts of Gisors mention Nicolas Poulain and his nail.

Henry Monnier: Henry Monnier (1799–1877), caricaturist and creator of Monsieur Prudhomme, a rich comic type of the dull, prosperous bourgeois of the 1830s, was one of the nineteenth century's best exponents of the then novel brand of 'English' humour.

Bouffé: perhaps a reference, designed to deflate Marambot's chauvinistic boasting, to Hugues-Marie-Désiré Bouffé (1800–88), who, though the son of an interior decorator, was in fact one of the leading actors of the Romantic stage. He had retired in 1855 but made one last appearance in 1878, when Maupassant might have seen him perform.

HAUTOT AND SON

First published in *L'Écho de Paris*, 5 January 1889; reprinted in *La Main gauche* (1889).

188 *rue de l'Éperlan*: like the rue des Trois Mares of page 191, an invention. However, the rue Beauvoisine, where Caroline works, was real enough.

193 *Great Exhibition*: of 1878. When this story appeared, preparations were already under way for the Exhibition of May 1889. It was to feature the new Eiffel Tower, which Maupassant thought an abomination and the symbol of the vulgarity of his age.

THE GROVE OF OLIVES

First published in *Le Figaro* of 19–23 February 1890; reprinted in *L'Inutile Beauté* (1890).

202 *Odéon*: the Théâtre de l'Odéon, founded in 1797, like the prestigious Théâtre Français, had close links with the

Conservatoire National de la Musique et de la Déclamation (1795), which, in its drama section, was charged with transmitting the French theatrical tradition to new generations. The Conservatoire course lasted two years, with a competitive examination at the end of each. The careers of students were determined by the results, the best appearing in productions staged by the two state theatres. By the chronology of the story, Vilbois's actress was following in famous footsteps: Sarah Bernhardt, who enrolled in the Conservatoire in 1860, was an immediate past pupil. The Divine Sarah, however, made her début in 1862 at the Théâtre Français.

207 *misspent youth*: Maupassant shared the widely held view that premature baldness was an early symptom of syphilis.

217 *Monte Cristo*: it has been suggested that this tale is a reduction of Alexandre Dumas's *The Count of Monte Cristo* (1844–5), an epic tale of injustice and revenge. Like Edmond Dantès, Abbé Vilbois is cheated of the woman he loves, spends many years in a prison of sorts, and finally acts as the agent of Providence. But in ethos and structure, this tale seems closer to other stories of frustrated parenthood, such as 'A Vendetta', 'Mother Savage', or 'Monsieur Parent'. Maupassant confessed in *Le Gaulois* (9 March 1882) that he had never read Dumas's novel to the end, finding 'the accumulation of so many incredible fantasies' irksome and boring. By 1889, he had revised his opinion and paid handsome tribute to the verve and imaginative genius of 'the Great Dumas'.

218 *near Meulan*: on the right bank of the Seine, 50 km from Paris, on the road to Mantes.

225 *taken his own life*: the original text published in *Le Figaro* ended on a more explicit and more moralistic note:

'Philippe-Auguste was tried at Aix-en-Provence and sentenced to death. To the last he protested his innocence with the energy of desperation, and several times unsettled his judges who were convinced of his guilt.

'But the case against him was overwhelming. It was clinched by the evidence given by the housekeeper.

'In his defence, he told a strange tale according to which he was the curé's illegitimate son. He was not believed. It never occurred to anyone that Abbé Vilbois might, just conceivably, have slit his own throat.

'As a last resort, the accused called upon a respected Senator, the Count de Pravallon, to testify on his behalf. But the evidence given by this witness was of such a damning nature that it finally swung the verdict against him.

'He was publicly guillotined.'

WHO CAN TELL?

First published in *L'Écho de Paris*, 6 April 1890; reprinted in *L'Inutile Beauté* (1890). It is one of Maupassant's very last stories.

228 *Sigurd*: an opera, in the Wagnerian manner, by Reyer (pseudonym of Ernest Rey, 1823–1909), friend and disciple of Berlioz, which had its Paris première on 12 June 1885. It aroused unfavourable comment because of the similarity of its subject, if not of its musical substance, to Wagner's handling of the Siegfried story.

233 *a trip to Italy*: the narrator's itinerary follows that described in Maupassant's travel book, *La Vie errante* (1890).

Eau de Robec: with its Renaissance houses, one of the oldest streets in Rouen. In *Madame Bovary* (ɪ, i), Flaubert sends Charles to live there for a time and comments: the river 'transforms this part of Rouen into a kind of ignoble Little Venice'. The stream is now culverted.

THE WORLD'S CLASSICS

A Select List

MOLIÈRE: Don Juan and Other Plays
Translated by George Graveley and Ian Maclean

GEORGE MOORE: Esther Waters
Edited by David Skilton

E. NESBIT: The Railway Children
Edited by Dennis Butts

ORIENTAL TALES
Edited by Robert L. Mack

OVID: Metamorphoses
Translated by A. D. Melville
Introduction and Notes by E. J. Kenney

EDGAR ALLAN POE: Selected Tales
Edited by Julian Symons

JEAN RACINE: Britannicus, Phaedra, Athaliah
Translated by C. H. Sisson

ANN RADCLIFFE: The Italian
Edited by Frederick Garber

THE MARQUIS DE SADE:
The Misfortune of Virtue and Other Early Tales
Translated and Edited by David Coward

PAUL SALZMAN (Ed.):
An Anthology of Elizabethan Prose Fiction

OLIVE SCHREINER: The Story of an African Farm
Edited by Joseph Bristow

SIR WALTER SCOTT: The Heart of Midlothian
Edited by Claire Lamont

MARY SHELLEY: Frankenstein
Edited by M. K. Joseph

STENDHAL: The Red and the Black
Translated by Catherine Slater

TOBIAS SMOLLETT: The Expedition of Humphry Clinker
Edited by Lewis M. Knapp
Revised by Paul-Gabriel Boucé

ROBERT LOUIS STEVENSON: Kidnapped and Catriona
Edited by Emma Letley

Treasure Island
Edited by Emma Letley

BRAM STOKER: Dracula
Edited by A. N. Wilson

JONATHAN SWIFT: Gulliver's Travels
Edited by Paul Turner

WILLIAM MAKEPEACE THACKERAY: Barry Lyndon
Edited by Andrew Sanders

LEO TOLSTOY: Anna Karenina
Translated by Louise and Aylmer Maude
Introduction by John Bayley

War and Peace
Translated by Louise and Aylmer Maude
Edited by Henry Gifford

ANTHONY TROLLOPE: The American Senator
Edited by John Halperin

Dr. Thorne
Edited by David Skilton

Dr. Wortle's School
Edited by John Halperin

Orley Farm
Edited by David Skilton

IVAN TURGENEV: First Love and Other Stories
Translated by Richard Freeborn

MARK TWAIN: Pudd'nhead Wilson and Other Tales
Edited by R. D. Gooder

GIORGIO VASARI: The Lives of the Artists
Translated and Edited by Julia Conaway Bondanella and Peter Bondanella

JULES VERNE: Journey to the Centre of the Earth
Translated and Edited by William Butcher

VIRGIL: The Aeneid
Translated by C. Day Lewis
Edited by Jasper Griffin

The Eclogues and The Georgics
Translated by C. Day Lewis
Edited by R. O. A. M. Lyne

HORACE WALPOLE : The Castle of Otranto
Edited by W. S. Lewis

IZAAK WALTON and CHARLES COTTON:
The Compleat Angler
Edited by John Buxton
Introduction by John Buchan

OSCAR WILDE: Complete Shorter Fiction
Edited by Isobel Murray

The Picture of Dorian Gray
Edited by Isobel Murray

MARY WOLLSTONECRAFT:
Mary *and* The Wrongs of Woman
Edited by Gary Kelly

VIRGINIA WOOLF: Mrs Dalloway
Edited by Claire Tomalin

ÉMILE ZOLA:
The Attack on the Mill and Other Stories
Translated by Douglas Parmée

Nana
Translated and Edited by Douglas Parmée